Virginia Woolf is now recognized as a major twentieth-century author, a great novelist and essayist, and a key figure in literary history as a feminist and a modernist. Born in 1882, she was the daughter of the editor and critic Leslie Stephen, and suffered a traumatic adolescence after the deaths of her mother, in 1895, and her step-sister Stella, in 1897, leaving her subject to breakdowns for the rest of her life. Her father died in 1904 and two years later her favourite brother Thoby died suddenly of typhoid. With her sister, the painter Vanessa Bell, she was drawn into the company of writers and artists such as Lytton Strachey and Roger Fry, later known as the Bloomsbury Group. Among them she met Leonard Woolf, whom she married in 1912, and together they founded the Hogarth Press in 1917, which was to publish the work of T. S. Eliot, E. M. Forster and Katherine Mansfield as well as the earliest translations of Freud. Woolf lived an energetic life among friends and family, reviewing and writing, and dividing her time between London and the Sussex Downs. In 1941, fearing another attack of mental illness, she drowned herself.

Her first novel, *The Voyage Out*, appeared in 1915, and she then worked through the transitional *Night and Day* (1919) to the highly experimental and impressionistic *Jacob's Room* (1922). From then on her fiction became a series of brilliant and extraordinarily varied experiments, each one searching for a fresh way of presenting the relationship between individual lives and the forces of society and history. She was particularly concerned with women's experience, not only in her novels but also in her essays and her two books of feminist polemic, *A Room of One's Own* (1929) and *Three Guineas* (1938). Her major novels include *Mrs Dalloway* (1925), the historical fantasy *Orlando* (1928), written for Vita Sackville-West, the extraordinarily poetic vision of *The Waves* (1931), the family saga of *The Years* (1937), and *Between the Acts* (1941). All these are published by Penguin, as are her *Diaries*, Volumes I–V, and selections from her essays and short stories.

Rachel Bowlby was born in Billingham-on-Tees. She was a student at Oxford and then at Yale, and now teaches English at Sussex University near Brighton, working on a range of topics linking consumerism, feminism, psychoanalysis and literature. She has written two books, *Just Looking* (1985) on femininity and consumerism in novels at the turn of the century, and *Virginia Woolf: Feminist Destinations* (1988). She also works as a translator from French into English.

Julia Briggs is General Editor for the works of Virginia Woolf in Penguin Twentieth-Century Classics.

A WOMAN'S ESSAYS

SELECTED ESSAYS: VOLUME ONE

———

VIRGINIA WOOLF

EDITED WITH AN INTRODUCTION
AND NOTES BY RACHEL BOWLBY

PENGUIN BOOKS

PENGUIN BOOKS

Published by the Penguin Group
Penguin Books Ltd, 27 Wrights Lane, London w8 5 tz, England
Penguin Books USA Inc., 375 Hudson Street, New York, New York 10014, USA
Penguin Books Australia Ltd, Ringwood, Victoria, Australia
Penguin Books Canada Ltd, 10 Alcorn Avenue, Toronto, Ontario, Canada m4v 3 b2
Penguin Books (NZ) Ltd, 182–190 Wairau Road, Auckland 10, New Zealand

Penguin Books Ltd, Registered Offices: Harmondsworth, Middlesex, England

This collection first published 1992

5

Filmset in 10/12 pt Monophoto Garamond

Printed in England by Clays Ltd, St Ives plc

CONTENTS

Bibliographical Note   vii
Introduction   ix
Further Reading   xxxiv
A Note on the Texts   xxxvi

A WOMAN'S ESSAYS   1
The Feminine Note in Fiction   3
The Decay of Essay-writing   5
The American Woman   8
Women Novelists   11
The Tunnel   15
Men and Women   18
Freudian Fiction   21
An Imperfect Lady   24
The Plumage Bill   27
The Intellectual Status of Women   30
The Modern Essay   40
Romance and the Heart   50
The Compromise   53
Montaigne   56
The Patron and the Crocus   65
Mr Bennett and Mrs Brown   69
Indiscretions   88
On Not Knowing Greek   93
The Duchess of Newcastle   107
Two Women   115
The Art of Fiction   121
Dorothy Osborne's Letters   126
Memories of a Working Women's Guild   133
Why?   148
Royalty   154
The Leaning Tower   159

Notes   179

Bibliographical Note

The following is a list of abbreviated titles used in this edition.

Diary: *The Diary of Virginia Woolf*, 5 vols., ed. Anne Olivier Bell (Hogarth Press, 1977; Penguin Books, 1979).

Letters: *The Letters of Virginia Woolf*, 6 vols., ed. Nigel Nicolson and Joanne Trautmann (Hogarth Press, 1975–80).

Passionate Apprentice: *A Passionate Apprentice: The Early Journals, 1897–1909*, ed. Mitchell A. Leaska (Hogarth Press, 1990).

Essays: *The Essays of Virginia Woolf*, 3 vols. (to be six vols.), ed. Andrew McNeillie (Hogarth Press, 1986).

CE: *Collected Essays*, 4 vols., ed. Leonard Woolf (Chatto & Windus, 1966, 1967).

Moments of Being: *Moments of Being: Unpublished Autobiographical Writings of Virginia Woolf*, ed. Jeanne Schulkind (Hogarth Press, 1985).

Introduction
A More Than Maternal Tie

Virginia Woolf the novelist and Virginia Woolf the essayist are two writers who might seem to have very little in common. One is famous, the other is not. One is a key figure in the history of modernism, the other was principally a journalist, working to commissions for weeklies and other periodicals. One wrote for art, the other (much of the time) for money. One is 'Virginia Woolf', the other often published anonymously in her many reviews for *The Times Literary Supplement*. One has been widely studied, and is the subject of numerous critical works; the other is little known, and often considered merely as an adjunct to the first, enhancing readers' understanding of the novels.

The essayist is, in every way, a more obscure figure, and not necessarily one whose works would seem to comprise any kind of unity. In her diaries Woolf does not refer to her essays in the way that she does her novels, as part of a continuing and conscious project. Their scattered nature – published here and there, on many topics and in many styles – is reflected in the heterogeneous volumes in which some of them (far from all) were put together, during and after her lifetime, beginning with the first *Common Reader* in 1925, and culminating in the four volumes of Leonard Woolf's *Collected Essays* – a selection, despite the comprehensive name. Only in the last few years, since Andrew McNeillie's six-volume edition of the total output began to come out, has the extraordinary range and quantity of the material been apparent to the common Woolf reader of today.

Previously the essays that were read at all widely themselves fell into two distinct categories. One or two of them ('Mr Bennett and Mrs Brown', 'Modern Fiction') were frequently cited as classics of modernist statements by modernist writers. Others have become known through the more recent interest in Woolf's feminism. To *A Room of One's Own* and *Three Gineas*, both longer essays published separately, Michèle Barrett's important anthology *Women and Writing* (1979) added more.

The writings on literature have usually been treated not in their own right, but as accessories to understanding what Woolf may have been trying to achieve in her fiction, considered as the true object of interest for her and for her readers. And the feminist writings, in contrast, have often been treated quite separately from the novels, according to a traditional division which assumes that what is touchingly called 'non-fiction', or just plain 'prose', is the proper place for polemical argument or explicit statement, while creative writing is separate from social concerns, and too ambiguous a medium for conveying them.

Woolf herself, in comments we find in her diaries and letters, as well as within the essays themselves, often substantiates the suggestion that her essays and her fiction should be considered as two very different kinds of undertaking. She will assert that political argument – attempting to change the reader's opinions – is appropriate in a journalistic piece, but out of place in art; or, in a related segregation of the practical from the aesthetic, she will bemoan the fact that she can't get on with the novel she is writing because of all the reviewing she has to do.

In the first of these modes, writing (as she often did) about her dislike of the novels of Arnold Bennett, John Galsworthy and H. G. Wells, she says:

> Sometimes I wonder if we are right to call them books at all. For they leave one with so strange a feeling of incompleteness and dissatisfaction. In order to complete them it seems necessary to do something – to join a society, or, more desperately, to write a cheque. (p. 77)

These are strict distinctions, recognizable as the concerns of some of Woolf's friends associated, like her, with the Bloomsbury Group of artists and intellectuals. In this representation, art is complete in itself, and separate from other spheres of life; it should be a provider of satisfaction, and this is incompatible with the moral instruction that might be inferred from it leaving us, instead, with the feeling that there is something to be done, that it is making demands on its readers. Art, moreover, has nothing to do with money or commitment.

Yet, at other moments, Woolf's views appear quite different to this. She originally intended the novel that became *The Years* to be a mixture of essays and fiction, without the relation between the two having an order of precedence. Rather than the essays simply illustrating or lending support to the fiction, this was to be a wholly new genre.[1] When she discusses the essay as such ('The Decay of Essay-writing', 'The Modern Essay'), her emphasis is not on its informative or persuasive uses, but rather on exactly the features which might be expected to go with literature:

> The principle which controls [the essay] is simply that it should give pleasure; the desire which impels us when we take it from the shelf is simply to receive pleasure. Everything in an essay must be subdued to that end. It should lay us under a spell with its first word, and we should only wake, refreshed, with its last. In the interval we may pass through the most various experiences of amusement, surprise, interest, indignation; we may soar to the heights of fantasy with Lamb or plunge to the depths of wisdom with Bacon, but we must never be roused. The essay must lap us about and draw its curtain across the world. (p. 40)

The drowsy hedonism of this – the reader as enchanted sleeper for the duration of the text – is only the complementary match for the writer of essays, able to indulge in personal ruminations and speculations which would be out of place elsewhere:

> Almost all essays begin with a capital I – 'I think', 'I feel' – and when you have said that, it is clear that you are not writing history or philosophy or biography or anything but an essay, which may be brilliant or profound, which may deal with the immortality of the soul, or the rheumatism in your left shoulder, but is primarily an expression of personal opinion. (p. 6)

After reading such an essay, you might feel, depending on the preoccupations of the particular writer, that it was 'necessary to do something'; but you might well feel more in that state of pleasurable satisfaction which the opening quotation associated with the experience of art. So the boundaries blur. The essay, just as much as the work of art, may be cut off like pleasant night-time dreams from the demands of daily life or from the implicitly more impersonal genres of history, philosophy or biography. Its personal aspect makes it distinctively modern, as Woolf says in the early essay just cited; and its openness to any subject at all brings it close to the capaciousness and adaptability associated with the novel. Woolf's novels were described at the time as 'experimental'; and in many respects her essays, too, can be seen as trials or attempts at new kinds of style, new possibilities for writing: as Montaigne coined the word for the genre which he initiated, an *essai* is literally a try.

There are certainly many points in common between Woolf's essays and her novels. Just as the novels break up the habitual progressions of narrative through easily identifiable beginnings, middles and ends, so, in her essays, Woolf tends to write in a way that is consciously exploratory, seeming to move from one point to the next in a tangential fashion rather than to develop logically in the traditional form of an argument. The essay will depart from the predictable expository step, wandering off into the sidelines, digressions, little stories that may then illuminate the starting point in an unexpected way, off the beaten track. In 'The Patron and the Crocus', the exigencies and opportunities of literary markets are discussed not in terms of a general survey, but literally from the grass roots, through the hypothetical example of the crocus that has to get itself communicated in words.

'The Patron and the Crocus' takes us to the second of Woolf's customary separations of essay-writing from art, this one to do with its status as paid work. In a situation where essay-writing was not the practice in which Woolf herself imagined her primary artistic ambition or vocation to lie, her diaries often testify to her sense of the way that a commissioned review or essay could function as a distraction from what she conceived as her real work, planning or writing the next novel. Following a pattern which often appears in the discussions of modern literature within the essays themselves, Woolf kept to a fairly clear-cut separation between the writing she did to earn money and the writing that was creative. The essays, in the first category, were subject to deadlines, contracts, payments and all the conditions of a particular publication and its particular readership. Novels, the place for artistic experimentation, were represented as being free from such constraints and demands (though no less arduous in terms of a different kind of commitment).

In reading Woolf's essays, we don't have to take her own valuation, dismissing them as mere hackwork to pay the bills or keep her hand in (although they were often that too).[2] But nor should we rush to the other extreme, and claim for the essays artistic value equal or superior to that of the novels. For one thing, there are great variations between the essays – in their pretensions, their style, their subject matter – which make their consideration as a self-contained corpus little more than a matter of classificatory convenience: the published writings, other than her novels or the primarily 'private' letters and diaries, of Virginia Woolf. But, more significantly, this initial division between writing as a job and writing as art is also, within the essays (and the novels too), a question and a problem for Woolf, just as it also frequently surfaces as an assumption to be taken for granted.

Woolf was fascinated by the history of writing as a profession, especially as it affected the changes in opportunities for women to write, which she saw as a significant part of the more general history of the changes in opportunities for women to do any kind of paid work at all. Though she spoke dismissively of the restrictions that accompanied journalistic writing assignments, she also regarded writing for money as a crucial possibility for freedom from other kinds of restriction: the constraint and the opening were not mutually exclusive, but they were related in complex ways that Woolf was constantly exploring, as we shall see.

It is in this essay whose title pair, patron and crocus, are so incongruous (to use a favourite word of Woolf's) that there occurs the enigmatic allusion to the 'more than maternal tie' which gives this introduction its title. The phrase is intriguing not only because the connection of mother and baby is usually taken to be the closest of all – what could be 'more' of a tie? – but also because it turns out to refer to a relationship which is neither biological nor familial, but economic. In its context, this oddly 'more than maternal tie' is nothing more or less than the bond between the writer and the 'patron' – the individual or organization which pays for and publishes the writing. Adding still further peculiarities, the two are then glossed in the following clauses as 'twins indeed, one dying if the other dies, one flourishing if the other flourishes' (p. 68). A kind of sibling symbiosis is represented as stronger than inter-generational links, at the same time as the force of this being a metaphor suggests that professional or literary bonds may themselves be stronger than the bodily proximities of either mother and child or babes in the womb.

Woolf wrote often and extensively, in her essays and in her novels, about literary ties of all kinds – between writers and between readers and writers, as well as between writers and patrons. She was fascinated by the question of what prompts people to want to write or to read; by the history of the conditions under which these activities have taken place; and by the relations of both to ties of love in the family and in social life more generally. And all this was itself part of a constant interest in the sources, the conditions and the complexity of human connections – biological, familial, amorous and social – and her relentless questioning of the standard ways of thinking about them, or refraining from thinking about them.

The maternal tie is paradigmatically an obvious, unquestionable one, absolutely compelling and undeniable for both parties in both its demands and its pleasures, its bonds of mastery and of love. Yet it also has the peculiarity of being a tie that has always already been broken. The 'more than maternal tie', in this sense, would be one which was never withdrawn, and which also, for the same reason, would not be charged with both the anxiety and the lure of a lost wholeness. By another inflection, the maternal tie is customarily seen as being 'more' than the paternal – both in a symbolic sense (the child's relation to its mother, but not to its biological father, is visibly proven), and because in common experience it is mothers, not fathers, who almost always establish the first and the stronger nurturing links with the newborn child. Later, we shall see how Woolf did, to a certain extent, imagine the essay, as opposed to the novel, along fatherly lines.

The essays in this volume all look, in different ways, at these many kinds of tie – literary, familial, social – and with an emphasis, as we shall see, which shows that the two topics for which Woolf's essays have been known – modern writing and feminism – are intimately connected, as modern writing daughters work out the strength of their ties, or lack of ties, to mothers, fathers and patrons of all sorts. For Woolf this was a question directly related to the fact of writing essays, rather than other genres.

Woolf took from Johnson (who used it in his 'Life of Gray') the phrase 'the common reader', which became her own title for the two volumes of her essays she put together herself. The genial, low-key style associated with other eighteenth-century essayists like Addison, to whom she often refers in her own essays, was something she emulated: while they may turn to fiction, swerving irresistibly from exposition to narrative, her essays are not, as most of her novels are often found to be, difficult to get into. She was conscious of this as a necessity as much as a personal choice. Essays tend to be written to fit the highly specific, short-term requirements of daily or weekly papers, and thus have less flexibility or finish than a longer published work:

> To write weekly, to write daily, to write shortly, to write for
> busy people catching trains in the morning or for tired people
> coming home in the evening, is a heart-breaking task for men
> who know good writing from bad. They do it, but instinctively
> draw out of harm's way anything precious that might be damaged
> by contact with the public, or anything sharp that might irritate
> its skin. (p. 47)

The rush evoked here for both writers and readers goes together with a high degree of routinized regularity, in the specification of the times and frequency of both activities. And to the extent that the writer, too, is just another 'man' with a deadline, his position does not differ from that of the fellow-commuter with a train to catch, except that he may have a sad awareness of the distinction between good and bad writing. Where the quotation above said that essays must not rouse their readers, here the emphasis is more negative, suggesting that the homogenized body of superficial readers (they are represented as a sensitive, potentially irritable, skin) are in a state that is not unlike apathy: they ask only not to be disturbed.

These practical controls for the journalistic essay follow the same line of division as the one suggested in Woolf's aesthetic criticism of the social criticism of the Edwardian novelists. But here the appeal to artistic criteria in the qualitative distinction between kinds of writing implies that if anything would move the public to respond, it is art: the daily or weekly piece not only does not, but must not. The terms have now been reversed so that, paradoxically, journalism resembles the good novel the Edwardians did not write, in that it must satisfy its readers, not rouse them to doing anything.

Interesting ambiguities of this kind appear everywhere when Woolf is discussing writing of all kinds and its relation to matters of art, daily life and the historical development of literature; and this is consistently connected, too, with the particular case of women's writing. One emphasis represents the writer as a worker, literally making with the pen what other craftsmen make with other equipment. The context of this – sometimes with a defensive glance towards her sister Vanessa Bell, who was a painter – is often implicitly an equation between pen and brush, and a claim that the skills necessary to write well are just as complex as those needed to paint well.

The effort implied here can also be associated with another kind of labour, in Woolf's development of a traditional metaphor likening the process of artistic creation to giving birth. In an essay on the literary critic Edmund Gosse, for instance, she gives another turn to the 'more than maternal' aspect of writing:

> Like all critics who persist in judging without creating he forgets the risk and agony of childbirth. His criticism becomes more and more criticism of the finished article, and not of the article in the making.[3]

Woolf comes close here to making babies, as well as books, into commodities, albeit authentically crafted ones; but 'the risk and agony' stresses, in both senses, that the process is at the same time painful, and one whose outcome is not known in advance.

This maternal making is related to another strand in Woolf's thinking about women and literary production. In 'Professions for Women', where the opening question is not about writing as an art, but about women's historical exclusion from paid employment, she points hyperbolically to the exceptional condition of writing as a type of work:

> The cheapness of writing paper is, of course, the reason why women have succeeded as writers before they have succeeded in the other professions.
>
> But to tell you my story – it is a simple one. You have only got to figure to yourselves a girl in a bedroom with a pen in her hand. She had only to move that pen from left to right – from ten o'clock to one. Then it occurred to her to do what is simple and cheap enough after all – to slip a few of those pages into an envelope, fix a penny stamp in the corner, and drop the envelope

into the red box at the corner. It was thus that I became a journalist; and my effort was rewarded on the first day of the following month – a very glorious day it was for me – by a letter from an editor containing a cheque for one pound ten shillings and sixpence.[4]

Room, paper and a little time are the sole conditions for this unusual occupation which, with a little help from the postal system, can be carried out entirely from the legitimately feminine sphere of the home.

But in the same essay, in a famous passage about the subtle, invisible censorship of a figure named (after Coventry Patmore's popular nineteenth-century poem) the Angel in the House, Woolf goes on to describe how writing for women is far more than a matter of pen and paper. To the Angel is attributed a block upon intellectual activity: '"Never let anybody guess that you have a mind of your own."'[5] It should not escape notice, though, that far from saying that women have no brains, the Angel assumes that they do: femininity is not the lack of a mind, but its concealment.

The repressive Angel can be dealt with, Woolf suggests (she suffers a violent end at the hands of the frustrated woman writer); but there is a second figure who proves less tractable, this one more masculine than feminine and curbing the writing of the body rather than that of the mind:

> The girl was roused from her dream. She was indeed in a state of the most acute and difficult distress. To speak without figure she had thought of something, something about the body, about the passions which it was unfitting for her as a woman to say. Men, her reason told her, would be shocked.[6]

Once again, rousing means trouble. This passage strongly resembles a moment early on in *A Room of One's Own* when the 'Oxbridge' official appears to inform the woman that she is out of bounds. Here, however, the censure emanates from what is ironically called her own 'reason', and concerns the loss of the female identity ('as a woman') she imagines as the false attribution or requirement on the part of the other sex. And it is precisely where the body and the passions – the principal differentials in standard representations of men and women – come into view that there is a break, a painful awakening from the 'dream'. Woolf does not disentangle or provide an answer to the complexities of this question, insisting that the 'obstacles' women experience are not only the visible outward ones – lack of space, opportunity or money – but also the inner 'ghosts', less simple to describe, and also less easy to remedy:

> That young woman had only to be herself. Ah, but what is 'herself'? I mean, what is a woman? I assure you, I do not know.[7]

It follows, from what Woolf says here and elsewhere, that even the attempt to adumbrate the difficulties faced by a woman who wants to be free to write is already a contribution to their undoing, bringing them to the surface and trying to put them at a distance and in the form of communicable words. Here the 'essay', halting and inconclusive, enacts the problem it is attempting to make visible. It is one thing to be able to afford paper, another (and with far more effort) to do away with the negative daughterly tie to the Angel as an anachronistic feminine ideal; but this still, it would seem, leaves a further masculine block to writing, or indeed – for the two come to stand for each other – to being 'herself'.

The style of 'Professions for Women' is speculative and hesitant: Woolf is not so much offering answers as trying to show how hard it is even to try out the questions at all. Further pieces, like 'Women and Fiction', are written in a similar mode; but at other times, with a different audience in mind, Woolf will adopt a trenchantly polemical style, mocking and debunking the sexism of particular books or articles, as in her retort to Desmond MacCarthy in 'The Intellectual Status of Women'. There is a versatility in Woolf's range of personae which itself complicates the appeal to a possible 'herself' who might be capable of getting herself wholly transferred to the page, or to her reader's mind. By her own strategic shifts, Woolf implies that the writer cannot really be thought of as an isolated identity, independently existing of any cultural mediation; and this is as much a pleasure (in being more than one person) as a restriction (the sense of some identities being ruled out, or of having to put on a mask). But precisely because the woman experiences herself as categorically ruled out, suppressed by the force of a masculine culture, so she can take on the appearance of an elusive and, this time, desirable phantom identity, the woman 'herself' – an essence impossibly held

within quotation marks, of whom women's writing is always en-
deavouring to catch hold.

Woolf's interest in issues of artistic creation and the differences
between the sexes is apparent throughout her essays and her novels.
But she also writes about other kinds of difference – social, national,
racial – as they may affect the possibilities for writing. In the essay
on 'American Fiction', for instance, she makes an analogy between
the situation of women writers in relation to men writers, and that
of American writers in relation to British ones. Because of the
common language, and the history of colonization, Americans, like
women, have found themselves caught up in gestures of defensive
vindication:

> Women writers have to meet many of the same problems that
> beset Americans. They too are conscious of their own peculiarities
> as a sex; apt to suspect insolence, quick to avenge grievances,
> eager to shape an art of their own.

The next sentence, however, seems to gesture towards what
would ideally be a removal of such differences as those of sex or
nationality, construed as merely contingent:

> In both cases all kinds of consciousness – consciousness of self,
> of race, of sex, of civilization – which have nothing to do with
> art, have got between them and the paper, with results that are,
> on the surface at least, unfortunate.[8]

In comments like this, Woolf treats differences of identity, whether
claimed or imposed, as detracting from what could otherwise emerge
as an art which implicitly should have none of them. Rather than
imagining ways in which such differences might alter the criteria for
what is to be considered interesting art, she insists – with the kind
of over-assertiveness she is quick to notice in some Americans,
among others – on a particular stabilizing view of it:

> To describe, to unify, to make order out of all these severed
> parts, a new art is needed and the control of a new tradition.[9]

So even while suggesting that there should be 'a new art', Woolf is
laying down prescriptions for what its function should be which
align it with the old and make it sound restrictive – a necessary

'control' in the same way that the figure of censure might be to the woman whose thought is interrupted as 'unfitting'.

This perspective on art as unifying and harmonizing recurs frequently in Woolf's writing, and occasionally – despite a habitual contempt for anything associated with the nineteenth century – takes on a tone of classicizing anti-modernism which in its phrasing and sentiments is not unlike that of a staunch Victorian such as Matthew Arnold. 'On Not Knowing Greek', which Leonard Woolf chose for the opening essay in his own collected edition of Woolf's essays, explores different possibilities as to why Greek literature should seem so interesting, such as 'reading into Greek poetry not what they have but what we lack' (p. 103), but finally comes to rest on a note of a Victorian appeal to classical solidity as a remedy for present-day bewilderment:

> Entirely aware of their own standing, yet alive to every tremor and gleam of existence, there they endure, and it is to the Greeks that we turn when we are sick of the vagueness, of the confusion, of the Christianity and its consolations, of our own age. (p. 106)

Apart from the Arnoldian associations, there is something of Pater's Platonism in the 'tremor and gleam' of this, too; and indeed the strand which sees the value of art in its separation from modern life and its restorative power of control is itself held in an unresolved tension with the many other moments in Woolf's work when the emphasis is, instead, on the pleasures and the desirability of dispensing with social and artistic forms identified as anachronistic and oppressive. There is no unity in Woolf's statements about the function of unity or the separation of 'art' from given social identities, and this makes the trials of her statements on these subjects frustrating and fascinating at the same time. But, in noting the contradictions, it would be a mistake to treat them as obvious flaws: this would be to demand the same kind of untroubled unity which looks so blandly disappointing when Woolf returns to it as a model.

The title, 'On Not Knowing Greek', is in part an allusion to the title of Keats's poem 'On First Looking Into Chapman's Homer' (1816). Implicitly, in referring not to the translation but to the original language, Woolf is calling attention to women's lack of access to the expensive classical education that was a matter of course for upper-middle-class English boys. This differentiation is a frequent theme of her essays and novels. She looks upon it as a deprivation, indicative of women's exclusion from the institutions of culture; but also, and thereby, as a kind of freedom, in that it exempted women, like other groups lacking these privileges, from either the complacency or the embarrassment of maintaining them.

Woolf's double vision in relation to these issues is itself, perhaps, a function of this ambiguous placing. On the one hand, she sees a need for symbols of order and stability, so that she will adopt a standard nineteenth-century valorization of Greek culture as a source of 'the stable, the permanent, the original human being' (p. 96), and assume universal criteria for artistic value. On the other hand, she rejects the narrowness of a tradition and an education which in reality is divisive and one-sided: so in a late essay, 'The Leaning Tower', she begins by emphasizing the class-specificity of authorship:

> if you look closely you will see that almost every writer who has practised his art successfully had been taught it. He had been taught it by about eleven years of education – at private schools, public schools, and universities. He sits upon a tower built first on his parents' station, then on his parents' gold. It is a tower of the utmost importance; it decides the angle of his vision; it affects his power of communication. (p. 166)

Those sitting on this tower before 'the crash' of the outbreak of the First World War in 1914 were not interested in politics, Woolf says, and she associates this with their capacity not to question their own privileged elevation. This is very far from her tone in other contexts, when she will make the opposite point – as later in the same essay when she comes to the thirties poets – that too much politics detracts from an art whose value lies precisely in its freedom from the particularities and polemics of contemporary life.

Such oscillations return again and again in Woolf's discussions of questions of class and economics in relation to art, and of the literary tradition as such. In 'Women and Fiction', an essay that is close in time and conception to the longer *A Room of One's Own*, she concludes by saying that the 'leisure, and money, and a room to themselves', which women have 'so long been denied', are prerequisite to the improvement of their writing.[10] But she also thinks that art ceases to be art if it is infiltrated by excessive consideration of the stuff and surroundings of everyday life: this is the burden of her recurrent criticism of the novelists (generally her 'Edwardians' – Bennett, Galsworthy and Wells) she calls 'materialists'. In 'Modern Fiction', she writes:

> We mean by it [the word 'materialists'] that they write of unimportant things; that they spend immense skill and immense industry making the trivial and the transitory appear the true and enduring.[11]

The material supports of existence are both crucial to a consideration of the conditions of literature (great art requires time, money and education) and, at the same time, only a background which should not intrude into the content of art itself, which is situated outside the contingencies of 'the trivial and the transitory'.

And yet it is Woolf herself who will elsewhere suggest that even definitions of what is trivial as opposed to important may themselves be subject to question. The following statement, unconditional in the assurance of its future tenses, comes from 'Women and Fiction':

> Thus, when a woman comes to write a novel, she will find that she is perpetually wishing to alter the established values – to make serious what appears insignificant to a man, and trivial what is to him important. And for that, of course, she will be criticized; for the critic of the opposite sex will be genuinely puzzled and surprised by an attempt to alter the current scale of values, and will see in it not merely a difference of view, but a view that is weak, trivial, or sentimental, because it differs from his own.[12]

From this point of view, the very definition 'the trivial and the transitory' is put into question; what endures – if endurance is still an issue for the woman – may well turn out to be art that is very differently focused from the art that has endured up to now.

And whatever her statements in another mode, Woolf's practices in relation to the existing 'scale of values' in literature were in most ways anything but conservative. She was acutely aware of literary history as a history of the social conditions in which it was produced, not simply a matter of exceptional talents flourishing here and there and then finding an appropriate audience. This historical interest extended not only to changes in markets and readerships and types of publishing venture, but also to the more general influences of what she sometimes calls the 'environment' on the kind of literature that emerges in a given culture. (The environment might be a question of the weather: 'On Not Knowing Greek' takes quite seriously the proposition that the difference between Greek and modern English sensibilities is best understood in terms of their respective outdoor and indoor modes of social life.) As we have seen, Woolf was forever tugging at issues to do with the effects upon writing of having or not having wealth, having or not having education. In relation to women, she was fascinated by the question of why it was that a relatively large number of middle-class women started writing novels in the eighteenth century; and character-istically, she put this question (in *A Room of One's Own* and in 'Women and Fiction') in terms of class as well as sex.

Woolf shared with both her father and her husband, Leonard Woolf, this interest in the history of literary production (so much so that Leonard Woolf saw fit to append historical corrections to the piece entitled 'Reviewing' when it was published in his edition of Woolf's essays). She also shared with her father an interest in biography: Leslie Stephen was principal editor of the respected and respectful Victorian project, the *Dictionary of National Biography*, which consisted of short lives of those deemed to have been import-ant British men (there were a few women too). In her many essays on biography and biographers, Woolf constructed various possible stories to describe and explain what she saw as the astonishing shifts of emphasis in the writings of this genre over the previous 200 years. Members of her own circle, in particular Lytton Strachey and Harold Nicolson, seemed to her to have broken away, by their shorter, less reverent texts, from the Victorian convention of biogra-phical monumentality which she associated with her father's work; Woolf herself experimented with the genre in her fictional pastiche and undermining of its conventions (*Orlando*, *Jacob's Room*), though less so in her actual biography of her friend Roger Fry.

If novels, as opposed to non-fiction, seem to be the area where Woolf more freely departed from paternal standards of writing, this is related to the fact that the essay was her father's genre: a 'man of letters' *par excellence*, Leslie Stephen did not write 'creative' literature. Stephen published widely, in both senses: he wrote many articles, which appeared in solid Victorian periodicals like the *Nineteenth Century* and the *Edinburgh Review*; and he wrote on a variety of topics, ranging from philosophy to theology to biography. Woolf's relation to this paternal background was almost inevitably ambivalent, and it influenced the structure of her perception of the relation between her essay-writing and her fiction-writing, as well as no doubt contributing to her modifications of the essay in the direction of narrative, as a move away from her father's analytic style. In writing essays, she was directly following her father's footsteps, in a move that was composed of both rivalry and honour; in fact she took over where he left off, quite literally, since she began publishing (as it happened, for a small religious weekly called the *Guardian*) just after he died, in 1904.

Woolf in fact wrote two essays on her father – as a personality rather than as an author – at different times in her life; their filial politeness interestingly contrasts with the remarks she was capable of making about him in diaries and letters. These sometimes seem to verge on the 'intemperate candour' which is her own phrase for her father's writing (in 'The Modern Essay'); yet the fact that they are available to us for comparison as readers today itself raises interesting questions of a kind which interested Woolf about the relation between the public (or published) and private attitudes of an author.

Woolf's adaptation of her father's preoccupation with biography took the form of an interest in what she called 'the lives of the obscure': those which were all but obliterated, but not quite, in the pages of volumes that are unread but none the less have some kind of existence as published volumes. Many of her essays begin with a scene of the reading of an out-of-the-way book in an out-of-the-way library; the history of the place and its dusty contents become inseparable from the thoughts suggested by the words on the page. The modern reader brings to life the otherwise dead occupant of an unread volume; but at the same time, the reader is afflicted with the lifelessness of her surroundings. 'The Lives of the Obscure', which will go on to details of unread Colchester memoirs from a century before, begins like this:

Five shillings, perhaps, will secure a life subscription to this faded, out-of-date, obsolete library, which, with a little help from the rates, is chiefly subsidized from the shelves of clergymen's widows, and country gentlemen inheriting more books than their wives like to dust. In the middle of the wide airy room, with windows that look to the sea and let in the shouts of men crying pilchards for sale on the cobbled street below, a row of vases stands, in which specimens of the local flowers droop, each with its name inscribed beneath. The elderly, the marooned, the bored, drift from newspaper to newspaper, or sit holding their heads over back numbers of the *Illustrated London News* and the *Wesleyan Chronicle*. No one has spoken aloud here since the room was opened in 1854. The obscure sleep on the walls, slouching against each other as if they were too drowsy to stand upright. Their backs are flaking off; their titles often vanished. Why disturb their sleep? Why reopen these peaceful graves, the librarian seems to ask, peering over his spectacles, and resenting the duty, which has indeed become laborious, of retrieving from among those nameless tombstones Nos. 1763, 1080, and 606 . . .

For one likes romantically to feel oneself a deliverer advancing with lights across the waste of years to the rescue of some stranded ghost . . . waiting, appealing, forgotten, in the growing gloom.[13]

In a similar vein, drawing out the implications of this strange continuation of a life in a 'Life' so that pre-biographical, pre-posthumous lives disappear altogether, Woolf writes at the beginning of 'The Art of Biography': 'For after all, of all the multitude of lives that are written, how few survive!'[14]

Woolf's rescuing of buried memoirs of unknown people represented a conscious departure from the Victorian reverence for 'great men' selected by social status or notable achievement. It would be wrong, though, to see this as simply in opposition to her father's views. The editor of the publication which represented the very standard of respect for great men's lives could himself come out with a statement which seems to take the same line: 'There is also an immense universe of second-rate people whose lives are full of suggestion to any intelligent reader.'[15] But for the summary dismissal of 'second-rate', both the sentence and the sentiment could have been his daughter's.

In other ways, too, father and daughter were not so distant in their attitudes to literature and scholarship. Both distrusted academic institutions and the pedantry they associated with academic scholarship, and strongly believed in the value of writing in a language that was not over-technical, but comprehensible to any moderately educated reader. And both were modest about the relative significance of the genre they wrote in. Leslie Stephen even identifies the essay as characteristically feminine in its readership and its concerns:

> All the best-known authors of the eighteenth century tried their hands at this form of composition, as our grandmothers and great-grandmothers had good cause to know. The essays were lay sermons, whose authors condescended, it was supposed, to turn from grave studies of philosophy or politics to topics at once edifying and intelligible to the weaker sex.[16]

With the same kind of ironic wit that Woolf was to deploy in feminist contexts, this is written from the point of view of the patronized women readers.

But if the essay is historically a women's genre in terms of its intended readers and their intended topics of interest, neither Stephen nor Woolf ever mentions a female practitioner of the craft. Woolf identifies essays as essentially modern, akin to biography in their shared preoccupation with, or indulgence for, the individual personality of writer or of subject. In 'The Decay of Essay-writing', one of her first published pieces (the Wildean title was not hers), she makes an exception for Montaigne, who is made an honorary modern. Her canon of essay-writers includes Addison, Lamb, Pater and (latterly) Max Beerbohm; and though the number of possible women essayists for consideration is surely less than that of women novelists, for instance, it is none the less puzzling that Woolf, with all her zeal for uncovering and appreciating forgotten women and forgotten writings, should not have included in her list, say, the remarkable essays of George Eliot, whose irony matches her own. Maternal ties, in this instance, do not seem strong, just as the paternal tie – to her actual father and to the forefathers of the genre, through whom she thinks back – remains, in this instance, a tight one. It is as though the thorough masculinization of the tradition of essay-writing, as opposed to the tradition of novel-writing, would then give all the more force to Woolf's own takeover of the genre for unfemininely feminist concerns.

'Memories of a Working Women's Guild' is suggestive in this regard, for this is a piece which tries to take up the difficulty, rather than the obviousness, for someone in Woolf's position, of immediate identification with the causes and the writings of other women. The piece was written as a preface to a collection of autobiographical letters to Margaret Llewellyn Davies, who had been president of the Women's Co-Operative Guild, and it is partly a retrospective analysis of the embarrassment for a 'lady' in attending a working women's conference and finding herself unable to feel at one with the demands for material improvements which were the main preoccupation of the participants. Years afterwards, reading the manuscripts sent her by her friend provided Woolf with a partial means of reconsidering and making amends, she found evidence of interest in reading and ideas which she had missed in the public emphasis on practical things at the conference.

This essay is no more agreeably easy-going to read than the sense of awkwardness it describes. It troubles any wish to imagine Woolf having a straightforwardly immediate feeling of sisterhood, whether political or literary, with other women, whatever their backgrounds. In some respects, too, it seems to lay itself open to a double charge of linguistic condescension, as these two extracts show:

> No, they were not in the least detached and easy and cosmopolitan. They were indigenous and rooted to one spot. Their very names were like the stones of the fields – common, grey, worn, obscure, docked of all the splendours of association and romance. (p. 137)

> How many words must lurk in those women's vocabularies that have faded from ours! How many scenes must lie dormant in their eyes unseen by ours! What images and saws and proverbial sayings must still be current with them that have never reached the surface of print, and very likely they still keep the power which we have lost of making new ones. (p. 140)

In the first example, the women and their names are primitive, or at best pre-literary, bare; in the second, their language has the naïvety of a childlike freshness. Leaving aside the differences of formation between 'indigenous' rural villagers and the working class of the early twentieth century, the two conflicting implied histories of the development of language – from bare, unadorned rocks in the first instance and from homely local colour in the second – both place the middle-class listener in a condition of greater linguistic refinement, whether this is seen as sophistication or as reduction.

Yet it is Woolf herself who makes a problem out of what she labels 'aesthetic sympathy' (p. 139), and to criticize the essay for not measuring up to comfortable standards of feminist opinion would be to miss its attempt at serious engagement with issues generally avoided or unmentionable for the 'cosmopolitan' woman with whom Woolf seems to identify herself. The stumblings of this essay – as though here in identification with the hesitant qualities it finds in the writing it sets out to describe – are often much more interesting than the moments in other essays on literature where Woolf falls smoothly back on to the props of conventional wisdom about artistic value.

There is a rather different analysis of the qualities of women's writing in the essay called 'Royalty', this time taking up the peculiarities of the top-most end of the social scale. Here Woolf uses an image of confinement and impediment – the royal 'cage' – analogous to the one that often occurs when she is speaking of women's writing in general as having been limited by their lack of access to a 'wider' field of experience. But, in this instance, the subjects are two women placed in the same, contradictory 'royal' position which has both shut them up 'as lions and tigers are kept, in a beautiful brightly lit room behind bars' (p. 154), and, at the same time, given them rare opportunities, of a kind from which ordinary women are debarred. Given this initial similarity, what interests Woolf is that the two women wrote in such different ways. Queen Victoria's stiffness is that of 'an old savage': 'This primitive little machine is all that she has with which to register some of the most extraordinary experiences that ever fell to a woman's lot' (p. 155). Her granddaughter, however, Queen Marie of Romania, is a real writer:

> ... by virtue of her pen she has won her freedom. She is no longer a royal queen in a cage. She ranges the world, free like any other human being to laugh, to scold, to say what she likes, to be what she is. (p. 157)

Where the linguistic simpleness of the working-class conference delegates was a collective quality, the difference between the 'primitive' Victoria and her cosmopolitan relation is a matter of the chance of personal gifts. Marie is a natural of a different kind from the 'savage': 'by some freak of fate ... [she] has been born with a pen in her hand' (p. 156). For all the iconoclastic reversal of post-Darwinian prejudices, whereby – as with Thorstein Veblen's wicked strategy in *The Theory of the Leisure Class* (1899) – it is the aristocrat who is identified with the primitive, lower stage of civilization, still it remains true that it is when considering her royals, not when considering the women from mining villages, that Woolf looks for individual differences rather than for group characteristics.

Yet the review concludes, after playful speculation about the future possibilities of royal authorship, with a strong statement linking literature to political powers for change:

> Words are dangerous things, let us remember. A republic might
> be brought into being by a poem. (p. 158)

This emphasis, on the ways in which writing, by shifting the normal views, might change minds and institutions, disordering traditional structures, stands alongside and itself disturbs that other emphasis, against 'rousing', where Woolf sees literature as supplying a missing image of stability. And it is notable that generally, as in 'Royalty', it is from women that the trouble emanates, as though their 'outsider' positions automatically made them more likely to be the bearers of dangerous words or new words: words 'unfitting' a woman, in the phrase attributed to the Angel in the House; and thereby unfitting too for the cultural order which depends on a woman fitting into her allotted place.

Sometimes Woolf's essays play with the idea of woman being inherently unruly, and disruptive of neat orders in language, literature and culture, and at such moments she tends to adopt a pastiche of eighteenth-century style. Here, she is beginning one of her numerous discussions of the current state of the novel:

> That fiction is a lady and a lady who has somehow got herself
> into trouble is a thought that must often have struck her admirers. Many gallant gentlemen have ridden to her rescue ...
> (p. 121)

and she continues further on:

> For possibly, if fiction is, as we suggest, in difficulties, it may be
> because nobody grasps her firmly and defines her severely. She
> has had no rules drawn up for her, very little thinking done on
> her behalf. And though rules may be wrong and must be broken,
> they have this advantage – they confer dignity and order upon
> their subject; they admit her to a place in civilized society; they
> prove that she is worthy of consideration. (p. 122)

While characteristically claiming a need for rules, Woolf also
jokingly genders the rule-makers and the rule-breakers, acknowledg-
ing too that the breaking occurs through the agency of a woman
who insists on slipping away from the grasp of men's attempts to
hold her in one place.

Other passages make similar identifications between the woman
and the contaminator of imagined purities – in this instance, also
disturbing a conventional image of linguistic origins as harmoniously maternal:

> Royal words mate with commoners. English words marry French
> words, German words, Indian words, Negro words, if they have
> a fancy. Indeed, the less we inquire into the past of our dear
> Mother English the better it will be for that lady's reputation.
> For she has gone a-roving, a-roving fair maid.[17]

At moments like these, Woolf is provocatively questioning a reassur-
ing association between femininity and stable values, substituting
for the good woman or mother the promiscuous wench, in an
exchange which is itself a parody of the stereotypical alternative
images by which women are identified.

In terms of overt arguments for change, as opposed to the interpretation of a writing style as indicative of a change, Woolf used the
focus on women's relative exclusion from culture most forcefully
when she wrote about war. *Three Guineas*, in 1938, developed the
'outsider' argument to suggest why it was not self-evident for men
to appeal to women for financial support even for a cause like
disarmament which they might strongly support, when they have
had no part in bringing about the situations which have led to the
need for these organizations in the first place. 'Thoughts on Peace
in an Air-Raid', written during the bombings of 1940, is a further

expansion of some of the questions raised in *Three Guineas* about the differences between the sexes and their relation to war and its prevention. Woolf's 'dangerous' assimilation here is to put the drawing-room on a level with the council of war, putting into practice her imagined reversal of trivial and serious preoccupations and arenas, and using her words to claim equal status and equal rights of argument for the sex differentiated by its categorical placement outside these concerns:

> All the idea-makers who are in a position to make ideas effective are men. That is a thought that damps thinking, and encourages irresponsibility. Why not bury the head in the pillow, plug the ears, and cease this futile activity of idea-making? Because there are other tables besides officer tables and conference tables. Are we not leaving the young Englishman without a weapon that might be of value to him if we give up private thinking, tea-table thinking, because it seems useless?[18]

The words here are dangerous because they too are identified as 'a weapon' to counter the weapons of war; it is the verbal weapons which may render the other kind obsolete or redundant.

This piece also raises an issue which remains unsettled for Woolf concerning the source and significance of the 'instincts' associated with the two sexes. Her suggestion that 'we must compensate the man for the loss of his gun' and her comparison of men's 'fighting instinct' with women's 'maternal instinct', each to his or her own, both sound as though they are taking for granted natural distinctions in the inclinations and interests of the sexes. This might then make arguments about war (or babies) just as futile as they seemed at the start, since changing the minds of those who are instinctive fighters would be impossible. But however comical its formulation (there is something of the dowager in that sentence worrying about what we can give the poor boy to make up for his gun), the point of the analogy is to say that the problem of why men make war is not one that can be dealt with simply, as though it were merely a matter of logical conviction or the removal of crude propaganda:

> The young airman up in the sky is driven not only by the voices of loud-speakers; he is driven by voices in himself – ancient instincts, instincts fostered and cherished by education and

tradition. Is he to be blamed for those instincts? Could we switch off the maternal instinct at the command of a table full of politicians?'[19]

Here, the source of the instincts which distinguish the sexes is not natural but the result of an 'ancient' accretion. In refusing the instantaneous solution – if it's social, not natural, then just switch it off – as being too simple, Woolf is suggesting that simply to advocate change would be to repeat the unthinking instructions of the 'loud-speaker', here standing in for thirties propaganda on both sides of the channel. Because she does not accept that minds can be altered or programmed at the touch of a button, Woolf does not provide the comforting illusion of quick answers, much as she recognizes their appeal.

Similar questions about the ways in which dispositions are shaped by the social forms of 'education and tradition' can be found throughout Woolf's writing – her writing about writing as much as her writing about the world that words dangerously order and challenge. She takes her verbal stand against ready assumptions about literature, culture and the place within them of women and other outsiders, but is also aware of a need for order which she wants to see as being independent of the restrictive manifestations it has had. Once women begin to write, to contribute from the tea-tables (and also from the mining villages) to thinking about the conditions of culture and their place in it, then the risks, as well as the chances, must be great.

In killing her Angel, Woolf imagined that the loss of the tie to a mother complicit with middle-class assumptions about women's place was a necessary preliminary to the opening up of new thoughts and freedoms for her daughters. But then a more serious opponent, less easily dismissed, appeared in the form of a masculine censure on thinking about the body. More than maternal, this tougher bond is not to be dislodged at a stroke, any more than women's minds and bodies would willingly accept the renunciation of a wish to have children which, when it exists, is far more than a matter of readily reversible conditioning. And perhaps, the essay implies, there may be no utterly free state outside the lines or the ties against which identities are drawn up. In their ambivalent combination of constraint and support, the links are there before any 'we' can even begin to talk a common language. But Woolf, among others, was interested in what kinds of connections might tie things and people together in new ways. Her essays, like her novels, try some out.

Rachel Bowlby 1991

The editor would like to thank Bet Inglis, Saul Frampton, Julia Briggs and Hero Chalmers for substantial contributions to the preparation of the notes and text of this volume.

NOTES

1. The drafts for this preliminary conception have been edited by Mitchell A. Leaska and published as *The Pargiters* (Hogarth Press, 1977).
2. And, interestingly, the novels too increasingly became sources of significant income, beginning with *To the Lighthouse* in 1927. There are many references (often full of material delight) in the diaries and letters to trade-offs between earnings and acquisitions: great excitement expressed, for instance, at the installation of an automatically flushing water closet in the house at Rodmell, paid for by *To the Lighthouse*.
3. 'Edmund Gosse', *CE*, IV, p. 86.
4. 'Professions for Women', *CE*, II, p. 284.
5. ibid., p. 285.
6. ibid., pp. 287–8.
7. ibid., p. 286.
8. 'American Fiction', *CE*, II, p. 113.
9. ibid., p. 120.
10. 'Women and Fiction', *CE*, II, p. 148.
11. 'Modern Fiction', *CE*, II, p. 105.
12. 'Women and Fiction', *CE*, II, p. 146.
13. 'The Lives of the Obscure', *CE*, IV, p. 120.
14. 'The Art of Biography', *CE*, IV, p. 221.
15. Leslie Stephen, 'National Biography', in *Studies of a Biographer* (G. P. Putnam & Sons, 1898, p. 27).
16. Leslie Stephen, 'The Evolution of Editors', ibid., pp. 45–6.
17. 'Craftsmanship', *CE*, II, p. 250.
18. 'Thoughts on Peace in an Air-Raid', *CE*, IV, pp. 173–4.
19. ibid., p. 175.

Further Reading

PRIMARY

The Essays of Virginia Woolf, 3 vols. (to be 6 vols.), ed. Andrew McNeillie (Hogarth Press, 1986).

Collected Essays, 4 vols., ed. Leonard Woolf (Hogarth Press, 1966, 1967).

Moments of Being: Unpublished Autobiographical Writings of Virginia Woolf, ed. Jeanne Schulkind (2nd edn, Hogarth Press, 1985).

The Diary of Virginia Woolf, 5 vols., ed. Anne Olivier Bell (Hogarth Press, 1977; Penguin Books, 1979).

A Passionate Apprentice: The Early Journals, 1897–1909, ed. Mitchell A. Leaska (Hogarth Press, 1990).

The Letters of Virginia Woolf, 6 vols., ed. Nigel Nicolson and Joanne Trautmann (Hogarth Press, 1975–80).

The Complete Shorter Fiction of Virginia Woolf, ed. Susan Dick (2nd edn, Hogarth Press, 1989).

The Pargiters, ed. Mitchell A. Leaska (Hogarth Press, 1977).

SECONDARY

Michèle Barrett, 'Introduction' to Virginia Woolf, in *Women and Writing* (Women's Press, 1979).

Gillian Beer, *Arguing With the Past* (Routledge, 1989).

Quentin Bell, *Virginia Woolf: A Biography*, 2 vols. (Hogarth Press, 1972).

Edward L. Bishop, 'Metaphor and the Subversive Process of Virginia Woolf's Essays', in *Style* (vol. 21, no. 4, Winter 1987, pp. 573–89).

Rachel Bowlby, *Virginia Woolf: Feminist Destinations* (Basil Blackwell, 1988).

Rachel Bowlby (ed.), 'Walking, Women and Writing: Virginia Woolf as Flâneuse', in *New Feminist Discourses* (ed. Isobel Armstrong, Routledge, 1991).

George Lukács, 'On the Nature and Form of the Essay: A Letter to

Leo Popper', in *Soul and Form* (trans. Anna Bostock, M.I.T. Press, 1974).

Jane Marcus, *Virginia Woolf and the Languages of Patriarchy* (Indiana University Press, 1987).

Perry Meisel, *The Absent Father: Virginia Woolf and Walter Pater* (Yale University Press, 1980).

Brenda R. Silver, *Viriginia Woolf's Reading Notebooks* (Princeton University Press, 1983).

Elizabeth Steele, *Virginia Woolf's Literary Sources and Allusions: A Guide to the Essays* (Garland, 1983).

Alex Zwerdling, *Virginia Woolf and the Real World* (University of California Press, 1986).

A Note on the Texts

The text of each essay follows that of first publication except when essays were reprinted in *The Common Reader* or *The Common Reader: Second Series*, where the later texts have been used and some variants given in the notes. The provenance of individual items is indicated at the start of each essay. For a fuller publication history readers are referred to Andrew McNeillie's six-volume edition of *The Essays of Virginia Woolf* (Hogarth Press), published from 1986 onwards. The *Collected Essays* edited in four volumes by Leonard Woolf (Hogarth Press, 1966, 1967) are not complete and the provision of dates and other details is erratic and sometimes inaccurate.

The present selection of essays on women and literature (sometimes the two together, sometimes one or the other) is in part a continuation of the questions raised in, and through, Michèle Barrett's anthology, *Women and Writing* (Women's Press, 1979). *A Woman's Essays* is intended as a companion to a second volume of Woolf's essays, *The Crowded Dance of Modern Life*, also published by Penguin. In many instances, there were reasons for considering a particular essay in relation to the themes of both books; the two, together with their introductions, are meant to be taken as a pair, not as presentations of unrelated aspects of Woolf's thought. In addition, there were copyright reasons for placing some essays (notably, 'Professions for Women') in the second volume, issued a year after the first.

A WOMAN'S ESSAYS

The Feminine Note in Fiction

A review of W. L. Courtney's *The Feminine Note in Fiction* (Chapman and Hall, 1904), first published in the *Guardian*, 25 January 1905.[1]

Mr Courtney is certain that there is such a thing as the feminine note in fiction; he desires, moreover, to define its nature in the book before us, though at the start he admits that the feminine and masculine points of view are so different that it is difficult for one to understand the other. At any rate, he has made a laborious attempt; it is, perhaps, partly for the reason just stated that he ends where he begins. He gives us eight very patient and careful studies in the works of living women writers, in which he outlines the plots of their most successful books in detail. But we would have spared him the trouble willingly in exchange for some definite verdict; we can all read Mrs Humphry Ward,[2] for instance, and remember her story, but we want a critic to separate her virtues and her failings, to assign her right place in literature and to decide which of her characteristics are essentially feminine and why, and what is their significance. Mr Courtney implies by his title that he will, at any rate, accomplish this last, and it is with disappointment, though not with surprise, that we discover that he has done nothing of the kind. Is it not too soon after all to criticize the 'feminine note' in anything? and will not the adequate critic of women be a woman?

Mr Courtney, we think, feels something of this difficulty; his introduction, in which we expected to find some kind of summing-up, contains only some very tentative criticisms and conclusions. Women, we gather, are seldom artists, because they have a passion for details which conflicts with the proper artistic proportion of their work. We would cite Sappho and Jane Austen as examples of two great women who combine exquisite detail with a supreme sense of artistic proportion. Women, again, excel in 'close analytic miniature work'; they are more happy when they reproduce than when they create; their genius is for psychological analysis – all of which we note with interest, though we reserve our judgement for the next hundred years or bequeath the duty to our successor. Yet it is worth noting, as proof of the difficulty of the task which Mr Courtney has set himself, that he finds two at least of his eight women writers 'artists' – that two others possess a strength which in this age one has to call masculine, and, in fact, that no pair of them come under any one heading, though, of course, in the same way as men, they can be divided roughly into schools. At any rate, it seems to be clear according to Mr Courtney that more and more novels are written by women for women, which is the cause, he declares, that the novel as a work of art is disappearing. The first part of his statement may well be true; it means that women having found their voices have something to say which is naturally of supreme interest and meaning to women, but the value of which we cannot yet determine. The assertion that the woman novelist is extinguishing the novel as a work of art seems to us, however, more doubtful. It is, at any rate, possible that the widening of her intelligence by means of education and study of the Greek and Latin classics[3] may give her that sterner view of literature which will make an artist of her, so that, having blurted out her message somewhat formlessly, she will in due time fashion it into permanent artistic shape. Mr Courtney has given us material for many questions such as these, but his book has done nothing to prevent them from still remaining questions.

The Decay of Essay-writing

First published in *Academy and Literature*, 25 February 1905.
According to Woolf, the *Academy* changed the title of this article
from 'A Plague of Essays' and 'cut out a good half'.

The spread of education and the necessity which haunts us to impart what we have acquired have led, and will lead still further, to some startling results. We read of the over-burdened British Museum – how even its appetite for printed matter flags, and the monster pleads that it can swallow no more. This public crisis has long been familiar in private houses. One member of the household is almost officially deputed to stand at the hall door with flaming sword and do battle with the invading armies. Tracts, pamphlets, advertisements, gratuitous copies of magazines, and the literary productions of friends come by post, by van, by messenger – come at all hours of the day and fall in the night, so that the morning breakfast-table is fairly snowed up with them.

This age has painted itself more faithfully than any other in a myriad of clever and conscientious though not supremely great works of fiction: it has tried seriously to liven the faded colours of bygone ages; it has delved industriously with spade and axe in the rubbish-heaps and ruins; and, so far, we can only applaud our use of pen and ink. But if you have a monster like the British public to feed you will try to tickle its stale palate in new ways: fresh and amusing shapes must be given to the old commodities – for we really have nothing so new to say that it will not fit into one of the familiar forms. So we confine ourselves to no one literary medium; we try to be new by being old; we review mystery-plays[1] and affect an archaic accent; we deck ourselves in the fine raiment of an embroidered style; we cast off all clothing and disport ourselves nakedly. In short, there is no end to our devices, and at this very moment probably some ingenious youth is concocting a fresh one which, be it ever so new, will grow stale in its turn. If there are thus an infinite variety of fashions in the external shapes of our wares, there are a certain number – naturally not so many – of wares that are new in substance and in form which we have either invented or very much developed. Perhaps the most significant of these literary inventions is the invention of the personal essay. It is true that it is at least as old as Montaigne,[2] but we may count him the first of the moderns. It has been used with considerable frequency since his day, but its popularity with us is so immense and so peculiar that we are justified in looking upon it as something of our own – typical, characteristic, a sign of the times which will strike the eye of our great-great-grandchildren. Its significance, indeed, lies not so much in the fact that we have attained any brilliant success in essay-writing – no one has approached the essays of Elia[3] – but in the undoubted facility with which we write essays as though this were beyond all others our natural way of speaking. The peculiar form of an essay implies a peculiar substance; you can say in this shape what you cannot with equal fitness say in any other. A very wide definition obviously must be that which will include all the varieties of thought which are suitably enshrined in essays; but perhaps if you say that an essay is essentially egoistical you will not exclude many essays and you will certainly include a portentous number. Almost all essays began with a capital I – 'I think', 'I feel' – and when you have said that, it is clear that you are not writing history or philosophy or biography or anything but an essay, which may be brilliant or profound, which may deal with the immortality of the soul, or the rheumatism in your left shoulder, but is primarily an expression of personal opinion.

We are not – there is, alas! no need to prove it – more subject to ideas than our ancestors; we are not, I hope, in the main more egoistical; but there is one thing in which we are more highly skilled than they are; and that is in manual dexterity with a pen. There can be no doubt that it is to the art of penmanship that we owe our present literature of essays. The very great of old – Homer and Aeschylus – could dispense with a pen; they were not inspired by sheets of paper and gallons of ink; no fear that their harmonies, passed from lip to lip, should lose their cadence and die. But our essayists write because the gift of writing has been bestowed on them. Had they lacked writing-masters we should have lacked essayists. There are, of course, certain distinguished people who use this medium from genuine inspiration because it best embodies the soul of their thought. But, on the other hand, there is a very large number who make the fatal pause, and the mechanical act of writing is allowed to set the brain in motion which should only be accessible to a higher inspiration.

The essay, then, owes its popularity to the fact that its proper use is to express one's personal peculiarities, so that under the decent veil of print one can indulge one's egoism to the full. You need know nothing of music, art, or literature to have a certain interest in their productions, and the great burden of modern criticism is simply the expression of such individual likes, and dislikes – the amiable garrulity of the tea-table – cast into the form of essays. If men and women must write, let them leave the great mysteries of art and literature unassailed; if they told us frankly not of the books that we can read and the pictures which hang for us all to see, but of that single book to which they alone have the key and of that solitary picture whose face is shrouded to all but one gaze – if they would write of themselves – such writing would have its own permanent value. The simple words 'I was born' have somehow a charm beside which all the splendours of romance and fairy-tale turn to moonshine and tinsel. But though it seems thus easy enough to write of one's self, it is, as we know, a feat but seldom accomplished. Of the multitude of autobiographies that are written, one or two alone are what they pretend to be. Confronted with the terrible spectre of themselves, the bravest are inclined to run away or shade their eyes. And thus, instead of the honest truth which we should all respect, we are given timid side-glances in the shape of essays, which, for the most part, fail in the cardinal virtue of sincerity. And those who do not sacrifice their beliefs to the turn of a phrase or the glitter of paradox think it beneath the dignity of the printed word to say simply what it means; in print that must pretend to an oracular and infallible nature. To say simply 'I have a garden, and I will tell you what plants do best in my garden' possibly justifies its egoism: but to say 'I have no sons, though I have six daughters, all unmarried, but I will tell you how I should have brought up my sons had I had any' is not interesting, cannot be useful, and is a specimen of the amazing and unclothed egoism for which first the art of penmanship and then the invention of essay-writing are responsible.

The American Woman

A review of Elizabeth McCracken's *The Women of America*
(Macmillan, 1904), first published in the *Guardian*, 31 May 1905.[1]

Miss McCracken, in her investigations into the natural history of
the American woman, travelled over nearly the whole of the United
States, in a journey which occupied six months, which she found to
be all too short. She came home with her boxes full of pamphlets
and calendars and her notebooks full of statistics. But when she
began to write she found it best to put aside all these and to draw
her picture from life. Instead of a scientific treatise on the nature of
woman or a Blue-book[2] upon her place in the national life, she
gives us fourteen snapshots of the woman herself as she works or
plays, in whatever position she happened to be found. This method
is admittedly superficial, but in the space of one short volume we
are taken over a great distance of country and shown many queer
people living out-of-the-way lives.

There are many types of the American woman – more, perhaps,
than of the English woman – but they have a curious unity. We
begin with the pioneer who is set down in the Western prairie
where 'one need not yet keep to the path, for there is none. You
make your own trail.' She and her husband have to make their own
house, their home, and their town, and the woman's work here is
even more important than the man's. 'I want to help try new ways,'
says one of these pioneer women who lives in a small cattle-ranch
thirty-five miles from the nearest town. 'We have our whole lives
before us. And we intend to make them *good*.' The woman in the
small town does, perhaps, the most important work done by women
in America. America, says Miss McCracken, is a nation of small
communities, and the influence of home, which is the influence of
woman, is paramount here. It is significant that almost all the public
libraries in these towns were founded by women, their librarians
were usually women, and the women read almost exclusively 'real
books'. In the South she found that the women who had suffered

most in the war were teaching the negroes and fitting them for public life.

Miss McCracken is a cordial admirer of her own sex, and in only one case does her sympathy fail. For the last ten years the women of Colorado have had the ballot, and, while she admits that they have done good work publicly by means of it, she thinks that it has been at the expense of their own womanliness. Charitable acts are done with a view to votes, and the woman's perception of right and wrong has been dulled. But it is open to remark that the same might be said as emphatically of the male politician, and that the real question is whether the use made by women of political freedom is sufficiently valuable to justify the alleged injury. It is characteristic that the American woman's club is almost invariably a kind of Charity Organization Society for the improvement of themselves and others, and the democratic motto of one of them, 'Of all, by all, for all', is appropriate to many. Indeed, the American view of charity is typical and peculiar. A charitable English lady, for example, may read to the blind in her village; but the work is personal, and probably ceases in the case of her illness or death. An American woman in the same circumstances at once organized a society from the members of her club to help the blind. Then, not content with this, she got a Commission appointed by the State of Massachusetts to inquire into the condition of the blind, with the result that the State will probably institute schools for the training of the blind at public expense. There are many other illustrations of the same genius for organization, and of the peculiar nature of American charity, which is not satisfied with relieving suffering, but must find out and, if possible, eliminate the cause of it.

We have not space to comment upon the many interesting lines of thought that Miss McCracken opens up. One remark of hers seems to us to suggest the essential difference between American and other women, which gives them their special interest, and which has made it possible to paint such a sketch as this of a whole race with marked and recognizable features. The province of the American writer, she says, is the short story, because American life lends itself to 'instantaneous portraiture'. 'It is so young, without any deep furrows on its face.' 'The oldest of us in America are still rather new,' said one lady, who went on to say that they were not old enough yet to be even really democratic. A mother can point to her own mother, herself, and her daughter as representing three stages of development, and can lay her finger on the causes which have made them different. So many causes have combined to make an Englishwoman, that it is impossible to trace their effects and the succession of influences may well have neutralized each other. But everything that alters her own or her country's life at present tells upon the American woman, and to watch the process is a study of exceeding interest.

Women Novelists

A review of R. Brimley Johnson's *The Women Novelists* (Collins, 1918), first published in *The Times Literary Supplement*, 17 October 1918.

By rights, or, more modestly, according to a theory of ours, Mr Brimley Johnson should have written a book amply calculated, according to the sex of the reader, to cause gratification or annoyance, but of no value from a critical point of view. Experience seems to prove that to criticize the work of a sex as a sex is merely to state with almost invariable acrimony prejudices derived from the fact that you are either a man or a woman. By some lucky balance of qualities Mr Brimley Johnson has delivered his opinion of women novelists without this fatal bias, so that, besides saying some very interesting things about literature, he says also many that are even more interesting about the peculiar qualities of literature that is written by women.

Given this unusual absence of partisanship, the interest and also the complexity of the subject can scarcely be over-stated. Mr Johnson, who has read more novels by women than most of us have heard of, is very cautious – more apt to suggest than to define, and much disposed to qualify his conclusions. Thus, though this book is not a mere study of the women novelists, but an attempt to prove that they have followed a certain course of development, we should be puzzled to state what his theory amounts to. The question is one not merely of literature, but to a large extent of social history. What, for example, was the origin of the extraordinary outburst in the eighteenth century of novel writing by women? Why did it begin then, and not in the time of Elizabethan renaissance? Was the motive which finally determined them to write a desire to correct the current view of their sex expressed in so many volumes and for so many ages by male writers? If so, their art is at once possessed of an element which should be absent from the work of all previous writers. It is clear enough, however, that the work of Miss Burney, the mother of English fiction, was not inspired by any single wish to redress a grievance: the richness of the human scene as Dr Burney's daughter[1] had the chance of observing it provided a sufficient stimulus; but however strong the impulse to write had become, it had at the outset to meet opposition not only of circumstance but of opinion. Her first manuscripts were burnt by her step-mother's orders, and needlework was inflicted as a penance, much as, a few years later, Jane Austen would slip her writing beneath a book if anyone came in, and Charlotte Brontë stopped in the middle of her work to pare the potatoes. But the domestic problem, being overcome or compromised with, there remained the moral one. Miss Burney had showed that it was 'possible for a woman to write novels and be respectable', but the burden of proof still rested anew upon each authoress. Even so late as the mid-Victorian days George Eliot was accused of 'coarseness and immorality' in her attempt 'to familiarize the minds of our young women in the middle and higher ranks with matters on which their fathers and brothers would never venture to speak in their presence.'

The effect of these repressions is still clearly to be traced in women's work, and the effect is wholly to the bad. The problem of art is sufficiently difficult in itself without having to respect the ignorance of young women's minds or to consider whether the public will think that the standard of moral purity displayed in your work is such as they have a right to expect from your sex. The attempt to conciliate, or more naturally to outrage, public opinion is equally a waste of energy and sin against art. It may have been not only with a view to obtaining impartial criticism that George Eliot and Miss Brontë adopted male pseudonyms[2] but in order to free their own consciousness as they wrote from the tyranny of what was expected from their sex. No more than men, however, could they free themselves from a more fundamental tyranny – the tyranny of sex itself. The effort to free themselves, or rather to enjoy what appears, perhaps erroneously, to be the comparative freedom of the male sex from that tyranny, is another influence which has told disastrously upon the writing of women. When Mr Brimley Johnson says that 'imitation has not been, fortunately, the besetting sin of women novelists,' he has in mind no doubt the work of the exceptional women who imitated neither a sex nor any individual of either sex. But to take no more thought of their sex when they wrote than of the colour of their eyes was one of their conspicuous distinctions, and of itself a proof that they wrote at the bidding of a profound and imperious instinct. The women who wished to be taken for men in what they wrote were certainly common enough; and if they have given place to the women who wish to be taken for women the change is hardly for the better, since any emphasis, either of pride or of shame, laid consciously upon the sex of a writer is not only irritating but superfluous. As Mr Brimley Johnson again and again remarks, a woman's writing is always feminine; it cannot help being feminine; at its best it is most feminine: the only difficulty lies in defining what we mean by feminine. He shows his wisdom not only by advancing a great many suggestions, but also by accepting the fact, upsetting though it is, that women are apt to differ. Still, here are a few attempts: – 'Women are born preachers and always work for an ideal.' 'Woman is the moral realist, and her realism is not inspired by any ideal of art, but of sympathy with life.' For all her learning, 'George Eliot's outlook remains thoroughly emotional and feminine.' Women are humorous and satirical rather than imaginative. They have a greater sense of emotional purity than men, but a less alert sense of humour.

No two people will accept without wishing to add to and qualify these attempts at a definition, and yet no one will admit that he can possibly mistake a novel written by a man for a novel written by a woman. There is the obvious and enormous difference of experience in the first place; but the essential difference lies in the fact not that men describe battles and women the birth of children, but that each sex describes itself. The first words in which either a man or a woman is described are generally enough to determine the sex of the writer; but though the absurdity of a woman's hero or a man's heroine is universally recognized, the sexes show themselves extremely quick at detecting each other's faults. No one can deny the authenticity of a Becky Sharp or of a Mr Woodhouse.[3] No doubt the desire and the capacity to criticize the other sex had its share in deciding women to write novels, for indeed that particular vein of comedy has been but slightly worked, and promises great richness. Then again, though men are the best judges of men and women of women, there is a side of each sex which is known only to the other, nor does this refer solely to the relationship of love. And finally (as regards this review at least) there rises for consideration the very difficult question of the difference between the man's and the woman's view of what constitutes the importance of any subject. From this spring not only marked differences of plot and incident, but infinite differences in selection, method, and style.

The Tunnel

A review of Dorothy M. Richardson's *The Tunnel* (Duckworth, 1919),
first published in *The Times Literary Supplement*, 13 February 1919.

Although *The Tunnel* is the fourth book[1] that Miss Richardson has
written, she must still expect to find her reviewers paying a great deal
of attention to her method. It is a method that demands attention, as a
door whose handle we wrench ineffectively calls our attention to the
fact that it is locked. There is no slipping smoothly down the
accustomed channels; the first chapters provide an amusing spectacle
of hasty critics seeking them in vain. If this were the result of
perversity, we should think Miss Richardson more courageous than
wise; but being as we believe, not wilful but natural, it represents a
genuine conviction of the discrepancy between what she has to say and
the form provided by tradition for her to say it in. She is one of the rare
novelists who believe that the novel is so much alive that it actually
grows. As she makes her advanced critic, Mr Wilson, remark: 'There
will be books with all that cut out – him and her – all that sort of thing.
The book of the future will be clear of all that.' And Miriam
Henderson herself reflects: 'but if books were written like that, sitting
down and doing it cleverly and knowing just what you were doing and
just how somebody else had done it, there was something wrong, some
mannish cleverness that was only half right. To write books knowing
all about style would be to become like a man.' So 'him and her' are cut
out, and with them goes the old deliberate business: the chapters that
lead up and the chapters that lead down; the characters who are always
characteristic; the scenes that are passionate and the scenes that are
humorous; the elaborate construction of reality; the conception that
shapes and surrounds the whole. All these things are cast away, and
there is left, denuded, unsheltered, unbegun and unfinished, the
consciousness of Miriam Henderson, the small sensitive lump of
matter, half transparent and half opaque, which endlessly reflects and
distorts the variegated procession, and is, we are bidden to believe, the
source beneath the surface, the very oyster within the shell.

The critic is thus absolved from the necessity of picking out the themes of the story. The reader is not provided with a story; he is invited to embed himself in Miriam Henderson's consciousness, to register one after another, and one on top of another, words, cries, shouts, notes of a violin, fragments of lectures, to follow these impressions as they flicker through Miriam's mind, waking incongruously other thoughts, and plaiting incessantly the many-coloured and innumerable threads of life. But a quotation is better than description.

> She was surprised now at her familiarity with the details of the room . . . that idea of visiting places in dreams. It was something more than that . . . all the real part of your life has a real dream in it; some of the real dream part of you coming true. You know in advance when you are really following your life. These things are familiar because reality is here. Coming events cast *light*. It is like dropping everything and walking backward to something you know is there. However far you go out you come back . . . I am back now where I was before I began trying to do things like other people. I left home to get here. None of those things can touch me here. They are mine.

Here we are thinking, word by word, as Miriam thinks. The method, if triumphant, should make us feel ourselves seated at the centre of another mind, and, according to the artistic gift of the writer, we should perceive in the helter-skelter of flying fragments some unity, significance, or design. That Miss Richardson gets so far as to achieve a sense of reality far greater than that produced by the ordinary means is undoubted. But, then, which reality is it, the superficial or the profound? We have to consider the quality of Miriam Henderson's consciousness, and the extent to which Miss Richardson is able to reveal it. We have to decide whether the flying helter-skelter resolves itself by degrees into a perceptible whole. When we are in a position to make up our minds we cannot deny a slight sense of disappointment. Having sacrificed not merely 'hims and hers', but so many seductive graces of wit and style for the prospect of some new revelation or greater intensity, we still find ourselves distressingly near the surface. Things look much the same as ever. It is certainly a very vivid surface. The consciousness of Miriam takes the reflection of a dentist's room to perfection. Her sense of touch, sight and hearing are all excessively acute. But sensations, impressions, ideas and emotions glance off her, unrelated and unquestioned, without shedding quite as much light as we had hoped into the hidden depths. We find ourselves in the dentist's room, in the street, in the lodging-house bedroom frequently and convincingly; but never, or only for a tantalizing second, in the reality which underlies these appearances. In particular, the figures of other people on whom Miriam casts her capricious light are vivid enough, but their sayings and doings never reach that degree of significance which we, perhaps unreasonably, expect. The old method seems sometimes the more profound and economical of the two. But it must be admitted that we are exacting. We want to be rid of realism, to penetrate without its help into the regions beneath it, and further require that Miss Richardson shall fashion this new material into something which has the shapeliness of the old accepted forms. We are asking too much; but the extent of our asking proves that *The Tunnel* is better in its failure than most books in their success.

Men and Women

A review of Léonie Villard's *La Femme anglaise au XIXe siècle et son évolution d'après le roman anglais contemporain* [*The English Woman in the Nineteenth Century and Her Evolution As Seen in the Contemporary English Novel*] (Henry Didier, 1920). First published in *The Times Literary Supplement*, 18 March 1920.

If you look at a large subject through the medium of a little book you see for the most part something of such vague and wavering outline that, though it may be a Greek gem, it may almost equally be a mountain or a bathing machine. But though Mlle Villard's book is small and her subject vast, her focus is so exact and her glass so clear that the outline remains sharp and the detail distinct. Thus we can read every word with interest because it is possible at a thousand points to check her statements; she is on every page dealing with the definite and the concrete. But how, in treating of a whole century, a whole country, and a whole sex, is it possible to be either definite or concrete? Mlle Villard has solved the problem by using fiction as her material; for, though she has read Blue-books[1] and biographies, her freshness and truth must be ascribed largely to the fact that she has preferred to read novels. In novels, she says, the thoughts, hopes and lives of women during the century and in the country of her most remarkable development are displayed more intimately and fully than elsewhere. One might indeed say that were it not for the novels of the nineteenth century we should remain as ignorant as our ancestors of this section of the human race. It has been common knowledge for ages that women exist, bear children, have no beards, and seldom go bald; but save in these respects, and in others where they are said to be identical with men, we know little of them and have little sound evidence upon which to base our conclusions. Moreover, we are seldom dispassionate.

Before the nineteenth century literature took almost solely the form of soliloquy, not of dialogue. The garrulous sex, against common repute, is not the female but the male; in all the libraries of the world the man is to be heard talking to himself and for the most part about himself. It is true that women afford ground for much speculation and are frequently represented; but it is becoming daily more evident that Lady Macbeth, Cordelia, Ophelia, Clarissa, Dora, Diana, Helen[2] and the rest are by no means what they pretend to be. Some are plainly men in disguise; others represent what men would like to be, or are conscious of not being; or again they embody that dissatisfaction and despair which afflict most people when they reflect upon the sorry condition of the human race. To cast out and incorporate in a person of the opposite sex all that we miss in ourselves and desire in the universe and detest in humanity is a deep and universal instinct on the part both of men and of women. But though it affords relief, it does not lead to understanding. Rochester[3] is as great a travesty of the truth about men as Cordelia is of the truth about women. Thus Mlle Villard soon finds herself confronted by the fact that some of the most famous heroines even of nineteenth-century fiction represent what men desire in women, but not necessarily what women are in themselves. Helen Pendennis, for example, tells us a great deal more about Thackeray than about herself. She tells us, indeed, that she has never had a penny that she could call her own, and no more education than serves to read the Prayer-book and the cookery-book. From her we learn also that when one sex is dependent upon the other it will endeavour for safety's sake to simulate what the dominant sex finds desirable. The women of Thackeray and the women of Dickens succeed to some extent in throwing dust in their masters' eyes though the peculiar repulsiveness of these ladies arises from the fact that the deception is not wholly successful. The atmosphere is one of profound distrust. It is possible that Helen herself flung off her widow's weeds, took a deep draught of beer, produced a short clay pipe, and stuck her legs on the mantelpiece directly her master was round the corner. At any rate, Thackeray cannot forbear one glance of suspicion as he turns his back. But midway through the nineteenth century the servile woman was stared out of countenance by two very uncompromising characters – Jane Eyre and Isopel Berners.[4] One insisted that she was poor and plain, and the other that she much preferred wandering on a heath to settling down and marrying anybody. Mlle Villard attributes the remarkable contrast between the servile and the defiant, the sheltered and the adventurous, to the introduction of machinery. Rather more than a century ago, after whirling for many thousands of years, the spinning-wheel became obsolete.

> *En fait, le désir de la femme de s'extérioriser, de dépasser les limites jusque-là assignées à son activité, prend naissance au moment même où sa vie est moins étroitement liée à toutes les heures aux tâches du foyer, aux travaux qui, une ou deux générations auparavant, absorbaient son attention et employaient ses forces. Le rouet, l'aiguille, la quenouille, la préparation des confitures et des conserves, voire des chandelles et du savon ... n'occupent plus les femmes et, tandis que l'antique ménagère disparaît, celle qui sera demain la femme nouvelle sent grandir en elle, avec le loisir de voir, de penser, de juger, la conscience d'elle-même et du monde où elle vit.*[5]

For the first time for many ages the bent figure with the knobbed hands and the bleared eyes, who, in spite of the poets, is the true figure of womanhood, rose from her wash-tub, took a stroll out of doors, and went into the factory. That was the first painful step on the road to freedom.

Any summary of the extremely intelligent pages in which Mlle Villard has told the story of the Englishwoman's progress from 1860 to 1914 is impossible. Moreover, Mlle Villard would be the first to agree that not even a woman, and a Frenchwoman at that, looking with the clear-sighted eyes of her race across the Channel, can say for certain what the words 'emancipation' and 'evolution' amount to. Granted that the woman of the middle class has now some leisure, some education, and some liberty to investigate the world in which she lives, it will not be in this generation or in the next that she will have adjusted her position or given a clear account of her powers. 'I have the feelings of a woman,' says Bathsheba in *Far from the Madding Crowd*,[6] 'but I have only the language of men.' From that dilemma arise infinite confusions and complications. Energy has been liberated, but into what forms is it to flow? To try the accepted forms, to discard the unfit, to create others which are more fitting, is a task that must be accomplished before there is freedom or achievement. Further, it is well to remember that woman was not created for the first time in the year 1860. A large part of her energy is already fully employed and highly developed. To pour such surplus energy as there may be into new forms without wasting a drop is the difficult problem which can only be solved by the simultaneous evolution and emancipation of man.

Freudian Fiction

A review of J. D. Beresford's *An Imperfect Mother* (Collins, 1920), first published in *The Times Literary Supplement*, 25 March 1920.

Mr Beresford is always a conscientious writer, but in *An Imperfect Mother* one cannot help feeling that conscience can at best play a stepmother's part in the art of fiction. She can keep things neat and orderly, see that no lies are told, and bring up her stepchildren to lead strenuous and self-respecting lives. But the joys of intimacy are not hers; there is something perfunctory in the relationship. In this case we hazard the opinion that, from the highest motives, Mr Beresford has acted the part of stepfather to some of the very numerous progeny of Dr Freud.[1] The chief characters, Cecilia, Stephen, and Margaret Weatherley, are his children and not Mr Beresford's. On page 12 there is certain proof of it:

> Something within him had inarticulately protested against his conscientious endeavours to submit himself to the idea of this new ambition ... He had been harassed, too, by a persistent nightmare, quite new in his experience – a nightmare of being confined in some intolerably dark and restricted place from which he struggled desperately to break out. Sometimes he had succeeded, and waked with a beautiful sense of relief.

After that one expects to find that Stephen is beginning, unconsciously, to fall in love with the schoolmaster's daughter; nor is one surprised to discover that he is the victim of an unacknowledged passion for his mother. It follows that she returns his affection in the inarticulate manner of those who lived before Freud, and, finding herself supplanted by Margaret Weatherley, decides to run away with Threlfall the organist. This is strictly in accordance with the new psychology, which in the sphere of medicine claims to have achieved positive results of great beneficence. A patient who has never heard a canary sing without falling down in a fit can now walk through an avenue of cages without a twinge of emotion since he has faced the fact that his mother kissed him in his cradle. The triumphs of science are beautifully positive. But for novelists the matter is much more complex; and should they, like Mr Beresford, possess a conscience, the question how far they should allow themselves to be influenced by the discoveries of the psychologists is by no means simple. Happily, that is their affair; our task in reviewing is comparatively easy, although we, too, are conscious of a division of mind which twenty or even ten years ago could hardly have afflicted our predecessors. Stated briefly, our dilemma resolves itself into this. Judged as an essay in morbid psychology, *An Imperfect Mother* is an interesting document; judged as a novel, it is a failure. All this talk, we find ourselves protesting when Mr Beresford in his able way describes Medboro', or the building of a factory, is irrelevant to the case. We cannot help adopting the professional manner of a doctor intent upon his diagnosis. A love scene interests us because something bearing significantly upon our patient's state of mind may emerge. Our attention is rewarded.

> She laughed at his deliberation. 'You *are* a funny boy,' she chided him. 'One might think I was your mother.' . . . The reference used as a simile finished Stephen. The obscure resistance that he had been fighting to overcome was no longer physical inertia; it had become a positive impulse.

Yes, says the scientific side of the brain, that is interesting; that explains a great deal. No, says the artistic side of the brain, that is dull and has no human significance whatever. Snubbed and discouraged, the artist retreats; and before the end of the book the medical man is left in possession of the field; all the characters have become cases; and our diagnosis is now so assured that a boy of six has scarcely opened his lips before we detect in him unmistakable symptoms of the prevailing disease.

There remains the question whether we are not pandering to some obsolete superstition when we thus decree that certain revelations are of medical significance, others of human; that some are only fit for the columns of the *Lancet*,[2] others for the pages of fiction. If it is true that our conduct in crucial moments is immensely influenced, if not decided, by some forgotten incident in childhood, then surely it is cowardice on the part of the novelist to persist in ascribing our behaviour to untrue causes. We must protest that we do not wish to debar Mr Beresford from making use of any key that seems to him to fit the human mind. Our complaint is rather that in *An Imperfect Mother* the new key is a patent key that opens every door. It simplifies rather than complicates, detracts rather than enriches. The door swings open briskly enough, but the apartment to which we are admitted is a bare little room with no outlook whatever. Partly, no doubt, this is to be attributed to the difficulty of adapting ourselves to any new interpretation of human character; but partly, we think, to the fact that, in the ardours of discovery, Mr Beresford has unduly stinted his people of flesh and blood. In becoming cases they have ceased to be individuals.

An Imperfect Lady

A review of Constance Hill's *Mary Russell Mitford and Her Surroundings*
(John Lane, 1920), first published in *The Times Literary Supplement*,
6 May 1920.

Little is known of Sappho, and that little is not wholly to her credit. Lady Jane Grey has merit, but is undeniably obscure. Of George Sand the more we know the less we approve. George Eliot was led into evil ways which not all her philosophy can excuse. The Brontës, however highly we rate their genius, lacked that indefinable something which marks the lady; Harriet Martineau was an atheist; Mrs Browning was a married woman; Jane Austen, Fanny Burney, and Maria Edgeworth[1] have been done already; so that, what with one thing and another, Mary Russell Mitford is the only woman left. This is no vain parade of erudition; we are trying to find out what considerations had weight with Miss Hill when she decided to write *Mary Russell Mitford and Her Surroundings*. Two emerge from the rest and may be held of paramount importance. In the first place, Miss Mitford was a lady; in the second, she was born in the year 1787.

There is no need to labour the extreme importance of the date when we see the word 'surroundings' on the back of a book. Surroundings, as they are called, are invariably eighteenth-century surroundings. When we come, as of course we do, to that phrase which relates how 'as we looked upon the steps leading down from the upper room, we fancied we saw the tiny figure jumping from step to step', it would be the grossest outrage upon our sensibilities to be told that those steps were Athenian, Elizabethan, or Parisian. They were, of course, eighteenth-century steps, leading down from the old panelled room into the shady garden, where, tradition has it, William Pitt[2] played marbles, or, if we like to be bold, where on still summer days we can almost fancy that we hear the drums of Bonaparte on the coast of France. Bonaparte is the limit of the imagination on one side, as Monmouth[3] is on the other; it would be fatal if the imagination took to toying with Prince Albert or sporting with

King John. But fancy knows her place, and there is no need to labour the point that her place is the eighteenth century. The other point is more obscure. One must be a lady. Yet what that means, and whether we like what it means, may both be doubtful. If we say that Jane Austen was a lady and that Charlotte Brontë was not one, we do as much as need be done in the way of definition, and commit ourselves to neither side.

It is undoubtedly because of their reticence that Miss Hill is on the side of the ladies. They sigh things off and they smile things off, but they never seize the silver table by the legs or dash the tea-cups on the floor. It is in many ways a great convenience to have a subject who can be trusted to live a long life without once raising her voice. Sixteen years is a considerable stretch of time, but of a lady it is enough to say, 'Here Mary Mitford passed sixteen years of her life and here she got to know and love not only their own beautiful grounds but also every turn of the surrounding shady lanes.' Her loves were vegetable, and her lanes were shady. Then, of course, she was educated at the school where Jane Austen and Mrs Sherwood[4] had been educated. She visited Lyme Regis, and there is mention of the Cobb.[5] She saw London from the top of St Paul's, and London was much smaller then than it is now. She changed from one charming house to another, and several distinguished literary gentlemen paid her compliments and came to tea. When the dining-room ceiling fell down it did not fall on her head, and when she took a ticket in a lottery she did win the prize. If in the foregoing sentences there are any words of more than two syllables, it is our fault and not Miss Hill's; and to do that writer justice there are not many whole sentences in the book which are neither quoted from Miss Mitford nor supported by the authority of Mr Crissy.[6]

But how dangerous a thing is life! Can one be sure that anything not wholly made of mahogany will to the very end stand empty in the sun? Even cupboards have their secret springs, and when, inadvertently we are sure, Miss Hill touches this one, out, terrible to relate, topples a stout old gentleman. In plain English, Miss Mitford had a father. There is nothing actually improper in that. Many women have had fathers. But Miss Mitford's father was kept in a cupboard; that is to say, he was not a nice father. Miss Hill even goes so far as to conjecture that when 'an imposing procession of neighbours and friends' followed him to the grave, 'we cannot help thinking that this was more to show sympathy and respect for Miss Mitford than from special respect for him.' Severe as the judgement is, the gluttonous, bibulous, amorous old man did something to deserve it. The less said about him the better. Only, if from your earliest childhood your father has gambled and speculated, first with your mother's fortune, then with your own, spent your earnings, driven you to earn more, and spent that too; if in old age he has lain upon a sofa and insisted that fresh air is bad for daughters, if, dying at length, he has left debts that can only be paid by selling everything you have or sponging upon the charity of friends – then even a lady sometimes raises her voice. Miss Mitford herself spoke out once, 'It was grief to go; there I had toiled and striven and tasted as deeply of bitter anxiety, of fear, and of hope as often falls to the lot of woman.' What language for a lady to use! for a lady, too, who owns a teapot.[7] There is a drawing of the teapot at the bottom of the page. But it is now of no avail; Miss Mitford has smashed it to smithereens. That is the worst of writing about ladies; they have fathers as well as teapots. On the other hand, some pieces of Dr Mitford's Wedgwood dinner service are still in existence, and a copy of Adam's Geography, which Mary won as a prize at school, is 'in our temporary possession'. If there is nothing improper in the suggestion, might not the next book be devoted entirely to them?

The Plumage Bill

First published in the *Woman's Leader*, 23 July 1920.

If I had the money and the time I should, after reading Wayfarer.[1] in the *Nation* of July 10th, go to Regent Street, buy an egret plume, and stick it – is it in the back or the front of the hat? – and this in spite of a vow taken in childhood and hitherto religiously observed. The Plumage Bill[2] has been smothered; millions of birds are doomed not only to extinction but to torture; and Wayfarer's comment is, 'What does one expect? They have to be shot in parenthood for child-bearing women to flaunt the symbols of it, and, as Mr Hudson says, one bird shot for its plumage means ten other deadly wounds and the starvation of the young. But what do women care? Look at Regent Street this morning!' One can look at Regent Street without leaving one's room. The lower half of the houses is composed of plate glass. One might string substantives and adjectives together for an hour without naming a tenth part of the dressing bags, silver baskets, boots, guns, flowers, dresses, bracelets and fur coats arrayed behind the glass. Men and women pass incessantly this way and that. Many loiter and perhaps desire, but few are in a position to enter the doors. Most of them merely steal a look and hurry on. And then comes on foot, so that we may have a good look at her, a lady of a different class altogether. A silver bag swings from her wrist. Her gloves are white. Her shoes lustrous. She holds herself upright. As an object of beauty her figure is incomparably more delightful than any other object in street or window. It is her face that one must discount, for, though discreetly tinted and powdered, it is a stupid face, and the look she sweeps over the shop windows has something of the greedy petulance of a pug-dog's face at tea-time. When she comes to the display of egret plumes, artfully arranged and centrally placed, she pauses. So do many women. For, after all, what can be more etherially and fantastically lovely? The plumes seem to be the natural adornment of spirited and fastidious life, the very symbols of pride and distinction. The lady of the stupid face and beautiful figure is going tonight to the opera; Clara Butt is singing Orpheus; Princess Mary will be present; a lemon-coloured egret is precisely what she wants to complete her toilet. In she goes; the silver bag disgorges I know not how many notes; and the fashion writers next day say that Lady So-and-So was 'looking lovely with a lemon-coloured egret in her hair'.

But since we are looking at pictures let us look at another which has the advantage of filling certain blank spaces in our rough sketch of Regent Street in the morning. Let us imagine a blazing South American landscape. In the foreground a bird with a beautiful plume circles round and round as if lost or giddy. There are red holes in its head where there should be eyes. Another bird, tied to a stake, writhes incessantly, for red ants devour it. Both are decoys. The fact is that before 'the child-bearing woman can flaunt the symbols of parenthood' certain acts have to be devised, done, and paid for. It is in the nesting season that the plumes are brightest. So, if we wish to go on making pictures, we must imagine innumerable mouths opening and shutting, opening and shutting, until – as no parent bird comes to feed them – the young birds rot where they sit. Then there are the wounded birds, trailing leg or wing, as they flutter off to droop and falter in the dust. But perhaps the most unpleasant sight that we must make ourselves imagine is the sight of the bird tightly held in one hand while another hand pierces the eyeballs with a feather. But these hands – are they the hands of men or of women? The Plumage Bill supporters say that the hunters 'are the very scum of mankind'. We may assume that the newspapers would have let us know if any of the other sex had been concerned in it. We may fairly suppose then that the birds are killed by men, starved by men, and tortured by men – not vicariously, but with their own hands. 'A small band of East End profiteers' supports the trade; and East End profiteers are apt also to be of the male sex. But now, as Wayfarer says, the birds 'have to be shot in parenthood for child-bearing women to flaunt the symbols of it'.

But what is the nature of this compulsion? Well, men must make their livings, must earn their profits, and must beget children. For though some people say that they can control their passions, the majority maintain that they should be protected from them rather than condemned for them. In other words, it is one thing to desire a woman; quite another to desire an egret plume.

There remains, however, a body of honourable and disinterested men who are neither plume hunters, profiteers, nor women. It is their duty, as it is within their power, to end the murder and torture of the birds, and to make it impossible for a single egret to be robbed of a single plume. The House of Commons took the matter up. The Plumage Bill was sent to Standing Committee C. With one exception each of its sixty-seven members was a man. And on five occasions it was impossible to get a quorum of twenty to attend. The Plumage Bill is for all practical purposes dead. But what do men care? Look wherever you like this morning! Still, one cannot imagine Wayfarer putting it like that. 'They have to be shot for child-begetting men to flaunt the symbols of it . . . But what do men care? Look at Regent Street this morning!' Such an outburst about a fishing-rod would be deemed sentimental in the extreme. Yet I suppose that salmon have their feelings.

So far as I know, the above, though much embittered by sex antagonism, is a perfectly true statement. But the interesting point is that in my ardour to confute Wayfarer, a journalist of admitted humanity, I have said more about his injustice to women than about the sufferings of birds. Can it be that it is a graver sin to be unjust to women than to torture birds?

The Intellectual Status of Women

In the Autumn of 1920 the successful Edwardian novelist
Arnold Bennett published a collection of his essays, *Our Women:
Chapters on the Sex-Discord*. Woolf, staying in the country and working
on *Jacob's Room*, found herself 'making up a paper on women, as a
counterblast to Mr Bennett's adverse views reported in the papers'
(*Diary*, II, 26 Sept. 1920, p. 69). Bennett's assertion that women
were intellectually the inferior of men provoked Woolf to think further
about the issue, which she later explored in *A Room of One's Own*
(1929). On 2 October her friend Desmond MacCarthy published
the following review of Bennett's book in the *New Statesman*,
under his pseudonym, Affable Hawk.

*Samuel Butler used to say when asked what he thought about women, 'I
think what every sensible man thinks'; and when pressed further he
would add, 'Sensible men never tell'. This was ominous and also
characteristic; the crusty bachelor was a strong strain in him. Mr
Arnold Bennett has written a book about women – not my women, you
observe, which is a title that would suit most other books written on the
subject. For though such books often profess to be results of detached
observation and to be about women in general, they usually contain only
notes about certain types familiar to the author. There seems an
irresistible tendency to generalize on the topic. It seems difficult to make
an observation about two or three women without at once turning into a
proposition about all women. I own I have done this myself, and said
many things which seemed to me clever and penetrating at the time,
but were not scientific. One such aphorism I recall because the first
half of it would meet, I think, with Mr Bennett's assent, since he quotes
with approval Lady Mary Montagu's remark,[1] 'I have never in all
my various travels seen but two sorts of people, and those very like
one another; I mean, men and women.' My aphorism ran thus: 'Men
and women are really more alike than they can believe each other to be;
but they ought not to behave to each other as though this were true.'*
Mr Bennett's book, unlike most books about women, is not an

30

essay on love. It is a book about economics. The influence of the economic factor on feminine characteristics and on the relations between men and women is the main theme of his discourse. It is a sensible book and like many books which strike one immediately as sensible and straightforward, superficial. It is readable but not at all brilliant.

He lets one cat out of the bag — oddly enough, rather nervously. The cat in question I should have thought had been scampering about people's minds too long to make apologies necessary, but Mr Bennett is perhaps extra reluctant to let it loose because he is a convinced feminist. He finds it difficult to say, yet say it he does, that women are inferior to men in intellectual power, especially in that kind of power which is described as creative. Certainly, that fact stares one in the face; and he admits that 'no amount of education and liberty of action will sensibly alter it.' 'The literature of the world can show at least fifty male poets greater than any woman poet . . .' (Yes; unless you believe with Samuel Butler that a woman wrote the Odyssey.[2]*) 'With the possible exception of Emily Brontë, no woman novelist has yet produced a novel to equal the great novels of men.' (On the whole that is true: assent is in this case a little more doubtful.) 'No woman at all has achieved either painting or sculpture that is better than second-rate, or music that is better than second-rate.' (True; remember the standard is the masterpieces of the world.) 'Nor has any woman come anywhere near the top in criticism.' (True.) 'Can anybody name a celebrated woman philosopher; or a woman who has made a first-rate scientific discovery; or a woman who has arrived at a first-rate generalization of any sort?' (No: I remember the standard again.) I cannot conceive anybody who considers facts impartially coming to any other conclusions. Though it is true that a small percentage of women are as clever as clever men, on the whole intellect is a masculine speciality. Some women undoubtedly have genius, but genius in a lesser degree than Shakespeare, Newton, Michael Angelo, Beethoven, Tolstoy. The average intellectual power of women also seems a good deal lower. If you tranferred the intellect of a clever but not remarkably clever man to a woman, you would make her at once into a remarkably clever woman, and I expect the same is true of general organizing capacity: a feminine Ford* [3] *would be one of the world's wonders.*

And what then? Well, intellect means in the long run, and on the whole, domination.

It is indubitable that if women were a nation instead of a sex, their country would not be considered to have contributed much to the world's art of discoveries. Is this a very depressing conclusion for women? I do not see why it should be; we most of us have got used to the idea that we are not going to be Aristotles or Rembrandts, and are quite satisfied to be in the running for the sixth or seventh places, let alone the second or third which women have reached.

There is a passage worth drawing attention to on p. 105: 'I shall continue to assert,' says Mr Bennett, 'not only that even in this very advanced year women as a sex love to be dominated, but that for some thousands of years, if not for ever, they always will love to be dominated. This desire to be dominated is in itself a proof of intellectual inferiority. It is distinctive and survives, despite a general impression in certain quarters that recent progressive events have in some mysterious way put an end to it.' Well, men of inferior intellect do not wish to be dominated, and it is often very unfortunate that they do not. Therefore this desire which Mr Bennett attributes to women has nothing to do with intellectual inferiority. He says it is 'instinctive', but leaves it at that. This is an example of his superficial treatment of his subject.

At the end of the book he gives an example of 'the sex-discord', that is to say the sort of way men and women misunderstand each other. The quarrel in this instance is over a gardener and some chrysanthemums. Jack and Jill fall out over this little matter, and as long as the quarrel lasts they think very badly of each other's character. Mr Bennett gets inside the head of each with great skill; but there is something queer about his version of matrimonial quarrels. I think what is wrong with it (I felt the same thing in These Twain[4]*) is that his couples do not strike one as people who are really intimate. It may be true that most married people are not intimate. Intimacy is a gift, and implies a power of being expressive and, above all, caring for intimacy. Anyhow, the lack of it between Jack and Jill make them uninteresting, and his little sketch does not get down too deep.*

About twelve years ago a book called Sex and Character, *by Otto Weininger, was published, which created some stir. (Translation published by Heinemann.) It was written by a young Jew who committed suicide, and it is said that it had such a depressing effect on feminine readers that at least two of them followed his example. It was an honest, wild book, full of ingenious, highly questionable reasoning, insight and unfairness. It began with a general characterization of Woman, 'W', which was then divided into two main types, the Courtesan and the Mother, differentiated by their preoccupation with lovers or with children. It ended with discourse upon abnormal types of women and a definition of hysteria as 'the organic mendacity of women'. In every human being there were mixed the two elements, 'M' (Man) and 'W' (Woman), just as these characteristics appear physiologically in each sex. To 'M' Weininger attributed all the admirable moral and intellectual qualities and to 'W' all the bad ones. Women therefore came out badly, for there was by hypothesis more 'W' in them than in the great majority of men.*

Another book on women has just appeared, The Good Englishwoman, *by Mr Orlo Williams. This is a collection of light, neatly written essays, of a friendly and soothing character. The author confines himself to the Englishwoman, and his book is more a study of manners and social habits than of sex. His address contains a good deal of flattery, but it is really more condescending. Mr Bennett is not condescending.*

Affable Hawk.

On 9 October the *New Statesman* printed the following letter from Woolf, followed by Affable Hawk's reply.

To the Editor of the New Statesman.

Sir, – Like most women, I am unable to face the depression and the loss of self respect which Mr Arnold Bennett's blame and Mr Orlo Williams's praise – if it is not the other way about – would certainly cause me if I read their books in the bulk. I taste them, therefore, in sips at the hands of reviewers. But I cannot swallow the teaspoonful administered in your columns last week by Affable Hawk. The fact that women are inferior to men in intellectual power, he says, 'stares him in the face'. He goes on to agree with Mr Bennett's conclusion that 'no amount of education and liberty of action will sensibly alter it'. How, then, does Affable Hawk account for the fact which stares me, and I should have thought any other impartial observer, in the face, that the seventeenth century produced more remarkable women than the sixteenth, the eighteenth than the seventeenth, and the nineteenth than all three put together? When I compare the Duchess of Newcastle with Jane Austen, the matchless Orinda and Emily Brontë, Mrs Heywood with George Eliot, Aphra Behn with Charlotte Brontë, Jane Grey with Jane Harrison,[5] the advance in intellectual power seems to me not only sensible but immense; the comparison with men not in the least one that inclines me to suicide; and the effects of education and liberty scarcely to be over-rated. In short, though pessimism about the other sex is always delightful and invigorating, it seems a little sanguine of Mr Bennett and Affable Hawk to indulge in it with such certainty on the evidence before them. Thus, though women have every reason to hope that the intellect of the male sex is steadily diminishing, it would be unwise, until they have more evidence than the great war and the great peace supply, to announce it as a fact. In conclusion, if Affable Hawk sincerely wishes to discover a great poetess, why does he let himself be fobbed off with a possible authoress of the *Odyssey*? Naturally, I cannot claim I know Greek as Mr Bennett and Affable Hawk know it, but I have often been told that Sappho was a woman, and that Plato and Aristotle placed her with Homer and Archilochus[6] among the greatest of their poets. That Mr Bennett can name fifty of the male sex who are indisputably her superiors is therefore a welcome surprise, and if he will publish their names I will promise, as an act of that submission which is so dear to my sex, not only to buy their works but, so far as my faculties allow, to learn them by heart. – Yours, etc.,

Virginia Woolf.

Affable Hawk writes: Sappho was at the height of her fame about 610 BC. She was a contemporary of Jeremiah and Nebuchadnezzar; when she wrote the Buddha was not born. This was a long time ago. Perhaps when Herculaneum[7] gives up its treasures her works will be found; at present we only possess two short odes and fragments preserved in quotation, or fragments of fragments stuck like the wings of flies in the solidified glue of ancient grammarians. Still, Sappho is a very great name. Whether she can be ranged among the fifty greatest poets of the 2,500 years which followed her leap from the Leucadian promontory is, in these circumstances, hard to decide. Perhaps, had other dialect poets, say Burns,[8] survived only in happy quotations, and been such themes for poetry in themselves as she, of whom it could be believed that she turned in falling into a swan, their reputations, too, might be as great. But 2,500 years is a long time to wait for a second poetess for whom that claim might even plausibly be made. Suppose Mr Bennett were to grant the point of Sappho, that long interval remains to be explained on another hypothesis than that the creative mind in fullest power seems to have been the property of few men. There was nothing else to prevent down the ages, so far as I can see, women who always played and sang and studied music producing as many musicians from among their number as men have done. Of the millions who led the contemplative religious life surely, otherwise, one or two might have equalled the achievements of Aquinas or Thomas à Kempis?[9] And when later painting was within their reach what great names can they show? If in the nineteenth century a woman had existed with the intellect of Mill, would she not have forced her way to the front as well as Harriet Martineau[10] did? Mill thought that Mrs Taylor was his superior in every respect; but no friend agreed with him. Newton was a small farmer's son, Herschel a member of a German band, Faraday a blacksmith's son, Laplace[11] the child of a poor peasant. Nothing will persuade me that if among their contemporaries a woman, more favourably placed than they, had shown the same instinctive intellectual passion and capacity, she could not have done their work. Granted the intellect and a garden of peas, and a monk may become a Mendel.[12] I maintain Mr Bennett's case is strong. Mrs Woolf asks how I account for the seventeenth century producing more remarkable women than the sixteenth, the eighteenth than the seventeenth, and the nineteenth than all three put together, if education is not the cause, and therefore the explanation also, of the smallness of women's achievement when education was withheld from most women. Of course it is education which has increased the number of remarkable women and the merit of their work, but the facts remain (1) that unfavourable in many respects as the conditions of women have been in the past, they have not been more unfavourable than many men possessing extraordinary intellectual powers have overcome; (2) that in directions to which those conditions were less unfavourable (literature, poetry, music and painting), they have hardly attained, with the possible exception of fiction, the highest achievements reached by men; (3) that, in spite of education, in pursuits requiring pure intellect they have not rivalled men. This does not imply, however, that a small percentage of women are not just as clever as any clever men, just as good artists, just as good correlators of facts, only that it seems that they fall short of the few men who are best of all.

On 16 October the *New Statesman* published Woolf's response to Affable Hawk's rejoinder.

To the Editor of the New Statesman.

Sir, – to begin with Sappho. We do not, as in the hypothetical case of Burns suggested by Affable Hawk, judge her merely by her fragments. We supplement our judgement by the opinions of those to whom her works were known in their entirety. It is true that she was born 2,500 years ago. According to Affable Hawk the fact that no poetess of her genius has appeared from 600 BC to the eighteenth century proves that during that time there were no poetesses of potential genius. It follows that the absence of poetesses of moderate merit during that period proves that there were no women writers of potential mediocrity. There was no Sappho; but also, until the seventeenth or eighteenth century, there was no Marie Corelli and no Mrs Barclay.[13]

To account for the complete lack not only of good women writers but also of bad women writers I can conceive no reason unless it be that there was some external restraint upon their powers. For Affable Hawk admits that there have always been women of second or third rate ability. Why, unless they were forcibly prohibited, did they not express these gifts in writing, music, or painting? The case of Sappho, though so remote, throws, I think, a little light upon the problem. I quote J. A. Symonds:[14]

> Several circumstances contributed to aid the development of lyric poetry in Lesbos. The customs of the Aeolians permitted more social and domestic freedom than was common in Greece.

Aeolian women were not confined to the harem like Ionians, or subjected to the rigorous discipline of the Spartans. While mixing freely with male society, they were highly educated and accustomed to express their sentiments to an extent unknown elsewhere in history – until, indeed, the present time.

And now to skip from Sappho to Ethel Smyth.[15]

'There was nothing else [but intellectual inferiority] to prevent down the ages, so far as I can see, women who always played, sang and studied music, producing as many musicians from among their number as men have done,' says Affable Hawk. Was there nothing to prevent Ethel Smyth from going to Munich? Was there no opposition from her father? Did she find that the playing, singing and study of music which well-to-do families provided for their daughters were such as to fit them to become musicians? Yet Ethel Smyth was born in the nineteenth century. There are no great women painters, says Affable Hawk, though painting is now within their reach. It is within reach – if that is to say there is sufficient money after the sons have been educated to permit of paints and studios for the daughters and no family reason requiring their presence at home. Otherwise they must make a dash for it and disregard a species of torture more exquisitely painful, I believe, than any that man can imagine. And this is in the twentieth century. But, Affable Hawk argues, a great creative mind would triumph over obstacles such as these. Can he point to a single one of the great geniuses of history who has sprung from a people stinted of education and held in subjection, as for example the Irish or the Jews? It seems to me indisputable that the conditions which make it possible for Shakespeare to exist are that he shall have had predecessors in his art, shall make one of a group where art is freely discussed and practised, and shall himself have the utmost freedom of action and experience. Perhaps in Lesbos, but never since, have these conditions been the lot of women. Affable Hawk then names several men who have triumphed over poverty and ignorance. His first example is Isaac Newton. Newton was the son of a farmer; he was sent to a grammar school; he objected to working on the farm; an uncle, a clergyman, advised that he should be exempted and prepared for college; and at the age of nineteen he was sent to Trinity College,

Cambridge. (See DNB.) Newton, that is to say, had to encounter about the same amount of opposition that the daughter of a country solicitor encounters who wishes to go to Newnham in the year 1920. But his discouragement is not increased by the works of Mr Bennett, Mr Orlo Williams and Affable Hawk.

Putting that aside, my point is that you will not get a big Newton until you have produced a considerable number of lesser Newtons. Affable Hawk will, I hope, not accuse me of cowardice if I do not take up your space with an inquiry into the careers of Laplace, Faraday, and Herschel, nor compare the lives and achievements of Aquinas and St Theresa, nor decide whether it was Mill or his friends who was mistaken about Mrs Mill. The fact, as I think we shall agree, is that women from the earliest times to the present day have brought forth the entire population of the universe. This occupation has taken much time and strength. It has also brought them into subjection to men, and incidentally – if that were to the point – bred in them some of the most lovable and admirable qualities of the race. My difference with Affable Hawk is not that he denies the present intellectual equality of men and women. It is that he, with Mr Bennett, asserts that the mind of woman is not sensibly affected by education and liberty; that it is incapable of the highest achievements; and that it must remain for ever in the condition in which it now is. I must repeat that the fact that women have improved (which Affable Hawk now seems to admit), shows that they might still improve; for I cannot see why a limit should be set to their improvement in the nineteenth century rather than in the one hundred and nineteenth. But it is not education only that is needed. It is that women should have liberty of experience; that they should differ from men without fear and express their differences openly (for I do not agree with Affable Hawk that men and women are alike); that all activity of the mind should be so encouraged that there will always be in existence a nucleus of women who think, invent, imagine, and create as freely as men do, and with as little fear of ridicule and condescension. These conditions, in my view of great importance, are impeded by such statements as those of Affable Hawk and Mr Bennett, for a man has still much greater facilities that a woman for making his views known and respected. Certainly

I cannot doubt that if such opinions prevail in the future we shall remain in a condition of half-civilized barbarism. At least that is how I define an eternity of dominion on the one hand and of servility on the other. For the degradation of being a slave is only equalled by the degradation of being a master. – Yours, etc.,

Virginia Woolf.

Affable Hawk writes: If the freedom and education of women is impeded by the expression of my views, I shall argue no more.

The Modern Essay

A revised version, published in *The Common Reader*, of a review of *Modern English Essays: 1870–1920* (5 vols., ed. Ernest Rhys, J. M. Dent, 1922), first published in *The Times Literary Supplement*, 30 November 1922.

As Mr Rhys truly says, [1] it is unnecessary to go profoundly into the history and origin of the essay – whether it derives from Socrates or Sirannez the Persian[2] – since, like all living things, its present is more important than its past. Moreover, the family is widely spread: and while some of its representatives have risen in the world and wear their coronets with the best, others pick up a precarious living in the gutter near Fleet Street. The form, too, admits variety. The essay can be short or long, serious or trifling, about God and Spinoza, or about turtles and Cheapside.[3] But as we turn over the pages of these five little volumes, containing essays written between 1870 and 1920, certain principles appear to control the chaos, and we detect in the short period under review something like the progress of history.

Of all forms of literature, however, the essay is the one which least calls for the use of long words. The principle which controls it is simply that it should give pleasure; the desire which impels us when we take it from the shelf is simply to receive pleasure. Everything in an essay must be subdued to that end. It should lay us under a spell with its first word, and we should only wake, refreshed, with its last. In the interval we may pass through the most various experiences of amusement, surprise, interest, indignation; we may soar to the height of fantasy with Lamb or plunge to the depths of wisdom with Bacon, but we must never be roused. The essay must lap us about and draw its curtain across the world.

So great a feat is seldom accomplished, though the fault may well be as much on the reader's side as on the writer's. Habit and lethargy have dulled his palate. A novel has a story, a poem rhyme; but what art can the essayist use in these short lengths of prose to sting us wide awake and fix us in a trance which is not sleep but rather an intensification of life – a basking, with every faculty alert, in the sun of pleasure? He must know – that is the first essential – how to write. His learning may be as profound as Mark Pattison's,[4] but in an essay it must be so fused by the magic of writing that not a fact juts out, not a dogma tears the surface of the texture. Macaulay in one way, Froude[5] in another, did this superbly over and over again. They have blown more knowledge into us in the course of one essay than the innumerable chapters of a hundred text-books. But when Mark Pattison has to tell us, in the space of thirty-five little pages, about Montaigne, we feel that he had not previously assimilated M. Grün. M. Grün was a gentleman who once wrote a bad book. M. Grün and his book should have been embalmed for our perpetual delight in amber. But the process is fatiguing; it requires more time and perhaps more temper than Pattison had at his command. He served M. Grün up raw, and he remains a crude berry among the cooked meats, upon which our teeth must grate for ever. Something of the sort applies to Matthew Arnold and a certain translator of Spinoza. Literal truth-telling and finding fault with a culprit for his good are out of place in an essay, where everything should be for our good and rather for eternity than for the March number of the *Fortnightly Review*.[6] But if the voice of the scold should never be heard in this narrow plot, there is another voice which is as a plague of locusts – the voice of a man stumbling drowsily among loose words, clutching aimlessly at vague ideas, the voice, for example, of Mr Hutton[7] in the following passage:

> Add to this that his married life was very brief, only seven years and a half, being unexpectedly cut short, and that his passionate reverence for his wife's memory and genius – in his own words, 'a religion' – was one which, as he must have been perfectly sensible, he could not make to appear otherwise than extravagant, not to say an hallucination, in the eyes of the rest of mankind, and yet that he was possessed by an irresistible yearning to attempt to embody it in all the tender and enthusiastic hyperbole of which it is so pathetic to find a man who gained his fame by his 'dry-light' a master, and it is impossible not to feel that the human incidents in Mr Mill's career are very sad.

A book could take that blow, but it sinks an essay. A biography in two volumes is indeed the proper depository; for there, where the licence is so much wider, and hints and glimpses of outside things make part of the feast (we refer to the old type of Victorian volume), these yawns and stretches hardly matter, and have indeed some positive value of their own. But that value, which is contributed by the reader, perhaps illicitly, in his desire to get as much into the book from all possible sources as he can, must be ruled out here.

There is no room for the impurities of literature in an essay. Somehow or other, by dint of labour or bounty of nature, or both combined, the essay must be pure – pure like water or pure like wine, but pure from dullness, deadness, and deposits of extraneous matter. Of all writers in the first volume, Walter Pater[8] best achieves this arduous task, because before setting out to write his essay ('Notes on Leonardo da Vinci') he has somehow contrived to get his material fused. He is a learned man, but it is not knowledge of Leonardo that remains with us, but a vision, such as we get in a good novel where everything contributes to bring the writer's conception as a whole before us. Only here, in the essay, where the bounds are so strict and facts have to be used in their nakedness, the true writer like Walter Pater makes these limitations yield their own quality. Truth will give it authority; from its narrow limits he will get shape and intensity; and then there is no more fitting place for some of those ornaments which the old writers loved and we, by calling them ornaments, presumably despise. Nowadays nobody would have the courage to embark on the once famous description of Leonardo's lady who has

> learned the secrets of the grave; and has been a diver in deep seas and keeps their fallen day about her; and trafficked for strange webs with Eastern merchants; and, as Leda, was the mother of Helen of Troy, and, as Saint Anne, the mother of Mary . . .

The passage is too thumb-marked to slip naturally into the context. But when we come unexpectedly upon 'the smiling of women and the motion of great waters,' or upon 'full of the refinement of the dead, in sad, earth-coloured raiment, set with pale stones', we suddenly remember that we have ears and we have eyes, and that the English language fills a long array of stout volumes with innumerable words, many of which are of more than one syllable.

The only living Englishman who ever looks into these volumes is, of course, a gentleman of Polish extraction.[9] But doubtless our abstention saves us much gush, much rhetoric, much high-stepping and cloud-prancing, and for the sake of the prevailing sobriety and hard-headedness we should be willing to barter the splendour of Sir Thomas Browne and the vigour of Swift.[10]

Yet, if the essay admits more properly than biography or fiction of sudden boldness and metaphor, and can be polished till every atom of its surface shines, there are dangers in that too. We are soon in sight of ornament. Soon the current, which is the lifeblood of literature, runs slow; and instead of sparkling and flashing or moving with a quieter impulse which has a deeper excitement, words coagulate together in frozen sprays which, like the grapes on a Christmas-tree, glitter for a single night, but are dusty and garish the day after. The temptation to decorate is great where the theme may be of the slightest. What is there to interest another in the fact that one has enjoyed a walking tour, or has amused oneself by rambling down Cheapside and looking at the turtles in Mr Sweeting's shop window? Stevenson[11] and Samuel Butler chose very different methods of exciting our interest in these domestic themes. Stevenson, of course, trimmed and polished and set out his matter in the traditional eighteenth-century form. It is admirably done, but we cannot help feeling anxious, as the essay proceeds, lest the material may give out under the craftsman's fingers. The ingot is so small, the manipulation so incessant. And perhaps that is why the peroration –

> To sit still and contemplate – to remember the faces of women without desire, to be pleased by the great deeds of men without envy, to be everything and everywhere in sympathy and yet content to remain where and what you are –

has the sort of insubstantiality which suggests that by the time he got to the end he had left himself nothing solid to work with. Butler adopted the very opposite method. Think your own thoughts, he seems to say, and speak them as plainly as you can. These turtles in the shop window which appear to leak out of their shells through heads and feet suggest a fatal faithfulness to a fixed idea. And so, striding unconcernedly from one idea to the next, we traverse a large stretch of ground; observe that a wound in the solicitor is a very serious thing;[12] that Mary Queen of Scots wears surgical boots and is subject to fits near the Horse Shoe in Tottenham Court Road;[13] take it for granted that no one really cares about Aeschylus; and so, with many amusing anecdotes and some profound reflections, reach the peroration, which is that, as he had been told not to see more in Cheapside than he could get into twelve pages of the *Universal Review*,[14] he had better stop. And yet obviously Butler is at least as careful of our pleasure as Stevenson; and to write like oneself and call it not writing is a much harder exercise in style than to write like Addison and call it writing well.

But, however much they differ individually, the Victorian essayists yet had something in common. They wrote at greater length than is now usual, and they wrote for a public which had not only time to sit down to its magazine seriously, but a high, if peculiarly Victorian, standard of culture by which to judge it. It was worth while to speak out upon serious matters in an essay; and there was nothing absurd in writing as well as one possibly could when, in a month or two, the same public which had welcomed the essay in a magazine would carefully read it once more in a book. But a change came from a small audience of cultivated people to a larger audience of people who were not quite so cultivated. The change was not altogether for the worse. In volume III we find Mr Birrell and Mr Beerbohm.[15] It might even be said that there was a reversion to the classic type, and that the essay by losing its size and something of its sonority was approaching more nearly the essay of Addison and Lamb. At any rate, there is a great gulf between Mr Birrell on Carlyle[16] and the essay which one may suppose that Carlyle would have written upon Mr Birrell. There is little similarity between *A Cloud of Pinafores*, by Max Beerbohm, and *A Cynic's Apology*,[17] by Leslie Stephen. But the essay is alive; there is no reason to despair. As the conditions change so the essayist, most sensitive of all plants to public opinion, adapts himself, and if he is good makes the best of the change, and if he is bad the worst. Mr Birrell is certainly good; and so we find that, though he has dropped a considerable amount of weight, his attack is much more direct and his movement more supple. But what did Mr Beerbohm give to the essay and what did he take from it? That is a much more complicated question, for here we have an essayist who has concentrated on the work and is without doubt the prince of his profession.

What Mr Beerbohm gave was, of course, himself. This presence, which has haunted the essay fitfully from the time of Montaigne, had been in exile since the death of Charles Lamb. Matthew Arnold was never to his readers Matt, nor Walter Pater affectionately abbreviated in a thousand homes to Wat. They gave us much, but that they did not give. Thus, some time in the nineties, it must have surprised readers accustomed to exhortation, information, and denunciation to find themselves familiarly addressed by a voice which seemed to belong to a man no larger than themselves. He was affected by private joys and sorrows, and had no gospel to preach and no learning to impart. He was himself, simply and directly, and himself he has remained. Once again we have an essayist capable of using the essayist's most proper but most dangerous and delicate tool. He has brought personality into literature, not unconsciously and impurely, but so consciously and purely that we do not know whether there is any relation between Max the essayist and Mr Beerbohm the man. We only know that the spirit of personality permeates every word that he writes. The triumph is the triumph of style. For it is only by knowing how to write that you can make use in literature of your self; that self which, while it is essential to literature, is also its most dangerous antagonist. Never to be yourself and yet always – that is the problem. Some of the essayists in Mr Rhys' collection, to be frank, have not altogether succeeded in solving it. We are nauseated by the sight of trivial personalities decomposing in the eternity of print. As talk, no doubt, it was charming, and certainly the writer is a good fellow to meet over a bottle of beer. But literature is stern; it is no use being charming, virtuous, or even learned and brilliant into the bargain, unless, she seems to reiterate, you fulfil her first condition – to know how to write.

This art is possessed to perfection by Mr Beerbohm. But he has not searched the dictionary for polysyllables. He has not moulded firm periods or seduced our ears with intricate cadences and strange melodies. Some of his companions – Henley[18] and Stevenson, for example – are momentarily more impressive. But *A Cloud of Pinafores* had in it that indescribable inequality, stir, and final expressiveness which belong to life and to life alone. You have not finished with it because you have read it, any more than friendship is ended because it is time to part. Life wells up and alters and adds. Even things in a bookcase change if they are alive; we find ourselves wanting to meet them again; we find them altered. So we look back upon essay after essay by Mr Beerbohm, knowing that, come September or May, we shall sit down with them and talk. Yet it is true that the essayist is the most sensitive of all writers to public opinion. The drawing-room[19] is the place where a great deal of reading is done nowadays, and the essays of Mr Beerbohm lie, with an exquisite appreciation of all that the position exacts, upon the drawing-room table. There is no gin about; no strong tobacco; no puns, drunkenness, or insanity. Ladies and gentlemen talk together, and some things, of course, are not said.

But if it would be foolish to attempt to confine Mr Beerbohm to one room, it would be still more foolish, unhappily, to make him, the artist, the man who gives us only his best, the representative of our age. There are no essays by Mr Beerbohm in the fourth or fifth volumes of the present collection. His age seems already a little distant, and the drawing-room table, as it recedes, begins to look rather like an altar where, once upon a time, people deposited offerings – fruit from their own orchards, gifts carved with their own hands. Now once more the conditions have changed. The public needs essays as much as ever, and perhaps even more. The demand for the light middle not exceeding fifteen hundred words, or in special cases seventeen hundred and fifty, much exceeds the supply. Where Lamb wrote one essay and Max perhaps writes two, Mr Belloc at a rough computation produces three hundred and sixty-five. They are very short, it is true. Yet with what dexterity the practised essayist will utilize his space – beginning as close to the top of the sheet as possible, judging precisely how far to go, when to turn, and how, without sacrificing a hair's-breadth of paper, to wheel about and alight accurately upon the last word his editor allows! As a feat of skill it is well worth watching. But the personality upon which Mr Belloc, like Mr Beerbohm, depends suffers in the process. It comes to us not with the natural richness of the speaking voice, but strained and thin and full of mannerisms and affections, like the voice of a man shouting through a megaphone[20] to a crowd on a windy day. 'Little friends, my readers', he says in the essay called 'An Unknown Country,' and he goes on to tell us how –

> There was a shepherd the other day at Findon Fair, who had come from the east by Lewes with sheep, and who had in his eyes that reminiscence of horizons which make the eyes of shepherds and of mountaineers different from the eyes of other men ... I went with him to hear what he had to say, for shepherds talk quite differently from other men.

Happily this shepherd had little to say, even under the stimulus of the inevitable mug of beer, about the Unknown Country,[21] for the only remark that he did make proves him either a minor poet, unfit for the care of sheep, or Mr Belloc himself masquerading with a fountain pen. That is the penalty which the habitual essayist must now be prepared to face. He must masquerade. He cannot afford the time either to be himself or to be other people. He must skim the surface of thought and dilute the strength of personality. He must give us a worn weekly halfpenny instead of a solid sovereign[22] once a year.

But it is not Mr Belloc only who has suffered from the prevailing conditions. The essays which bring the collection to the year 1920 may not be the best of their author's work, but, if we except writers like Mr Conrad and Mr Hudson, who have strayed into essay writing accidentally, and concentrate upon those who write essays habitually, we shall find them a good deal affected by the change in their circumstances. To write weekly, to write daily, to write shortly, to write for busy people catching trains in the morning or for tired people coming home in the evening, is a heart-breaking task for men who know good writing from bad. They do it, but instinctively draw out of harm's way anything precious that might be damaged by contact with the public, or anything sharp that might irritate its skin. And so, if one reads Mr Lucas, Mr Lynd, or Mr Squire in the bulk, one feels that a common greyness silvers everything.[23] They are as far removed from the extravagant beauty of Walter Pater as they are from the intemperate candour of Leslie Stephen. Beauty and courage are dangerous spirits to bottle in a column and a half; and thought, like a brown paper parcel in a waist-coat pocket, has a way of spoiling the symmetry of an article. It is a kind, tired, apathetic world for which they write, and the marvel is that they never cease to attempt, at least, to write well.

But there is no need to pity Mr Clutton-Brock[24] for this change in the essayist's conditions. He has clearly made the best of his circumstances and not the worst. One hesitates even to say that he has had to make any conscious effort in the matter, so naturally has he effected the transition from the private essayist to the public, from the drawing-room to the Albert Hall. Paradoxically enough, the shrinkage in size has brought about a corresponding expansion of individuality. We have no longer the 'I' of Max[25] and of Lamb, but the 'we' of public bodies and other sublime personages. It is 'we' who go to hear the *Magic Flute*; 'we' who ought to profit by it; 'we', in some mysterious way, who, in our corporate capacity, once upon a time actually wrote it. For music and literature and art must submit to the same generalization or they will not carry to the farthest recesses of the Albert Hall. That the voice of Mr Clutton-Brock, so sincere and so disinterested, carries such a distance and reaches so many without pandering to the weakness of the mass or its passions must be a matter of legitimate satisfaction to us all. But while 'we' are gratified, 'I', that unruly partner in the human fellowship, is reduced to despair. 'I' must always think things for himself, and feel things for himself. To share them in a diluted form with the majority of well-educated and well-intentioned men and women is for him sheer agony; and while the rest of us listen intently and profit profoundly, 'I' slips off to the woods and the fields and rejoices in a single blade of grass or a solitary potato.

In the fifth volume of modern essays, it seems, we have got some way from pleasure and the art of writing. But in justice to the essayists of 1920 we must be sure that we are not praising the famous because they have been praised already and the dead because we shall never meet them wearing spats in Piccadilly. We must know what we mean when we say that they can write and give us pleasure. We must compare them; we must bring out the quality. We must point to this and say it is good because it is exact, truthful, and imaginative:

Nay, retire men cannot when they would; neither will they,

when it were Reason; but are impatient of Privateness, even in age and sickness, which require the shadow: like old Townsmen: that will still be sitting at their street door, though thereby they offer Age to Scorn . . .[26]

and to this, and say it is bad because it is loose, plausible, and commonplace:

With courteous and precise cynicism on his lips, he thought of quiet virginal chambers, of waters singing under the moon, of terraces where taintless music sobbed into the open night, of pure maternal mistresses with protecting arms and vigilant eyes, of fields slumbering in the sunlight, of leagues of ocean heaving under warm tremulous heavens, of hot ports, gorgeous and perfumed. . . .[27]

It goes on, but already we are bemused with sound and neither feel nor hear. The comparison makes us suspect that the art of writing has for backbone some fierce attachment to an idea. It is on the back of an idea, something believed in with conviction or seen with precision and thus compelling words to its shape, that the diverse company which includes Lamb and Bacon, and Mr Beerbohm and Hudson, and Vernon Lee and Mr Conrad, and Leslie Stephen and Butler and Walter Pater reaches the farther shore. Very various talents have helped or hindered the passage of the idea into words. Some scrape through painfully; others fly with every wind favouring. But Mr Belloc and Mr Lucas and Mr Squire are not fiercely attached to anything in itself. They share the contemporary dilemma – that lack of an obstinate conviction which lifts ephemeral sounds through the misty sphere of anybody's language to the land where there is a perpetual marriage, a perpetual union.[28] Vague as all definitions are, a good essay must have this permanent quality about it; it must draw its curtain round us, but it must be a curtain that shuts us in, not out.

Romance and the Heart

A review of *The Grand Tour* by Romer Wilson (Methuen, 1923) and *Revolving Lights* by Dorothy Richardson (Duckworth, 1923) first published in the *Nation and Athenaeum*, 19 May 1923.

Both Miss Wilson and Miss Richardson are serious novelists, and we must therefore put our minds at their service with the consciousness that, though criticize them we must, something of positive value, which that criticism should reveal, remains. And in trying to make out what this gift of theirs amounts to it is not necessary to go with great detail into the particular examples before us. Each writer is mature; each has written many books, and here, again, each is doing her own work in her own way.

Miss Wilson is a romantic. That is the first impression which her vigour and freedom make upon us. While other novelists sit studying the skeleton of humanity and painfully tracing the relations of tiny fibres, Miss Wilson hurls a sponge at the blackboard, takes her way into the forest, flings herself on a couch of amaranth,[1] and revels in the thunder. For her not only the sky, but the soul too, is always thundering and lightening. There are no mouse-coloured virtues; no gradual transitions; all is genius, violence, and rhapsody, and her thick crowded utterance, often eloquent and sometimes exquisite, recalls the stammer of a bird enraptured with life in June. Yet she is not, as this description might imply, sentimentally lyrical, and frequently, if pardonably, absurd. One of the remarkable qualities of her work is that she handles the great explosives with complete good faith. She believes in thunder, violence, genius, and rhapsody. Therefore, no one is going to sneer at her for saying so. Moreover, she constantly renews her sense of the marvellous by touching the earth, if only with the tip of her toe. She can be sardonic and caustic; she can mention the stomach.

Why is it, then, that she fails to convince us of the reality of her romance? It is because her sense of it is more conventional than original. She has taken it from poetry rather than from life, and from minor poetry more frequently than from major. She has not, like Meredith, used her freedom from the ties of realism to reveal something new in the emotions of human beings when they are most roused to excitement. Nor has she gone the other way to work. She has not taken the usual and made it blossom into the extraordinary. When we begin a play by Ibsen we say that there can be nothing romantic about a room with bookcases and upholstered furniture. But in the end we feel that all the forests and nightingales in the world cannot be so romantic as a room with bookcases and upholstered furniture. That is an exaggeration, however; we have overshot the mark. Nightingales and forests are for ever romantic, and it is merely cowardice to be afraid of saying so. But writers are afraid, and very naturally afraid, lest their own feeling for such famous things may not be strong enough to persist against the multitude of other people's feelings. Miss Wilson has no such fear. And thus she has the romantic power of making us feel the stir and tumult of life as a whole. She gives us a general, not a particular, sense of excitement. When at the end of the book Marichaud exclaims: 'Life is the thing, Paul. Life is to be the thing,' we feel that at last someone has put into words what we have been feeling for two hundred and fifty pages. And to have made us feel that life is the thing for two hundred and fifty pages is a real achievement.

There is no one word, such as romance or realism, to cover, even roughly, the works of Miss Dorothy Richardson. Their chief characteristic, if an intermittent student be qualified to speak, is one for which we still seek a name. She has invented, or, if she has not invented, developed and applied to her own uses, a sentence which we might call the psychological sentence of the feminine gender. It is of a more elastic fibre than the old, capable of stretching to the extreme, of suspending the frailest particles, of enveloping the vaguest shapes. Other writers of the opposite sex have used sentences of this description and stretched them to the extreme. But there is a difference. Miss Richardson has fashioned her sentence consciously, in order that it may descend to the depths and investigate the crannies of Miriam Henderson's consciousness. It is a woman's sentence, but only in the sense that it is used to describe a woman's mind by a writer who is neither proud nor afraid of anything that she may discover in the psychology of her sex. And therefore we feel that the trophies that Miss Richardson brings to the surface, however we may dispute their size, are undoubtedly genuine. Her discoveries are concerned with states of being and not with states of doing. Miriam is aware of 'life itself'; of the atmosphere of the table rather than of the table; of the silence rather than of the sound. Therefore she adds an element to her perception of things which has not been noticed before, or, if noticed, has been guiltily suppressed. A man might fall dead at her feet (it is not likely), and Miriam might feel that a violet-coloured ray of light was an important element in her consciousness of the tragedy. If she felt it, she would say it. Therefore, in reading *Revolving Lights*[2] we are often made uncomfortable by feeling that the accent upon the emotions has shifted. What was emphatic is smoothed away. What was important to Maggie Tulliver[3] no longer matters to Miriam Henderson. At first, we are ready to say that nothing is important to Miriam Henderson. That is the way we generally retaliate when an artist tells us that the heart is not, as we should like it to be, a stationary body, but a body which moves perpetually, and is thus always standing in a new relation to the emotions which are its sun. Chaucer, Donne, Dickens – each, if you read him, shows this change of the heart. That is what Miss Richardson is doing on an infinitely smaller scale. Miriam Henderson is pointing to her heart and saying she feels a pain on her right, and not on her left. She points too didactically. Her pain, compared with Maggie Tulliver's, is a very little pain. But, be that as it may, here we have both Miss Wilson and Miss Richardson proving that the novel is not hung upon a nail and festooned with glory, but, on the contrary, walks the high road, alive and alert, and brushes shoulders with real men and women.

The Compromise

A review of Janet Penrose Trevelyan's *The Life of Mrs Humphry Ward*
(Constable, 1923), first published in the *Nation and Athenaeum*,
29 September 1923.

None of the great Victorian reputations has sunk lower than that of
Mrs Humphry Ward. Her novels, already strangely out of date,
hang in the lumber-room of letters like the mantles of our aunts,
and produce in us the same desire that they do to smash the window
and let in the air, to light the fire and pile the rubbish on top. Some
books fade into a gentle picturesqueness with age. But there is a
quality, perhaps a lack of quality, about the novels of Mrs Ward
which makes it improbable that, however much they fade, they will
ever become picturesque. Their large bunches of jet, their intricate
festoons of ribbon, skilfully and firmly fabricated as they are, obstin-
ately resist the endearments of time. But Mrs Trevelyan's life of her
mother makes us consider all this from a different angle. It is an
able and serious book, and like all good biographies so permeates
us with the sense of the presence of a human being that by the time
we have finished it we are more disposed to ask questions than to
pass judgements. Let us attempt, in a few words, to hand on the
dilemma to our readers.

Of Mrs Ward's descent there is no need to speak. She had by
birth and temperament all those qualities which fitted her, before
she was twenty, to be the friend of Mark Pattison, and 'the best
person', in the opinion of J. R. Green,[1] to be asked to contribute a
volume to a history of Spain. There was little, even at the age of
twenty, that this ardent girl did not know about the Visigothic
Invasion or the reign of Alfonso el Sabio. One of her first pieces of
writing, 'A Morning in the Bodleian', records in priggish but
burning words her scholar's enthusiasm: '. . . let not the young
man reading for his pass, the London copyist, or the British
Museum illuminator', hope to enjoy the delights of literature; that
deity will only yield her gifts to 'the silent ardour, the thirst, the

disinterestedness of the true learner'. With such an inscription above
the portal, her fate seems already decided. She will marry a Don;
she will rear a small family; she will circulate 'Plain Facts on Infant
Feeding' in the Oxford slums; she will help to found Somerville
College; she will sit up writing learned articles for the *Dictionary of
Christian Biography*; and at last, after a hard life of unremunerative
toil, she will finish the book which fired her fancy as a girl and will
go down to posterity as the author of a standard work upon the
origins of modern Spain. But, as everyone knows, the career which
seemed so likely, and would have been so honourable, was interrupted by the melodramatic success of *Robert Elsmere*.[2] History was
forsaken for fiction, and the *Origins of Modern* Spain became trans-
muted into the *Origins of Modern France*, a phantom book which the
unfortunate Robert Elsmere never succeeded in writing.

It is here that we begin to scribble in the margin of Mrs Ward's
life those endless notes of interrogation. After *Robert Elsmere* –
which we may grant to have been inevitable – we can never cease to
ask ourselves, why? Why desert the charming old house in Russell
Square for the splendours and expenses of Grosvenor Place? Why
wear beautiful dresses, why keep butlers and carriages, why give
luncheon parties and weekend parties, why buy a house in the
country and pull it down and build it up again, when all this can be
achieved by writing at breathless speed novels which filial piety
calls autumnal, but the critic, unfortunately, must call bad? Mrs
Ward might have replied that the compromise, if she agreed to call
it so, was entirely justified. Who but a coward would refuse, when
cheques for £7,000 dropped out of George Smith's pocket[3] before
breakfast, to spend the money as the great ladies of the Renaissance
would have spent it, upon society and entertainment and phil-
anthropy? Without her novel-writing there would have been no
centre for good talk in the pretty room overlooking the grounds of
Buckingham Palace. Without her novel-writing thousands of poor
children would have ranged the streets unsheltered. It is impossible
to remain a schoolgirl in the Bodleian for ever, and, once you breast
the complicated currents of modern life at their strongest, there is
little time to ask questions, and none to answer them. One thing
merges in another; one thing leads to another. After an exhausting
At Home in Grosvenor Place, she would snatch a meal and drive

off to fight the cause of Play Centres in Bloomsbury. Her success in that undertaking involved her, against her will,[4] in the Anti-Suffrage campaign. Then, when the war came, this elderly lady of weak health was selected by the highest authorities to peer into shell-holes, and be taken over men-of-war by admirals. Sometimes, says Mrs Trevelyan, eighty letters were dispatched from Stocks in a single day; five hats were bought in the course of one drive to town – 'on spec., darling'; and what with grandchildren and cousins and friends; what with being kind and being unmethodical and being energetic; what with caring more and more passionately for politics, and finding the meetings of Liberal Churchmen 'desperately, perhaps disproportionately' interesting, there was only one half-hour in the whole day left for reading Greek.

It is tempting to imagine what the schoolgirl in the Bodleian would have said to her famous successor. 'Literature has no guerdon for bread-students, to quote the expressive German phrase . . . only to the silent ardour, the thirst, the disinterestedness of the true learner, is she prodigal of all good gifts.' But Mrs Humphry Ward, the famous novelist, might have rounded upon her critic of twenty. 'It is all very well,' she might have said, 'to accuse me of having wasted my gifts; but the fault lay with you. Yours was the age for seeing visions; and you spent it in dreaming how you stopped the Princess of Wales' runaway horses, and were rewarded by "a command" to appear at Buckingham Palace. It was you who starved my imagination and condemned it to the fatal compromise.' And here the elder lady undoubtedly lays her finger upon the weakness of her own work. For the depressing effects of her books must be attributed to the fact that while her imagination always attempts to soar, it always agrees to perch. That is why we never wish to open them again.

In Mrs Trevelyan's biography these startling discrepancies between youth and age, between ideal and accomplishment, are successfully welded together, as they are in life, by an infinite series of details. She makes it apparent that Mrs Ward was beloved, famous, and prosperous in the highest degree. And if to achieve all this implies some compromise, still – but here we reach the dilemma which we intend to pass on to our readers.

Montaigne

This is a slightly modified version (taken from *The Common Reader*) of
a review of Charles Cotton's translation of the *Essays of Montaigne*
(The Navarre Society, 5 vols., 1923), first published in *The Times
Literary Supplement*, 31 January 1924.

Once at Bar-Le-Duc Montaigne saw a portrait which René, King of
Sicily, had painted of himself, and asked, 'Why is it not, in like
manner, lawful for everyone to draw himself with a pen, as he did
with a crayon?'[1] Offhand one might reply, Not only is it lawful, but
nothing could be easier. Other people may evade us, but our own
features are almost too familiar. Let us begin. And then, when we
attempt the task, the pen falls from our fingers; it is a matter of
profound, mysterious, and overwhelming difficulty.

After all, in the whole of literature, how many people have
succeeded in drawing themselves with a pen? Only Montaigne and
Pepys and Rousseau[2] perhaps. The *Religio Medici*[3] is a coloured glass
through which darkly one sees[4] racing stars and a strange and
turbulent soul. A bright polished mirror reflects the face of Boswell
peeping between other people's shoulders in the famous biography.
But this talking of oneself, following one's own vagaries, giving the
whole map, weight, colour, and circumference of the soul in its
confusion, its variety, its imperfection – this art belonged to one
man only: to Montaigne. As the centuries go by, there is always a
crowd before that picture, gazing into its depths, seeing their own
faces reflected in it, seeing more the longer they look, never being
able to say quite what it is that they see. New editions testify to the
perennial fascination. Here is the Navarre Society in England re-
printing in five fine volumes Cotton's translation; while in France
the firm of Louis Conard is issuing the complete works of Montaigne with the various readings in an edition to which Dr Arma-
ingaud has devoted a long lifetime of research

To tell the truth about oneself, to discover oneself near at hand,
is not easy.

> We hear of but two or three of the ancients who have beaten this road [said Montaigne]. No one since has followed the track; 'tis a rugged road, more so than it seems, to follow a pace so rambling and uncertain, as that of the soul; to penetrate the dark profundities of its intricate internal windings; to choose and lay hold of so many little nimble motions; 'tis a new and extraordinary undertaking, and that withdraws us from the common and most recommended employments of the world.[5]

There is, in the first place, the difficulty of expression. We all indulge in the strange, pleasant process called thinking, but when it comes to saying, even to someone opposite, what we think, then how little we are able to convey! The phantom is through the mind and out of the window before we can lay salt on its tail, or slowly sinking and returning to the profound darkness which it has lit up momentarily with a wandering light. Face, voice, and accent eke out our words and impress their feebleness with character in speech. But the pen is a rigid instrument; it can say very little; it has all kinds of habits and ceremonies of its own. It is dictatorial too: it is always making ordinary men into prophets, and changing the natural stumbling trip of human speech into the solemn and stately march of pens. It is for this reason that Montaigne stands out from the legions of the dead with such irrepressible vivacity. We can never doubt for an instant that his book was himself. He refused to teach; he refused to preach; he kept on saying that he was just like other people. All his effort was to write himself down, to communicate, to tell the truth, and that is a 'rugged road, more than it seems'.

For beyond the difficulty of communicating oneself, there is the supreme difficulty of being oneself. This soul, or life within us, by no means agrees with the life outside us. If one has the courage to ask her what she thinks, she is always saying the very opposite to what other people say. Other people, for instance, long ago made up their minds that old invalidish gentlemen ought to stay at home and edify the rest of us by the spectacle of their connubial fidelity. The soul of Montaigne said, on the contrary, that it is in old age that one ought to travel, and marriage, which, rightly, is very seldom founded on love, is apt to become, towards the end of life, a formal tie better broken up. Again with politics, statesmen are always praising the greatness of Empire, and preaching the moral duty of civilizing the savage. But look at the Spanish in Mexico, cried Montaigne in a burst of rage. 'So many cities levelled with the ground, so many nations exterminated . . . and the richest and most beautiful part of the world turned upside down for the traffic of pearl and pepper! Mechanic victories!'[6] And then when the peasants came and told him that they had found a man dying of wounds and deserted him for fear lest justice might incriminate them, Montaigne asked:

> What could I have said to these people? 'Tis certain that this office of humanity would have brought them into trouble . . . There is nothing so much, nor so grossly, nor so ordinarily faulty as the laws.[7]

Here the soul, getting restive, is lashing out at the more palpable forms of Montaigne's great bugbears, convention and ceremony. But watch her as she broods over the fire in the inner room of that tower which,[8] though detached from the main building, has so wide a view over the estate. Really she is the strangest creature in the world, far from heroic, variable as a weathercock, 'bashful, insolent; chaste, lustful; prating, silent; laborious, delicate; ingenious, heavy; melancholic, pleasant; lying, true; knowing, ignorant; liberal, covetous, and prodigal'[9] – in short, so complex, so indefinite, corresponding so little to the version which does duty for her in public, that a man might spend his life merely in trying to run her to earth. The pleasure of the pursuit more than rewards one for any damage that it may inflict upon one's worldly prospects. The man who is aware of himself is henceforward independent; and he is never bored, and life is only too short, and he is steeped through and through with a profound yet temperate happiness. He alone lives, while other people, slaves of ceremony, let life slip past them in a kind of dream. Once conform, once do what other people do because they do it, and a lethargy steals over all the finer nerves and faculties of the soul. She becomes all outer show and inward emptiness; dull, callous, and indifferent.

Surely then, if we ask this great master of the art of life to tell us his secret, he will advise us to withdraw to the inner room of our tower and there turn the pages of books, pursue fancy after fancy as they chase each other up the chimney, and leave the government of the world to others. Retirement and contemplation – these must be the main elements of his prescription. But no; Montaigne is by no means explicit. It is impossible to extract a plain answer from that subtle, half smiling, half melancholy man, with the heavy-lidded eyes and the dreamy, quizzical expression. The truth is that life in the country, with one's books and vegetables and flowers, is often extremely dull. He could never see that his own peas were so much better than other people's. Paris was the place he loved best in the whole world – *'jusques à ses verrues et à ses taches'*.[10] As for reading, he could seldom read any book for more than an hour at a time, and his memory was so bad that he forgot what was in his mind as he walked from one room to another. Book learning is nothing to be proud of, and as for the achievements of science, what do they amount to? He had always mixed with clever men, and his father had a positive veneration for them, but he had observed that, though they have their fine moments, their rhapsodies, their visions, the cleverest tremble on the verge of folly. Observe yourself: one moment you are exalted; the next a broken glass puts your nerves on edge. All extremes are dangerous. It is best to keep in the middle of the road, in the common ruts, however muddy. In writing choose the common words; avoid rhapsody and eloquence – yet, it is true, poetry is delicious; the best prose is that which is most full of poetry.

It appears, then, that we are to aim at a democratic simplicity. We may enjoy our room in the tower, with the painted walls and the commodious bookcases, but down in the garden there is a man digging who buried his father this morning, and it is he and his like who live the real life and speak the real language. There is certainly an element of truth in that. Things are said very finely at the lower end of the table. There are perhaps more of the qualities that matter among the ignorant than among the learned. But again, what a vile thing the rabble is! 'The mother of ignorance, injustice, and inconstancy. Is it reasonable that the life of a wise man should depend upon the judgement of fools?'[11] Their minds are weak, soft and without power of resistance. They must be told what it is expedient for them to know. It is not for them to face facts as they are. The truth can only be known by the well-born soul – *'l'âme bien née'*. Who, then, are these well-born souls, whom we would imitate if only Montaigne would enlighten us more precisely?

But no. '*Je n'enseigne poinct; je raconte.*'[12] After all, how could he explain other people's souls when he could say nothing 'entirely simply and solidly, without confusion or mixture, in one word',[13] about his own, when indeed it became daily more and more in the dark to him? One quality or principle there is perhaps – that one must not lay down rules. The souls whom one would wish to resemble, like Etienne de La Boétie,[14] for example, are always the supplest. '*C'est estre, mais ce n'est pas vivre, que de se tenir attaché et obligé par necessité à un seul train.*'[15] The laws are mere conventions, utterly unable to keep touch with the vast variety and turmoil of human impulses; habits and customs are a convenience devised for the support of timid natures who dare not allow their souls free play. But we, who have a private life and hold it infinitely the dearest of our possessions, suspect nothing so much as an attitude. Directly we begin to protest, to attitudinize, to lay down laws, we perish. We are living for others, not for ourselves. We must respect those who sacrifice themselves in the public service, load them with honours, and pity them for allowing, as they must, the inevitable compromise; but for ourselves let us fly fame, honour, and all offices that put us under an obligation to others. Let us simmer over our incalculable cauldron, our enthralling confusion, our hotch-potch of impulses, our perpetual miracle – for the soul throws up wonders every second. Movement and change are the essence of our being; rigidity is death; conformity is death: let us say what comes into our heads, repeat ourselves, contradict ourselves, fling out the wildest nonsense, and follow the most fantastic fancies without caring what the world does or thinks or says. For nothing matters except life; and, of course, order.

This freedom, then, which is the essence of our being, has to be controlled. But it is difficult to see what power we are to invoke to help us, since every restraint of private opinion or public law has been derided, and Montaigne never ceases to pour scorn upon the misery, the weakness, the vanity of human nature. Perhaps, then, it will be well to turn to religion to guide us? 'Perhaps' is one of his favourite expressions; 'perhaps' and 'I think' and all those words which qualify the rash assumptions of human ignorance. Such words help one to muffle up opinions which it would be highly impolitic to speak outright. For one does not say everything; there are some things which at present it is advisable only to hint. One writes for a very few people, who understand. Certainly, seek the Divine guidance by all means, but meanwhile there is, for those who live a private life, another monitor, an invisible censor within, *'un patron au dedans'*,[16] whose blame is much more to be dreaded than any other because he knows the truth; nor is there anything sweeter than the chime of his approval. This is the judge to whom we must submit; this is the censor who will help us to achieve that order which is the grace of a well-born soul. For *'C'est une vie exquise, celle qui se maintient en ordre jusques en son privé'*.[17] But he will act by his own light; by some internal balance will achieve that precarious and everchanging poise which, while it controls, in no way impedes the soul's freedom to explore and experiment. Without other guide, and without precedent, undoubtedly it is far more difficult to live well the private life than the public. It is an art which each must learn separately, though there are, perhaps, two or three men, like Homer, Alexander the Great, and Epaminondas[18] among the ancients, and Etienne de La Boétie among the moderns, whose example may help us. But it is an art; and the very material in which it works is variable and complex and infinitely mysterious – human nature. To human nature we must keep close '. . . *il faut vivre entre les vivants'*.[19] We must dread any eccentricity or refinement which cuts us off from our fellow-beings. Blessed are those who chat easily with their neighbours about their sport or their buildings or their quarrels, and honestly enjoy the talk of carpenters and gardeners. To communicate is our chief business; society and friendship our chief delights; and reading, not to acquire knowledge, not to earn a living, but to extend our intercourse beyond our own time and province. Such wonders there are in the world; halcyons[20] and undiscovered lands, men with dogs' heads and eyes in their chests, and laws and customs, it may well be, far superior to our own. Possibly we are asleep in this world; possibly there is some other which is apparent to beings with a sense which we now lack.

Here then, in spite of all contradictions and all qualifications, is something definite. These essays are an attempt to communicate a soul. On this point at least he is explicit. It is not fame that he wants; it is not that men shall quote him in years to come; he is setting up no statue in the market-place; he wishes only to communicate his soul. Communication is health; communication is truth; communication is happiness. To share is our duty; to go down boldly and bring to light those hidden thoughts which are the most diseased; to conceal nothing; to pretend nothing; if we are ignorant to say so; if we love our friends to let them know it.

> ... car, comme je scay par une trop certaine expérience, il n'est aucune si douce consolation en la perte de nos amis que celle que nous aporte la science de n'avoir rien oublié à leur dire et d'avoir eu avec eux une parfaite et entière communication.[21]

There are people who, when they travel, wrap themselves up, 'se défendans de la contagion d'un air incogneu'[22] in silence and suspicion. When they dine they must have the same food they get at home. Every sight and custom is bad unless it resembles those of their own village. They travel only to return. That is entirely the wrong way to set about it. We should start without any fixed idea where we are going to spend the night, or when we propose to come back; the journey is everything. Most necessary of all, but rarest good fortune, we should try to find before we start some man of our own sort who will go with us and to whom we can say the first thing that comes into our heads. For pleasure has no relish unless we share it. As for the risks – that we may catch cold or get a headache – it is always worth while to risk a little illness for the sake of pleasure. 'Le plaisir est des principales espèces du profit.'[23] Besides if we do what we like, we always do what is good for us. Doctors and wise men may object, but let us leave doctors and wise men to their own dismal philosophy. For ourselves, who are ordinary men and women, let us return thanks to Nature for her bounty by using every one of the senses she has given us; vary our state as much as possible; turn now this side, now that, to the warmth, and relish to the full before the sun goes down the kisses of youth and the echoes of a beautiful voice singing Catullus.[24] Every season is likeable, and wet days and fine, red wine and white, company and solitude. Even sleep, that deplorable curtailment of the joy of life, can be full of dreams; and the most common actions – a walk, a talk, solitude in one's own orchard – can be enhanced and lit up by the association of the mind. Beauty is everywhere, and beauty is only two fingers' breadth from goodness. So, in the name of health and sanity, let us not dwell on the end of the journey. Let death come upon us planting our cabbages, or on horseback, or let us steal away to some cottage and there let strangers close our eyes, for a servant sobbing or the touch of a hand would break us down. Best of all, let death find us at our usual occupations, among girls and good fellows who make no protests, no lamentations; let him find us *parmy les jeux, les festins, faceties, entretiens communs et populaires, et la musique, et des vers amoureux*.[25] But enough of death; it is life that matters.

It is life that emerges more and more clearly as these essays reach not their end, but their suspension in full career. It is life that becomes more and more absorbing as death draws near, one's self, one's soul, every fact of existence: that one wears silk stockings summer and winter; puts water in one's wine; has one's hair cut after dinner; must have glass to drink from; has never worn spectacles; has a loud voice; carries a switch in one's hand; bites one's tongue; fidgets with one's feet; is apt to scratch one's ears; likes meat to be high; rubs one's teeth with a napkin (thank God, they are good!); must have curtains to one's bed; and, what is rather curious, began by liking radishes, then disliked them, and now likes them again. No fact is too little to let it slip through one's fingers, and besides the interest of facts themselves there is the strange power we have of changing facts by the force of the imagination. Observe how the soul is always casting her own lights and shadows; makes the substantial hollow and the frail substantial; fills broad daylight with dreams; is as much excited by phantoms as by reality; and in the moment of death sports with a trifle. Observe, too, her duplicity, her complexity. She hears of a friend's loss and sympathizes, and yet has a bitter-sweet malicious pleasure in the sorrows of others. She believes; at the same time she does not believe. Observe her extraordinary susceptibility to impressions, especially in youth. A rich man steals because his father kept him short of money as a boy. This wall one builds not for oneself, but because one's father loved building. In short, the soul is all laced about with nerves and sympathies which affect her every action, and yet, even now in 1580, no one has any clear knowledge – such cowards we are, such lovers of the smooth conventional ways – how she works or what she is except that of all things she is the most mysterious, and one's self the greatest monster and miracle in the world. '... *plus je me*

hante et connois, plus ma difformité m'estonne, moins, je m'entens en moy.' [26]
Observe, observe perpetually, and, so long as ink and paper exist,
'*sans cesse et sans travail*' [27] Montaigne will write.

But there remains one final question which, if we could make
him look up from his enthralling occupation, we should like to put
to this great master of the art of life. In these extraordinary volumes
of short and broken, long and learned, logical and contradictory
statements, we have heard the very pulse and rhythm of the soul,
beating day after day, year after year, through a veil which, as time
goes on, fines itself almost to transparency. Here is someone who
succeeded in the hazordous enterprise of living; who served his
country and lived retired; and landlord, husband, father; entertained
kings, loved women, and mused for hours alone over old books. By
means of perpetual experiment and observation of the subtlest he
achieved at last a miraculous adjustment of all these wayward parts
that constitute the human soul. He laid hold of the beauty of the
world with all his fingers. He achieved happiness. If he had had to
live again, he said, he would have lived the same life over. But, as
we watch with absorbed interest the enthralling spectacle of a soul
living openly beneath our eyes, the question frames itself, Is pleasure
the end of all? Whence this overwhelming interest in the nature of
the soul? Why this overmastering desire to communicate with
others? Is the beauty of this world enough, or is there, elsewhere, some explanation of the mystery? To this what answer can
there be? [28] There is none. There is only one more question: '*Que
scais-je?*' [29]

The Patron and The Crocus

This essay was first published in the *Nation and Athenaeum*, 12 April 1924; the revised version, reprinted here, was originally published in *The Common Reader*.

Young men and women beginning to write are generally given the plausible but utterly impracticable advice to write what they have to write as shortly as possible, as clearly as possible, and without other thought in their minds except to say exactly what is in them. Nobody ever adds on these occasions the one thing needful: 'And be sure you choose your patron wisely', though that is the gist of the whole matter. For a book is always written for somebody to read, and, since the patron is not merely the paymaster, but also in a very subtle and insidious way the instigator and inspirer of what is written, it is of the utmost importance that he should be a desirable man.

But who, then, is the desirable man – the patron who will cajole the best out of the writer's brain and bring to birth¹ the most varied and vigorous progeny of which he is capable? Different ages have answered the question differently. The Elizabethans, to speak roughly, chose the aristocracy to write for and the playhouse public. The eighteenth-century patron was a combination of coffee-house wit and Grub Street bookseller. In the nineteenth century the great writers wrote for the half-crown magazines and the leisured classes. And looking back and applauding the splendid results of these different alliances, it all seems enviably simple, and plain as a pike-staff compared with our own predicament – for whom should we write? For the present supply of patrons is of unexampled and bewildering variety. There is the daily Press, the weekly Press, the monthly Press; the English public and the American public; the best-seller public and the worst-seller public; the high-brow public and the red-blood public; all now organized self-conscious entities capable through their various mouthpieces of making their needs known and their approval or displeasure felt. Thus the writer who has been moved by the sight of the first crocus in Kensington Gardens has, before he sets pen to paper, to choose from a crowd of competitors the particular patron who suits him best. It is futile to say, 'Dismiss them all; think only of your crocus', because writing is a method of communication; and the crocus is an imperfect crocus until it has been shared. The first man or the last may write for himself alone, but he is an exception and an unenviable one at that, and the gulls are welcome to his works if the gulls can read them.

Granted, then, that every writer has some public or other at the end of his pen, the high-minded will say that it should be a submissive public, accepting obediently whatever he likes to give it. Plausible as the theory sounds, great risks are attached to it. For in that case the writer remains conscious of his public, yet is superior to it – an uncomfortable and unfortunate combination, as the works of Samuel Butler, George Meredith, and Henry James may be taken to prove. Each despised the public; and each desired a public; each failed to attain a public; and each wreaked his failure upon the public by a succession, gradually increasing in intensity, of angularities, obscurities, and affectations which no writer whose patron was his equal and friend would have thought it necessary to inflict. Their crocuses, in consequence, are tortured plants, beautiful and bright, but with something wry-necked about them, malformed, shrivelled on the one side, overblown on the other. A touch of the sun would have done them a world of good. Shall we then rush to the opposite extreme and accept (if in fancy alone) the flattering proposals which the editors of *The Times* and the *Daily News* may be supposed to make us – 'Twenty pounds down for your crocus in precisely fifteen hundred words, which shall blossom upon every breakfast table from John o' Groats to the Land's End before nine o'clock tomorrow morning with the writer's name attached'?

But will one crocus be enough, and must it not be a very brilliant yellow to shine so far, to cost so much, and to have one's name attached to it? The Press is undoubtedly a great multiplier of crocuses. But if we look at some of these plants, we shall find that they are only very distantly related to the original little yellow or purple flower which pokes up through the grass in Kensington Gardens early in March every year. The newspaper crocus is an amazing but still a very different plant. It fills precisely the space allotted to it. It radiates a golden glow. It is genial, affable,[2] warm-hearted. It is beautifully finished, too, for let nobody think that the art of 'our dramatic critic' of *The Times* or of Mr Lynd of the *Daily News* is an easy one. It is no despicable feat to start a million brains running at nine o'clock in the morning, to give two-million eyes something bright and brisk and amusing to look at. But the night comes and these flowers fade. So little bits of glass lose their lustre if you take them out of the sea; great prima donnas howl like hyenas if you shut them up in telephone boxes; and the most brilliant of articles when removed from its element is dust and sand and the husks of straw. Journalism embalmed in a book is unreadable.

The patron we want, then, is one who will help us to preserve our flowers from decay. But as his qualities change from age to age, and it needs considerable integrity and conviction not to be dazzled by the pretensions or bamboozled by the persuasions of the competing crowd, this business of patron-finding is one of the tests and trials of authorship. To know whom to write for is to know how to write. Some of the modern patron's qualities are, however, fairly plain. The writer will require at this moment, it is obvious, a patron with the book-reading habit rather than the play-going habit. Nowadays, too, he must be instructed in the literature of other times and races. But there are other qualities which our special weaknesses and tendencies demand in him. There is the question of indecency, for instance, which plagues us and puzzles us much more than it did the Elizabethans. The twentieth-century patron must be immune from shock. He must distinguish infallibly between the little clod of manure which sticks to the crocus of necessity, and that which is plastered to it out of bravado. He must be judge, too, of those social influences which inevitably play so large a part in modern literature, and able to say which matures and fortifies, which inhibits and makes sterile. Further, there is emotion for him to pronounce on, and in no department can he do more useful work than in bracing a writer against sentimentality on the one hand and a craven fear of expressing his feeling on the other. It is worse, he will say, and perhaps more common, to be afraid of feeling than to feel too much. He will add, perhaps, something about language, and point out how many words Shakespeare used and how much grammar

Shakespeare violated, while we, though we keep our fingers so demurely to the black notes on the piano, have not appreciably improved upon *Antony and Cleopatra*. And if you can forget your sex altogether, he will say, so much the better; a writer has none. But all this is by the way – elementary and disputable. The patron's prime quality is something different, only to be expressed perhaps by the use of that convenient word which cloaks so much – atmosphere. It is necessary that the patron should shed and envelop the crocus in an atmosphere which makes it appear a plant of the very highest importance, so that to misrepresent it is the one outrage not to be forgiven this side of the grave. He must make us feel that a single crocus, if it be a real crocus, is enough for him; that he does not want to be lectured, elevated, instructed, or improved; that he is sorry that he bullied Carlyle into vociferation, Tennyson into idyllics, and Ruskin into insanity; that he is now ready to efface himself or assert himself as his writers require; that he is bound to them by a more than maternal tie; that they are twins indeed, one dying if the other dies, one flourishing if the other flourishes; that the fate of literature depends upon their happy alliance – all of which proves, as we began by saying, that the choice of patron is of the highest importance. But how to choose rightly? How to write well? Those are the questions.

Mr Bennett and Mrs Brown

An earlier version of this essay appeared in the *Nation and Athenaeum* on 1 December 1923; it was then substantially revised, read to the Cambridge Heretics on 18 May 1924, and published under the title 'Character in Fiction' in the *Criterion*, July 1924. On 30 October 1924 it was published as a separate pamphlet, 'Mr Bennett and Mrs Brown', by the Hogarth Press (the version reprinted here).[1]

It seems to me possible, perhaps desirable, that I may be the only person in this room who has committed the folly of writing, trying to write, or failing to write, a novel. And when I asked myself, as your invitation to speak to you about modern fiction made me ask myself, what demon whispered in my ear and urged me to my doom, a little figure rose before me – the figure of a man, or of a woman, who said, 'My name is Brown. Catch me if you can.'

Most novelists have the same experience. Some Brown, Smith, or Jones comes before them and says in the most seductive and charming way in the world, 'Come and catch me if you can.' And so, led on by this will-o'-the-wisp, they flounder through volume after volume, spending the best years of their lives in the pursuit, and receiving for the most part very little cash in exchange. Few catch the phantom; most have to be content with a scrap of her dress or a wisp of her hair.

My belief that men and women write novels because they are lured on to create some character which has thus imposed itself upon them has the sanction of Mr Arnold Bennett. In an article from which I will quote he says: 'The foundation of good fiction is character-creating and nothing else . . . Style counts; plot counts; originality of outlook counts. But none of these counts anything like so much as the convincingness of the characters. If the characters are real the novel will have a chance; if they are not, oblivion will be its portion . . .'[2] And he goes on to draw the conclusion that we have no young novelists of first-rate importance at the present moment, because they are unable to create characters that are real, true, and convincing.

These are the questions that I want with greater boldness than discretion to discuss tonight. I want to make out what we mean when we talk about 'character' in fiction; to say something about the question of reality which Mr Bennett raises; and to suggest some reasons why the younger novelists fail to create characters, if, as Mr Bennett asserts, it is true that fail they do. This will lead me, I am well aware, to make some very sweeping and some very vague assertions. For the question is an extremely difficult one. Think how little we know about character – think how little we know about art. But, to make a clearance before I begin, I will suggest that we range Edwardians and Georgians[3] into two camps; Mr Wells, Mr Bennett, and Mr Galsworthy I will call the Edwardians; Mr Forster, Mr Lawrence, Mr Strachey, Mr Joyce, and Mr Eliot I will call the Georgians. And if I speak in the first person, with intolerable egotism, I will ask you to excuse me. I do not want to attribute to the world at large the opinions of one solitary, ill-informed, and misguided individual.

My first assertion is one that I think you will grant – that every one in this room is a judge of character. Indeed it would be impossible to live for a year without disaster unless one practised character-reading and had some skill in the art. Our marriages, our friendships depend on it; our business largely depends on it; every day questions arise which can only be solved by its help. And now I will hazard a second assertion, which is more disputable perhaps, to the effect that in or about December 1910[4] human character changed.

I am not saying that one went out, as one might into a garden, and there saw that a rose had flowered, or that a hen had laid an egg. The change was not sudden and definite like that. But a change there was, nevertheless; and, since one must be arbitrary, let us date it about the year 1910. The first signs of it are recorded in the books of Samuel Butler, in *The Way of All Flesh*[5] in particular; the plays of Bernard Shaw continue to record it. In life one can see the change, if I may use a homely illustration, in the character of one's cook. The Victorian cook lived like a leviathan in the lower depths, formidable, silent, obscure, inscrutable; the Georgian cook is a creature of sunshine and fresh air; in and out of the drawing-room, now to borrow the *Daily Herald*,[6] now to ask advice about a hat. Do you ask for more solemn instances of the power of the human race to change? Read the *Agamemnon*,[7] and see whether, in process of time, your sympathies are not almost entirely with Clytemnestra. Or consider the married life of the Carlyles,[8] and bewail the waste, the futility, for him and for her, of the horrible domestic tradition which made it seemly for a woman of genius to spend her time chasing beetles, scouring saucepans, instead of writing books. All human relations have shifted – those between masters and servants, husbands and wives, parents and children. And when human relations change there is at the same time a change in religion, conduct, politics, and literature. Let us agree to place one of these changes about the year 1910.

I have said that people have to acquire a good deal of skill in character-reading if they are to live a single year of life without disaster. But it is the art of the young. In middle age and in old age the art is practised mostly for its uses, and friendships and other adventures and experiments in the art of reading character are seldom made. But novelists differ from the rest of the world because they do not cease to be interested in character when they have learnt enough about it for practical purposes. They go a step further; they feel that there is something permanently interesting in character in itself. When all the practical business of life has been discharged, there is something about people which continues to seem to them of overwhelming importance, in spite of the fact that it has no bearing whatever upon their happiness, comfort, or income. The study of character becomes to them an absorbing pursuit; to impart character an obsession. And this I find it very difficult to explain: what novelists mean when they talk about character, what the impulse is that urges them so powerfully every now and then to embody their view in writing.

So, if you will allow me, instead of analysing and abstracting, I will tell you a simple story which, however pointless, has the merit of being true, of a journey from Richmond to Waterloo,[9] in the hope that I may show you what I mean by character in itself; that you may realize the different aspects it can wear; and the hideous perils that beset you directly you try to describe it in words.

One night some weeks ago, then, I was late for the train and jumped into the first carriage I came to. As I sat down I had the strange and uncomfortable feeling that I was interrupting a conversation between two people who were already sitting there. Not that they were young or happy. Far from it. They were both elderly, the woman over sixty, the man well over forty. They were sitting opposite each other, and the man, who had been leaning over and talking emphatically to judge by his attitude and the flush on his face, sat back and became silent. I had disturbed him, and he was annoyed. The elderly lady, however, whom I will call Mrs Brown, seemed rather relieved. She was one of those clean, threadbare old ladies whose extreme tidiness – everything buttoned, fastened, tied together, mended and brushed up – suggests more extreme poverty than rags and dirt. There was something pinched about her – a look of suffering, of apprehension, and, in addition, she was extremely small. Her feet, in their clean little boots, scarcely touched the floor. I felt that she had nobody to support her; that she had to make up her mind for herself; that, having been deserted, or left a widow, years ago, she had led an anxious, harried life, bringing up an only son, perhaps, who, as likely as not, was by this time beginning to go to the bad. All this shot through my mind as I sat down, being uncomfortable, like most people, at travelling with fellow passengers unless I have somehow or other accounted for them. Then I looked at the man. He was no relation of Mrs Brown's I felt sure; he was of a bigger, burlier, less refined type. He was a man of business I imagined, very likely a respectable corn-chandler[10] from the North, dressed in good blue serge with a pocket-knife and a silk handkerchief, and a stout leather bag. Obviously, however, he had an unpleasant business to settle with Mrs Brown; a secret, perhaps sinister business, which they did not intend to discuss in my presence.

'Yes, the Crofts have had very bad luck with their servants,' Mr Smith (as I will call him) said in a considering way, going back to some earlier topic, with a view to keeping up appearances.

'Ah, poor people,' said Mrs Brown, a trifle condescendingly. 'My grandmother had a maid who came when she was fifteen and stayed till she was eighty' (this was said with a kind of hurt and aggressive pride to impress us both perhaps).

'One doesn't often come across that sort of thing nowadays,' said Mr Smith in conciliatory tones.

Then they were silent.

'It's odd they don't start a golf club there – I should have thought one of the young fellows would,' said Mr Smith, for the silence obviously made him uneasy.

Mrs Brown hardly took the trouble to answer.

'What changes they're making in this part of the world,' said Mr Smith looking out of the window, and looking furtively at me as he did so.

It was plain, from Mrs Brown's silence, from the uneasy affability with which Mr Smith spoke, that he had some power over her which he was exerting disagreeably. It might have been her son's downfall, or some painful episode in her past life, or her daughter's. Perhaps she was going to London to sign some document to make over some property. Obviously against her will she was in Mr Smith's hands. I was beginning to feel a great deal of pity for her, when she said, suddenly and inconsequently,

'Can you tell me if an oak-tree dies when the leaves have been eaten for two years in succession by caterpillars?'

She spoke quite brightly, and rather precisely, in a cultivated, inquisitive voice.

Mr Smith was startled, but relieved to have a safe topic of conversation given him. He told her a great deal very quickly about plagues of insects. He told her that he had a brother who kept a fruit farm in Kent. He told her what fruit farmers do every year in Kent, and so on, and so on. While he talked a very odd thing happened. Mrs Brown took out her little white handkerchief and began to dab her eyes. She was crying. But she went on listening quite composedly to what he was saying, and he went on talking, a little louder, a little angrily, as if he had seen her cry often before; as if it were a painful habit. At last it got on his nerves. He stopped abruptly, looked out of the window, then leant towards her as he had been doing when I got in, and said in a bullying, menacing way, as if he would not stand any more nonsense,

'So about that matter we were discussing. It'll be all right? George will be there on Tuesday?'

'We shan't be late,' said Mrs Brown, gathering herself together with superb dignity.

Mr Smith said nothing. He got up, buttoned his coat, reached his bag down, and jumped out of the train before it had stopped at Clapham Junction. He had got what he wanted, but he was ashamed of himself; he was glad to get out of the old lady's sight.

Mrs Brown and I were left alone together. She sat in her corner opposite, very clean, very small, rather queer, and suffering intensely. The impression she made was overwhelming. It came pouring out like a draught, like a smell of burning. What was it composed of – that overwhelming and peculiar impression? Myriads of irrelevant and incongruous ideas crowd into one's head on such occasions; one sees the person, one sees Mrs Brown, in the centre of all sorts of different scenes. I thought of her in a seaside house, among queer ornaments: sea-urchins, models of ships in glass cases. Her husband's medals were on the mantelpiece. She popped in and out of the room, perching on the edges of chairs, picking meals out of saucers, indulging in long, silent stares. The caterpillars and the oak-trees seemed to imply all that. And then, into this fantastic and secluded life, in broke Mr Smith. I saw him blowing in, so to speak, on a windy day. He banged, he slammed. His dripping umbrella made a pool in the hall. They sat closeted together.

And then Mrs Brown faced the dreadful revelation. She took her heroic decision. Early, before dawn, she packed her bag and carried it herself to the station. She would not let Smith touch it. She was wounded in her pride, unmoored from her anchorage; she came of gentlefolks who kept servants – but details could wait. The important thing was to realize her character, to steep oneself in her atmosphere. I had no time to explain why I felt it somewhat tragic, heroic, yet with a dash of the flighty, and fantastic, before the train stopped, and I watched her disappear, carrying her bag, into the vast blazing station. She looked very small, very tenacious; at once very frail and very heroic. And I have never seen her again, and I shall never know what became of her.

The story ends without any point to it. But I have not told you this anecdote to illustrate either my own ingenuity or the pleasure of travelling from Richmond to Waterloo. What I want you to see in it is this. Here is a character imposing itself upon another person. Here is Mrs Brown making someone begin almost automatically to write a novel about her. I believe that all novels begin with an old lady in the corner opposite. I believe that all novels, that is to say, deal with character, and that it is to express character – not to preach doctrines, sing songs, or celebrate the glories of the British Empire, that the form of the novel, so clumsy, verbose, and un-dramatic, so rich, elastic, and alive, has been evolved. To express character, I have said; but you will at once reflect that the very widest interpretation can be put upon those words. For example, old Mrs Brown's character will strike you very differently according to the age and country in which you happen to be born. It would be easy enough to write three different versions of that incident in the train, an English, a French, and a Russian. The English writer would make the old lady into a 'character'; he would bring out her oddities and mannerisms; her buttons and wrinkles; her ribbons and warts. Her personality would dominate the book. A French writer would rub out all that; he would sacrifice the individual Mrs Brown to give a more general view of human nature; to make a more abstract, proportioned, and harmonious whole. The Russian would pierce through the flesh; would reveal the soul – the soul alone, wandering out into the Waterloo Road, asking of life some tremend-ous question which would sound on and on in our ears after the book was finished. And then besides age and country there is the writer's temperament to be considered. You see one thing in charac-ter, and I another. You say it means this, and I that. And when it comes to writing each makes a further selection on principles of his own. Thus Mrs Brown can be treated in an infinite variety of ways, according to the age, country, and temperament of the writer.

But now I must recall what Mr Arnold Bennett says. He says that it is only if the characters are real that the novel has any chance of surviving. Otherwise, die it must. But, I ask myself, what is reality? And who are the judges of reality? A character may be real to Mr Bennett and quite unreal to me. For instance, in this article he says that Dr Watson in *Sherlock Holmes*[11] is real to him: to me Dr Watson is a sack stuffed with straw, a dummy, a figure of fun. And so it is with character after character – in book after book. There is nothing that people differ about more than the reality of characters, especially in contemporary books. But if you take a larger view I think that Mr Bennett is perfectly right. If, that is, you think of the novels which seem to you great novels – *War and Peace, Vanity Fair, Tristram Shandy, Madame Bovary, Pride and Prejudice, The Mayor of*

Casterbridge, Villette[12] – if you think of these books, you do at once think of some character who has seemed to you so real (I do not by that mean so lifelike) that it has the power to make you think not merely of it itself, but all sorts of things through its eyes – of religion, of love, of war, of peace, of family life, of balls in county towns, of sunsets, moonrises, the immortality of the soul. There is hardly any subject of human experience that is left out of *War and Peace* it seems to me. And in all these novels all these great novelists have brought us to see whatever they wish us to see through some character. Otherwise, they would not be novelists; but poets, historians, or pamphleteers.

But now let us examine what Mr Bennett went on to say – he said that there was no great novelist among the Georgian writers because they cannot create characters who are real, true, and convincing. And there I cannot agree. There are reasons, excuses, possibilities which I think put a different colour upon the case. It seems so to me at least, but I am well aware that this is a matter about which I am likely to be prejudiced, sanguine, and near-sighted. I will put my view before you in the hope that you will make it impartial, judicial, and broad-minded. Why, then, is it so hard for novelists at present to create characters which seem real, not only to Mr Bennett, but to the world at large? Why, when October comes round,[13] do the publishers always fail to supply us with a masterpiece?

Surely one reason is that the men and women who began writing novels in 1910 or thereabouts had this great difficulty to face – that there was no English novelist living from whom they could learn their business. Mr Conrad is a Pole; which sets him apart, and makes him, however admirable, not very helpful. Mr Hardy has written no novel since 1895. The most prominent and successful novelists in the year 1910 were, I suppose, Mr Wells, Mr Bennett, and Mr Galsworthy.[14] Now it seems to me that to go to these men and ask them to teach you how to write a novel – how to create characters that are real – is precisely like going to a bootmaker and asking him to teach you how to make a watch. Do not let me give you the impression that I do not admire and enjoy their books. They seem to me of great value, and indeed of great necessity. There are seasons when it is more important to have boots than to have watches. To drop metaphor, I think that after the creative activity of the Victorian age it was quite necessary, not only for literature but for life, that someone should write the books that Mr Wells, Mr Bennett, and Mr Galsworthy have written. Yet what odd books they are! Sometimes I wonder if we are right to call them books at all. For they leave one with so strange a feeling of incompleteness and dissatisfaction. In order to complete them it seems necessary to do something – to join a society, or, more desperately, to write a cheque. That done, the restlessness is laid, the book finished; it can be put upon the shelf, and need never be read again. But with the work of other novelists it is different. *Tristram Shandy* or *Pride and Prejudice* is complete in itself; it is self-contained; it leaves one with no desire to do anything, except indeed to read the book again, and to understand it better. The difference perhaps is that both Sterne and Jane Austen were interested in things in themselves; in character in itself; in the book in itself. Therefore everything was inside the book, nothing outside. But the Edwardians were never interested in character in itself; or in the book in itself. They were interested in something outside. Their books, then, were incomplete as books, and required that the reader should finish them, actively and practically, for himself.

Perhaps we can make this clearer if we take the liberty of imagining a little party in the railway carriage – Mr Wells, Mr Galsworthy, Mr Bennett are travelling to Waterloo with Mrs Brown. Mrs Brown, I have said, was poorly dressed and very small. She had an anxious, harassed look. I doubt whether she was what you call an educated woman. Seizing upon all these symptoms of the unsatisfactory condition of our primary schools with a rapidity to which I can do no justice, Mr Wells would instantly project upon the window-pane a vision of a better, breezier, jollier, happier, more adventurous and gallant world, where these musty railway carriages and fusty old women do not exist; where miraculous barges bring tropical fruit to Camberwell by eight o'clock in the morning; where there are public nurseries, fountains, and libraries, dining-rooms, drawing-rooms, and marriages; where every citizen is generous and candid, manly and magnificent, and rather like Mr Wells himself. But nobody is in the least like Mrs Brown. There are no Mrs Browns in Utopia. Indeed I do not think that Mr Wells, in his passion to make her what she ought to be, would waste a thought upon her as she is.

And what would Mr Galsworthy see? Can we doubt that the walls of Doulton's factory would take his fancy? There are women in that factory who make twenty-five dozen earthenware pots every day. There are mothers in the Mile End Road[15] who depend upon the farthings which those women earn. But there are employers in Surrey[16] who are even now smoking rich cigars while the nightingale sings. Burning with indignation, stuffed with information, arraigning civilization, Mr Galsworthy would only see in Mrs Brown a pot broken on the wheel and thrown into the corner.

Mr Bennett, alone of the Edwardians, would keep his eyes in the carriage. He, indeed, would observe every detail with immense care. He would notice the advertisements; the pictures of Swanage and Portsmouth;[17] the way in which the cushion bulged between the buttons; how Mrs Brown wore a brooch which had cost three-and-ten-three at Whitworth's bazaar; and had mended both gloves – indeed the thumb of the left-hand glove had been replaced. And he would observe, at length, how this was the non-stop train from Windsor which calls at Richmond for the convenience of middle-class residents, who can afford to go to the theatre but have not reached the social rank which can afford motor-cars, though it is true, there are occasions (he would tell us what), when they hire them from a company (he would tell us which). And so he would gradually sidle sedately towards Mrs Brown, and would remark how she had been left a little copyhold, not freehold,[18] property at Datchet, which, however, was mortgaged to Mr Bungay the solicitor – but why should I presume to invent Mr Bennett? Does not Mr Bennett write novels himself? I will open the first book that chance puts in my way – *Hilda Lessways*.[19] Let us see how he makes us feel that Hilda is real, true, and convincing, as a novelist should. She shut the door in a soft, controlled way, which showed the constraint of her relations with her mother. She was fond of reading *Maud*;[20] she was endowed with the power to feel intensely. So far, so good; in his leisurely, surefooted way Mr Bennett is trying in these first pages, where every touch is important, to show us the kind of girl she was.

But then he begins to describe, not Hilda Lessways, but the view from her bedroom window, the excuse being that Mr Skellorn, the man who collects rents, is coming along that way. Mr Bennett proceeds:

The bailiwick of Turnhill lay behind her; and all the murky district of the Five Towns, of which Turnhill is the northern outpost, lay to the south. At the foot of Chatterley Wood the canal wound in large curves on its way towards the undefiled plains of Cheshire and the sea. On the canal-side, exactly opposite to Hilda's window, was a flour-mill, that sometimes made nearly as much smoke as the kilns and the chimneys closing the prospect on either hand. From the flour-mill a bricked path, which separated a considerable row of new cottages from their appurtenant gardens, led straight into Lessways Street, in front of Mrs Lessways' house. By this path Mr Skellorn should have arrived, for he inhabited the farthest of the cottages.

One line of insight would have done more than all those lines of description; but let them pass as the necessary drudgery of the novelist. And now – where is Hilda? Alas. Hilda is still looking out of the window. Passionate and dissatisfied as she was, she was a girl with an eye for houses. She often compared this old Mr Skellorn with the villas she saw from her bedroom window. Therefore the villas must be described. Mr Bennett proceeds:

The row was called Freehold Villas: a consciously proud name in a district where much of the land was copyhold and could only change owners subject to the payment of 'fines', and to the feudal consent of a 'court' presided over by the agent of a lord of the manor. Most of the dwellings were owned by their occupiers, who, each an absolute monarch of the soil, niggled in his sooty garden of an evening amid the flutter of drying shirts and towels. Freehold Villas symbolized the final triumph of Victorian economics, the apotheosis of the prudent and industrious artisan. It corresponded with a Building Society Secretary's dream of paradise. And indeed it was a very real achievement. Nevertheless, Hilda's irrational contempt would not admit this.

Heaven be praised, we cry! At last we are coming to Hilda herself. But not so fast. Hilda may have been this, that, and the other; but Hilda not only looked at houses, and thought of houses; Hilda lived in a house. And what sort of a house did Hilda live in? Mr Bennett proceeds:

It was one of the two middle houses of a detached terrace of four houses build by her grandfather Lessways, the tea-pot manufacturer; it was the chief of the four, obviously the habitation of the proprietor of the terrace. One of the corner houses comprised a grocer's shop, and this house had been robbed of its just proportion of garden so that the seigneurial garden-plot might be triflingly larger than the other. The terrace was not a terrace of cottages, but of houses rated at from twenty-six to thirty-six pounds a year; beyond the means of artisans and petty insurance agents and rent-collectors. And further, it was well built, generously built; and its architecture, though debased, showed some faint traces of Georgian amenity. It was admittedly the best row of houses in that newly settled quarter of the town. In coming to it out of Freehold Villas Mr Skellorn obviously came to something superior, wider, more liberal. Suddenly Hilda heard her mother's voice . . .

But we cannot hear her mother's voice, or Hilda's voice; we can only hear Mr Bennett's voice telling us facts about rents and freeholds and copyholds and fines. What can Mr Bennett be about? I have formed my own opinion of what Mr Bennett is about – he is trying to make us imagine for him; he is trying to hypnotize us into the belief that, because he has made a house, there must be a person living there. With all his powers of observation, which are marvellous, with all his sympathy and humanity, which are great, Mr Bennett has never once looked at Mrs Brown in her corner. There she sits in the corner of the carriage – that carriage which is travelling, not from Richmond to Waterloo, but from one age of English literature to the next, for Mrs Brown is eternal, Mrs Brown is human nature, Mrs Brown changes only on the surface, it is the novelists who get in and out – there she sits and not one of the Edwardian writers has so much as looked at her. They have looked very powerfully, searchingly, and sympathetically out of the window; at factories, at Utopias, even at the decoration and upholstery of the carriage; but never at her, never at life, never at human nature. And so they have developed a technique of novel-writing which suits their purpose; they have made tools and established conventions which do their business. But those tools are not our tools, and that business is not our business. For us those conventions are ruin, those tools are death.

You may well complain of the vagueness of my language. What is a convention, a tool, you may ask, and what do you mean by saying that Mr Bennett's and Mr Wells's and Mr Galsworthy's conventions are the wrong conventions for the Georgians? The question is difficult: I will attempt a short cut. A convention in writing is not much different from a convention in manners. Both in life and in literature it is necessary to have some means of bridging the gulf between the hostess and her unknown guest on the one hand, the writer and his unknown reader on the other. The hostess bethinks her of the weather, for generations of hostesses have established the fact that this is a subject of universal interest in which we all believe. She begins by saying that we are having a wretched May, and having thus got into touch with her unknown guest, proceeds to matter of greater interest. So it is in literature. The writer must get into touch with his reader by putting before him something which he recognizes, which therefore stimulates his imagination, and makes him willing to co-operate in the far more difficult business of intimacy. And it is of the highest importance that this common meeting place should be reached easily, almost instinctively, in the dark, with one's eyes shut. Here is Mr Bennett making use of this common ground in the passage which I have quoted. The problem before him was to make us believe in the reality of Hilda Lessways. So he began, being an Edwardian, by describing accurately and minutely the sort of house Hilda lived in, and the sort of house she saw from the window. House property was the common ground from which the Edwardians found it easy to proceed to intimacy. Indirect as it seems to us, the convention worked admirably, and thousands of Hilda Lessways were launched upon the world by this means. For that age and generation, the convention was a good one.

But now, if you will allow me to pull my own anecdote to pieces, you will see how keenly I felt the lack of a convention, and how serious a matter it is when the tools of one generation are useless for the next. The incident had made a great impression on me. But how was I to transmit it to you? All I could do was to report as accurately as I could what was said, to describe in detail what was worn, to say, despairingly, that all sorts of scenes rushed into my mind, to proceed to tumble them out pell-mell, and to describe this vivid, this overmastering impression by likening it to a draught or a smell of burning. To tell you the truth, I was also strongly tempted to manufacture a three-volume novel,[21] about the old lady's son, and his adventures crossing the Atlantic, and her daughter, and how she kept a milliner's shop in Westminster, the past life of Smith himself, and his house at Sheffield, though such stories seem to me the most dreary, irrelevant, and humbugging[22] affairs in the world.

But if I had done that I should have escaped the appalling effort of saying what I meant. And to have got at what I meant I should have had to go back and back and back; to experiment with one thing and another; to try this sentence and that, referring each word to my vision, matching it as exactly as possible, and knowing that somehow I had to find a common ground between us, a convention which would not seem to you too odd, unreal, and far-fetched to believe in. I admit that I shirked that arduous undertaking. I let my Mrs Brown slip through my fingers. I have told you nothing whatever about her. But that is partly the great Edwardians' fault. I asked them – they are my elders and betters – How shall I begin to describe this woman's character? And they said, 'Begin by saying that her father kept a shop in Harrogate. Ascertain the rent. Ascertain the wages of shop assistants in the year 1878. Discover what her mother died of. Describe cancer. Describe calico. Describe—' But I cried, 'Stop! Stop!' And I regret to say that I threw that ugly, that clumsy, that incongruous tool out of the window, for I knew that if I began describing the cancer and the calico, my Mrs Brown, that vision to which I cling though I know no way of imparting it to you, would have been dulled and tarnished and vanished for ever.

That is what I mean by saying that the Edwardian tools are the wrong ones for us to use. They have laid an enormous stress upon the fabric of things. They have given us a house in the hope that we may be able to deduce the human beings who live there. To give them their due, they have made that house much better worth living in. But if you hold that novels are in the first place about people, and only in the second about the houses they live in, that is the wrong way to set about it. Therefore, you see, the Georgian writer had to begin by throwing away the method that was in use at the moment. He was left alone there facing Mrs Brown without any method of conveying her to the reader. But that is inaccurate. A writer is never alone. There is always the public with him – if not on the same seat, at least in the compartment next door. Now the public is a strange travelling companion. In England it is a very suggestible and docile creature, which, once you get it to attend, will believe implicitly what it is told for a certain number of years. If you say to the public with sufficient conviction, 'All women have tails, and all men humps,' it will actually learn to see women with tails and men with humps, and will think it very revolutionary and probably improper if you say, 'Nonsense. Monkeys have tails and camels humps. But men and women have brains, and they have hearts; they think and they feel' – that will seem to it a bad joke, and an improper one into the bargain.

But to return. Here is the British public sitting by the writer's side and saying in its vast and unanimous way, 'Old women have houses. They have fathers. They have incomes. They have servants. They have hot-water bottles. That is how we know that they are old women. Mr Wells and Mr Bennett and Mr Galsworthy have always taught us that this is the way to recognize them. But now with your Mrs Brown – how are we to believe in her? We do not even know whether her villa was called Albert or Balmoral;[23] what she paid for her gloves; or whether her mother died of cancer or of consumption.[24] How can she be alive? No; she is a mere figment of your imagination.'

And old women of course ought to be made of freehold villas and copyhold estates, not of imagination.

The Georgian novelist, therefore, was in an awkward predicament. There was Mrs Brown protesting that she was different, quite different, from what people made out, and luring the novelist to her rescue by the most fascinating if fleeting glimpse of her charms; there were the Edwardians handing out tools appropriate to house building and house breaking; and there was the British public assever-ating[25] that they must see the hot-water bottle first. Meanwhile the train was rushing to that station where we must all get out.

Such, I think, was the predicament in which the young Georgians found themselves about the year 1910. Many of them – I am thinking of Mr Forster and Mr Lawrence in particular – spoilt their early work because, instead of throwing away those tools, they tried to use them. They tried to compromise. They tried to combine their own direct sense of the oddity and significance of some character with Mr Galsworthy's knowledge of the Factory Acts,[26] and Mr Bennett's knowledge of the Five Towns.[27] They tried it, but they had too keen, too overpowering a sense of Mrs Brown and her peculiarities to go on trying it much longer. Something had to be done. At whatever cost of life, limb, and damage to valuable property Mrs Brown must be rescued, expressed, and set in her high relations to the world before the train stopped and she disappeared for ever. And so the smashing and the crashing began. Thus it is that we hear all round us, in poems and novels and biographies, even in newspaper articles and essays, the sound of breaking and falling, crashing and destruction. It is the prevailing sound of the Georgian age – rather a melancholy one if you think what melodious days there have been in the past, if you think of Shakespeare and Milton and Keats or even of Jane Austen and Thackeray and Dickens, if you think of the language, and the heights to which it can soar when free, and see the same eagle captive, bald, and croaking.

In view of these facts – with these sounds in my ears and these fancies in my brain – I am not going to deny that Mr Bennett has some reason when he complains that our Georgian writers are unable to make us believe that our characters are real. I am forced to agree that they do not pour out three immortal masterpieces with Victorian regularity every autumn. But instead of being gloomy, I am sanguine. For this state of things is, I think, inevitable whenever from hoar old age or callow youth the convention ceases to be a means of communication between writer and reader, and becomes instead an obstacle and an impediment. At the present moment we are suffering, not from decay, but from having no code of manners which writers and readers accept as a prelude to the more exciting intercourse of friendship. The literary convention of the time is so artificial – you have to talk about the weather and nothing but the weather throughout the entire visit – that, naturally, the feeble are tempted to outrage, and the strong are led to destroy the very foundations and rules of literary society. Signs of this are everywhere apparent. Grammar is violated; syntax disintegrated; as a boy staying with an aunt for the weekend rolls in the geranium bed out of sheer desperation as the solemnities of the sabbath wear on. The more adult writers do not, of course, indulge in such wanton exhibitions of spleen. Their sincerity is desperate, and their courage tremendous; it is only that they do not know which to use, a fork or their fingers. Thus, if you read Mr Joyce and Mr Eliot you will be struck by the indecency of the one, and the obscurity of the other. Mr Joyce's indecency in *Ulysses*[28] seems to me the conscious and calculated indecency of a desperate man who feels that in order to breathe he must break the windows. At moments, when the window is broken, he is magnificent. But what a waste of energy! And, after all, how dull indecency is, when it is not the overflowing of a super-abundant energy or savagery, but the determined and public-spirited act of a man who needs fresh air! Again, with the obscurity of Mr Eliot. I think that Mr Eliot has written some of the loveliest single lines of modern poetry. But how intolerant he is of the old usages and politenesses of society – respect for the weak, consideration for the dull! As I sun myself upon the intense and ravishing beauty of one of his lines, and reflect that I must make a dizzy and dangerous leap to the next, and so on from line to line, like an acrobat flying precariously from bar to bar, I cry out, I confess, for the old decorums, and envy the indolence of my ancestors who, instead of spinning madly through mid-air, dreamt quietly in the shade with a book. Again, in Mr Strachey's books,[29] *Eminent Victorians* and *Queen Victoria*, the effort and strain of writing against the grain and current of the times is visible too. It is much less visible, of course, for not only is he dealing with facts, which are stubborn things, but he has fabricated, chiefly from eighteenth-century material, a very discreet code of manners of his own, which allows him to sit at table with the highest in the land and to say a great many things under cover of that exquisite apparel which, had they gone naked, would have been chased by the men-servants from the room. Still, if you compare *Eminent Victorians* with some of Lord Macaulay's essays, though you will feel that Lord Macaulay is always wrong, and Mr Strachey always right, you will also feel a body, a sweep, a richness in Lord Macaulay's essays[30] which show that his age was behind him; all his strength went straight into his work; none was used for purposes of concealment or of conversion. But Mr Strachey has had to open our eyes before he made us see; he has had to search out and sew together a very artful manner of speech; and the effort, beautifully though it is concealed, has robbed his work of some of the force that should have gone into it, and limited his scope.

For these reasons, then, we must reconcile ourselves to a season of failures and fragments. We must reflect that where so much strength is spent on finding a way of telling the truth the truth itself is bound to reach us in rather an exhausted and chaotic condition. Ulysses, Queen Victoria, Mr Prufrock[31] – to give Mrs Brown some of the names she has made famous lately – is a little pale and dishevelled by the time her rescuers reach her. And it is the sound of their axes that we hear – a vigorous and stimulating sound in my ears – unless of course you wish to sleep, when, in the bounty of his concern, Providence has provided a host of writers anxious and able to satisfy your needs.

Thus I have tried, at tedious length, I fear, to answer some of the questions which I began by asking. I have given an account of some of the difficulties which in my view beset the Georgian writer in all his forms. I have sought to excuse him. May I end by venturing to remind you of the duties and responsibilities that are yours as partners in this business of writing books, as companions in the railway carriage, as fellow travellers with Mrs Brown? For she is just as visible to you who remain silent as to us who tell stories about her. In the course of your daily life this past week you have had far stranger and more interesting experiences than the one I have tried to describe. You have overheard scraps of talk that filled you with amazement. You have gone to bed at night bewildered by the complexity of your feelings. In one day thousands of ideas have coursed through your brains; thousands of emotions have met, collided, and disappeared in astonishing disorder. Nevertheless, you allow the writers to palm off upon you a version of all this, an image of Mrs Brown, which has no likeness to that surprising apparition whatsoever. In your modesty you seem to consider that writers are of different blood and bone from yourselves; that they know more of Mrs Brown than you do. Never was there a more fatal mistake. It is this division between reader and writer, this humility on your part, these professional airs and graces on ours, that corrupt and emasculate the books which should be the healthy offspring of a close and equal alliance between us. Hence spring those sleek, smooth novels, those portentous and ridiculous biographies, that milk and watery criticism, those poems melodiously celebrating the innocence of roses and sheep which pass so plausibly for literature at the present time.

Your part is to insist that writers shall come down off their plinths and pedestals, and describe beautifully if possible, truthfully at any rate, our Mrs Brown. You should insist that she is an old lady of unlimited capacity and infinite variety;[32] capable of appearing in any place; wearing any dress; saying anything and doing heaven knows what. But the things she says and the things she does and her eyes and her nose and her speech and her silence have an overwhelming fascination, for she is, of course, the spirit we live by, life itself.

But do not expect just at present a complete and satisfactory presentment of her. Tolerate the spasmodic, the obscure, the fragmentary, the failure. Your help is invoked in a good cause. For I will make one final and surpassingly rash prediction – we are trembling on the verge of one of the great ages of English literature. But it can only be reached if we are determined never, never to desert Mrs Brown.

Indiscretions

First published in *Vogue*, November 1924. It was originally subtitled,
'"Never Seek to Tell Thy Love, Love that Never Told Can Be" –
but One's Feelings for Some Writers Outrun all Prudence.'[1]

It is always indiscreet to mention the affections. Yet how they prevail, how they permeate all our intercourse! Boarding an omnibus we like the conductor; in a shop take for or against the young lady serving; through all traffic and routine, liking and disliking we go our ways, and our whole day is stained and steeped by the affections. And so it must be in reading. The critic may be able to abstract the essence and feast upon it undisturbed, but for the rest of us in every book there is something – sex, character, temperament – which, as in life, rouses affection or repulsion; and, as in life, sways and prejudices; and again, as in life, is hardly to be analysed by the reason.

George Eliot is a case in point. Her reputation, they say, is on the wane, and, indeed, how could it be otherwise? Her big nose, her little eyes, her heavy, horsey head loom from behind the printed page and make a critic of the other sex uneasy. Praise he must, but love he cannot; and however absolute and austere his devotion to the principle that art has no truck with personality, still there has crept into his voice, into textbooks and articles, as he analyses her gifts and unmasks her pretensions, that it is not George Eliot he would like to pour out tea. On the other hand, exquisitely and urbanely, from the chastest urn into the finest china Jane Austen pours, and, as she pours, smiles, charms, appreciates – that too has made its way into the austere pages of English criticism.

But now perhaps it may be pertinent, since women not only read but sometimes scribble a note of their opinions, to inquire into their preferences, their equally suppressed but equally instinctive response to the lure of personal liking in the printed page. The attractions and repulsions of sex are naturally among the most emphatic. One may hear them crackling and spitting and lending an agreeable vivacity to the insipidity of weekly journalism. In higher spheres these same impurities serve to fledge the arrows and wing the mind more swiftly if more capriciously in its flight. Some adjustment before reading is essential. Byron is the first name that comes to mind. But no woman ever loved Byron; they bowed to convention; did what they were told to do; ran mad to order. Intolerably condescending, ineffably vain, a barber's block[2] to look at, compound of bully and lap-dog, now hectoring, now swimming in vapours of sentimental twaddle, tedious, egotistical, melodramatic, the character of Byron is the least attractive in the history of letters. But no wonder that every man was in love with him. In their company he must have been irresistible; brilliant and courageous; dashing and satirical; downright and tremendous; the conqueror of women and companion of heroes – everything that strong men believe themselves to be and weak men envy them for being. But to fall in love with Byron, to enjoy Don Juan and the letters to the full, obviously one must be a man; or, if of the other sex, disguise it.

No such disguise is necessary with Keats. His name, indeed, is to be mentioned with diffidence lest the thought of a character endowed as his was with the rarest qualities that human beings can command – genius, sensibility, dignity, wisdom – should mislead us into mere panegyric. There, if ever, was a man whom both sexes must unite to honour; towards whom the personal bias must incline all in the same direction. But there is a hitch; there is Fanny Brawne.[3] She danced too much at Hampstead, Keats complained. The divine poet was a little sultanic in his behaviour; after the manly fashion of his time apt to treat his adored both as angel and cockatoo. A jury of maidens would bring in a verdict in Fanny's favour. It was to his sister, whose education he supervised and whose character he formed, that he showed himself the man of all others which 'had he been put on would have prov'd most royally'.[4] Sisterly his women readers must suppose themselves to be; and sisterly to Wordsworth,[5] who should have had no wife, as Tennyson should have had none, nor Charlotte Brontë her Mr Nicholls.[6]

To put oneself at the best post of observation for the study of Samuel Johnson needs a little circumspection. He was apt to tear the tablecloth to ribbons; he was a disciplinarian and a sentimentalist; very rude to women, and at the same time the most devoted, respectful and devout of their admirers. Neither Mrs Thrale,[7] whom he harangued, nor the pretty young woman who sat on his knee is to be envied altogether. Their positions are too precarious. But some sturdy matchseller or apple woman well on in years, some old struggler who had won for herself a decent independence would have commanded his sympathy, and, standing at a stall on a rainy night in the Strand, one might perhaps have insinuated oneself into his service, washed up his tea-cups and thus enjoyed the greatest felicity that could fall to the lot of woman.

These instances, however, are all of a simple character; the men have been supposed to remain men, the women women when they write. They have exerted the influence of their sex directly and normally. But there is a class which keeps itself aloof from any such contamination.[8] Milton is their leader; with him are Landor, Sappho, Sir Thomas Browne, Marvell.[9] Feminists or anti-feminists, passionate or cold – whatever the romances or adventures of their private lives not a whiff of that mist attaches itself to their writing. It is pure, uncontaminated, sexless as the angels are said to be sexless. But on no account is this to be confused with another group which has the same peculiarity. To which sex do the works of Emerson, Matthew Arnold, Harriet Martineau, Ruskin[10] and Maria Edgeworth belong? It is uncertain. It is, moreover, quite immaterial. They are not men when they write, nor are they women. They appeal to that large tract of the soul which is sexless; they excite no passions; they exalt, improve, instruct, and man or woman can profit equally by their pages, without indulging in the folly of affection or the fury of partisanship.

Then, inevitably, we come to the harem, and tremble slightly as we approach the curtain and catch glimpses of women behind it and even hear ripples of laughter and snatches of conversation. Some obscurity still veils the relations of women to each other. A hundred years ago it was simple enough; they were stars who shone only in male sunshine; deprived of it, they languished into nonentity – sniffed, bickered, envied each other – so men said. But now it must be confessed things are less satisfactory. Passions and repulsions manifest themselves here too, and it is by no means certain that every woman is inspired by pure envy when she reads what another has written. More probably Emily Brontë was the passion of her youth; Charlotte even she loved with nervous affection; and cherished a quiet sisterly regard for Anne. Mrs Gaskell[11] wields a maternal sway over readers of her own sex; wise, witty and very large-minded, her readers are devoted to her as to the most admirable of mothers; whereas George Eliot is an Aunt, and, as an Aunt, inimitable. So treated she drops the apparatus of masculinity which Herbert Spencer[12] necessitated; indulges herself in memory; and pours forth, no doubt with some rustic accent, the genial stores of her youth, the greatness and profundity of her soul. Jane Austen we needs must adore; but she does not want it; she wants nothing; our love is a by-product, an irrelevance; with that mist or without it her moon shines on. As for loving foreigners, some say it is an impossibility; but if not, it is to Madame de Sévigné[13] that we must turn.

But all these preferences are partialities, all these adjustments and attempts of the mind to relate itself harmoniously with another, pale, as the flirtations of a summer compared with the consuming passions of a lifetime, when we consider the great devotions which one, or at most two, names in the whole of literature inspire. Of Shakespeare we need not speak. The nimble little birds of field and hedge, lizards, shrews and dormice, do not pause in their dallyings and sportings to thank the sun for warming them; nor need we, the light of whose literature comes from Shakespeare, seek to praise him. But there are other names, more retired, less central, less universally gazed upon than his. There is a poet, whose love of women was all stuck about with briars; who railed and cursed; was fierce and tender; passionate and obscene. In the very obscurity of his mind there is something that intrigues us on; his rage scorches but sets on fire; and in the thickest of his thorn bushes are glimpses of the highest heavens, and ecstasies and pure and windless calms. Whether as a young man gazing from narrow Chinese eyes upon a world that half allures, half disgusts him, or with his flesh dried on his cheek bones, wrapped in by winding sheet, excruciated, dead in St Paul's, one cannot help but love John Donne. With him is associated a man of the very opposite sort – large, lame, simple-minded; a scribbler of innumerable novels not a line of which is harsh, obscure or anything but propriety itself; a landed gentleman with a passion for Gothic architecture; a man who, if he had lived today, would have been the upholder of all the most detestable institutions of his country, but for all that a great writer – no woman can read the life of this man and his diary and his novels without being head over ears in love with Walter Scott.

On Not Knowing Greek

First published in *The Common Reader*, 1925.

For it is in vain and foolish to talk of knowing Greek, since in our ignorance we should be at the bottom of any class of schoolboys, since we do not know how the words sounded, or where precisely we ought to laugh, or how the actors acted, and between this foreign people and ourselves there is not only difference of race and tongue but a tremendous breach of tradition. All the more strange, then, is it that we should wish to know Greek, try to know Greek, feel for ever drawn back to Greek, and be for ever making up some notion of the meaning of Greek, though from what incongruous odds and ends, with what slight resemblance to the real meaning of Greek, who shall say?

It is obvious in the first place that Greek literature is the impersonal literature. Those few hundred years that separate John Paston[1] from Plato, Norwich from Athens, make a chasm which the vast tide of European chatter can never succeed in crossing. When we read Chaucer, we are floated up to him insensibly on the current of our ancestors' lives, and later, as records increase and memories lengthen, there is scarcely a figure which has not its nimbus[2] of association, its life and letters, its wife and family, its house, its character, its happy or dismal catastrophe. But the Greeks remain in a fastness of their own. Fate has been kind there too. She has preserved them from vulgarity. Euripides[3] was eaten by dogs; Aeschylus killed by a stone;[4] Sappho leapt from a cliff. We know no more of them than that. We have their poetry, and that is all.

But that is not, and perhaps never can be, wholly true. Pick up any play by Sophocles, read –

Son of him who led our hosts at Troy of old, son of Agamemnon,[5]

and at once the mind begins to fashion itself surroundings. It makes some background, even of the most provisional sort, for Sophocles;

it imagines some village, in a remote part of the country, near the sea. Even nowadays such villages are to be found in the wilder parts of England, and as we enter them we can scarcely help feeling that here, in this cluster of cottages, cut off from rail or city, are all the elements of a perfect existence. Here is the Rectory; here the Manor house, the farm and the cottages; the church for worship, the club for meeting, the cricket field for play. Here life is simply sorted out into its main elements. Each man and woman has his work; each works for the health or happiness of others. And here, in this little community, characters become part of the common stock; the eccentricities of the clergyman are known; the great ladies' defects of temper; the blacksmith's feud with the milkman, and the loves and matings of the boys and girls. Here life has cut the same grooves for centuries; customs have arisen; legends have attached themselves to hill-tops and solitary trees, and the village has its history, its festivals, and its rivalries.

It is the climate that is impossible. If we try to think of Sophocles here, we must annihilate the smoke and the damp and the thick wet mists. We must sharpen the lines of the hills. We must imagine a beauty of stone and earth rather than of woods and greenery. With warmth and sunshine and months of brilliant, fine weather, life of course is instantly changed; it is transacted out of doors, with the result, known to all who visit Italy, that small incidents are debated in the street, not in the sitting-room, and become dramatic; make people voluble; inspire in them that sneering, laughing, nimbleness of wit and tongue peculiar to the southern races, which has nothing in common with the slow reserve, the low half-tones, the brooding introspective melancholy of people accustomed to live more than half the year indoors.

That is the quality that first strikes us in Greek literature, the lightning-quick, sneering, out-of-doors manner. It is apparent in the most august as well as in the most trivial places. Queens and Princesses in this very tragedy by Sophocles stand at the door bandying words like village women, with a tendency, as one might expect, to rejoice in language, to split phrases into slices, to be intent on verbal victory. The humour of the people was not good-natured like that of our postmen and cab-drivers. The taunts of men lounging at the street corners had something cruel in them as well as witty. There is a cruelty in Greek tragedy which is quite unlike our English brutality. Is not Pentheus,[6] for example, that highly respectable man, made ridiculous in the *Bacchae* before he is destroyed? In fact, of course, these Queens and Princesses were out of doors, with the bees buzzing past them, shadows crossing them, and the wind taking their draperies. They were speaking to an enormous audience[7] rayed round them on one of those brilliant southern days when the sun is so hot and yet the air so exciting. The poet, therefore, had to bethink him, not of some theme which could be read for hours by people in privacy, but of something emphatic, familiar, brief, that would carry, instantly and directly, to an audience of seventeen thousand people perhaps, with ears and eyes eager and attentive, with bodies whose muscles would grow stiff if they sat too long without diversion. Music and dancing he would need, and naturally would choose one of those legends, like our Tristram and Iseult,[8] which are known to every one in outline, so that a great fund of emotion is ready prepared, but can be stressed in a new place by each new poet.

Sophocles would take the old story of Electra,[9] for instance, but would at once impose his stamp upon it. Of that, in spite of our weakness and distortion, what remains visible to us? That his genius was of the extreme kind in the first place; that he chose a design which, if it failed, would show its failure in gashes and ruin, not in the gentle blurring of some insignificant detail; which, if it succeeded, would cut each stroke to the bone, would stamp each finger-print in marble. His Electra stands before us like a figure so tightly bound that she can only move an inch this way, an inch that. But each movement must tell to the utmost, or, bound as she is, denied the relief of all hints, repetitions, suggestions, she will be nothing but a dummy, tightly bound. Her words in crisis are, as a matter of fact, bare; mere cries of despair joy, hate

> οἲ 'γὼ τάλαιν', ὄλωλα τῇδ' ἐν ἡμέρᾳ.
> παῖσον, εἰ σθένεις, διπλῆν.[10]

But these cries give angle and outline to the play. It is thus, with a thousand differences of degree, that in English literature Jane Austen shapes a novel. There comes a moment – 'I will dance with you,'[11] says Emma – which rises higher than the rest, which, though not eloquent in itself, or violent, or made striking by beauty of language, has the whole weight of the book behind it. In Jane Austen, too, we have the same sense, though the ligatures are much less tight, that her figures are bound, and restricted to a few definite movements. She, too, in her modest, everyday prose, chose the dangerous art where one slip means death.

But it is not so easy to decide what it is that gives these cries of Electra in her anguish their power to cut and wound and excite. It is partly that we know her, that we have picked up from little turns and twists of the dialogue hints of her character, of her appearance, which, characteristically, she neglected; of something suffering in her, outraged and stimulated to its utmost stretch of capacity, yet, as she herself knows ('my behaviour is unseemly and becomes me ill'), blunted and debased by the horror of her position, an unwed girl made to witness her mother's vileness and denounce it in loud, almost vulgar, clamour to the world at large. It is partly, too, that we know in the same way that Clytemnestra is no unmitigated villainess. 'δεινὸν τὸ τίκτειν ἐστίν,' she says – 'there is a strange power in motherhood'.[12] It is no murderess, violent and un-redeemed, whom Orestes kills within the house and Electra bids him utterly destroy – 'Strike again.' No; the men and women stand-ing out in the sunlight before the audience on the hill-side were alive enough, subtle enough, not mere figures, or plaster casts of human beings.

Yet it is not because we can analyse them into feelings that they impress us. In six pages of Proust[13] we can find more complicated and varied emotions than in the whole of the *Electra*. But in the *Electra* or in the *Antigone*[14] we are impressed by something different, by something perhaps more impressive – by heroism itself, by fidelity itself. In spite of the labour and the difficulty it is this that draws us back and back to the Greeks; the stable, the permanent, the original human being is to be found there. Violent emotions are indeed to rouse him into action, but when thus stirred by death, by betrayal, by some other primitive calamity, Antigone and Ajax and Electra behave in the way in which we should behave thus struck down; the way in which everybody has always behaved; and thus we understand them more easily and more directly than we understand the characters in the *Canterbury Tales*.[15] These are the originals, Chaucer's the varieties of the human species.

It is true, of course, that these types of the original man or woman, these heroic Kings, these faithful daughters, these tragic Queens who stalk through the ages always planting their feet in the same places, twitching their robes with the same gestures, from habit not from impulse,[16] are among the greatest bores and the most demoralizing companions in the world. The plays of Addison, Voltaire,[17] and a host of others are there to prove it. But encounter them in Greek. Even in Sophocles, whose reputation for restraint and mastery has filtered down to us from the scholars, they are decided, ruthless, direct. A fragment of their speech broken off would, we feel, colour oceans and oceans of the respectable drama. Here we meet them before their emotions have been worn into uniformity. Here we listen to the nightingale whose song echoes through English literature singing in her own Greek tongue. For the first time Orpheus with his lute makes men and beasts follow him. Their voices ring out clear and sharp; we see the hairy, tawny bodies at play in the sunlight among the olive trees, not posed gracefully, on granite plinths in the pale corridors of the British Museum.[18] And then suddenly, in the midst of all this sharpness and compression, Electra, as if she swept her veil over her face and forbade us to think of her any more, speaks of that very nightingale: 'that bird distraught with grief, the messenger of Zeus. Ah, queen of sorrow, Niobe, thee I deem divine – thee; who evermore weepest in thy rocky tomb.'[19]

And as she silences her own complaint, she perplexes us again with the insoluble question of poetry and its nature, and why, as she speaks thus, her words put on the assurance of immortality. For they are Greek; we cannot tell how they sounded; they ignore the obvious source of excitement; they owe nothing of their effect to any extravagant expression, and certainly they throw no light upon the speaker's character or the writer's. But they remain, something that has been stated and must eternally endure.

Yet in a play how dangerous this poetry, this lapse from the particular to the general must of necessity be, with the actors standing there in person, with their bodies and their faces passively waiting to be made use of! For this reason the later plays of Shakespeare, where there is more of poetry than of action, are better read than seen, better understood by leaving out the actual body than by having the body, with all its associations and move-ments, visible to the eye. The intolerable restrictions of the drama could be loosened, however, if a means could be found by which what was general and poetic, comment, not action, could be freed without interrupting the movement of the whole. It is this that the choruses[20] supply; the old men or women who take no active part in the drama, the undifferentiated voices who sing like birds in the pauses of the wind; who can comment, or sum up, or allow the poet to speak himself or supply, by contrast, another side to his concep-tion. Always in imaginative literature, where characters speak for themselves and the author has no part, the need of that voice is making itself felt. For though Shakespeare (unless we consider that his fools and madmen supply the part) dispensed with the chorus, novelists are always devising some substitute – Thackeray speaking in his own person, Fielding coming out and addressing the world before his curtain rises. So to grasp the meaning of the play the chorus is of the utmost importance. One must be able to pass easily into those ecstasies, those wild and apparently irrelevant utterances, those sometimes obvious and commonplace statements, to decide their relevance or irrelevance, and give them their relation to the play as a whole.

We must 'be able to pass easily'; but that of course is exactly what we cannot do. For the most part the choruses, with all their ob-scurities, must be spelt out and their symmetry mauled. But we can guess that Sophocles used them not to express something outside the action of the play, but to sing the praises of some virtue, or the beauties of some place mentioned in it. He selects what he wishes to emphasize and sings of white Colonus and its nightingale,[21] or of love unconquered in fight. Lovely, lofty, and serene, his choruses grow naturally out of his situations, and change, not the point of view, but the mood. In Euripides, however, the situations are not contained within themselves; they give off an atmosphere of doubt, of suggestion, of questioning; but if we look to the choruses to make this plain we are often baffled rather than instructed. At once in the *Bacchae* we are in the world of psychology and doubt; the world where the mind twists facts and changes them and makes the familiar aspects of life appear new and questionable. What is Bacchus, and who are the Gods, and what is man's duty to them, and what the rights of his subtle brain? To these questions the chorus makes no reply, or replies mockingly, or speaks darkly as if the straitness of the dramatic form had tempted Euripides to violate it, in order to relieve his mind of its weight. Time is so short and I have so much to say, that unless you will allow me to place together two apparently unrelated statements and trust to you to pull them together, you must be content with a mere skeleton of the play I might have given you. Such is the argument. Euripides therefore suffers less than Sophocles and less than Aeschylus from being read privately in a room, and not seen on a hill-side in the sunshine. He can be acted in the mind; he can comment upon the questions of the moment; more than the others he will vary in popularity from age to age.

If then in Sophocles the play is concentrated in the figures themselves, and in Euripides is to be retrieved from flashes of poetry and questions far flung and unanswered, Aeschylus makes these little dramas (the *Agamemnon* has 1663 lines;[22] *Lear* about 2600) tremendous by stretching every phrase to the utmost, by sending them floating forth in metaphors, by bidding them rise up and stalk eyeless and majestic through the scene. To understand him it is not so necessary to understand Greek as to understand poetry. It is necessary to take that dangerous leap through the air without the support of words which Shakespeare also asks of us. For words, when opposed to such a blast of meaning, must give out, must be blown astray, and only by collecting in companies convey the meaning which each one separately is too weak to express. Connecting them in a rapid flight of the mind we know instantly and instinctively what they mean, but could not decant that meaning afresh into any other words. There is an ambiguity which is the mark of the highest poetry; we cannot know exactly what it means. Take this from the *Agamemnon* for instance –

ὀμμάτων δ' ἐν ἀχηνίαις ἔρρει πᾶσ' Ἀφροδίτα.[23]

The meaning is just on the far side of language. It is the meaning which in moments of astonishing excitement and stress we perceive in our minds without words; it is the meaning that Dostoevsky[24] (hampered as he was by prose and as we are by translation) leads us to by some astonishing run up the scale of emotions and points at but cannot indicate; the meaning that Shakespeare succeeds in snaring.

Aeschylus thus will not give, as Sophocles gives, the very words that people might have spoken, only so arranged that they have in some mysterious way a general force, a symbolic power, not like Euripides will he combine incongruities and thus enlarge his little space, as a small room is enlarged by mirrors in odd corners.[25] By the bold and running use of metaphor he will amplify and give us, not the thing itself, but the reverberation, and reflection which, taken into his mind, the thing has made; close enough to the original to illustrate it, remote enough to heighten, enlarge, and make splendid.

For none of these dramatists had the licence which belongs to the novelist, and, in some degree, to all writers of printed books, of modelling their meaning with an infinity of slight touches which can only be properly applied by reading quietly, carefully, and sometimes two or three times over. Every sentence had to explode on striking the ear, however slowly and beautifully the words might then descend, and however enigmatic might their final purport be. No splendour or richness of metaphor could have saved the *Agamemnon* if either images or allusions of the subtlest or most decorative had got between us and the naked cry

ὀτοτοτοῖ πόποι δᾶ. ὦ ᾿πολλον, ὦ ᾿πολλον.[26]

Dramatic they had to be at whatever cost.

But winter fell on these villages, darkness and extreme cold descended on the hill-side. There must have been some place indoors where men could retire, both in the depths of winter and in the summer heats, where they could sit and drink, where they could lie stretched at their ease, where they could talk. It is Plato, of course, who reveals the life indoors, and describes how, when a party of friends met and had eaten not at all luxuriously and drunk a little wine, some handsome boy ventured a question, or quoted an opinion, and Socrates took it up, fingered it, turned it round, looked at it this way and that, swiftly stripped it of its inconsistencies and falsities and brought the whole company by degrees to gaze with him at the truth. It is an exhausting process; to contract painfully upon the exact meaning of words; to judge what each admission

involves; to follow intently, yet critically, the dwindling and changing of opinion as it hardens and intensifies into truth. Are pleasure
and good the same? Can virtue be taught? Is virtue knowledge? The
tired or feeble mind may easily lapse as the remorseless questioning
proceeds; but no one, however weak, can fail, even if he does not
learn more from Plato, to love knowledge better. For as the argument mounts from step to step,[27] Protagoras[28] yielding, Socrates
pushing on, what matters is not so much the end we reach as our
manner of reaching it. That all can feel – the indomitable honesty,
the courage, the love of truth which draw Socrates and us in his
wake to the summit where, if we too may stand for a moment, it is
to enjoy the greatest felicity of which we are capable.

Yet such an expression seems ill fitted to describe the state of
mind of a student to whom, after painful argument, the truth has
been revealed. But truth is various; truth comes to us in different
disguises; it is not with the intellect alone that we perceive it. It is a
winter's night; the tables are spread at Agathon's house;[29] the girl is
playing the flute; Socrates has washed himself and put on sandals;
he has stopped in the hall; he refuses to move when they send for
him. Now Socrates has done; he is bantering Alcibiades;[30] Alcibiades
takes a fillet and binds it round 'this wonderful fellow's head'. He
praises Socrates. 'For he cares not for mere beauty, but despises
more than any one can imagine all external possessions, whether it
be beauty or wealth or glory, or any other thing for which the
multitude felicitates the possessor. He esteems these things and us
who honour them, as nothing, and lives among men, making all the
objects of their admiration the playthings of his irony. But I know
not if any one of you has ever seen the divine images which are
within, when he has been opened and is serious. I have seen them,
and they are so supremely beautiful, so golden, divine, and wonderful, that everything which Socrates commands surely ought to be
obeyed even like the voice of a God.' All this flows over the
arguments of Plato – laughter and movement; people getting up
and going out; the hour changing; tempers being lost; jokes cracked;
the dawn rising. Truth, it seems, is various; Truth is to be pursued
with all our faculties. Are we to rule out the amusements, the
tenderness, the frivolities of friendship because we love truth? Will
truth be quicker found because we stop our ears to music and drink

no wine, and sleep instead of talking through the long winter's night? It is not to the cloistered disciplinarian mortifying himself in solitude that we are to turn, but to the well-sunned nature, the man who practises the art of living to the best advantage, so that nothing is stunted but some things are permanently more valuable than others.

So in these dialogues we are made to seek truth with every part of us. For Plato, of course, had the dramatic genius. It is by means of that, by an art which conveys in a sentence or two the setting and the atmosphere, and then with perfect adroitness insinuates itself into the coils of the argument without losing its liveliness and grace, and then contracts to bare statement, and then, mounting, expands and soars in that higher air which is generally reached only by the more extreme measures of poetry – it is this art which plays upon us in so many ways at once and brings us to an exultation of mind which can only be reached when all the powers are called upon to contribute their energy to the whole.

But we must beware. Socrates did not care for 'mere beauty', by which he meant, perhaps, beauty as ornament. A people who judged as much as the Athenians did by ear, sitting out-of-doors at the play or listening to argument in the market-place, were far less apt than we are to break off sentences and appreciate them apart from the context. For them there were no Beauties of Hardy, Beauties of Meredith, Sayings from George Eliot. The writer had to think more of the whole and less of the detail. Naturally, living in the open, it was not the lip or the eye that struck them, but the carriage of the body and the proportions of its parts. Thus when we quote and extract we do the Greeks more damage than we do the English. There is a bareness and abruptness in their literature which grates upon a taste accustomed to the intricacy and finish of printed books. We have to stretch our minds to grasp a whole devoid of the prettiness of detail or the emphasis of eloquence. Accustomed to look directly and largely rather than minutely and aslant, it was safe for them to step into the thick of emotions which blind and bewilder an age like our own. In the vast catastrophe of the European war[31] our emotions had to be broken up for us, and put at an angle from us, before we could allow ourselves to feel them in poetry or fiction. The only poets who spoke to the purpose spoke in the sidelong, satiric manner of Wilfred Owen and Siegfried Sassoon.[32] It was not possible for them to be direct without being clumsy; or to speak simply of emotion without being sentimental. But the Greeks could say, as if for the first time, 'Yet being dead they have not died'. They could say, 'If to die nobly is the chief part of excellence, to us out of all men Fortune gave this lot; for hastening to set a crown of freedom on Greece we lie possessed of praise that grows not old'.[33] They could march straight up, with their eyes open; and thus fearlessly approached, emotions stand still and suffer themselves to be looked at.

But again (the question comes back and back), Are we reading Greek as it was written when we say this? When we read these few words cut on a tombstone, a stanza in a chorus, the end of the opening of a dialogue of Plato's, a fragment of Sappho, when we bruise our minds upon some tremendous metaphor in the *Agamemnon* instead of stripping the branch of its flowers instantly as we do in reading *Lear* – are we not reading wrongly? losing our sharp sight in the haze of associations? reading into Greek poetry not what they have but what we lack? Does not the whole of Greece heap itself behind every line of its literature? They admit us to a vision of the earth unravaged, the sea unpolluted, the maturity, tried but unbroken, of mankind. Every word is reinforced by a vigour which pours out of olive-tree and temple and the bodies of the young. The nightingale has only to be named by Sophocles and she sings; the grove has only to be called ἄβατον, 'untrodden', and we imagine the twisted branches and the purple violets. Back and back we are drawn to steep ourselves in what, perhaps, is only an image of the reality, not the reality itself, a summer's night imagined in the heart of a northern winter. Chief among these sources of glamour and perhaps misunderstanding is the language. We can never hope to get the whole fling of a sentence in Greek as we do in English. We cannot hear it, now dissonant, now harmonious, tossing sound from line to line across a page. We cannot pick up infallibly one by one all those minute signals by which a phrase is made to hint, to turn, to live. Nevertheless, it is the language that has us most in bondage; the desire for that which perpetually lures us back. First there is the compactness of the expression. Shelley takes twenty-one words[34] in English to translate thirteen words of

Greek – πᾶς γοῦν ποιητὴς γίγνεται, κἂν ἄμουσος ᾖ τὸ πρίν, οὗ ἂν Ἔρως ἅψηται ('. . . for everyone, even if before he were ever so undisciplined, becomes a poet as soon as he is touched by love').

Every ounce of fat has been pared off, leaving the flesh firm. Then, spare and bare as it is, no language can move more quickly, dancing, shaking, all alive, but controlled. Then there are the words themselves which, in so many instances, we have made expressive to us of our own emotions, θάλασσα, θάνατος, ἄνθος, ἀστήρ, σελήνη[35] – to take the first that come to hand; so clear, so hard, so intense, that to speak plainly yet fittingly without blurring the outline or clouding the depths Greek is the only expression. It is useless then, to read Greek in translations. Translators can but offer us a vague equivalent; their language is necessarily full of echoes and associations. Professor Mackail says 'wan',[36] and the age of Burne-Jones and Morris[37] is at once evoked. Nor can the subtler stress, the flight and the fall of the words, be kept even by the most skilful of scholars –

> . . . thee, who evermore weepest in thy rocky tomb

is not

> ἅτ' ἐν τάφῳ πετραίῳ
> αἰεὶ δακρύεις.[38]

Further, in reckoning the doubts and difficulties there is this important problem – Where are we to laugh in reading Greek? There is a passage in the *Odyssey* where laughter begins to steal upon us, but if Homer[39] were looking we should probably think it better to control our merriment. To laugh instantly it is almost necessary (though Aristophanes may supply us with an exception) to laugh in English. Humour, after all, is closely bound up with a sense of the body. When we laugh at the humour of Wycherley,[40] we are laughing with the body of that burly rustic who was our common ancestor on the village green. The French, the Italians, the Americans, who derive physically from so different a stock, pause, as we pause in reading Homer, to make sure that they are laughing in the right place, and the pause is fatal. Thus humour is the first of the gifts to perish in a foreign tongue, and when we turn from Greek to English literature it seems, after a long silence, as if our great age were ushered in by a burst of laughter.

These are all difficulties, sources of misunderstanding, of distorted and romantic, of servile and snobbish passion. Yet even for the unlearned some certainties remain. Greek is the impersonal literature; it is also the literature of masterpieces. There are no schools; no forerunners; no heirs. We cannot trace a gradual process working in many men imperfectly until it expresses itself adequately at last in one. Again, there is always about Greek literature that air of vigour which permeates an 'age', whether it is the age of Aeschylus, or Racine,[41] or Shakespeare. One generation at least in that fortunate time is blown on to be writers to the extreme; to attain that unconsciousness which means that the consciousness is stimulated to the highest extent; to surpass the limits of small triumphs and tentative experiments. Thus we have Sappho with her constellations of adjectives; Plato daring extravagant flights of poetry in the midst of prose; Thucydides, constricted and contracted; Sophocles gliding like a shoal of trout smoothly and quietly, apparently motionless, and then, with a flicker of fins, off and away; while in the *Odyssey* we have what remains the triumph of narrative, the clearest and at the same time the most romantic story of the fortunes of men and women.

The *Odyssey* is merely a story of adventure, the instinctive story-telling of a sea-faring race. So we may begin it, reading quickly in the spirit of children wanting amusement to find out what happens next. But here is nothing immature; here are full-grown people, crafty, subtle, and passionate. Nor is the world itself a small one, since the sea which separates island from island has to be crossed by little hand-made boats and is measured by the flight of the sea-gulls. It is true that the islands are not thickly populated, and the people, though everything is made by hands, are not closely kept at work. They have had time to develop a very dignified, a very stately society, with an ancient tradition of manners behind it, which makes every relation at once orderly, natural, and full of reserve. Penelope crosses the room; Telemachus goes to bed; Nausicaa[42] washes her linen; and their actions seem laden with beauty because they do not know that they are beautiful, have been born to their possessions, are no more self-conscious than children, and yet, all those thousands of years ago, in their little islands, know all that is to be known. With the sound of the sea in their ears, vines, meadows, rivulets about them, they are even more aware than we are of a ruthless fate. There is a sadness at the back of life which they do not attempt to mitigate. Entirely aware of their own standing in the shadow, and yet alive to every tremor and gleam of existence, there they endure, and it is to the Greeks that we turn when we are sick of the vagueness, of the confusion, of the Christianity and its consolations, of our own age.

The Duchess of Newcastle

First published in *The Common Reader*, 1925.

'. . . All I desire is fame,'[1] wrote Margaret Cavendish, Duchess of Newcastle. And while she lived her wish was granted. Garish in her dress,[2] eccentric in her habits, chaste in her conduct, coarse in her speech, she succeeded during her lifetime in drawing upon herself the ridicule of the great and the applause of the learned. But the last echoes of that clamour have now all died away; she lives only in the few splendid phrases that Lamb scattered upon her tomb;[3] her poems, her plays, her philosophies, her orations, her discourses – all those folios and quartos in which, she protested, her real life was shrined – moulder in the gloom of public libraries, or are decanted into tiny thimbles which hold six drops of their profusion. Even the curious student, inspired by the words of Lamb, quails before the mass of her mausoleum, peers in, looks about him, and hurries out again, shutting the door.

But that hasty glance has shown him the outlines of a memorable figure. Born (it is conjectured) in 1624, Margaret was the youngest child of a Thomas Lucas, who died when she was an infant, and her upbringing was due to her mother, a lady of remarkable character, of majestic grandeur and beauty 'beyond the ruin of time'.[4] 'She was very skilful in leases, and setting of lands and court keeping, ordering of stewards, and the like affairs.' The wealth which thus accrued she spent, not on marriage portions, but on generous and delightful pleasures, 'out of an opinion that if she bred us with needy necessity it might chance to create in us sharking qualities'. Her eight sons and daughters were never beaten, but reasoned with, finely and gaily dressed, and allowed no conversation with servants, not because they are servants but because servants 'are for the most part ill-bred as well as meanly born'. The daughters were taught the usual accomplishments 'rather for formality than for benefit', it being their mother's opinion that character, happiness, and honesty were of greater value to a woman than fiddling and singing, or 'the prating of several languages'.

Already Margaret was eager to take advantage of such indulgence to gratify certain tastes. Already she liked reading better than needle-work, dressing and 'inventing fashions' better than reading, and writing best of all. Sixteen paper books of no title, written in straggling letters, for the impetuosity of her thought always outdid the pace of her fingers,[5] testify to the use she made of her mother's liberality. The happiness of their home life had other results as well. They were a devoted family. Long after they were married, Margaret noted, these handsome brothers and sisters, with their well-proportioned bodies, their clear complexions, brown hair, sound teeth, 'tunable voices', and plain way of speaking, kept themselves 'in a flock together'. The presence of strangers silenced them. But when they were alone, whether they walked in Spring Gardens or Hyde Park, or had music, or supped in barges upon the water, their tongues were loosed and they made 'very merry amongst themselves . . . judging, condemning, approving, commending, as they thought good'.

The happy family life had its effect upon Margaret's character. As a child, she would walk for hours alone, musing and contemplating and reasoning with herself of 'everything her senses did present'. She took no pleasure in activity of any kind. Toys did not amuse her, and she could neither learn foreign languages nor dress as other people did. Her great pleasure was to invent dresses for herself, which nobody else was to copy, 'for', she remarks, 'I always took delight in a singularity, even in accoutrements of habits.'

Such a training, at once so cloistered and so free, should have bred a lettered old maid, glad of her seclusion, and the writer perhaps of some volume of letters or translations from the classics, which we should still quote as proof of the cultivation of our ancestresses. But there was a wild streak in Margaret, a love of finery and extravagance and fame, which was for ever upsetting the orderly arrangements of nature. When she heard that the Queen, since the outbreak of the Civil War,[6] had fewer maids-of-honour than usual, she had 'a great desire' to become one of them. Her mother let her go against the judgement of the rest of the family, who, knowing that she had never left home and had scarcely been beyond their sight, justly thought that she might behave at Court to her disadvantage. 'Which indeed I did,' Margaret confessed; 'for I was so bashful when I was out of my mother's, brothers', and sisters' sight that ... I durst neither look up with my eyes, nor speak, nor be any way sociable, insomuch as I was thought a natural fool.' The courtiers laughed at her; and she retaliated in the obvious way. People were censorious; men were jealous of brains in a woman; women suspected intellect in their own sex; and what other lady, she might justly ask, pondered as she walked on the nature of matter and whether snails have teeth? But the laughter galled her, and she begged her mother to let her come home. This being refused, wisely as the event turned out, she stayed on for two years (1643–5), finally going with the Queen to Paris, and there, among the exiles who came to pay their respects to the Court, was the Marquis of Newcastle. To the general amazement, the princely nobleman, who had led the King's forces to disaster with indomitable courage but little skill, fell in love with the shy, silent, strangely dressed maid-of-honour. It was not 'amorous love, but honest, honourable love', according to Margaret. She was no brilliant match; she had gained a reputation for prudery and eccentricity. What, then, could have made so great a nobleman fall at her feet? The onlookers were full of derision, disparagement, and slander. 'I fear,' Margaret wrote to the Marquis, 'others foresee we shall be unfortunate, though we see it not ourselves, or else there would not be such pains to untie the knot of our affections.' Again, 'Saint Germains is a place of much slander, and thinks I send too often to you.' 'Pray consider,' she warned him, 'that I have enemies.'[7] But the match was evidently perfect. The Duke, with his love of poetry and music and play-writing, his interest in philosophy, his belief 'that nobody knew or could know the cause of anything',[8] his romantic and generous temperament, was naturally drawn to a woman who wrote poetry herself, was also a philosopher of the same way of thinking, and lavished upon him not only the admiration of a fellow artist, but the gratitude of a sensitive creature who had been shielded and succoured by his extraordinary magnanimity. 'He did approve,'[9] she wrote, 'of those bashful fears which many condemned ... and though I did dread marriage and shunned men's company as much as I could, yet I ... had not the power to refuse him.' She kept him company during the long years of exile; she entered with sympathy, if not with understanding, into the conduct and acquirements of those horses which he trained to such perfection that the Spaniards crossed themselves and cried 'Miraculo!' as they witnessed their corvets, voltoes,[10] and pirouettes; she believed that the horses even made a 'trampling action' for joy when he came into the stables; she pleaded his cause in England during the Protectorate;[11] and, when the Restoration[12] made it possible for them to return to England, they lived together in the depths of the country in the greatest seclusion and perfect contentment, scribbling plays, poems, philosophies, greeting each other's works with raptures of delight, and confabulating, doubtless, upon such marvels of the natural world as chance threw their way. They were laughed at by their contemporaries; Horace Walpole sneered at them.[13] But there can be no doubt that they were perfectly happy.

For now Margaret could apply herself uninterruptedly to her writing. She could devise fashions for herself and her servants. She could scribble more and more furiously with fingers that became less and less able to form legible letters. She could even achieve the miracle of getting her plays acted in London and her philosophies humbly perused by men of learning. There they stand, in the British Museum, volume after volume, swarming with a diffused, uneasy, contorted vitality. Order, continuity, the logical development of her argument are all unknown to her. No fears impede her. She has the irresponsibility of a child and the arrogance of a Duchess. The wildest fancies come to her, and she canters away on their backs. We seem to hear her, as the thoughts boil and bubble, calling to John, who sat with a pen in his hand next door, to come quick, 'John, John, I conceive!' And down it goes – whatever it may be; sense or nonsense; some thought on women's education – 'Women live like Bats or Owls, labour like Beasts, and die like Worms . . .[14] the best bred women are those whose minds are civilest';[15] some speculation that had struck her, perhaps, walking that afternoon alone – why 'hogs have the measles',[16] why 'dogs that rejoice swing their tails', or what the stars are made of, or what this chrysalis is that her maid has brought her, and she keeps warm in a corner of her room. On and on, from subject to subject she flies, never stopping to correct, 'for there is more pleasure in making than in mending',[17] talking aloud to herself of all those matters that filled her brain to her perpetual diversion – of wars, and boarding-schools, and cutting down trees, of grammar and morals, of monsters and the British, whether opium in small quantities is good for lunatics, why it is that musicians are mad. Looking upwards, she speculates still more ambitiously upon the nature of the moon, and if the stars are blazing jellies; looking downwards she wonders if the fishes know that the sea is salt; opines that our heads are full of fairies, 'dear to God as we are';[18] muses whether there are not other worlds than ours, and reflects that the next ship may bring us word of a new one. In short, 'we are in utter darkness'.[19] Meanwhile, what a rapture is thought!

As the vast books appeared from the stately retreat at Welbeck the usual censors made the usual objections, and had to be answered, despised, or argued with, as her mood varied, in the preface to every work. They said, among other things, that her books were not her own, because she used learned terms, and 'wrote of many matters outside her ken'. She flew to her husband for help, and he answered, characteristically, that the Duchess 'had never conversed with any professed scholar in learning except her brother and myself'. The Duke's scholarship, moreover, was of a peculiar nature. 'I have lived in the great world a great while, and have thought of what has been brought to me by the senses, more than was put into me by learned discourse; for I do not love to be led by the nose, by authority, and old authors; *ipse dixit* will not serve my turn.'[20] And then she takes up the pen and proceeds, with the importunity and indiscretion of a child, to assure the world that her ignorance is of the finest quality imaginable. She has only seen Des Cartes and Hobbes, not questioned them; she did indeed ask Mr Hobbes to dinner, but he could not come; she often does not listen to a word that is said to her; she does not know any French, though she lived abroad for five years; she has only read the old philosophers in Mr Stanley's account[21] of them; of Des Cartes she has read but half of his work on Passion;[22] and of Hobbes only 'the little book called *De Cive*',[23] all of which is infinitely to the credit of her native wit, so abundant that outside succour pained it, so honest that it would not accept help from others. It was from the plain of complete ignorance, the untilled field of her own consciousness, that she proposed to erect a philosophic system that was to oust all others. The results were not altogether happy. Under the pressure of such vast structures, her natural gift, the fresh and delicate fancy which had led her in her first volume to write charmingly of Queen Mab and fairyland, was crushed out of existence.

> The palace of the Queen wherein she dwells,
> Its fabric's built all of hodmandod shells;
> The hangings of a Rainbow made that's thin,
> Shew wondrous fine, when one first enters in;
> The chambers made of Amber that is clear,
> Do give a fine sweet smell, if fire be near;
> Her bed a cherry stone, is carved throughout,
> And with a butterfly's wing hung about;
> Her sheets are of the skin of Dove's eyes made
> Where on a violet bud her pillow's laid.[24]

So she could write when she was young. But her fairies, if they survived at all, grew up into hippopotami. Too generously her prayer was granted:

> Give me the free and noble style,
> Which seems uncurb'd, though it be wild.

She became capable of involutions, and contortions and conceits of which the following is among the shortest, but not the most terrific:

> The human head may be likened to a town:
> The mouth when full, begun
> Is market day, when empty, market's done;
> The city conduct, where the water flows,
> Is with two spouts, the nostrils and the nose.

She similized, energetically, incongruously, eternally; the sea became a meadow, the sailors shepherds, the mast a maypole. The fly was the bird of summer, trees were senators, houses ships, and even the fairies, whom she loved better than any earthly thing, except the Duke, are changed into blunt atoms and sharp atoms, and take part in some of those horrible manoeuvres in which she delighted to marshal the universe. Truly, 'my Lady Sanspareille hath a strange spreading wit'.[25] Worse still, without an atom of dramatic power, she turned to play-writing. It was a simple process. The unwieldly thoughts which turned and tumbled within her were christened Sir Golden Riches, Moll Meanbred, Sir Puppy Dogman, and the rest,[26] and sent revolving in tedious debate upon the parts of the soul, or whether virtue is better than riches, round a wise and learned lady who answered their questions and corrected their fallacies at considerable length in tones which we seem to have heard before.

Sometimes, however, the Duchess walked abroad. She would issue out in her own proper person, dressed in a thousand gems and furbelows, to visit the houses of the neighbouring gentry. Her pen made instant report of these excursions. She recorded how Lady C.R. 'did beat her husband in a public assembly'; Sir F.O. 'I am sorry to hear hath undervalued himself so much below his birth and wealth as to marry his kitchen-maid'; 'Miss P.I. has become a sanctified soul, a spiritual sister, she has left curling her hair, black patches are become abominable to her, laced shoes and Galoshoes are steps to pride – she asked me what posture I thought was the best to be used in prayer.' Her answer was probably unacceptable. 'I shall not rashly go there again,' she says of one such 'gossip-making'. She was not, we may hazard, a welcome guest or an altogether hospitable hostess. She had a way of 'bragging of myself'[27] which frightened visitors so that they left, nor was she sorry to see them go. Indeed, Welbeck was the best place for her, and her own company the most congenial, with the amiable Duke wandering in and out, with his plays and his speculations, always ready to answer a question or refute a slander. Perhaps it was this solitude that led her, chaste as she was in conduct, to use language which in time to come much perturbed Sir Egerton Brydges. She used, he complained,[28] 'expressions and images of extraordinary coarseness as flowing from a female of high rank brought up in courts'. He forgot that this particular female had long ceased to frequent the Court; she consorted chiefly with fairies; and her friends were among the dead. Naturally, then, her language was coarse. Nevertheless, though her philosophies are futile, and her plays intolerable, and her verses mainly dull, the vast bulk of the Duchess is leavened by a vein of authentic fire. One cannot help following the lure of her erratic and lovable personality as it meanders and twinkles through page after page. There is something noble and Quixotic and high-spirited, as well as crack-brained and bird-witted, about her. Her simplicity is so open; her intelligence so active; her sympathy with fairies and animals so true and tender. She has the freakishness of an elf, the irresponsibility of some non-human creature, its heartlessness, and its charm. And although 'they', those terrible critics who had sneered and jeered at her ever since, as a shy girl, she had not dared look her tormentors in the face at Court, continued to mock, few of her critics, after all, had the wit to trouble about the nature of the universe, or cared a straw for the sufferings of the hunted hare, or longed, as she did, to talk to some one 'of Shakespeare's fools'.[29] Now, at any rate, the laugh is not all on their side.

But laugh they did. When the rumour spread that the crazy Duchess was coming up from Welbeck to pay her respects at Court, people crowded the streets to look at her, and the curiosity of Mr Pepys twice brought him to wait in the Park to see her pass. But the pressure of the crowd about her coach was too great. He could only catch a glimpse of her in her silver coach with her footmen all in velvet, a velvet cap on her head, and her hair about her ears. He could only see for a moment between the white curtains the face of 'a very comely woman',[30] and on she drove through the crowd of staring Cockneys, all pressing to catch a glimpse of that romantic lady, who stands, in the picture at Welbeck, with large melancholy eyes, and something fastidious and fantastic in her bearing, touching a table with the tips of long pointed fingers, in the calm assurance of immortal fame.

Two Women

This is a review of the *Letters of Lady Augusta Stanley* (ed. the Dean of Windsor and Hector Bolitho, Gerald Howe, 1927) and Lady Barbara Stephen's *Emily Davies and Girton College* (Constable, 1927), first published in the *Nation and Athenaeum*, 23 April 1927.

Up to the beginning of the nineteenth century the distinguished woman had almost invariably been an aristocrat. It was the great lady who ruled and wrote letters and influenced the course of politics. From the huge middle class few women rose to eminence, nor has the drabness of their lot received the attention which has been bestowed upon the splendours of the great and the miseries of the poor. There they remain, even in the early part of the nineteenth century, a vast body, living, marrying, bearing children in dull obscurity until at last we begin to wonder whether there was something in their condition itself – in the age at which they married, the number of children they bore, the privacy they lacked, the incomes they had not, the conventions which stifled them, and the education they never received which so affected them that though the middle class is the great reservoir from which we draw our distinguished men it has thrown up singularly few women to set beside them.

The profound interest of Lady Stephen's life of Miss Emily Davies lies in the light it throws upon this dark and obscure chapter of human history. Miss Davies was born in the year 1830, of middle-class parents who could afford to educate their sons but not their daughters. Her education was, she supposed, much the same as that of other clergymen's daughters at that time. 'Do they go to school? No. Do they have governesses at home? No. They have lessons and get on as they can.' But if their positive education had stopped at a little Latin, a little history, a little housework, it would not so much have mattered. It was what may be called the negative education, that which decrees not what you may do but what you may not do, that cramped and stifled. 'Probably only women who have laboured under it can understand the weight of discouragement produced by being perpetually told that, as women, nothing much is ever expected of them ... Women who have lived in the atmosphere produced by such teaching know how it stifles and chills; how hard it is to work courageously through it.' Preachers and rulers of both sexes nevertheless formulated the creed and enforced it vigorously. Charlotte Yonge wrote: 'I have no hesitation in declaring my full belief in the inferiority of women, nor that she brought it upon herself.'[1] She reminded her sex of a painful incident with a snake in a garden which had settled their destiny, Miss Yonge said, for ever. The mention of Woman's Rights made Queen Victoria so furious[2] that 'she cannot contain herself'. Mr Greg, underlining his words, wrote that 'the essentials of a woman's being are *that they are supported by, and they minister to men.*'[3] The only other occupation allowed them, indeed, was to become a governess or a needlewoman, 'and both these employments were naturally overstocked'. If women wanted to paint there was, up to the year 1858, only one life class in London where they could learn. If they were musical there was the inevitable piano, but the chief aim was to produce a brilliant mechanical execution, and Trollope's picture of four girls[4] all in the same room playing on four pianos all of them out of tune seems to have been, as Trollope's pictures usually are, based on fact. Writing was the most accessible of the arts, and write they did, but their books were deeply influenced by the angle from which they were forced to observe the world. Half occupied, always interrupted, with much leisure but little time to themselves and no money of their own, these armies of listless women were either driven to find solace and occupation in religion, or, if that failed, they took, as Miss Nightingale said, 'to that perpetual day dreaming which is so dangerous'.[5] Some indeed envied the working classes, and Miss Martineau frankly hailed[6] the ruin of her family with delight. 'I, who had been obliged to write before breakfast, or in some private way, had henceforth liberty to do my own work in my own way, for we had lost our gentility.' But the time had come when there were occasional exceptions both among parents and among daughters. Mr Leigh Smith, for example, allowed his daughter Barbara the same income that he gave his sons. She at once started a school of an advanced character. Miss Garrett became a doctor because her parents, though shocked and anxious, would be reconciled if she were a success. Miss Davies had a brother who sympathized and helped her in her determination to reform the education of women. With such encouragement the three young women started in the middle of the nineteenth century to lead the army of the unemployed in search of work. But the war of one sex upon the rights and possessions of the other is by no means a straightforward affair of attack and victory or defeat. Neither the means nor the end itself is clear-cut and recognized. There is the very potent weapon, for example, of feminine charm – what use were they to make of that? Miss Garrett said[7] she felt 'so mean in trying to come over the doctors by all kinds of little feminine dodges'. Mrs Gurney[8] admitted the difficulty, but pointed out that 'Miss Marsh's success among the navvies'[9] had been mainly won by these means, which, for good or for bad, were certainly of immense weight. It was agreed therefore that charm was to be employed. Thus we have the curious spectacle, at once so diverting and so humiliating, of grave and busy women doing fancy work and playing croquet in order that the male eye might be gratified and deceived. 'Three lovely girls' were placed conspicuously in the front row at a meeting, and Miss Garrett herself sat there looking 'exactly like one of the girls whose instinct it is to do what you tell them'. For the arguments that they had to meet by these devious means were in themselves extremely indefinite. There was a thing called 'the tender home-bloom of maidenliness' which must not be touched. There was chastity, of course, and her handmaidens innocence, sweetness, unselfishness, sympathy; all of which might suffer if women were allowed to learn Latin and Greek. The *Saturday Review*[10] gave cogent expression to what men feared for women and needed of women in the year 1864. The idea of submitting young ladies to local university examinations 'almost takes one's breath away', the writer said. If examined they must be, steps must be taken to see that 'learned men advanced in years' were the examiners, and that the presumably aged wives of these aged gentlemen should occupy 'a commanding position in the gallery'. Even so it would be 'next to impossible to persuade the world that a pretty first-class woman came by her honours fairly'. For the truth was, the reviewer wrote, that 'there is a strong and ineradicable male instinct that a learned, or even an accomplished young woman is the most intolerable monster in creation'. It was against instincts and prejudices

A WOMAN'S ESSAYS

such as these, tough as roots but intangible as sea mist, that Miss Davies had to fight. Her days passed in a round of the most diverse occupations. Besides the actual labour of raising money and fighting prejudice she had to decide the most delicate moral questions which, directly victory was within sight, began to be posed by the students and their parents. A mother, for example, would only entrust her with her daughter's education on condition that she should come home 'as if nothing had happened', and not 'take to anything eccentric'. The students, on the other hand, bored with watching the Edinburgh express slip a carriage at Hitchin or rolling the lawn with a heavy iron roller, took to playing football, and then invited their teachers to see them act scenes from Shakespeare and Swinburne dressed in men's clothes. This, indeed, was a very serious matter; the great George Eliot was consulted; Mr Russell Gurney was consulted, and also Mr Tomkinson. They decided that it was unwomanly; Hamlet must be played in a skirt.

Miss Davies herself was decidedly austere. When money for the college flowed in she refused to spend it on luxuries. She wanted rooms – always more and more rooms to house those unhappy girls dreaming their youth away in indolence or picking up a little knowledge in the family sitting-room. 'Privacy was the one luxury Miss Davies desired for the student, and in her eyes it was not a luxury – she despised luxuries – but a necessity.' But one room to themselves was enough. She did not believe that they needed armchairs to sit in or pictures to look at. She herself lived austerely in lodgings till she was seventy-two, combative, argumentative, frankly preferring a labour meeting at Venice to the pictures and the palaces, consumed with an abstract passion for justice to women which burnt up trivial personalities and made her a little intolerant of social frivolities. Was it worth while, she once asked, in her admirable, caustic manner, after meeting Lady Augusta Stanley, to go among the aristocracy? 'I felt directly that if I went to Lady Stanley's again, I must get a new bonnet. And is it well to spend one's money in bonnets and flys instead of on instructive books?' she wondered. For Miss Davies perhaps was a little deficient in feminine charm.

That was a charge that nobody could bring against Lady Augusta Stanley. No two women could on the surface have less in common. Lady Augusta, it is true, was no more highly educated in a bookish sense than the middle-class women whom Miss Davies championed. But she was the finest flower of the education which for some centuries the little class of aristocratic women had enjoyed. She had been trained in her mother's drawing-room in Paris. She had talked to all the distinguished men and women of her time – Lamartine, Mérimée, Victor Hugo, the Duc de Broglie, Sainte-Beuve, Renan, Jenny Lind, Turgenev[11] – everybody came to talk to old Lady Elgin and to be entertained by her daughters. There she developed that abounding sensibility, that unquenchable sympathy which were to be so lavishly drawn upon in after years. For she was very young when she entered the Duchess of Kent's household. For fifteen years of her youth she lived there. For fifteen years she was the life and soul of that 'quiet affectionate dull household of old people at Frogmore and Clarence House'. Nothing whatever happened. They drove out and she thought how charming the village children looked. They walked and the Duchess picked heather. They came home and the Duchess was tired. Yet not for a moment, pouring her heart out in profuse letters to her sisters, does she complain or wish for any other existence.

Seen through her peculiar magnifying glass, the slightest event in the life of the Royal family was either harrowing in the extreme or beyond words delightful. Prince Arthur was more handsome than ever. The Princess Helena was so lovely. Princess Ada fell from her pony. Prince Leo was naughty. The Beloved Duchess wanted a green umbrella. The measles had come out, but, alas, they threatened to go in again. One might suppose, to listen to Lady Augusta exclaiming and protesting in alternate rapture and despair, that to read aloud to the old Duchess of Kent was the most exciting of occupations, and that the old ladies' rheumatisms and headaches were catastrophes of the first order. For inevitably the power of sympathy when so highly developed and discharged solely upon personal relations tends to produce a hothouse atmosphere in which domestic details assume prodigious proportions and the mind feeds upon every detail of death and disease with a gluttonous relish. The space devoted in this volume to illness and marriage entirely out-weighs any reference to art, literature or politics. It is all personal, emotional, and detailed as one of the novels which were written so inevitably by women.

It was such a life as this and such an atmosphere as this that Mr Greg and the *Saturday Review* and many men who had themselves enjoyed the utmost rigours of education wished to see preserved. And perhaps there was some excuse for them. It is difficult to be sure, after all, that a college don is the highest type of humanity known to us; and there is something in Lady Augusta's power to magnify the common and illumine the dull which seems to imply a very arduous education of some sort behind it. Nevertheless, as one studies the lives of the two women side by side, one cannot doubt that Miss Davies got more interest, more pleasure, and more use out of one month of her life than Lady Augusta out of a whole year of hers. Some inkling of the fact seems to have reached Lady Augusta even at Windsor Castle. Perhaps being a woman of the old type is a little exhausting; perhaps it is not altogether satisfying. Lady Augusta at any rate seems to have got wind of other possibilities. She liked the society of literary people best, she said. 'I had always said that I had wished to be a fellow of a college,' she added surprisingly. At any rate she was one of the first to support Miss Davies in her demand for a university education for women. Did Miss Davies then sacrifice her book and buy her bonnet? Did the two women, so different in every other way, come together over this – the education of their sex? It is tempting to think so, and to imagine sprung from that union of the middle-class woman and the court lady some astonishing phoenix of the future who shall combine the new efficiency with the old amenity, the courage of the indomitable Miss Davies and Lady Augusta's charm.

The Art of Fiction

A review of E. M. Forster's *Aspects of the Novel* (Edward Arnold,
1927), published in the *Nation and Athenaeum*, 12 November 1927. A
slightly different version had appeared the previous month in the
New York Herald Tribune.

That fiction is a lady and a lady who has somehow got herself into
trouble is a thought that must often have struck her admirers. Many
gallant gentlemen have ridden to her rescue, chief among them Sir
Walter Raleigh and Mr Percy Lubbock.[1] But both were a little
ceremonious in their approach; both, one felt, had a great deal of
knowledge of her, but not much intimacy with her. Now comes Mr
Forster, who disclaims knowledge but cannot deny that he knows
the lady well. If he lacks something of the others' authority, he
enjoys the privileges which are allowed the lover. He knocks at the
bedroom door and is admitted when the lady is in slippers and
dressing gown. Drawing up their chairs to the fire they talk easily,
wittily, subtly, like old friends who have no illusions, although in
fact the bedroom is a lecture-room, and the place the highly austere
city of Cambridge.

This informal attitude on Mr Forster's part is, of course, deliberate. He is not a scholar; he refuses to be a pseudo-scholar. There
remains a point of view which the lecturer can adopt usefully if
modestly. He can, as Mr Forster puts it, 'visualize the English
novelists, not as floating down that stream which bears all its sons
away unless they are careful, but as seated together in a room, a
circular room – a sort of British Museum reading-room – all writing
their novels simultaneously'. So simultaneous are they, indeed, that
they persist in writing out of their turn. Richardson insists that he is
contemporary with Henry James. Wells will write a passage which
might be written by Dickens. Being a novelist himself, Mr Forster
is not annoyed at this discovery. He knows from experience what a
muddled and illogical machine the brain of a writer is. He knows
how little they think about methods; how completely they forget

their grandfathers; how absorbed they tend to become in some vision of their own. Thus though the scholars have all his respect, his sympathies are with the untidy and harassed people who are scribbling away at their books. And looking down on them not from any great height, but, as he says, over their shoulders, he makes out, as he passes, that certain shapes and ideas tend to recur in their minds whatever their period. Since story-telling began, stories have always been made out of much the same elements; and these, which he calls The Story, People, Plot, Fantasy, Prophecy, Pattern, and Rhythm, he now proceeds to examine.

Many are the judgements that we would willingly argue, many are the points over which we would willingly linger, as Mr Forster passes lightly on his way. That Scott is a story-teller and nothing more; that a story is the lowest of literary organisms; that the novelist's unnatural preoccupation with love is largely a reflection of his own state of mind while he composes – every page has a hint or a suggestion which makes us stop to think or wish to contradict. Never raising his voice above the speaking level, Mr Forster has the art of saying things which sink airily enough into the mind to stay there and unfurl like those Japanese flowers which open up in the depths of the water. But greatly though these sayings intrigue us we want to call a halt at some definite stopping place; we want to make Mr Forster stand and deliver. For possibly, if fiction is, as we suggest, in difficulties, it may be because nobody grasps her firmly and defines her severely. She has had no rules drawn up for her, very little thinking done on her behalf. And though rules may be wrong, and must be broken, they have this advantage – they confer dignity and order upon their subject; they admit her to a place in civilized society; they prove that she is worthy of consideration. But this part of his duty, if it is his duty, Mr Forster expressly disowns. He is not going to theorize about fiction except incidentally; he doubts even whether she is to be approached by a critic, and if so, with what critical equipment. All we can do is to edge him into a position which is definite enough for us to see where he stands. And perhaps the best way to do this is to quote, much summarized, his estimates of three great figures – Meredith,[2] Hardy, and Henry James. Meredith is an exploded philosopher. His vision of nature is 'fluffy and lush'. When he gets serious and noble, he becomes a bully. 'And his novels; most of the social values are faked. The tailors are not tailors, the cricket matches are not cricket.' Hardy is a far greater writer. But he is not so successful as a novelist because his characters are 'required to contribute too much to the plot; except in their rustic humours, their vitality has been impoverished, they have gone thin and dry – he has emphasized causality more strongly than his medium permits.' Henry James pursued the narrow path of aesthetic duty and was successful. But at what a sacrifice? 'Most of human life has to disappear before he can do us a novel. Maimed creatures can alone breathe in his novels. His characters are few in number and constructed on stingy lines.'

Now if we look at these judgements and place beside them certain admissions and omissions, we shall see that, if we cannot pin Mr Forster to a creed, we can commit him to a point of view. There is something – we hesitate to be more precise – which he calls 'life'. It is to this that he brings the books of Meredith, Hardy, or James for comparison. Always their failure is some failure in relation to life. It is the humane as opposed to the aesthetic view of fiction. It maintains that the novel is 'sogged with humanity'; that 'human beings have their great chance in the novel'; a triumph won at the expense of life is, in fact, a defeat. Thus we arrive at the notably harsh judgement of Henry James. For Henry James brought into the novel something besides human beings. He created patterns which, though beautiful in themselves, are hostile to humanity. And for his neglect of life, says Mr Forster, he will perish.

But at this point the pertinacious pupil may demand, 'What is this "Life" that keeps on cropping up so mysteriously and so complacently in books about fiction? Why is it absent in a pattern and present in a tea party? Why is the pleasure that we get from the pattern in *The Golden Bowl*[3] less valuable than the emotion which Trollope gives us when he describes a lady drinking tea in a parsonage? Surely the definition of life is too arbitrary and requires to be expanded.' To all of this Mr Forster would reply, presumably, that he lays down no laws; the novel somehow seems to him too soft a substance to be carved like the other arts; he is merely telling us what moves him and what leaves him cold. Indeed, there is no other criterion. So then we are back in the old bog; nobody knows anything about the laws of fiction; or what its relation is to life; or to what effects it can lend itself. We can only trust our instincts. If instinct leads one reader to call Scott a story-teller, another to call him a master of romance; if one reader is moved by art, another by life, each is right, and each can pile a card-house of theory on top of his opinion as high as he can go. But the assumption that fiction is more intimately and humbly attached to the service of human beings than the other arts leads to a further position which Mr Forster's book again illustrates. It is unnecessary to dwell upon her aesthetic functions because they are so feeble that they can safely be ignored. Thus, though it is impossible to imagine a book on painting in which not a word should be said about the medium in which a painter works, a wise and brilliant book, like Mr Forster's, can be written about fiction without saying more than a sentence or two about the medium in which a novelist works. Almost nothing is said about words. One might suppose, unless one had read them, that a sentence means the same thing and is used for the same purposes by Sterne and by Wells. One might conclude that *Tristram Shandy*[4] gains nothing from the language in which it is written. So with the other aesthetic qualities. Pattern, as we have seen, is recognized, but severely censured for her tendency to obscure the human features.[5] Beauty occurs, but she is suspect. She makes one furtive appearance – 'beauty at which a novelist should never aim, though he fails if he does not achieve it' – and the possibility that she may emerge again as rhythm is briefly discussed in a few interesting pages at the end. But for the rest, fiction is treated as a parasite which draws its sustenance from life, and must, in gratitude, resemble life or perish. In poetry, in drama, words may excite and stimulate and deepen without this allegiance; but in fiction they must, first and foremost, hold themselves at the service of the teapot and the pug dog,[6] and to be found wanting is to be found lacking.

Strange though this unaesthetic attitude would be in the critic of any other art, it does not surprise us in the critic of fiction. For one thing, the problem is extremely difficult. A book fades like a mist, like a dream. How are we to take a stick and point to that tone, that relation, in the vanishing pages, as Mr Roger Fry[7] points with his wand at a line or a colour in the picture displayed before him? Moreover, a novel in particular has roused a thousand ordinary human feelings in its progress. To drag in art in such a connection seems priggish and cold-hearted. It may well compromise the critic as a man of feeling and domestic ties. And so, while the painter, the musician, and the poet come in for their share of criticism, the novelist goes unscathed. His character will be discussed; his morality, it may be his genealogy, will be examined; but his writing will go scot free. There is not a critic alive now who will say that a novel is a work of art and that as such he will judge it.

And perhaps, as Mr Forster insinuates, the critics are right. In England, at any rate, the novel is not a work of art. There are none to be stood beside *War and Peace*, *The Brothers Karamazov*, or *A la Recherche du Temps Perdu*.[8] But while we accept the fact, we cannot suppress one last conjecture. In France and Russia they take fiction seriously. Flaubert[9] spends a month seeking a phrase to describe a cabbage. Tolstoy writes *War and Peace* seven times over. Something of their pre-eminence may be due to the pains they take, something to the severity with which they are judged. If the English critic were less domestic, less assiduous to protect the rights of what it pleases him to call life, the novelist might be bolder too. He might cut adrift from the eternal tea-table and the plausible and preposterous formulas which are supposed to represent the whole of our human adventure. But then the story might wobble; the plot might crumble; ruin might seize upon the characters. The novel in short might become a work of art.[10]

Such are the dreams that Mr Forster leads us to cherish. For his is a book to encourage dreaming. None more suggestive has been written about the poor lady whom, with perhaps mistaken chivalry, we still persist in calling the art of fiction.

Dorothy Osborne's Letters

A review of *The Letters of Dorothy Osborne to William Temple*
(Clarendon Press, 1928), first published in the *New Republic*, 24
October 1928. The slightly modified version reprinted here was
published in *The Common Reader: Second Series* (Hogarth Press, 1932).

It must sometimes strike the casual reader of English literature that
there is a bare season in it, sometimes like early spring in our
country-side. The trees stand out; the hills are unmuffled in green;
there is nothing to obscure the mass of the earth or the lines of the
branches. But we miss the tremor and murmur of June, when the
smallest wood seems full of movement, and one has only to stand
still to hear the whispering and the pattering of nimble inquisitive
animals going about their affairs in the undergrowth. So in English
literature we have to wait till the sixteenth century is over and the
seventeenth well on its way before the bare landscape becomes full
of stir and quiver and we can fill in the spaces between the great
books with the voices of people talking.

Doubtless great changes in psychology were needed and great
changes in material comfort – armchairs and carpets and good roads
– before it was possible for human beings to watch each other
curiously or to communicate their thoughts easily. And it may be
that our early literature owes something of its magnificence to the
fact that writing was an uncommon art, practised, rather for fame
than for money, by those whose gifts compelled them. Perhaps the
dissipation of our genius in biography, and journalism, and letter-
and memoir-writing has weakened its strength in any one direction.
However this may be, there is a bareness about an age that has
neither letter-writers nor biographers. Lives and characters appear
in stark outline. Donne, says Sir Edmund Gosse,[1] is inscrutable;
and that is largely because, though we know what Donne thought
of Lady Bedford, we have not the slightest inkling what Lady
Bedford thought of Donne. She had no friend to whom she described the effect of that strange visitor; nor, had she had a confi-

dante, could she have explained for what reasons Donne seemed to her strange.

And the conditions that made it impossible for Boswell or Horace Walpole[2] to be born in the sixteenth century were obviously likely to fall with far heavier force upon the other sex. Besides the material difficulty – Donne's small house at Mitcham with its thin walls and crying children typifies the discomfort in which the Elizabethans lived – the woman was impeded also by her belief that writing was an act unbefitting her sex. A great lady here and there whose rank secured her the toleration and it may be the adulation of a servile circle, might write and print her writings. But the act was offensive to a woman of lower rank. 'Sure the poore woman is a little distracted, she could never bee soe ridiculous else as to venture writeing book's and in verse too', Dorothy Osborne exclaimed when the Duchess of Newcastle[3] published one of her books. For her own part, she added, 'If I could not sleep this fortnight I should not come to that.' And the comment is the more illuminating in that it was made by a woman of great literary gift. Had she been born in 1827, Dorothy Osborne would have written novels; had she been born in 1527, she would never have written at all. But she was born in 1627, and at that date though writing books was ridiculous for a woman there was nothing unseemly in writing a letter. And so by degrees the silence is broken; we begin to hear rustlings in the undergrowth; for the first time in English literature we hear men and women talking together over the fire.

But the art of letter-writing in its infancy was not the art that has since filled so many delightful volumes. Men and women were ceremoniously Sir and Madam; the language was still too rich and stiff to turn and twist quickly and freely upon half a sheet of notepaper. The art of letter-writing is often the art of essay-writing in disguise. But such as it was, it was an art that a woman could practise without unsexing herself.[4] It was an art that could be carried on at odd moments, by a father's sick-bed, among a thousand interruptions, without exciting comment, anonymously as it were, and often with the pretence that it served some useful purpose. Yet into these innumerable letters, lost now for the most part, went powers of observation and of wit that were later to take rather a different shape in *Evelina*[5] and in *Pride and Prejudice*.[6] They were only letters, yet some pride went to their making. Dorothy, without admitting it, took pains with her own writing and had views as to the nature of it: '. . . great Schollers are not the best writer's (of Letters I mean, of books perhaps they are) . . . all letters mee thinks should be free and easy as one's discourse'. She was in agreement with an old uncle of hers who threw his standish[7] at his secretary's head for saying 'put pen to paper' instead of simply 'wrote'. Yet there were limits, she reflected, to free-and-easiness: '. . . many pritty things shuffled together' do better spoken than in a letter. And so we come by a form of literature, if Dorothy Osborne will let us call it so, which is distinct from any other, and much to be regretted now that it has gone from us, as it seems for ever.

For Dorothy Osborne, as she filled her great sheets by her father's bed or by the chimney-corner, gave a record of life, gravely yet playfully, formally yet with intimacy, to a public of one, but to a fastidious public, as the novelist can never give it, or the historian either. Since it is her business to keep her lover informed of what passes in her home, she must sketch the solemn Sir Justinian Isham – Sir Solomon Justinian, she calls him – the pompous widower with four daughters and a great gloomy house in Northamptonshire who wished to marry her. 'Lord what would I give that I had a Lattin letter of his for you', she exclaimed, in which he describes her to an Oxford friend and specially commended her that she was 'capable of being company and conversation for him'; she must sketch her valetudinarian Cousin Molle waking one morning in fear of the dropsy and hurrying to the doctor at Cambridge; she must draw her own picture wandering in the garden at night and smelling the 'Jessomin', 'and yet I was not pleased' because Temple[8] was not with her. Any gossip that comes her way is sent on to amuse her lover. Lady Sunderland, for instance, has condescended to marry plain Mr Smith, who treats her like a princess, which Sir Justinian thinks a bad precedent for wives. But Lady Sunderland tells everyone she married him out of pity, and that, Dorothy comments, 'was the pittyfull'st sayeing that ever I heard'. Soon we have picked up enough about all her friends to snatch eagerly at any further addition to the picture which is forming in our mind's eye.

Indeed, our glimpse of the society of Bedfordshire in the seventeenth century is the more intriguing for its intermittency. In they

come and out they go – Sir Justinian and Lady Diana, Mr Smith
and his countess – and we never know when or whether we shall
hear of them again. But with all this haphazardry, the *Letters*, like
the letters of all born letter-writers, provide their own continuity.
They make us feel that we have our seat in the depths of Dorothy's
mind, at the heart of the pageant which unfolds itself page by page
as we read. For she possesses indisputably the gift which counts for
more in letter-writing than wit or brilliance or traffic with great
people. By being herself without effort or emphasis, she envelops
all these odds and ends in the flow of her own personality. It was a
character that was both attractive and a little obscure. Phrase by
phrase we come closer into touch with it. Of the womanly virtues
that befitted her age she shows little trace. She says nothing of
sewing or baking. She was a little indolent by temperament. She
browsed casually on vast French romances. She roams the commons,
loitering to hear the milkmaids sing; she walks in the garden by the
side of a small river, 'where I sitt downe and wish you were with
mee'. She was apt to fall silent in company and dream over the fire
till some talk of flying, perhaps, roused her, and she made her
brother laugh by asking what they were saying about flying, for the
thought had struck her, if she could fly she could be with Temple.
Gravity, melancholy were in her blood. She looked, her mother
used to say, as if all her friends were dead. She is oppressed by a
sense of fortune and its tyranny and the vanity of things and the
uselessness of effort. Her mother and sister were grave women too,
the sister famed for her letters, but fonder of books than of company,
the mother 'counted as wise a woman as most in England', but
sardonic. 'I have lived to see that 'tis almost impossible to think
People worse than they are and soe will you' – Dorothy could
remember her mother saying that. To assuage her spleen, Dorothy
herself had to visit the wells at Epsom[9] and to drink water that steel
had stood in.

With such a temperament her humour naturally took the form of
irony rather than of wit. She loved to mock her lover and to pour a
fine raillery over the pomps and ceremonies of existence. Pride of
birth she laughed at. Pompous old men were fine subjects for her
satire. A dull sermon moved her to laughter. She saw through
parties; she saw through ceremonies; she saw through worldliness

and display. But with all this clear-sightedness there was something that she did not see through. She dreaded with a shrinking that was scarcely sane the ridicule of the world. The meddling of aunts and the tyranny of brothers exasperated her. 'I would live in a hollow Tree,' she said, 'to avoyde them.' A husband kissing his wife in public seemed to her as 'ill a sight as one would wish to see'. Though she cared no more whether people praised her beauty or her wit than whether 'they think my name Eliz: or Dor:', a word of gossip about her own behaviour would set her in a quiver. Thus when it came to proving before the eyes of the world that she loved a poor man and was prepared to marry him, she could not do it. 'I confess that I have an humor that will not suffer mee to Expose myself to People's Scorne,' she wrote. She could be 'sattisfyed within as narrow a compasse as that of any person liveing of my rank', but ridicule was intolerable to her. She shrank from any extravagance that could draw the censure of the world upon her. It was a weakness for which Temple had sometimes to reprove her.

For Temple's character emerges more and more clearly as the letters go on – it is a proof of Dorothy's gift as a correspondent. A good letter-writer so takes the colour of the reader at the other end, that from reading the one we can imagine the other. As she argues, as she reasons, we hear Temple almost as clearly as we hear Dorothy herself. He was in many ways the opposite of her. He drew out her melancholy by rebutting it; he made her defend his dislike of marriage by opposing it. Of the two Temple was by far the more robust and positive. Yet there was perhaps something – a little hardness, a little conceit – that justified her brother's dislike of him. He called Temple the 'proudest imperious insulting ill-natured man that ever was'. But, in the eyes of Dorothy, Temple had qualities that none of her other suitors possessed. He was not a mere country gentleman, nor a pompous Justice of the Peace, nor a town gallant, making love to every woman he met, nor a travelled Monsieur; for had he been any one of these things, Dorothy, with her quick sense of the ridiculous, would have had none of him. To her he had some charm, some sympathy, that the others lacked; she could write to him whatever came into her head; she was at her best with him; she loved him; she respected him. Yet suddenly she declared that marry him she would not. She turned violently against marriage indeed, and cited failure after failure. If people knew each other before marriage, she thought, there would be an end of it. Passion was the most brutish and tyrannical of all our senses. Passion had made Lady Anne Blount the 'talk of all the footmen and Boy's in the street'. Passion had been the undoing of the lovely Lady Izabella – what use was her beauty now married to 'that beast with all his estate'? Torn asunder by her brother's anger, by Temple's jealousy, and by her own dread of ridicule, she wished for nothing but to be left to find 'an early and a quiet grave'. That Temple overcame her scruples and overrode her brother's opposition is much to the credit of his character. Yet it is an act that we can hardly help deploring. Married to Temple, she wrote to him no longer. The letters almost immediately cease. The whole world that Dorothy had brought into existence is extinguished. It is then that we realize how round and populous and stirring that world has become. Under the warmth of her affection for Temple the stiffness had gone out of her pen. Writing half asleep by her father's side, snatching the back of an old letter to write upon, she had come to write easily though always with the dignity proper to that age, of the Lady Dianas, and the Ishams, of the aunts and the uncles – how they come, how they go; what they say; whether she finds them dull, laughable, charming, or much as usual. More than that, she has suggested, writing her mind out to Temple, the deeper relationships, the more private moods, that gave her life its conflict and its consolation – her brother's tyranny; her own moodiness and melancholy; the sweetness of walking in the garden at night; of sitting lost in thought by the river; of longing for a letter and finding one. All this is around us; we are deep in this world, seizing its hints and suggestions when, in the moment, the scene is blotted out. She married, and her husband was a rising diplomat. She had to follow his fortunes in Brussels, at The Hague,[10] wherever they called him. Seven children were born and seven children died 'almost all in their cradle'. Innumerable duties and responsibilities fell to the lot of the girl who had made fun of pomp and ceremony, who loved privacy and had wished to live secluded out of the world and 'grow old together in our little cottage'. Now she was mistress of her husband's house at The Hague with its splendid buffet of plate. She was his confidante in the many troubles of his difficult career. She stayed behind in

London to negotiate if possible the payment of his arrears of salary. When her yacht was fired on, she behaved, the King said, with greater courage than the captain himself. She was everything that the wife of an ambassador should be: she was everything, too, that the wife of a man retired from the public service should be. And troubles came upon them – a daughter died; a son, inheriting perhaps his mother's melancholy, filled his boots with stones and leapt into the Thames. So the years passed; very full, very active, very troubled. But Dorothy maintained her silence.

At last, however, a strange young man came to Moor Park as secretary to her husband. He was difficult, ill-mannered, and quick to take offence. But it is through Swift's eyes that we see Dorothy once more in the last years of her life. 'Mild Dorothea, peaceful, wise, and great', Swift called her;[11] but the light falls upon a ghost. We do not know that silent lady. We cannot connect her after all these years with the girl who poured her heart out to her lover. 'Peaceful, wise, and great' – she was none of those things when we last met her, and much though we honour the admirable ambassadress who made her husband's career her own, there are moments when we would exchange all the benefits of the Triple Alliance[12] and all the glories of the Treaty of Nimuegen[13] for the letters that Dorothy did not write.

Memories of a Working Women's Guild

This was written as an introduction to a volume entitled *Life As We Have Known It* by Co-Operative Working Women (ed. Margaret Llewellyn Davies, Hogarth Press, 1931). It was first published, however, in the *Yale Review*, September 1930, with some differences that also appear in subsequent reprints by Leonard Woolf, some of which are recorded in the notes for their interest.

When you asked me to write a preface to a book which you had collected of papers by working women I replied that I would be drowned rather than write a preface to any book whatsoever. Books should stand on their own feet, my argument was (and I think it is a sound one). If they need shoring up by a preface here, an introduction there, they have no more right to exist than a table that needs a wad of paper under one leg in order to stand steady. But you left me the papers, and, turning them over, I saw that on this occasion the argument did not apply; this book is not a book. Turning the pages, I began to ask myself what is that book then, if it is not a book? What quality has it? What ideas does it suggest? What old arguments and memories does it rouse in me? And as all this had nothing to do with an introduction or a preface, but brought you to mind and certain pictures from the past, I stretched my hand for a sheet of notepaper and wrote the following letter addressed not to the public but to you.

You have forgotten (I wrote) a hot June morning in Newcastle[1] in the year 1913, or at least you will not remember what I remember, because you were otherwise engaged. Your attention was entirely absorbed by a green table, several sheets of paper, and a bell. Moreover you were frequently interrupted. There was a woman wearing something like a Lord Mayor's chain round her shoulders; she took her seat perhaps at your right; there were other women without ornament save fountain pens and despatch boxes – they sat perhaps at your left. Soon a row had been formed up there on the platform, with tables and inkstands and tumblers of water; while we, many hundreds of us, scraped and shuffled and filled the entire body of some vast municipal building beneath. The proceedings somehow opened. Perhaps an organ played. Perhaps songs were sung. Then the talking and the laughing suddenly subsided. A bell struck; a figure rose; a woman took her way from among us; she mounted a platform; she spoke for precisely five minutes; she descended. Directly she sat down another woman rose; mounted the platform; spoke for precisely five minutes and descended; then a third rose, then a fourth – and so it went on, speaker following speaker, one from the right, one from the left, one from the middle, one from the background – each took her way to the stand, said what she had to say, and gave place to her successor. There was something military in the regularity of the proceeding. They were like marksmen, I thought, standing up in turn with rifle raised to aim at a target. Sometimes they missed, and there was a roar of laughter; sometimes they hit, and there was a roar of applause. But whether the particular shot hit or missed there was no doubt about the carefulness of the aim. There was no beating the bush;[2] there were no phrases of easy eloquence. The speaker made her way to the stand primed with her subject. Determination and resolution were stamped on her face. There was so much to be said between the strokes of the bell that she could not waste one second. The moment had come for which she had been waiting, perhaps for many months. The moment had come for which she had stored hat, shoes and dress – there was an air of discreet novelty about her clothing. But above all the moment had come when she was going to speak her mind, the mind of her constituency, the mind of the women who had sent her from Devonshire, perhaps, or Sussex, or some black mining village in Yorkshire to speak their mind for them in Newcastle.

It soon became obvious that the mind which lay spread over so wide a stretch of England was a vigorous mind working with great activity. It was thinking in June 1913 of the reform of the Divorce Laws; of the taxation of land values; of the Minimum Wage. It was concerned with the care of maternity; with the Trades Board Act; with the education of children over fourteen; it was unanimously of opinion that Adult Suffrage should become a Government measure – it was thinking in short about every sort of public question, and it was thinking constructively and pugnaciously. Accrington did not see eye to eye with Halifax, nor Middlesbrough with Plymouth. There was argument and opposition; resolutions were lost and amendments won. Hands shot up stiff as swords, or were pressed as stiffly to the side. Speaker followed speaker; the morning was cut up into precise lengths of five minutes by the bell.

Meanwhile – let me try after seventeen years to sum up the thoughts that passed through the minds of your guests, who had come from London and elsewhere, not to take part, but to listen – meanwhile what was it all about? What was the meaning of it? These women were demanding divorce, education, the vote – all good things. They were demanding higher wages and shorter hours – what could be more reasonable? And yet, though it was all so reasonable, much of it so forcible, some of it so humorous, a weight of discomfort was settling and shifting itself uneasily from side to side in your visitors' minds. All these questions – perhaps this was at the bottom of it – which matter so intensely to the people here, questions of sanitation and education and wages, this demand for an extra shilling, for another year at school, for eight hours instead of nine behind a counter or in a mill, leave me, in my own blood and bones, untouched. If every reform they demand was granted this very instant it would not touch one hair of my comfortable capitalistic head.[3] Hence my interest is merely altruistic. It is thin spread and moon coloured. There is no lifeblood or urgency about it. However hard I clap my hands or stamp my feet there is a hollowness in the sound which betrays me. I am a benevolent spectator. I am irretrievably cut off from the actors. I sit here hypocritically clapping and stamping, an outcast from the flock. On top of this too, my reason (it was in 1913, remember) could not help assuring me that even if the resolution, whatever it was, were carried unanimously the stamping and the clapping was an empty noise. It would pass out of the open window and become part of the clamour of the lorries and the striving of the hooves on the cobbles of Newcastle beneath – an inarticulate uproar. The mind might be active; the mind might be aggressive; but the mind was without a body; it had no legs or arms with which to enforce its will. In all that audience, among all those women who worked, who bore children, who scrubbed and cooked and bargained, there was not a single woman with a vote. Let them fire off their rifles if they liked, but they would hit no target; there were only blank cartridges inside. The thought was irritating and depressing in the extreme.

The clock had now struck half-past eleven. Thus there were still then many hours to come. And if one had reached this stage of irritation and depression by half-past eleven in the morning, into what depths of boredom and despair would one not be plunged by half-past five in the evening? How could one sit out another day of speechifying? How could one, above all, face you, our hostess, with the information that your Congress had proved so insupportably exacerbating that one was going back to London by the very first train? The only chance lay in some happy conjuring trick, some change of attitude by which the mist and blankness of the speeches could be turned to blood and bone. Otherwise they remained intolerable. But suppose one played a childish game; suppose one said, as a child says, 'Let's pretend.' 'Let's pretend,' one said to oneself, looking at the speaker, 'that I am Mrs Giles of Durham City.' A woman of that name had just turned to address us. 'I am the wife of a miner. He comes back thick with grime. First he must have his bath. Then he must have his supper. But there is only a copper. My range is crowded with saucepans. There is no getting on with the work. All my crocks are covered with dust again. Why in the Lord's name have I not hot water and electric light laid on when middle-class women . . .' So up I jump and demand passionately 'labour saving appliances and housing reform.' Up I jump in the person of Mrs Giles of Durham; in the person of Mrs Phillips of Bacup; in the person of Mrs Edwards of Wolverton. But after all the imagination is largely the child of the flesh. One could not be Mrs Giles of Durham because one's body had never stood at the wash-tub; one's hands had never wrung and scrubbed and chopped up whatever the meat may be that makes a miner's supper. The picture therefore was always letting in irrelevancies. One sat in an armchair or read a book. One saw landscapes and seascapes, perhaps Greece or Italy, where Mrs Giles or Mrs Edwards must have seen slag heaps and rows upon rows of slate-roofed houses. Something was always creeping in from a world that was not their world and making the picture false and the game too much of a game to be worth playing.

It was true that one could always correct these fancy portraits by taking a look at the actual person – at Mrs Thomas, or Mrs Langrish, or Miss Bolt of Hebden Bridge. They were worth looking at. Certainly, there were no armchairs, or electric light, or hot water laid on in their lives; no Greek hills or Mediterranean bays in their dreams. Bakers and butchers did not call for orders. They did not sign a cheque to pay the weekly bills, or order, over the telephone, a cheap but quite adequate seat at the Opera. If they travelled it was on excursion day, with food in string bags and babies[4] in their arms. They did not stroll through the house and say, that cover must go to the wash, or those sheets need changing. They plunged their arms in hot water and scrubbed the clothes themselves. In consequence their bodies were thick-set and muscular, their hands were large, and they had the slow emphatic gestures of people who are often stiff and fall tired in a heap on hard-backed chairs. They touched nothing lightly. They gripped papers and pencils as if they were brooms. Their faces were firm and heavily folded and lined with deep lines. It seemed as if their muscles were always taut and on the stretch. Their eyes looked as if they were always set on something actual – on saucepans that were boiling over, on children who were getting into mischief. Their lips never expressed the lighter and more detached emotions that come into play when the mind is perfectly at ease about the present. No, they were not in the least detached and easy and cosmopolitan. They were indigenous and rooted to one spot. Their very names were like the stones of the fields – common, grey, worn, obscure, docked of all splendours of association and romance. Of course they wanted baths and ovens and education and seventeen shillings instead of sixteen, and freedom and air and . . . 'And,' said Mrs Winthrop of Spennymoor, breaking into these thoughts with words that sounded like a refrain, 'we can wait.' . . . 'Yes,' she repeated, as if she had waited so long that the last lap of that immense vigil meant nothing for the end was in sight, 'we can wait.' And she got down rather stiffly from her perch and made her way back to her seat, an elderly woman dressed in her best clothes.

Then Mrs Potter spoke. Then Mrs Elphick. Then Mrs Holmes of Edgbaston. So it went on, and at last after innumerable speeches, after many communal meals at long tables and many arguments –

the world was to be reformed, from top to bottom, in a variety of ways – after seeing Co-operative jams bottled and Co-operative biscuits made, after some song singing and ceremonies with banners, the new President received the chain of office with a kiss from the old President; the Congress dispersed; and the separate members who had stood up so valiantly and spoken out so boldly while the clock ticked its five minutes went back to Yorkshire and Wales and Sussex and Devonshire, and hung their clothes in the wardrobe and plunged their hands in the wash-tub again.

Later that summer the thoughts here so inadequately described, were again discussed, but not in a public hall hung with banners and loud with voices. The head office of the Guild, the centre from which speakers, papers, inkstands and tumblers, as I suppose, issued, was then in Hampstead. There, if I may remind you again of what you may well have forgotten, you invited us to come; you asked us to tell you how the Congress had impressed us. But I must pause on the threshold of that very dignified old house, with its eighteenth-century carvings and panelling, as we paused then in truth, for one could not enter and go upstairs without encountering Miss Kidd. Miss Kidd sat at her typewriter in the outer office. Miss Kidd, one felt, had set herself as a kind of watch-dog to ward off the meddle-some middle-class wasters of time who come prying into other people's business. Whether it was for this reason that she was dressed in a peculiar shade of deep purple I do not know. The colour seemed somehow symbolical. She was very short, but, owing to the weight which sat on her brow and the gloom which seemed to issue from her dress, she was also very heavy. An extra share of the world's grievances seemed to press upon her shoulders. When she clicked her typewriter one felt that she was making that instru-ment transmit messages of foreboding and ill-omen to an unheeding universe. But she relented, and like all relentings after gloom hers came with a sudden charm. Then we went upstairs, and upstairs we came upon a very different figure – upon Miss Lilian Harris,[5] indeed, who, whether it was due to her dress which was coffee coloured, or to her smile which was serene, or to the ash-tray in which many cigarettes had come amiably to an end,[6] seemed the image of detachment and equanimity. Had one not known that Miss Harris was to the Congress what the heart is to the remoter veins –

that the great engine at Newcastle would not have thumped and throbbed without her – that she had collected and sorted and summoned and arranged that very intricate but orderly assembly of women – she would never have enlightened one. She had nothing whatever to do; she licked a few stamps and addressed a few envelopes – it was a fad of hers – that was what her manner conveyed. It was Miss Harris who moved the papers off the chairs and got the tea-cups out of the cupboard. It was she who answered questions about figures and put her hand on the right file of letters infallibly and sat listening, without saying very much, but with calm comprehension, to whatever was said.

Again let me telescope into a few sentences, and into one scene many random discussions on various occasions at various places. We said then – for you now emerged from an inner room, and if Miss Kidd was purple and Miss Harris was coffee coloured, you, speaking pictorially (and I dare not speak more explicitly) were kingfisher blue and as arrowy and decisive as that quick bird – we said then that the Congress had roused thoughts and ideas of the most diverse nature. It had been a revelation and a disillusionment. We had been humiliated and enraged. To begin with, all their talk, we said, or the greater part of it, was of matters of fact. They want baths and money.[7] To expect us, whose minds, such as they are, fly free at the end of a short length of capital to tie ourselves down again to that narrow plot of acquisitiveness and desire is impossible. We have baths and we have money. Therefore, however much we had sympathized our sympathy was largely fictitious. It was aesthetic sympathy, the sympathy of the eye and of the imagination, not of the heart and of the nerves; and such sympathy is always physically uncomfortable. Let us explain what we mean, we said. The Guild's women are magnificent to look at. Ladies in evening dress are lovelier far, but they lack the sculpturesque quality that these working women have. And though the range of expression is narrower in working women, their few expressions have a force and an emphasis, of tragedy or humour, which the faces of ladies lack. But, at the same time, it is much better to be a lady; ladies desire Mozart and Einstein[8] – that is, they desire things that are ends, not things that are means. Therefore to deride ladies and to imitate, as some of the speakers did, their mincing speech and little knowledge of what it pleases them to call 'reality' is, so it seems to us, not merely foolish but gives away the whole purpose of the Congress, for if it is better to be working women by all means let them remain so and not undergo the contamination which wealth and comfort bring. In spite of this, we went on, apart from prejudice and bandying compliments, undoubtedly the women at the Congress possess something which ladies lack, and something which is desirable, which is stimulating, and yet very difficult to define. One does not want to slip easily into fine phrases about 'contact with life', about 'facing facts' and 'the teaching of experience', for they invariably alienate the hearer, and moreover no working man or woman works harder or is in closer touch with reality than a painter with his brush or a writer with his pen.[9] But the quality that they have, judging from a phrase caught here and there, from a laugh, or a gesture seen in passing, is precisely the quality that Shakespeare would have enjoyed. One can fancy him slipping away from the brilliant salons of educated people to crack a joke in Mrs Robson's back kitchen. Indeed, we said, one of our most curious impressions at your Congress was that the 'poor', 'the working classes', or by whatever name you choose to call them, are not downtrodden, envious and exhausted; they are humorous and vigorous and thoroughly independent. Thus if it were possible to meet them not as masters or mistresses or customers with a counter between us, but over the wash-tub or in the parlour casually and congenially as fellow-beings with the same wishes and ends in view, a great liberation would follow, and perhaps friendship and sympathy would supervene. How many words must lurk in those women's vocabularies that have faded from ours! How many scenes must lie dormant in their eyes which are unseen by ours! What images and saws and proverbial sayings must still be current with them that have never reached the surface of print, and very likely they still keep the power which we have lost of making new ones. There were many shrewd sayings in the speeches at Congress which even the weight of a public meeting could not flatten out entirely. But, we said, and here perhaps fiddled with a paper knife, or poked the fire impatiently by way of expressing our discontent, what is the use of it all? Our sympathy is fictitious, not real. Because the baker calls and we pay our bills with cheques, and our clothes are washed for us and we do not know the liver from the lights[10] we are condemned to remain forever shut up in the confines of the middle classes, wearing tail coats and silk stockings, and called Sir or Madam as the case may be, when we are all, in truth, simply Johns and Susans. And they remain equally deprived. For we have as much to give them as they to give us – wit and detachment, learning and poetry, and all those good gifts which those who have never answered bells or minded machines enjoy by right. But the barrier is impassable. And nothing perhaps exacerbated us more at the Congress (you must have noticed at times a certain irritability) than the thought that this force of theirs, this smouldering heat which broke the crust now and then and licked the surface with a hot and fearless flame, is about to break through and melt us together so that life will be richer and books more complex and society will pool its possessions instead of segregating them – all this is going to happen inevitably, thanks to you, very largely, and to Miss Harris and to Miss Kidd – but only when we are dead.

It was thus that we tried in the Guild Office that afternoon to explain the nature of fictitious sympathy and how it differs from real sympathy and how defective it is because it is not based upon sharing the same important emotions unconsciously. It was thus that we tried to describe the contradictory and complex feelings which beset the middle-class visitor when forced to sit out a Congress of working women in silence.

Perhaps it was at this point that you unlocked a drawer and took out a packet of papers. You did not at once untie the string that fastened them. Sometimes, you said, you got a letter which you could not bring yourself to burn; once or twice a Guildswoman had at your suggestion written a few pages about her life. It might be that we should find these papers interesting; that if we read them the women would cease to be symbols and would become instead individuals. But they were very fragmentary and ungrammatical; they had been jotted down in the intervals of housework. Indeed you could not at once bring yourself to give them up, as if to expose them to other eyes were a breach of confidence. It might be that their crudity[11] would only perplex, that the writing of people who do not know how to write – but at this point we burst in. In the first place, every Englishwoman knows how to write; in the second, even if she does not she has only to take her own life for subject and write the truth about that and not fiction or poetry for our interest to be so keenly roused that – that in short we cannot wait but must read the packet at once.

Thus pressed you did by degrees and with many delays – there was the war for example, and Miss Kidd died, and you and Lilian Harris retired from the Guild, and a testimonial was given you in a casket, and many thousands of working women tried to say how you had changed their lives – tried to say what they will feel for you to their dying day – after all these interruptions you did at last gather the papers together and finally put them in my hands early this May. There they were, typed and docketed with a few snapshots and rather faded photographs stuck between the pages. And when at last I began to read, there started up in my mind's eye the figures that I had seen all those years ago at Newcastle with such bewilderment and curiosity. But they were no longer addressing a large meeting in Newcastle from a platform, dressed in their best clothes. The hot June day with its banners and its ceremonies had vanished, and instead one looked back into the past of the women who had stood there; into the four-roomed houses of miners, into the homes of small shopkeepers and agricultural labourers, into the fields and factories of fifty or sixty years ago. Mrs Burrows, for example, had worked in the Lincolnshire fens when she was eight with forty or fifty other children, and an old man had followed the gang with a long whip in his hand 'which he did not forget to use'. That was a strange reflection. Most of the women had started work at seven or eight, earning a penny on Saturday for washing a doorstep, or twopence a week for carrying suppers to the men at the iron foundry. They had gone into factories when they were fourteen. They had worked from seven in the morning till eight or nine at night and had made thirteen or fifteen shillings a week. Out of this money they had saved some pence with which to buy their mother gin – she was often very tired in the evening and had borne perhaps thirteen children in as many years; or they fetched opium to assuage some miserable old woman's ague in the fens. Old Betty Rollett killed herself when she could get no more. They had seen half-starved women standing in rows to be paid for their match-boxes while they snuffed the roast meat of their employer's dinner cooking within. The smallpox had raged in Bethnal Green and they had known that the boxes went on being made in the sick-room and were sold to the public with the infection still thick on them. They had been so cold working in the wintry fields that they could not run when the ganger[12] gave them leave. They had waded through floods when the Wash overflowed its banks. Kind old ladies had given them parcels of food which had turned out to contain only crusts of bread and rancid bacon rind. All this they had done and seen and known when other children were still dabbling in seaside pools and spelling out fairy tales by the nursery fire. Naturally their faces had a different look on them. But they were, one remembered, firm faces, faces with something indomitable in their expression. Astonishing though it seems, human nature is so tough that it will take such wounds, even at the tenderest age, and survive them. Keep a child mewed up in Bethnal Green and she will somehow snuff the country air from seeing the yellow dust on her brother's boots, and nothing will serve her but she must go there and see the 'clean ground', as she calls it, for herself. It was true that at first the 'bees were very frightening', but all the same she got to the country and the blue smoke and the cows came up to her expectation. Put girls, after a childhood of minding smaller brothers and washing doorsteps, into a factory when they are fourteen and their eyes will turn to the window and they will be happy because, as the workroom is six storeys high, the sun can be seen breaking over the hills, 'and that was always such a comfort and a help'. Still stranger, if one needs additional proof of the strength of the human instinct to escape from bondage and attach itself whether to a country road or to a sunrise over the hills, is the fact that the highest ideals of duty flourish in an obscure hat factory as surely as on a battlefield. There were women in Christies' felt-hat factory, for example, who worked for 'honour'. They gave their lives to the cause of putting straight stitches into the bindings of men's hat brims. Felt is hard and thick; it is difficult to push the needle through; there are no rewards or glory to be won; but such is the incorrigible idealism of the human mind that there were 'trimmers' in those obscure places who would never put a crooked stitch in their work and ruthlessly tore out the crooked stitches of others. And as they drove in their straight stitches they reverenced Queen Victoria and thanked God, drawing up to the fire, that they were all married to good Conservative working men.

Certainly that story explained something of the force, of the obstinacy, which one had seen in the faces of the speakers at Newcastle. And then, if one went on reading these papers, one came upon other signs of the extraordinary vitality of the human spirit. That inborn energy which no amount of childbirth and washing up can quench had reached out, it seemed, and seized upon old copies of magazines; had attached itself to Dickens; had propped the poems of Burns against a dish cover to read while cooking. They read at meals; they read before going to the mill. They read Dickens and Scott and Henry George and Bulwer Lytton and Ella Wheeler Wilcox and Alice Meynell[13] and would like 'to get hold of any good history of the French Revolution, not Carlyle's, please',[14] and B. Russell on China,[15] and William Morris and Shelley and Florence Barclay and Samuel Butler's Notebooks – they read with the indiscriminate greed of a hungry appetite, that crams itself with toffee and beef and tarts and vinegar and champagne all in one gulp. Naturally such reading led to argument. The younger generation had the audacity to say that Queen Victoria was no better than an honest charwoman who had brought up her children respectably. They had the temerity to doubt whether to sew straight stitches into men's hat brims should be the sole aim and end of a woman's life. They started arguments and even held rudimentary debating societies on the floor of the factory. In time the old trimmers even were shaken in their beliefs and came to think that there might be other ideals in the world besides straight stitches and Queen Victoria. Strange ideas indeed were seething in their brain. A girl, for instance, would reason, as she walked along the streets of a factory town, that she had no right to bring a child into the world if that child must earn its living in a mill. A chance saying in a book would fire her imagination to dream of future cities where there were to be baths and kitchens and washhouses and art galleries and museums and parks. The minds of working women were humming and their imaginations were awake. But how were they to realize their ideals? How were they to express their needs? It was hard enough for middle-class women with some amount of money and some degree of education behind them. But how could women whose hands were full of work, whose kitchens were thick with steam, who had neither education nor encouragement nor leisure remodel the world according to the ideas of working women? It was then, I suppose, sometime in the eighties, that the Women's Guild crept modestly and tentatively into existence. For a time it occupied an inch or two of space in the *Co-operative News* which called itself The Women's Corner. It was there that Mrs Acland asked, 'Why should we not hold our Co-operative mothers' meetings, when we may bring our work and sit together, one of us reading some Co-operative work aloud, which may afterwards be discussed?' And on April 18th, 1883, she announced that the Women's Guild now numbered seven members. It was the Guild then that drew to itself all that restless wishing and dreaming. It was the Guild that made a central meeting place where formed and solidified all that was else so scattered and incoherent. The Guild must have given the older women, with their husbands and children, what 'clean ground' had given to the little girl in Bethnal Green, or the view of day breaking over the hills had given the girls in the hat factory. It gave them in the first place the rarest of all possessions – a room where they could sit down and think remote from boiling saucepans and crying children; and then that room became not merely a sitting-room and a meeting place, but a workshop where, laying their heads together, they could remodel their houses, could remodel their lives, could beat out this reform and that. And, as the membership grew, and twenty or thirty women made a practice of meeting weekly, so their ideas increased, and their interests widened. Instead of discussing merely their own taps and their own sinks and their own long hours and little pay, they began to discuss education and taxation and the conditions of work in the country at large. The women who had crept modestly in 1883 into Mrs Acland's sitting-room to sew and 'read some Co-operative work aloud', learnt to speak out, boldly and authoritatively, about every question of civic life. Thus it came about that Mrs Robson and Mrs Potter and Mrs Wright at Newcastle in 1913 were asking not only for baths and wages and electric light, but also for Adult Suffrage and the Taxation of Land Values and Divorce Law Reform. Thus in a year or two they were to demand peace and disarmament and the spread of Co-operative principles, not only among the working people of Great Britain, but among the nations of the world. And the force that lay behind their speeches and drove them home beyond the reach of eloquence was compact of many things – of men with whips, of sick-rooms where match-boxes were made, of hunger and cold, of many and difficult child-births, of much scrubbing and washing up, of reading Shelley and William Morris and Samuel Butler over the kitchen table, of weekly meetings of the Women's Guild, of Committees and Congresses at Manchester and elsewhere. And this lay behind the speeches of Mrs Robson and Mrs Potter and Mrs Wright. The papers which you sent me certainly threw some light upon the old curiosities and bewilderments which had made that Congress so memorable, and so thick with unanswered questions.

But that the pages here printed should mean all this to those who cannot supplement the written word with the memory of faces and the sound of voices is perhaps unlikely. It cannot be denied that the chapters here put together do not make a book – that as literature they have many limitations. The writing, a literary critic might say, lacks detachment and imaginative breadth, even as the women them-selves lacked variety and play of feature. Here are no reflections, he might object, no view of life as a whole, and no attempt to enter into the lives of other people. Poetry and fiction seem far beyond their horizon. Indeed, we are reminded of those obscure writers before the birth of Shakespeare who never travelled beyond the borders of their own parishes, who read no language but their own, and wrote with difficulty, finding few words and those awkwardly. And yet since writing is a complex art, much infected by life, these pages have some qualities even as literature that the literate and instructed might envy. Listen, for instance, to Mrs Scott, the felt-hat worker: 'I have been over the hill-tops when the snow drifts were over three feet high, and six feet in some places. I was in a blizzard in Hayfield and thought I should never get round the corners. But it was life on the moors; I seemed to know every blade of grass and where the flowers grew and all the little streams were my companions.' Could she have said that better if Oxford had made her a Doctor of Letters? Or take Mrs Layton's description of a match-box factory in Bethnal Green and how she looked through the fence and saw three ladies 'sitting in the shade doing some kind of fancy work'. It has something of the accuracy and clarity of a description by Defoe. And when Mrs Burrows brings to mind that bitter day when the children were about to eat their cold dinner and drink their cold tea under the hedge and the ugly woman asked them into her parlour saying, 'Bring these children into my house and let them eat their dinner there,' the words are simple, but it is difficult to see how they could say more. And then there is a fragment of a letter from Miss Kidd – the sombre purple figure who typed as if the weight of the world were on her shoulders. 'When I was a girl of seventeen,' she writes, 'my then employer, a gentleman of good position and high standing in the town, sent me to his home one night, ostensibly to take a parcel of books, but really with a very different object. When I arrived at the house all the family were away, and before he would allow me to leave he forced me to yield to him. At eighteen I was a mother.' Whether that is literature or not literature I do not presume to say, but that it explains much and reveals much is certain. Such then was the burden that rested on that sombre figure as she sat typing your letters, such were the memories she brooded as she guarded your door with her grim and indomitable fidelity.

But I will quote no more. These pages are only fragments. These voices are beginning only now to emerge from silence into half articulate speech. These lives are still half hidden in profound obscurity. To express even what is expressed here has been a work of labour and difficulty. The writing has been done in kitchens, at odds and ends of leisure, in the midst of distractions and obstacles – but really there is no need for me, in a letter addressed to you, to lay stress upon the hardship of working women's lives. Have not you and Lilian Harris given your best years – but hush! you will not let me finish that sentence and therefore, with the old messages of friendship and admiration, I will make an end.

Why?

This was first published in *Lysistrata*, an Oxford student magazine, in 1934. The magazine took its name from the eponymous heroine of Aristophanes' play, who led the women of Athens and Sparta in a revolt against the war.

When the first number of *Lysistrata* appeared, I confess that I was deeply disappointed. It was so well-printed, on such good paper. It looked established, prosperous. As I turned the pages it seemed to me that wealth must have descended upon Somerville,[1] and I was about to answer the request of the editor for an article with a negative when I read, greatly to my relief, that one of the writers was badly dressed, and gathered from another that the women's colleges still lack power and prestige. At this I plucked up heart, and a crowd of questions that have been pressing to be asked rushed to my lips saying: Here is our chance.

I should explain that like so many people nowadays I am pestered with questions. I find it impossible to walk down the street without stopping, it may be in the middle of the road, to ask Why? Churches, public-houses, parliaments, shops, loud-speakers, motor-cars, the drone of an aeroplane in the clouds, and men and women, all inspire questions. Yet what is the point of asking questions of oneself? They should be asked openly in public. But the great obstacle to asking questions in public is, of course, wealth. The little twisted sign that comes at the end of a question has a way of making the rich writhe; power and prestige come down upon it with all their weight. Questions, therefore, being sensitive, impulsive, and often foolish, have a way of picking their asking place with care. They shrivel up in an atmosphere of power, prosperity, and time-worn stone. They die by the dozen on the threshold of great newspaper offices. They slink away to less favoured, less flourishing quarters where people are poor and therefore have nothing to give, where they have no power and therefore have nothing to lose. Now the questions that have been pestering me to ask them decided, whether rightly or wrongly, that they could be asked in *Lysistrata*. They said, 'We do not expect you to ask us in—' here they named some of our most respectable dailies and weeklies; 'nor in—' here they named some of our most venerable institutions. 'But, thank Heaven!' they exclaimed, 'are not women's colleges poor and young? Are they not inventive, adventurous? Are they not out to create a new—'

'The editor forbids feminism,' I interposed severely.

'What is feminism?' they screamed with one accord, and as I did not answer at once, a new question was flung at me, 'Don't you think it high time that a new—?' But I stopped them by reminding them that they had only two thousand words at their disposal, upon which they consulted together, and finally put forward the request that I should introduce one or two of the simplest, tamest, and most obvious among them. For example, there is the question that always bobs up at the beginning of term when Societies issue their invitations and universities open their doors – why lecture, why be lectured?

In order to place this question fairly before you, I will describe, for memory has kept the picture bright, one of those rare but, as Queen Victoria would have put it, never-to-be-sufficiently-lamented occasions when in deference to friendship, or in a desperate attempt to acquire information about, perhaps, the French Revolution, it seemed necessary to attend a lecture. The room to begin with had a hybrid look – it was not for sitting in, nor yet for eating in. Perhaps there was a map on the wall; certainly there was a table on a platform, and several rows of rather small, rather hard, comfortless little chairs. These were occupied intermittently, as if they shunned each other's company, by people of both sexes, and some had notebooks and were tapping their fountain pens, and some had none and gazed with the vacancy and placidity of bull frogs at the ceiling. A large clock displayed its cheerless face, and when the hour struck in strode a harried-looking man, a man from whose face nervousness, vanity, or perhaps the depressing and impossible nature of his task had removed all traces of ordinary humanity. There was a momentary stir. He had written a book, and for a moment it is interesting to see people who have written books. Everybody gazed at him. He was bald and not hairy; had a mouth and a chin; in short he was a man like another, although he had written a book. He cleared his throat and the lecture began. Now, the human voice is an instrument of varied power; it can enchant and it can soothe; it can rage and it can despair; but when it lectures it almost always bores. What he said was sensible enough; there was learning in it and argument and reason; but as the voice went on attention wandered. The face of the clock seemed abnormally pale; the hands too suffered from some infirmity. Had they the gout? Were they swollen? They moved so slowly. They reminded one of the painful progress of a three-legged fly that has survived the winter. How many flies on an average survive the English winter, and what would be the thoughts of such an insect on waking to find itself lectured on the French Revolution? The inquiry was fatal. A link had been lost – a paragraph dropped. It was useless to ask the lecturer to repeat his words; on he plodded with dogged pertinacity. The origin of the French Revolution was being sought for – also the thoughts of flies. Now there came one of those flat stretches of discourse when minute objects can be seen coming for two or three miles ahead. 'Skip!' we entreated him – vainly. He did not skip. He went on. Then there was a joke; then it seemed that the windows wanted washing; then a woman sneezed; then the voice quickened; then there was a peroration; and then – thank Heaven! the lecture was over.

Why, since life holds only so many hours, waste one of them on being lectured? Why, since printing presses have been invented these many centuries, should he not have printed his lecture instead of speaking it? Then, by the fire in winter, or under an apple-tree in summer, it could have been read, thought over, discussed; the difficult ideas pondered, the argument debated. It could have been thickened, and stiffened. There would have been no need of those repetitions and dilutions with which lectures have to be watered down and brightened up so as to attract the attention of a miscellaneous audience too apt to think about noses and chins, women sneezing and the longevity of flies.

It may be, I told these questions, that there is some reason, imperceptible to outsiders, which makes lectures an essential part of university discipline. But why – here another rushed to the forefront – why, if lectures are necessary as a form of education should they not be abolished as a form of entertainment? Never does the crocus flower or the beech-tree redden but there issue simultaneously from all the universities of England, Scotland and Ireland, a shower of notes in which desperate secretaries entreat So-and-So and So-and-So to come up and address them upon art or literature, or politics, or morality – and why?

In the old days, when newspapers were scarce and carefully lent about from Hall to Rectory, such laboured methods of rubbing up minds and imparting ideas were no doubt essential. But now, when every day of the week scatters our tables with articles and pamphlets in which every shade of opinion is expressed, far more tersely than by word of mouth, why continue an obsolete custom which not merely wastes time and temper, but incites the most debased of human passions – vanity, ostentation, self-assertion, and the desire to convert? Why encourage your elders to turn themselves into prigs and prophets, when they are ordinary men and women? Why force them to stand on a platform for forty minutes while you reflect upon the colour of their hair and the longevity of flies? Why not let them talk to you and listen to you, naturally and happily, on the floor? Why not create a new form of society founded on poverty and equality? Why not bring together people of all ages and both sexes of all shades of fame and obscurity so that they can talk, without mounting platforms, or reading papers, or wearing expensive clothes, or eating expensive food? Would not such a society be worth, even as a form of education, all the papers on art and literature that have ever been read since the world began? Why not abolish prigs and prophets? Why not invent human intercourse? Why not try?

Here, being sick of the word 'why', I was about to indulge myself with a few reflections of a general nature upon society as it was, as it is, as it might be, with some fancy pictures of Mrs Thrale entertaining Dr Johnson, of Lady Holland abusing Lord Macaulay thrown in, when such a clamour arose among the questions that I could hardly hear myself think. The cause of the clamour was soon apparent. I had incautiously and foolishly used the word 'literature'. Now if there is one word that excites questions and puts them in a fury it is this word 'literature'. There they were, screaming and crying, asking questions about poetry and fiction and criticism, each demanding to be heard, each certain that his was the only question that deserved an answer. At last, when they had destroyed all my fancy pictures of Lady Holland and Dr Johnson, one insisted, for he said that foolish and rash as he might be he was less so than the others, that he should be asked. And his question was, why learn English literature at universities when you can read it for yourselves in books? But I said it is foolish to ask a question that has already been answered – English literature is, I believe, already taught at the universities. Besides, if we are going to start an argument about it, we should need at least twenty volumes, whereas we have only about seven hundred words left to us. Still, as he was importunate, I said I would ask the question and introduce it to the best of my ability, without expressing any opinion of my own, by copying down the following fragment of dialogue.

The other day I went to call upon a friend of mine who earns her living as a publisher's reader. The room was a little dark it seemed to me when I went in. Yet, as the window was open and it was a fine spring day, the darkness must have been spiritual – the effect of some private sorrow I feared. Her first words as I came in confirmed my fears. 'Alas, poor boy!' she exclaimed, tossing the manuscript she was reading to the ground, with a gesture of despair.

Had some accident happened to one of her relations, I asked, motoring or climbing?

'If you call three hundred pages on the evolution of the Eliza-bethan sonnet an accident,' she said.

'Is that all?' I replied with relief.

'All?' she retaliated. 'Isn't it enough?' And, beginning to pace up and down the room, she exclaimed, 'Once he was a clever boy; once he was worth talking to; once he cared about English literature. But now—' She threw out her hands as if words failed her – but not at all. There followed such a flood of lamentation and vituperation – but reflecting how hard her life was, reading manuscripts day in and day out, I excused her – that I could not follow the argument. All I could gather was that this lecturing about English literature – 'If you want to teach them to read English,' she threw in, 'teach them to read Greek' – all this passing of examinations in English litera-ture, which led to all this writing about English literature, was sure in the end to be the death and burial of English literature. 'The tombstone,' she was proceeding, 'will be a bound volume of—' when I stopped her and told her not to talk such nonsense. 'Then tell me,' she said, standing over me with her fists clenched. 'Do they write the better for it? is poetry better, is fiction better, is criticism better, now that they have been taught how to read English literature?'

As if to answer her own question she read a passage from the manuscript on the floor. 'And each the spit and image of the other!' she groaned, lifting it wearily to its place with the manuscripts on the shelf.

'But think of all they must know?' I tried to argue. 'Know?' she echoed me. 'Know? What d'you mean by "know"?' As that was a difficult question to answer offhand, I passed it over by saying, 'Well, at any rate, they'll be able to make their livings and teach other people.' Whereupon she lost her temper and, seizing the unfortunate work upon the Elizabethan sonnet, whizzed it across the room. The rest of the visit passed in picking up the fragments of a vase that had belonged to her grandmother.

Now, of course, a dozen other questions clamour to be asked; about churches and parliaments and public-houses and shops and loud-speakers and men and women; but mercifully time is up; silence falls.

Royalty

This is a review of *The Story of My Life* by Marie, Queen of Romania, first published in *Time and Tide*, 1 December 1934. Queen Marie was a much-celebrated European royal, and was the daughter of a Duchess of Edinburgh who was herself the daughter of a Tsar. On 26 April 1924, the *Illustrated London News* described Marie as 'an extraordinarily magnetic and fascinating personality, in addition to being very good indeed to look at'.

Many important autobiographies have appeared this autumn, but none stranger or in certain respects more interesting than *The Story of My Life*, by Marie, Queen of Romania. The reasons seem to be that she is royal; that she can write; that no royal person has ever been able to write before; and that the consequences may well be extremely serious.

Royalty to begin with, merely as an experiment in the breeding of human nature, is of great psychological interest. For centuries a certain family has been segregated; bred with a care only lavished upon race horses; splendidly housed, clothed and fed; abnormally stimulated in some ways, suppressed in others; worshipped, stared at, and kept shut up, as lions and tigers are kept, in a beautiful brightly lit room behind bars. The psychological effect upon them must be profound; and the effect upon us is as remarkable. Sane men and women as we are, we cannot rid ourselves of the superstition that there is something miraculous about these people shut up in their cage. Common sense may deny it; but take common sense for a walk through the streets of London on the Duke of Kent's wedding-day.[1] Not only will he find himself in a minority, but as the gold coach passes and the bride bows, his hand will rise to his head; off will come his hat, or on the contrary it will be rammed firmly on his head. In either case he will recognize the divinity of royalty.

Now one of these royal animals, Queen Marie of Romania, has done what had never been done before; she has opened the door of the cage and sauntered out into the street. Queen Marie can write; in a second, therefore, the bars are down. Instead of the expected suavities and sweetnesses we come upon sharp little words; Uncle Bertie laughs, 'his laugh was a sort of crackle'; Kitty Renwick kept the medicine chest; 'the castor-oil pills looked like transparent white grapes with the oil moving about inside'; there were 'little squares of burnt skin' on the pudding at Windsor; Queen Victoria's teeth were 'small like those of a mouse'; she had a way of shrugging her shoulders when she laughed; when they rode on the sands at evening 'the shadows become so long that it is as though our horses were walking on stilts'; there was a marvellous stone in the museum, like a large piece of shortbread, that 'swayed slightly up and down when held at one end'. This little girl, in short, smelt, touched and saw as other children do; but she had an unusual power of following her feeling until she had coined the word for it. That is to say, she can write.

If we want an example of the difference between writing and non-writing we have only to compare a page of Queen Marie with a page of Queen Victoria. The old Queen was, of course, an author. She was forced by the exigencies of her profession to fill an immense number of pages, and some of these have been printed and bound between covers. But between the old Queen and the English language lay an abyss which no depth of passion and no strength of character could cross. Her works make very painful reading on that account. She has to express herself in words; but words will not come to her call. When she feels strongly and tries to say so, it is like hearing an old savage beating with a wooden spoon on a drum. '. . . this last refusal of Servia . . . almost *forces us* to SEE *that* there is *no* false play.' Rhythm is broken; the few poverty stricken words are bruised and battered; now hooked together with hyphens, now desperately distended with italics and capital letters – it is all no good. In the same way her descriptions of celebrated people slip through the fingers like water. 'I waited a moment in the Drawing-room to speak to Irving and Ellen Terry.[2] He is very gentleman-like, and she, very pleasing and handsome.' This primitive little machine is all that she has with which to register some of the most extraordinary experiences that ever fell to a woman's lot. But probably she owed much of her prestige to her inability to express herself. The majority of her subjects, knowing her through her writing, came to feel that only a woman immune from the usual frailties and passions of human nature could write as Queen Victoria wrote. It added to her royalty.

But now by some freak of fate, which Queen Victoria would have been the first to deplore, her granddaughter, the eldest child of the late Duke and Duchess of Edinburgh, has been born with a pen in her hand. Words do her bidding. Her own account of it is illuminating: 'Even as a child,' she says, 'I possessed a vivid imagination and I liked telling stories to my sisters . . . Then one of my children said to me: "Mama, you ought to write all this down, it is a pity to allow so many beautiful pictures to fade away." . . . I knew nothing whatever about writing, about style or composition, or about the "rules of the game", but I did know how to conjure up beauty, also at times, emotion. I also had a vast store of words.' It is true; she knows nothing about 'the rules of the game'; words descend and bury whole cities under them; sights that should have been seen once and for all are distracted and dissipated; she ruins her effects and muffs her chances; but still because she feels abundantly, because she rides after her emotion fearlessly and takes her fences without caring for falls, she conjures up beauty and conveys emotion. Nor is it merely that by a happy fluke she is able to hit off a moment's impression, a vivid detail; she has the rarer power of sweeping these figures along in a torrent of language; lives grow and change beneath our eyes; scenes form themselves; details arrange themselves; all the actors come alive. Her most remarkable achievement in this way is her portrait of 'Aunty' – that Queen Elizabeth of Romania who called herself Carmen Sylva. As it happened, Queen Victoria also tried her hand at a portrait of this lady. 'The dear charming Queen [she writes] came to luncheon . . . She spoke with resignation and courage of her many trials and difficulties . . . I gave her a Celtic brooch and Balmoral shawl, also some books . . . the Queen read to us one of her plays, an ancient Greek story, very tragic. She read it to us almost wonderfully and beautifully, and had quite an inspired look as she did so . . . Many could, of course, not understand, as she read it in German, but all were interested.'

In Queen Marie's hands this 'dear charming Queen' develops out of all recognition. She becomes a complex, contradictory human being, wearing floating veils and a motoring cap, at once 'splendid and absurd'. We see her posing in bed under a top light; dramatizing herself melodramatically; luxuriating in the flattery of sycophants; declaiming poetry through a megaphone to ships at sea; waving a napkin to grazing cows whom she mistakes for loyal subjects – deluded and fantastic, but at the same time generous and sincere. So the picture shapes itself, until all the different elements are shown in action. Two scenes stand out with genuine vitality – one where the romantic impulsive old lady seeks to enchant an ancient flame – the late Duke of Edinburgh – by dragging him to a hill top where hidden minstrels spring out from behind rocks and bawl native melodies into his disgusted ears; the other where Queen Elizabeth of Romania and Queen Emma of Holland sit at their needlework while the Italian secretary reads aloud. He chose Maeterlinck,[3] and as he declaimed the famous passage where the Queen bee soars higher and higher in her nuptial ecstasy till at last the male insect, ravaged by passion, drops dismembered to the ground, Carmen Sylva raised her beautiful white hands in rapture. But Queen Emma gave one look at the reader and went on hemming her duster.

Vivid as it all is, nobody is going to claim that Queen Marie ranks with Saint Simon or with Proust. Yet it would be equally absurd to deny that by virtue of her pen she has won her freedom. She is no longer a royal queen in a cage. She ranges the world, free like any other human being to laugh, to scold, to say what she likes, to be what she is. And if she has escaped, so too thanks to her, have we. Royalty is no longer quite so royal. Uncle Bertie, Onkel, Aunty, Nando, and the rest are not mere effigies bowing and smiling, opening bazaars, expressing exalted sentiments and remembering faces always with the same sweet smile. They are violent and eccentric; charming and ill-tempered; some have blood-shot eyes; others handle flowers with a peculiar tenderness. In short, they are very like ourselves. They live as we do. And the effect is surprising. A month or two ago, the late Duke of Edinburgh was as dead as the Dodo. Now, thanks to his daughter, we know that he liked beer; that he liked to sip it while he read his paper; that he hated music; that he loathed Romanian melodies; and that he sat on a rock in a rage.

But what will be the consequences if this familiarity between them and us increases? Can we go on bowing and curtseying to people who are just like ourselves? Are we not already a little ashamed of the pushing and the staring now that we know from these two stout volumes that one at least of the animals can talk? We begin to wish that the Zoo should be abolished; that the royal animals should be given the run of some wider pasturage – a royal Whipsnade.[4] And another question suggests itself. When a gift for writing lodges in a family, it often persists and improves; and if Queen Marie's descendants improve upon her gift as much as she has improved upon Queen Victoria's is it not quite possible that a real poet will be King of England in a hundred years' time? And suppose that among the autumn books of 2034 is *Prometheus Unbound*, by George the Sixth, or *Wuthering Heights*,[5] by Elizabeth the Second, what will be the effect upon their loyal subjects? Will the British Empire survive? Will Buckingham Palace look as solid then as it does now? Words are dangerous things let us remember. A republic might be brought into being by a poem.

The Leaning Tower

A paper read to the Workers' Educational Association, Brighton, May 1940. First published in *Folios of New Writing*, Autumn 1940.

A writer is a person who sits at a desk and keeps his eye fixed, as intently as he can, upon a certain object – that figure of speech may help to keep us steady on our path if we look at it for a moment. He is an artist who sits with a sheet of paper in front of him trying to copy what he sees. What is his object – his model? Nothing so simple as a painter's model; it is not a bowl of flowers, a naked figure, or a dish of apples and onions. Even the simplest story deals with more than one person, with more than one time. Characters begin young; they grow old; they move from scene to scene, from place to place. A writer has to keep his eye upon a model that moves, that changes, upon an object that is not one object but innumerable objects. Two words alone cover all that a writer looks at – they are, human life.

Let us look at the writer next. What do we see – only a person who sits with a pen in his hand in front of a sheet of paper? That tells us little or nothing. And we know very little. Considering how much we talk about writers, how much they talk about themselves, it is odd how little we know about them. Why are they so common sometimes; then so rare? Why do they sometimes write nothing but masterpieces, then nothing but trash?[1] And why should a family, like the Shelleys, like the Keatses, like the Brontës, suddenly burst into flame and bring to birth Shelley, Keats and the Brontës? What are the conditions that bring about that explosion? There is no answer – naturally. Since we have not yet discovered the germ of influenza, how should we yet have discovered the germ of genius? We know even less about the mind than about the body. We have less evidence. It is less than two hundred years since people took an interest in themselves;[2] Boswell was almost the first writer who thought that a man's life was worth writing a book about. Until we have more facts, more biographies, more autobiographies, we cannot know much about ordinary people, let alone about extraordinary people. Thus at present we have only theories about writers – a great many theories, but they all differ. The politician says that a writer is the product of the society in which he lives, as a screw is the product of a screw machine; the artist, that a writer is a heavenly apparition that slides across the sky, grazes the earth and vanishes. To the psychologists a writer is an oyster; feed him on gritty facts, irritate him with ugliness and by way of compensation as they call it, he will produce a pearl. The genealogists say that certain stocks, certain families, breed writers as fig-trees breed figs – Dryden, Swift and Pope they tell us were all cousins. This proves that we are in the dark about writers; anybody can make a theory; the germ of a theory is almost always the wish to prove what the theorist wishes to believe.

Theories then are dangerous things. All the same we must risk making one this afternoon since we are going to discuss modern tendencies. Directly we speak of tendencies or movements we commit ourselves to the belief that there is some force, influence, outer pressure which is strong enough to stamp itself upon a whole group of different writers so that all their writing has a certain common likeness. We must then have a theory as to what this influence is. But let us always remember – influences are infinitely numerous; writers are infinitely sensitive; each writer has a different sensibility. That is why literature is always changing, like the weather, like the clouds in the sky. Read a page of Scott; then of Henry James; try to work out the influences that have transformed the one page into the other. It is beyond our skill. We can only hope therefore to single out the most obvious influences that have formed writers into groups. Yet there are groups. Books descend from books as families descend from families. Some descend from Jane Austen; others from Dickens. They resemble their parents, as human children resemble their parents; yet they differ as children differ, and revolt as children revolt. Perhaps it will be easier to understand living writers as we take a quick look at some of their forebears. We have not time to go far back – certainly we have not time to look closely. But let us glance at English writers as they were a hundred years ago – that may help us to see what we ourselves look like.

In 1815 England was at war, as England is now. And it is natural to ask, how did their war – the Napoleonic war[3] – affect them? Was that one of the influences that formed them into groups? The answer is a very strange one. The Napoleonic wars did not affect the great majority of those writers at all. The proof of that is to be found in the work of two great novelists – Jane Austen and Walter Scott. Each lived through the Napoleonic wars; each wrote through them. But, though novelists live very close to the life of their time, neither of them in all their novels mentioned the Napoleonic wars. This shows that their model, their vision of human life, was not disturbed or agitated or changed by war. Nor were they themselves. It is easy to see why that was so. Wars were then remote; wars were carried on by soldiers and sailors, not by private people. The rumour of battles took a long time to reach England. It was only when the mail coaches clattered along the country roads hung with laurels that the people in villages like Brighton[4] knew that a victory had been won and lit their candles and stuck them in their windows. Compare that with our state today.[5] Today we hear the gunfire in the channel. We turn on the wireless;[6] we hear an airman telling us how this very afternoon he shot down a raider; his machine caught fire; he plunged into the sea; the light turned green and then black; he rose to the top and was rescued by a trawler. Scott never saw the sailors drowning at Trafalgar; Jane Austen never heard the cannon roar at Waterloo.[7] Neither of them heard Napoleon's voice as we hear Hitler's voice as we sit at home of an evening.

That immunity from war lasted all through the nineteenth century. England, of course, was often at war – there was the Crimean War; the Indian Mutiny; all the little Indian frontier wars, and at the end of the century the Boer War.[8] Keats, Shelley, Byron, Dickens, Thackeray, Carlyle, Ruskin, the Brontës, George Eliot, Trollope, the Brownings – all lived through all those wars. But did they ever mention them? Only Thackeray I think; in *Vanity Fair* he described the Battle of Waterloo long after it was fought; but only as an illustration, as a scene. It did not change his characters' lives; it merely killed one of his heroes. Of the poets only Byron and Shelley felt the influence of the nineteenth-century wars profoundly.

War then we can say, speaking roughly, did not affect either the writer or his vision of human life in the nineteenth century. But peace – let us consider the influence of peace? Were the nineteenth-century writers affected by the settled, the peaceful and prosperous state of England? Let us collect a few facts before we launch out into the dangers and delights of theory. We know for a fact, from their lives, that the nineteenth-century writers were all of them fairly well-to-do middle-class people. Most had been educated either at Oxford or at Cambridge. Some were civil servants like Trollope and Matthew Arnold. Others, like Ruskin, were professors. It is a fact that their work brought them considerable fortunes. There is visible proof of that in the houses they built. Look at Abbotsford, bought out of the proceeds of Scott's novels; or at Farringford, built by Tennyson from his poetry. Look at Dickens's great house in Marylebone; and at his great house at Gadshill. All these are houses needing many butlers, maids, gardeners, grooms to keep the tables spread, the cans carried, and the gardens neat and fruitful. Not only did they leave behind them large houses; they left too an immense body of literature – poems, plays, novels, essays, histories, criticism. It was a very prolific, creative rich century – the nineteenth century. Now let us ask – is there any connection between that material prosperity and that intellectual creativeness? Did one lead to the other? How difficult it is to say – for we know so little about writers, and what conditions help them, what hinder them. It is only a guess, and a rough guess; yet I think that there is a connection. 'I think' – perhaps it would be nearer the truth to say 'I see'. Thinking should be based on facts; and here we have intuitions rather than facts – the lights and shades that come after books are read, the general shifting surface of a large expanse of print. What I see, glancing over that shifting surface, is the picture I have already shown you; the writer seated in front of human life in the nineteenth century; and, looking at it through their eyes, I see that life divided up, herded together, into many different classes. There is the aristocracy; the landed gentry; the professional class; the commercial class; the working class; and there, in one dark blot, is the great class which is called simply and comprehensively 'The Poor'. To the nineteenth-century writer human life must have looked like a landscape cut up into separate fields. In each field was gathered a different group of people. Each to some extent had its own traditions; its own manners, its own speech; its own dress; its own occupation. But owing to that peace, to that prosperity each group was tethered; stationary – a herd grazing within its own hedges. And the nineteenth-century writer did not seek to change those divisions; he accepted them. He accepted them so completely that he became unconscious of them. Does that serve to explain why it is that the nineteenth-century writers are able to create so many characters who are not types but individuals? Is it because he did not see the hedges that divide classes; he saw only the human beings that live within those hedges? Is that why he could get beneath the surface and create many-sided characters – Pecksniff, Becky Sharp, Mr Woodhouse[9] – who change with the years, as the living change? To us now the hedges are visible. We can see now that each of those writers only dealt with a very small section of human life – all Thackeray's characters are upper middle-class people; all Dickens's characters come from the lower or middle class. We can see that now; but the writer himself seems unconscious that he is only dealing with one type; with the type formed by the class into which the writer was born himself, with which he is most familiar. And that unconsciousness was an immense advantage to him.

Unconsciousness, which means presumably that the under mind works at top speed while the upper mind drowses, is a state we all know. We all have experience of the work done by unconsciousness in our own daily lives. You have had a crowded day, let us suppose, sightseeing in London. Could you say what you had seen and done when you came back? Was it not all a blur, a confusion? But after what seemed a rest, a chance to turn aside and look at something different, the sights and sounds and sayings that had been of most interest to you swam to the surface, apparently of their own accord; and remained in memory; what was unimportant sunk into forgetfulness. So it is with the writer. After a hard day's work, trudging round, seeing all he can, feeling all he can, taking in the book of his mind innumerable notes, the writer becomes – if he can – unconscious.[10] In fact, his under mind works at top speed while his upper mind drowses. Then, after a pause the veil lifts; and there is the thing – the thing he wants to write about – simplified, composed. Do we strain Wordsworth's famous saying about emotion recollected in tranquillity[11] when we infer that by tranquillity he meant that the writer needs to become unconscious before he can create?

If we want to risk a theory then, we can say that peace and prosperity were influences that gave the nineteenth-century writers a family likeness. They had leisure; they had security; life was not going to change; they themselves were not going to change. They could look; and look away. They could forget; and then – in their books – remember. Those then are some of the conditions that brought about a certain family likeness, in spite of the great individual differences, among the nineteenth-century writers. The nineteenth century ended; but the same conditions went on. They lasted, roughly speaking, till the year 1914. Even in 1914 we can still see the writer sitting as he sat all through the nineteenth century looking at human life; and that human life is still divided into classes; he still looks most intently at the class from which he himself springs; the classes are still so settled that he has almost forgotten that there are classes; and he is still so secure himself that he is almost unconscious of his own position and of its security. He believes that he is looking at the whole of life; and will always so look at it. That is not altogether a fancy picture. Many of those writers are still alive. Sometimes they describe their own position as young men, beginning to write, just before August 1914. How did you learn your art? one can ask them. At College they say – by reading; by listening; by talking. What did they talk about? Here is Mr Desmond MacCarthy's answer,[12] as he gave it, a week or two ago, in the *Sunday Times*. He was at Cambridge just before the war began and he says: 'We were not very much interested in politics. Abstract speculation was much more absorbing; philosophy was more interesting to us than public causes . . . What we chiefly discussed were those "goods", which were ends in themselves . . . the search for truth, aesthetic emotions, and personal relations.' In addition they read an immense amount; Latin and Greek, and of course French and English. They wrote too – but they were in no hurry to publish. They travelled; – some of them went far afield – to India, to the South Seas. But for the most part they rambled happily in the long summer holidays through England, through France, through Italy. And now and then they published books – books like Rupert Brooke's poems;[13] novels like E. M. Forster's *Room with a View*;[14] essays like G. K. Chesterton's essays,[15] and reviews. It seemed to them that they were to go on living like that, and writing like that for ever and ever. Then suddenly, like a chasm in a smooth road, the war came.

But before we go on with the story of what happened after 1914, let us look more closely for a moment, not at the writer himself, nor at his model; but at his chair. A chair is a very important part of a writer's outfit. It is the chair that gives him his attitude towards his model; that decides what he sees of human life; that profoundly affects his power of telling us what he sees. By his chair we mean his upbringing, his education. It is a fact, not a theory, that all writers from Chaucer to the present day, with so few exceptions that one hand can count them, have sat upon the same kind of chair – a raised chair. They have all come from the middle class; they have had good, at least expensive, educations. They have all been raised above the mass of people upon a tower of stucco – that is their middle-class birth; and of gold – that is their expensive education. That was true of all the nineteenth-century writers, save D. H. Lawrence. Let us run through what are called 'representative names': G. K. Chesterton; T. S. Eliot; Belloc; Lytton Strachey; Somerset Maugham; Hugh Walpole; Wilfred Owen; Rupert Brooke; J. E. Flecker; E. M. Forster; Aldous Huxley; G. M. Trevelyan; O. and S. Sitwell; Middleton Murry.[16] Those are some of them; and all, with the exception of D. H. Lawrence, came of the middle class, and were educated at public schools and universities. There is another fact, equally indisputable: the books that they wrote were among the best books written between 1910 and 1925. Now let us ask, is there any connection between those facts? Is there a connection between the excellence of their work and the fact that they came of families rich enough to send them to public schools and universities?

Must we not decide, greatly though those writers differ, and shallow as we admit our knowledge of influences to be, that there must be a connection between their education and their work? It cannot be a mere chance that this minute class of educated people has produced so much that is good as writing; and that the vast mass of people without education has produced so little that is good. It is a fact, however. Take away all that the working class has given to English literature and that literature would scarcely suffer; take away all that the educated class has given, and English literature would scarcely exist. Education must then play a very important part in a writer's work.

That seems so obvious, that it is astonishing how little stress has been laid upon the writer's education. Perhaps it is because a writer's education is so much less definite than other educations. Reading, listening, talking, travel, leisure – many different things it seems are mixed together. Life and books must be shaken and taken in the right proportions. A boy brought up alone in a library turns into a book worm; brought up alone in the fields he turns into an earth worm. To breed the kind of butterfly a writer is you must let him sun himself for three or four years at Oxford or Cambridge – so it seems. However it is done, it is there that it is done – there that he is taught his art. And he has to be taught his art. Again, is that strange? Nobody thinks it strange[17] if you say that a painter has to be taught his art; or a musician; or an architect. Equally a writer has to be taught. For the art of writing is at least as difficult as the other arts. And though, perhaps because the education is indefinite, people ignore this education, if you look closely you will see that almost every writer who has practised his art successfully had been taught it. He had been taught it by about eleven years of education – at private schools, public schools and universities. He sits upon a tower raised above the rest of us; a tower built first on his parents' station, then on his parents' gold. It is a tower of the utmost importance; it decides his angle of vision; it affects his power of communication.

All through the nineteenth century, down to August 1914, that tower was a steady tower. The writer was scarcely conscious either of his high station, or of his limited vision. Many of them had sympathy, great sympathy, with other classes; they wished to help the working class to enjoy the advantages of the tower class; but they did not wish to destroy the tower, or to descend from it – rather to make it accessible to all. Nor had the model, human life changed essentially since Trollope looked at it, since Hardy looked at it: and Henry James, in 1914, was still looking at it. Also, the tower itself held firm beneath the writer during all the most impressionable years, when he was learning his art, and receiving all those complex influences and instructions that are summed up by the word education. These were conditions that influenced their work profoundly. For when the crash came in 1914 all those young men who were to be the representative writers of their time, had their past, their education, safe behind them, safe within them. They had known security; they had the memory of a peaceful boyhood, the knowledge of a settled civilization. Even though the war cut into their lives, and ended some of them, they wrote, and still write, as if the tower were firm beneath them. In one word, they are aristocrats; the unconscious inheritors of a great tradition. Put a page of their writing under the magnifying glass and you will see, far away in the distance, the Greeks, the Romans; coming nearer the Elizabethans; coming nearer still Dryden, Swift, Voltaire, Jane Austen, Dickens, Henry James. Each, however much he differs individually from the others, is a man of education; a man who has learnt his art.

From that group let us pass to the next – to the group which began to write about 1925 and, it may be, came to an end as a group in 1939. If you read current literary journalism you will be able to rattle off a string of names – Day Lewis, Auden, Spender, Isherwood, Louis MacNeice and so on. They adhere much more closely than the names of their predecessors. But at first sight there seems little difference, in station, in education. Mr Auden in a poem written to Mr Isherwood says:[18] Behind us we have stucco suburbs and expensive educations. They are tower dwellers like their predecessors, the sons of well-to-do parents, who could afford to send them to public schools and universities. But what a difference in the tower itself, in what they saw from the tower! When they looked at human life what did they see? Everywhere change; everywhere revolution. In Germany, in Russia, in Italy, in Spain,[19] all the old hedges were being rooted up; all the old towers were being thrown to the ground. Other hedges were being planted; other towers were being raised. There was communism in one country; in another fascism. The whole of civilization, of society, was changing. There was, it is true, neither war nor revolution in England itself. All those writers had time to write many books before 1939. But even in England towers that were built of gold and stucco were no longer steady towers. They were leaning towers. The books were written under the influence of change, under the threat of war. That perhaps is why the names adhere so closely; there was one influence that affected them all and made them, more than their predecessors, into groups. And that influence, let us remember, may well have excluded from that string of names the poets whom posterity will value most highly, either because they could not fall into step, as leaders or as followers, or because the influence was adverse to poetry, and until that influence relaxed, they could not write. But the tendency that makes it possible for us to group the names of these writers together, and gives their work a common likeness, was the tendency of the tower they sat on – the tower of middle-class birth and expensive education – to lean.

Let us imagine, to bring this home to us, that we are actually upon a leaning tower and note our sensations. Let us see whether they correspond to the tendencies we observe in those poems, plays and novels. Directly we feel that a tower leans we become acutely conscious that we are upon a tower. All those writers too are acutely tower conscious; conscious of their middle-class birth; of their expensive educations. Then when we come to the top of the tower how strange the view looks – not altogether upside down, but slanting, sidelong. That too is characteristic of the leaning-tower writers; they do not look any class straight in the face; they look either up, or down, or sidelong. There is no class so settled that they can explore it unconsciously. That perhaps is why they create no characters. Then what do we feel next, raised in imagination on top of the tower? First discomfort; next self-pity for that discomfort; which pity soon turns to anger – to anger against the builder, against society, for making us uncomfortable. Those too seem to be tendencies of the leaning-tower writers. Discomfort; pity for themselves; anger against society. And yet – here is another tendency – how can you altogether abuse a society that is giving you after all a very fine view and some sort of security? You cannot abuse that society wholeheartedly while you continue to profit by that society. And so very naturally you abuse society in the person of some retired admiral or spinster or armament manufacturer; and by abusing them hope to escape whipping yourself. The bleat of the scapegoat sounds loud in their work, and the whimper of the schoolboy crying 'Please Sir it was the other fellow, not me.' Anger; pity; scapegoat bleating; excuse finding – these are all very natural tendencies; if we were in their position we should tend to do the same. But we are not in their position; we have not had eleven years of expensive education. We have only been climbing an imaginary tower. We can cease to imagine. We can come down.

But they cannot. They cannot throw away their education; they cannot throw away their upbringing. Eleven years at school and college have been stamped upon them indelibly. And then, to their credit but to their confusion, the leaning tower not only leant in the thirties, but it leant more and more to the left. Do you remember what Mr MacCarthy said about his own group at the university in 1914? 'We were not very much interested in politics . . . philosophy was more interesting to us than public causes'? That shows that his tower leant neither to the right nor to the left. But in 1930 it was impossible – if you were young, sensitive, imaginative – not to be interested in politics; not to find public causes of much more pressing interest than philosophy. In 1930 young men at college were forced to be aware of what was happening in Russia; in Germany; in Italy; in Spain. They could not go on discussing aesthetic emotions and personal relations. They could not confine their reading to the poets; they had to read the politicians. They read Marx. They become communists; they became anti-fascists. The tower they realized was founded upon injustice and tyranny; it was wrong for a small class to possess an education that other people paid for; wrong to stand upon the gold that a bourgeois father had made from his bourgeois profession. It was wrong; yet how could they make it right? Their education could not be thrown away; as for their capital – did Dickens, did Tolstoy ever throw away their capital? Did D. H. Lawrence, a miner's son, continue to live like a miner? No; for it is death for a writer to throw away his capital; to be forced to earn his living in a mine or a factory. And thus, trapped by their education, pinned down by their capital they remained on top of their leaning tower, and their state of mind as we see it reflected in their poems and plays and novels is full of discord and bitterness, full of confusion and of compromise.

These tendencies are better illustrated by quotation than by analysis. There is a poem, by one of those writers, Louis MacNeice, called *Autumn Journal*.[20] It is dated March 1939. It is feeble as poetry, but interesting as autobiography. He begins of course with a snipe at the scapegoat – the bourgeois, middle-class family from which he sprang. The retired admirals, the retired generals and the spinster lady have breakfasted off bacon and eggs served on a silver dish, he tells us. He sketches that family as if it were already a little remote and more than a little ridiculous. But they could afford to send him to Marlborough[21] and then to Merton, Oxford. This is what he learnt at Oxford:

> We learned that a gentleman never misplaces his accents,
> That nobody knows how to speak, much less how to write
> English who has not hob-nobbed with the great-grandparents of
>   English.

Besides that he learnt at Oxford Latin and Greek; and philosophy, logic and metaphysics:

> Oxford [he says] crowded the mantelpiece with gods –
>   Scaliger, Heinsius, Dindorf, Bentley, Wilamowitz

It was at Oxford that the tower began to lean. He felt that he was living under a system –

> That gives the few at fancy prices their fancy lives
> While ninety-nine in the hundred who never attend the banquet
> Must wash the grease of ages off the knives.

But at the same time, an Oxford education had made him fastidious:

> It is so hard to imagine
> A world where the many would have their chance without
> A fall in the standard of intellectual living
> And nothing left that the highbrow cares about.

At Oxford he got his honours degree; and that degree – in humane letters[22] – put him in the way of a 'cushy job' – seven hundred a year, to be precise, and several rooms of his own.

> If it were not for Lit. Hum. I might be climbing
> A ladder with a hod
> And seven hundred a year
> Will pay the rent and the gas and the phone and the grocer –

And yet, again, doubts break in; the 'cushy job' of teaching more Latin and Greek to more undergraduates does not satisfy him –

> . . . the so-called humane studies
> May lead to cushy jobs
> But leave the men who land them spiritually bankrupt,
> Intellectual snobs.

And what is worse, that education and that cushy job cut one off, he complains, from the common life of one's kind.

> All that I would like to be is human, having a share
> In a civilized, articulate and well-adjusted
> Community where the mind is given its due
> But the body is not distrusted.

Therefore, in order to bring about that well-adjusted community he must turn from literature to politics, remembering, he says,

> Remembering that those who by their habit
> Hate politics, can no longer keep their private
> Values unless they open the public gate
> To a better political system.

So, in one way or another, he takes part in politics, and finally he ends:

> What is it we want really?
> For what end and how?
> If it is something feasible, obtainable,
> Let us dream it now,
> And pray for a possible land
> Not of sleep-walkers, not of angry puppets,
> But where both heart and brain can understand
> The movements of our fellows
> Where life is a choice of instruments and none
> Is debarred his natural music . . .
> Where the individual, no longer squandered
> In self-assertion, works with the rest . . .

Those quotations give a fair description of the influences that have told upon the leaning-tower group. Others could easily be discovered. The influence of the films explains the lack of transitions in their work and the violently opposed contrasts. The influence of poets like Mr Yeats and Mr Eliot explains the obscurity. They took over from the elder poets a technique which, after many years of experiment, those poets used skilfully, and used it clumsily and often inappropriately. But we have time only to point to the most obvious influences; and these can be summed up as Leaning Tower Influences. If you think of them, that is, as people trapped on a leaning tower from which they cannot descend, much that is puzzling in their work is easier to understand. It explains the violence of their attack upon bourgeois society and also its half-heartedness. They are profiting by a society which they abuse. They are flogging a dead or dying horse because a living horse, if flogged, would kick them off its back. It explains the destructiveness of their work; and also its emptiness. They can destroy bourgeois society, in part at least; but what have they put in its place? How can a writer who has no first-hand experience of a towerless, of a classless society create that society? Yet as Mr MacNeice bears witness, they feel compelled to preach, if not by their living, at least by their writing, the creation of a society in which every one is equal and every one is free. It explains the pedagogic, the didactic, the loud speaker strain[23] that dominates their poetry. They must teach; they must preach. Everything is a duty – even love. Listen to Mr Day Lewis ingeminating love.[24] 'Mr Spender,' he says, 'speaking from the living unit of himself and his friends appeals for the contraction of the social group to a size at which human contact may again be established and demands the destruction of all impediments to love. Listen.' And we listen to this:

> We have come at last to a country
> Where light, like shine from snow, strikes all faces
> Here you may wonder
> How it was that works, money, interest, building could ever
> Hide the palpable and obvious love of man for man.

We listen to oratory not to poetry. It is necessary, in order to feel the emotion of those lines, that other people should be listening too. We are in a group, in a class-room[25] as we listen.

Listen now to Wordsworth:

> Lover had he known in huts where poor men dwell
> His daily teachers had been woods and rills,

The silence that is in the starry sky,
The sleep that is among the lonely hills[26]

We listen to that when we are alone. We remember that in solitude. Is that the difference between politician's poetry and poet's poetry? We listen to the one in company; to the other when we are alone. But the poet in the thirties was forced to be a politician. That explains why the artist in the thirties was forced to be a scapegoat. If politics were 'real', the ivory tower was an escape from 'reality'. That explains the curious bastard language in which so much of this leaning over the prose and poetry is written. It is not the rich speech of the aristocrat: it is not the racy speech of the peasant. It is betwixt and between. The poet is a dweller in two worlds, one dying, the other struggling to be born.[27] And so we come to what is perhaps the most marked tendency of leaning-tower literature – the desire to be whole; to be human. 'All that I would like to be is human' – that cry rings through their books – the longing to be closer to their kind, to write the common speech of their kind, to share the emotions of their kind, no longer to be isolated and exalted in solitary state upon their tower, but to be down on the ground with the mass of human kind.

These then, briefly and from a certain angle, are some of the tendencies of the modern writer who is seated upon a leaning tower. No other generation has been exposed to them. It may be that none has had such an appallingly difficult task. Who can wonder if they have been incapable of giving us great poems, great plays, great novels? They had nothing settled to look at; nothing peaceful to remember; nothing certain to come. During all the most impressionable years of their lives they were stung into consciousness – into self-consciousness, into class-consciousness, into the consciousness of things changing, of things falling, of death perhaps about to come. There was no tranquillity in which they could recollect. The inner mind was paralysed, because the surface mind was always hard at work.

Yet if they have lacked the creative power of the poet and the novelist, the power – does it come from a fusion of the two minds, the upper and the under? – that creates characters that live, poems that we all remember, they have had a power which, if literature continues, may prove to be of great value in the future. They have been great egotists. That too was forced upon them by their circumstances. When everything is rocking round one, the only person who remains comparatively stable is oneself. When all faces are changing and obscured, the only face one can see clearly is one's own. So they wrote about themselves – in their plays, in their poems, in their novels. No other ten years can have produced so much autobiography as the ten years between 1930 and 1940. No one, whatever his class or his obscurity, seems to have reached the age of thirty without writing his autobiography. But the leaning-tower writers wrote about themselves honestly, therefore creatively. They told the unpleasant truths, not only the flattering truths. That is why their autobiography is so much better than their fiction or their poetry. Consider how difficult it is to tell the truth about oneself – the unpleasant truth; to admit that one is petty, vain, mean, frustrated, tortured, unfaithful, and unsuccessful. The nineteenth-century writers never told that kind of truth, and that is why so much of the nineteenth-century writing is worthless; why, for all their genius, Dickens and Thackeray seem so often to write about dolls and puppets,[28] not about full-grown men and women; why they are forced to evade the main themes and make do with diversions instead. If you do not tell the truth about yourself you cannot tell it about other people. As the nineteenth century wore on, the writers knew that they were crippling themselves, diminishing their material, falsifying their object. 'We are condemned,' Stevenson wrote,[29] 'to avoid half the life that passes us by. What books Dickens could have written had he been permitted! Think of Thackeray as unfettered as Flaubert or Balzac! What books I might have written myself? But they give us a little box of toys and say to us "You mustn't play with anything but these"!' Stevenson blamed society – bourgeois society was his scapegoat too. Why did he not blame himself? Why did he consent to go on playing with his little box of toys?

The leaning-tower writer has had the courage, at any rate, to throw that little box of toys out of the window. He has had the courage to tell the truth, the unpleasant truth, about himself. That is the first step towards telling the truth about other people. By analysing themselves honestly, with help from Dr Freud,[30] these writers have done a great deal to free us from nineteenth-century suppressions. The writers of the next generation may inherit from them a whole state of mind, a mind no longer crippled, evasive, divided. They may inherit that unconsciousness which as we guessed – it is only a guess – at the beginning of this paper is necessary if writers are to get beneath the surface, and to write something that people remember when they are alone. For that great gift of unconsciousness the next generation will have to thank the creative and honest egotism of the leaning-tower group.

The next generation – there will be a next generation, in spite of this war and whatever it brings. Have we time then for a rapid glance, for a hurried guess at the next generation? The next generation will be, when peace comes, a post-war generation too. Must it too be a leaning-tower generation – an oblique, sidelong self-centred, self-conscious generation – with a foot in two worlds? Or will there be no more towers and no more classes and shall we stand, without hedges between us, on the common ground?

There are two reasons which lead us to think, perhaps to hope, that the world after the war will be a world without classes or towers. Every politician who has made a speech since September 1939 has ended with a peroration in which he has said that we are not fighting this war for conquest; but to bring about a new order in Europe. In that order, they tell us, we are all to have equal opportunities, equal chances of developing whatever gifts we may possess. That is one reason why, if they mean what they say, and can effect it, classes and towers will disappear. The other reason is given by the income tax. The income tax is already doing in its own way what the politicians are hoping to do in theirs. The income tax is saying to middle-class parents: You cannot afford to send your sons to public schools any longer; you must send them to the elementary schools. One of these parents wrote to the *New Statesman*[31] a week or two ago. Her little boy, who was to have gone to Winchester,[32] had been taken away from his elementary school and sent to the village school. 'He has never been happier in his life,' she wrote. 'The question of class does not arise; he is merely interested to find how many different kinds of people there are in the world . . .' And she is only paying twopence half-penny a week for that happiness and instruction instead of 35 guineas[33] a term and extras. If the pressure of the income tax continues, classes will disappear. There will be no more upper classes; middle classes; lower classes. All classes will be merged in one class. How will that change affect the writer who sits at his desk looking at human life? It will not be divided by hedges any more. Very likely that will be the end of the novel, as we know it. Literature, as we know it, is always ending, and beginning again. Remove the hedges from Jane Austen's world, from Trollope's world, and how much of their comedy and tragedy would remain? We shall regret our Jane Austens and our Trollopes; they gave us comedy, tragedy and beauty. But much of that old-class literature was very petty; very false; very dull. Much is already unreadable. The novel of a classless and towerless world should be a better novel than the old novel. The novelist will have more interesting people to describe – people who have had a chance to develop their humour, their gifts, their tastes; real people, not people cramped and squashed into featureless masses[34] by hedges. The poet's gain is less obvious; for he has been less under the dominion of hedges. But he should gain words; when we have pooled all the different dialects, the clipped and cabined vocabulary[35] which is all that he uses now should be enriched. Further, there might then be a common belief which he could accept, and thus shift from his shoulders the burden of didacticism, of propaganda. These then are a few reasons, hastily snatched, why we can look forward hopefully to a stronger, a more varied literature in the classless and towerless society of the future.

But it is in the future; and there is a deep gulf to be bridged between the dying world, and the world that is struggling to be born. For there are still two worlds, two separate worlds. 'I want,' said the mother who wrote to the paper the other day about her boy, 'the best of both worlds for my son.' She wanted, that is, the village school, where he learnt to mix with the living; and the other school – Winchester it was – where he mixed with the dead. 'Is he to continue,' she asked, 'under the system of free national education, or shall he go on – or should I say back – to the old public school system which really is so very, very private?' She wanted the new world and the old world to unite, the world of the present and the world of the past.

But there is still a gulf between them, a dangerous gulf, in which, possibly, literature may crash and come to grief. It is easy to see that gulf; it is easy to lay the blame for it upon England. England has crammed a small aristocratic class with Latin and Greek and logic and metaphysics and mathematics until they cry out like the young men on the leaning tower, 'All that I would like to be is human'. She has left the other class, the immense class to which almost all of us must belong, to pick up what we can in village schools; in factories; in workshops; behind counters; and at home. When one thinks of that criminal injustice one is tempted to say England deserves to have no literature. She deserves to have nothing but detective stories, patriotic songs and leading articles for generals, admirals and business men to read themselves to sleep with when they are tired of winning battles and making money. But let us not be unfair; let us avoid if we can joining the embittered and futile tribe of scapegoat hunters. For some years now England has been making an effort – at last – to bridge the gulf between the two worlds. Here is one proof of that effort – this book. This book was not bought; it was not hired. It was borrowed from a public library. England lent it to a common reader,[36] saying 'It is time that even you, whom I have shut out from all my universities for centuries, should learn to read your mother tongue. I will help you.' If England is going to help us, we must help her. But how? Look at what is written in the book she has lent us. 'Readers are requested to point out any defects[37] that they may observe to the local librarian.' That is England's way of saying: 'If I lend you books, I expect you to make yourselves critics.'

We can help England very greatly to bridge the gulf between the two worlds if we borrow the books she lends us and if we read them critically. We have got to teach ourselves to understand literature. Money is no longer going to do our thinking for us. Wealth will no longer decide who shall be taught and who not. In future it is we who shall decide whom to send to public schools and universities; how they shall be taught; and whether what they write justifies their exemption from other work. In order to do that we must teach ourselves to distinguish – which is the book that is going to pay dividends of pleasure[38] for ever; which is the book that will pay not a penny in two years' time? Try it for yourselves on new books as they come out; decide which are the lasting, which are the perishing. That is very difficult. Also we must become critics because in future we are not going to leave writing to be done for us by a small class of well-to-do young men who have only a pinch, a thimbleful of experience to give us. We are going to add our own experience, to make our own contribution. That is even more difficult. For that too we need to be critics. A writer, more than any other artist, needs to be a critic because words are so common, so familiar, that he must sieve them and sift them if they are to become enduring. Write daily; write freely; but let us always compare what we have written with what the great writers have written. It is humiliating, but it is essential. If we are going to preserve and to create, that is the only way. And we are going to do both. We need not wait till the end of the war. We can begin now. We can begin, practically and prosaically, by borrowing books from public libraries; by reading omnivorously, simultaneously, poems, plays, novels, histories, biographies, the old and the new. We must sample before we can select.[39] It never does to be a nice feeder; each of us has an appetite that must find for itself the food that nourishes it. Nor let us shy away from the kings because we are commoners. That is a fatal crime in the eyes of Aeschylus, Shakespeare, Virgil and Dante, who, if they could speak – and after all they can – would say, 'Don't leave me to the wigged and gowned.[40] Read me, read me for yourselves.' They do not mind if we get our accents wrong, or have to read with a crib in front of us. Of course – are we not commoners, outsiders? – we shall trample many flowers and bruise much ancient grass. But let us bear in mind a piece of advice that an eminent Victorian who was also an eminent pedestrian[41] once gave to walkers: 'Whenever you see a board up with "Trespassers will be prosecuted", trespass at once.'

Let us trespass at once. Literature is no one's private ground; literature is common ground. It is not cut up into nations; there are no wars there. Let us trespass freely and fearlessly and find our own way for ourselves. It is thus that English literature will survive this war and cross the gulf – if commoners and outsiders like ourselves make that country our own country, if we teach ourselves how to read and write, how to preserve and how to create.

Notes

THE FEMININE NOTE IN FICTION

1. See *Passionate Apprentice*, p. 276.
2. *Mrs Humphry Ward*: Victorian novelist and philanthropist, (1851–1920), whose biography is reviewed in 'The Compromise', pp. 53ff.
3. *study of the Greek and Latin classics*: Woolf had herself been engaged in such studies from 1902, under the supervision of Janet Case. Middle-class girls' exclusion from this aspect of their brothers' education was a theme she often addressed, both explicitly and implicitly (for instance, in 'On Not Knowing Greek', pp. 93ff).

THE DECAY OF ESSAY-WRITING

1. *mystery-plays*: medieval religious drama.
2. *it is at least as old as Montaigne*: his *Essais*, the first examples of the form, were published in 1580 – see 'Montaigne', pp. 56ff.
3. *the essays of Elia*: by Charles Lamb, published in the *London Magazine* and elsewhere in the 1820s and 1830s.

THE AMERICAN WOMAN

1. see *Passionate Apprentice*, pp. 219, 276.
2. *Blue-book*: an official parliamentary report.

WOMEN NOVELISTS

1. *Dr Burney's daughter*: Fanny Burney's father was a musician.
2. *male pseudonyms*: Charlotte Brontë initially published under the name Currer Bell; George Eliot's real name was Marian Evans.
3. *a Becky Sharp ... a Mr Woodhouse*: characters in *Vanity Fair* (1848), by Thackeray, and *Emma* (1816), by Jane Austen.

THE TUNNEL

1. *the fourth book*: The Tunnel was part of Dorothy Richardson's 'Pilgrimage' sequence, which ran to twelve volumes. Woolf's

review of the seventh, *Revolving Lights*, is in 'Romance and the Heart' (pp. 50 ff). She felt a degree of unease in reviewing Richardson's work since they had comparable aims and she found herself 'looking for faults; hoping for them' (*Diary*, I, 28 Nov. 1919, p. 315).

MEN AND WOMEN

1. *Blue-books*: see 'The American Woman', Note 2.
2. *Lady Macbeth . . . Helen*: Lady Macbeth is from Shakespeare's *Macbeth* (1606); Cordelia is from *King Lear* (1606); Ophelia is from *Hamlet* (1603); Clarissa is from Samuel Richardson's novel of the same name, (1748); Dora is from Dickens' *David Copperfield* (1850); Diana is from Meredith's *Diana of the Crossways* (1885); and Helen is from Thackeray's *Pendennis* (1850).
3. *Rochester*: Jane Eyre's lover in Charlotte Brontë's *Jane Eyre* (1847).
4. *Isopel Berners*: a character in George Borrow's novels *Lavengro* (1851), and *The Romany Rye* (1857).
5. *En fait, le désir . . . où elle vit*: the passage may be translated:

   In fact, the woman's desire to get outside herself, to surpass the limits up till then assigned to her activity, is born at the very moment when her life is less narrowly tied at every minute to domestic tasks, the jobs which, one or two generations before, absorbed her attention and used her strengths. The spinning-wheel, the needle, the distaff, the preparation of jams and preserves, and even of candles and soaps . . . no longer occupy women, and whereas the old-fashioned housewife is disappearing, the one who will tomorrow be the new woman feels growing in her, together with the leisure to see, to think, to judge, a consciousness of herself and the world in which she lives.

6. *Bathsheba in Far from the Madding Crowd*: Hardy's novel was published by Smith, Elder & Co. in 1874; the quotation is from chapter LI: 'It is difficult for a woman to define her feelings in a language which is chiefly made by men to express theirs.'

FREUDIAN FICTION

1. *Dr Freud*: (1856–1939), Woolf was familiar with his work from an early stage since it was translated into English by her friend James Strachey, Lytton's brother, and published by the Hogarth Press from 1922 onwards.
2. *the Lancet*: a highly respected medical journal.

AN IMPERFECT LADY

1. *Little is known of Sappho . . . Maria Edgeworth:* for a similar parody of clichés about authors, see 'Indiscretions', pp. 88ff. Sappho (lived seventh century BC), the lyric poet born in Lesbos; Lady Jane Grey (1537–54), the great-granddaughter of Henry VII, was forced to become Queen and was subsequently executed – she was the author of letters and religious writings; George Sand (1804–76), the prolific French romantic novelist; Harriet Martineau (1802–76), wrote on a variety of social and political issues; Maria Edgeworth (1767–1849), the novelist and woman of letters.
2. *William Pitt*: (1759–1806), was Britain's youngest ever Prime Minister at the age of twenty-four.
3. *Monmouth*: the Duke of Monmouth, leader of the rebellion (1685).
4. *Mrs Sherwood*: Mary Sherwood (1775–1851), the highly didactic children's writer, author of *The Fairchild Family* (1816).
5. *the Cobb*: the famous landmark at Lyme Regis is the site of Louisa Musgrove's fall in Jane Austen's *Persuasion* (1818).
6. *Mr Crissy*: the publisher of *The Works of M. R. Mitford, Prose and Verse* (1840).
7. *for a lady, too, who owns a teapot:* Woolf is satirizing Hill's obsession with domestic ephemera.

THE PLUMAGE BILL

1. *Wayfarer*: the pen-name of H. W. Massingham, editor of the *Nation*. The following month, in the context of a diatribe against journalism associated with the relief of getting back to the country after London, Woolf referred to this piece as her 'vendetta against Massingham, against whom my arrow was launched' (*Diary*, II 17 Aug. 1920, p. 58). In 1919, she had had a more personal cause for irritation with Wayfarer, who had included in his column a

paragraph putting down Woolf's novel *Night and Day*, which had just appeared (see *Diary*, I, 5 Nov. 1919, p. 316).

2. *The Plumage Bill*: though its failure this time had been the subject of Wayfarer's column, this bill for restrictions on the import of birds and feathers was passed the following year.

THE INTELLECTUAL STATUS OF WOMEN

1. *Lady Mary Montagu's remark*: in a letter to Lady Bute, 5 January 1748 (*The Complete Letters of Lady Mary Wortley Montagu*, 3 vols., ed. Robert Halsband, OUP, 1965–7, II, p. 392).

2. *Yes; unless you believe . . . a woman wrote the Odyssey*: in *The Authoress of the Odyssey* (1897), Samuel Butler had suggested that the epic had been written by a woman, arguing that it featured so many and such interesting women.

3. *Ford*: Henry Ford (1863–1947), the American industrialist and advocate of mass-production, founder of the Ford Motor Co. (1903).

4. *These Twain*: (1916) a novel by Arnold Bennett.

5. *When I compare the Duchess of Newcastle with . . . Jane Harrison*: Woolf drew up a similar list of women writers at the beginning of 'An Imperfect Lady'. The 'matchless Orinda' was the seventeenth-century poet Kathleen Philips (1631–64), thus described on her title pages; Eliza Heywood (1693–1756) was an actress, playwright and novelist; Aphra Behn (1640–89) was a prolific playwright, poet and novelist, and one of the first women to earn a living by writing; Jane Grey (1537–54), the great-granddaughter of Henry VII and queen for nine days, wrote letters and prayers; Jane Harrison (1850–1928) was a classical scholar whose work on the representation of women in pre-classical Greece was much admired by Woolf.

6. *Archilochus*: the Greek satiric poet (714–676 BC).

7. *Herculaneum*: the Roman city buried under volcanic lava from nearby Vesuvius.

8. *Burns*: Robert Burns (1756–96), the Scottish dialect poet.

9. *Aquinas or Thomas à Kempis*: Thomas Aquinas (*c.* 1225–74) and Thomas à Kempis (*c.* 1380–1471) were both major religious thinkers of the Middle Ages.

10. *Harriet Martineau . . . Mrs Taylor*: Harriet Martineau (1802–76) was a well-known woman of letters. The Victorian philosopher John Stuart Mill thought Harriet Taylor (1808–59), later his wife, his intellectual superior. She was a strong advocate of women's rights,

and it was under her influence that he wrote *The Subjection of Women* (1869), a substantial contribution to the subject.

11. *Herschel ... Faraday ... Laplace*: Sir William Herschel (1738–1822), a pioneering astronomer, discovered the planet Uranus and the moons of Saturn; Michael Faraday (1791–1867), a chemist and physicist, made important discoveries concerning electricity; Pierre Simon de Laplace (1749–1827) was an astronomer and mathematician who theorized about the creation of the universe.

12. *Mendel*: Gregor Mendel (1822–84) was an Austrian monk who formulated the laws of genetics.

13. *Marie Corelli ... Mrs Barclay*: Woolf's 'bad women writers' – Corelli (1855–1924) and Florence Barclay (1862–1921) – were authors of popular romances.

14. *J. A. Symonds*: from his *Studies of the Greek Poets* (2 vols., 3rd edn, 1893, I, p. 291).

15. *Ethel Smyth*: (1858–1944) a composer and committed feminist. Woolf had read her memoirs, *Impressions that Remained* (1919), the previous year (see *Diary*, I, 28 Nov. 1919, p. 315), though it was not until 1930 that the two women met and became friends.

THE MODERN ESSAY

1. *As Mr Rhys truly says*: in his introduction to volume I.

2. *Sirannez the Persian*: was quoted in Montaigne's essay 'Of the Art of Discussion' as having said, 'that he was master of his plans, but of the outcome of his affairs Fortune was his mistress.'

3. *God and Spinoza ... turtles and Cheapside*: Matthew Arnold's 'A Word about Spinoza', a criticism of Robert Willis's translation of Spinoza's *Tractatus Theologico-Politicus*, appears in volume I of Rhys's anthology; the turtles are in a shop window in Samuel Butler's 'Ramblings in Cheapside' in volume II.

4. *as profound as Mark Pattison's*: Mark Pattison's essay 'Montaigne', a criticism of M. Grün's book on Montaigne, appears in volume I.

5. *Macaulay ... Froude*: Thomas Macaulay (1800–59), the politician, historian and essayist whose *History of England* (1849–55) was a celebrated bestseller; J. A. Froude (1818–94) was Regius Professor of Modern History at Oxford and an essayist.

6. *Fortnightly Review*: founded in 1865 as an organ of advanced liberalism, and initially edited by G. H. Lewes; it rapidly became monthly rather than fortnightly.

7. *Mr Hutton*: R. H. Hutton's essay 'Autobiography', is in volume I.

8. *Walter Pater*: Pater (1839–94), was a leading influence on the aesthetic movement of the 1880s; Wilde called his *Studies in the History of the Renaissance* (1873) 'the holy writ of beauty'. Pater's 'Notes on Leonardo da Vinci' is extracted in volume I.

9. *a gentleman of Polish extraction*: Joseph Conrad (1857–1924), Polish-born novelist and short-story writer, author of *Nostromo* (1904).

10. *the vigour of Swift*: in the earlier version, 'the vigour of Bacon'.

11. *Stevenson*: Robert Louis Stevenson's essay, in volume II, is called 'Walking Tours'. Woolf contrasts his style with that of Samuel Butler.

12. *a wound in the solicitor is a very serious thing*: in his essay, Butler is saying that a man can no more cut himself off from his financial and legal ties than he can cut off a leg; he then makes the metaphor literal with the chilling thought of injuring one's solicitor.

13. *Mary Queen of Scots wears surgical boots ... Tottenham Court Road*: Butler's point is that normal people can resemble the famous and long dead.

14. *Universal Review*: started in 1859 and intermittently issued until 1890.

15. *Mr Birrell and Mr Beerbohm*: Augustine Birrell's 'The Essays of Elia', and Max Beerbohm's 'A Cloud of Pinafores' are in volume III.

16. *Mr Birrell on Carlyle*: 'Carlyle', in volume II.

17. *A Cynic's Apology*: appeared in volume II; Leslie Stephen (1832–1904) was Virginia Woolf's father.

18. *Henley*: W. E. Henley's 'William Hazlitt' appeared in volume III.

19. *The drawing-room*: the Victorian drawing-room was common to both sexes, so everything in it had to suit accepted ideas of good taste.

20. *megaphone*: Woolf often uses the megaphone to suggest a crudeness in modern mass communication.

21. *An Unknown Country*: Hilaire Belloc's essay 'On an Unknown Country' appeared in volume IV.

22. *halfpenny ... sovereign*: the smallest and largest units of currency.

23. *Mr Conrad ... silvers everything*: Joseph Conrad's 'Tales of the Sea' appeared in volume IV; W. H. Hudson's 'The Samphire Gatherer' in volume V; E. V. Lucas's 'A Philosopher that Failed' in volume IV; Robert Lynd's 'Hawthorne' and J. C. Squire's 'A Dead Man' (subsequently quoted) in volume V. The phrase 'A common greyness silvers everything' is line 35 of Robert Browning's poem 'Andrea del Sarto' (*Men and Women*, II, 1855).

24. *Mr Clutton-Brock*: the essay by A. Clutton-Brock reviewing a produc-

tion of Mozart's *The Magic Flute* at the Albert Hall is in the final volume.

25. *Max*: Max Beerbohm.
26. *Nay, retire men ... to Scorn*: from Francis Bacon's essay, 'Of Great Place' (first published in his *Essays*, 1612).
27. *With courteous and polite cynicism ... perfumed*: from J. C. Squire's essay, 'A Dead Man'.
28. *a perpetual union*: in the earlier version, 'a perpetual life'.

ROMANCE AND THE HEART

1. *amaranth*: an imaginary flower that never fades.
2. *Revolving Lights*: Dorothy Richardson's novel was the seventh in her 'Pilgrimage' sequence; a review of the fourth, *The Tunnel*, is reprinted on pp. 15ff.
3. *Maggie Tulliver*: the heroine of George Eliot's novel *The Mill on the Floss* (1860).

THE COMPROMISE

1. *Mark Pattison ... J. R. Green*: Pattison (1813–84) the essayist and Rector of Lincoln College, Oxford; Green (1837–83) the historian and clergyman, and author of *The History of the English People* (1877–80).
2. *Robert Elsmere:* published in 1888.
3. *George Smith's pocket*: Mrs Ward's books were published by Smith, Elder & Co.
4. *against her will*: although Mrs Humphry Ward had always disapproved of women's suffrage she was at first reluctant to oppose it actively.

MONTAIGNE

1. *Why is it not ... crayon*: from Montaigne's *Essays*, Book II, 'Of Presumption'.
2. *Rousseau*: Jean-Jacques Rousseau (1712–78), the social, political and educational theorist and novelist, wrote his own *Confessions*.
3. *Religio Medici*: by Sir Thomas Browne; first published in 1642.
4. *a coloured glass through which darkly one sees*: cf. 1 Cor. 13:12.
5. *We hear of but ... employments of the world*: Montaigne's *Essays*, Book II, 'Of Exercitation'.
6. *So many cities ... Mechanic victories!*: from Book II, 'Of Experience'.

7. *What could I have said ... the laws*: from Book II, 'Of Experience'.

8. *as she broods over the fire in the inner room of that tower which ...*:
   Montaigne's study was in a tower but Woolf combines this image
   with that of the feminine soul ('l'âme') to personify inconstancy. So
   Montaigne's description of the inconstancy of his actions (quoted
   below) becomes a personification of the inconstancy of our *consciousness*. Woolf's characterization of this philosophical retreat –
   'to withdraw to the inner room of our tower and there turn the
   pages of books, pursue fancy after fancy as they chase each other
   up the chimney' – is also reminiscent of her essay on the Duchess of
   Newcastle (reprinted on pp. 107ff):

   > They lived together in the depths of the country in the greatest
   > seclusion and perfect contentment, scribbling plays, poems,
   > philosophies, greeting each other's works with raptures of
   > delight and confabulating, doubtless, upon such marvels of
   > the natural world as chance threw their way.

9. *bashful ... prodigal*: from Book II, 'Of the Inconstancy of our
   Actions'.

10. *jusques à ses verrues et à ses taches*: translated by Charles Cotton as,
    'even to her warts and blemishes', from Book III, 'Of Vanity'. (All
    other translations given here are taken from Cotton's version.)

11. *the mother of ignorance ... of fools*: from Book II, 'Of Glory'.

12. *Je n'enseigne poinct; je raconte*: 'I do not teach; I only relate,' from
    Book II, 'Of Repentance'.

13. *entirely ... word*: from Book II, 'Of the Inconstancy of our Actions'.

14. *Étienne de La Boétie*: (1530–63) was Montaigne's best friend and the
    inspiration for his essay 'Of Friendship' in Book I.

15. *C'est estre, mais ce n'est pas vivre, que de se tenir attaché et obligé par
    necessité à un seul train*: ''Tis to be, but not to live, to keep man's self
    tied and bound by necessity to one only course', from Book II, 'Of
    Three Employments'.

16. *un patron au dedans*: 'a pattern within ourselves', from Book II, 'Of Re-
    pentance'.

17. *C'est une vie ... son prive*: ''Tis an exact life that maintains itself in
    due order in private', from Book II, 'Of Repentance'.

18. *Epaminondas*: (410–362 BC) the Theban statesman and military tac-
    tician responsible for breaking the military dominance of Sparta.

19. *il faut vivre entre les vivants*: 'we must live among the living', from
    Book III, 'Of the Art of Conferring'.

20. *halcyons*: kingfishers.

21. *car, comme je scay . . . communication*: 'for, as I myself know by too certain experience, there is no so sweet consolation in the loss of friends as the conscience of having had no reserve or secret for them, and to have had with them a perfect and entire communication', from Book II, 'Of the Affection of Fathers for their Children'.

22. *se défendans . . . incogneu*: 'preserving themselves from the contagion of an unknown air', from Book II, 'Of Vanity'.

23. *Le plaisir . . . profit*: 'pleasure is one of the chiefest kinds of profit', from Book II, 'Of Experience'.

24. *Catullus*: (84?–54? BC) the best known of the Silver Latin lyric poets.

25. *parmy les jeux . . . amoureux*: 'amongst sports, feastings, wit and mirth, common and indifferent discourses, music, and amorous verses', from Book II, 'Of Vanity'.

26. *plus je me hante . . . en moy*: 'the more I frequent and the better I know myself, the more does my own deformity astonish me, the less I understand myself', from Book III, 'Of Cripples'.

27. *sans cesse et sans travail*: 'incessantly and without labour', from Book II, 'Of Vanity'.

28. *To this what answer can there be?*: in the earlier version, 'But to this there is no answer, only one more question . . .'

29. *Que scais-je?*: 'What do I know?', the motto that many consider to be Montaigne's central question, from Book II, 'Apology for Raymond Sebond'.

THE PATRON AND THE CROCUS

1. *bring to birth*: one of many uses in Woolf's metaphors of midwifery and maternity for the process of writing.

2. *affable*: the word is a pointed one in this context; Affable Hawk was the pen-name of Desmond MacCarthy, with whom Woolf had an argument in print over his *New Statesman* column on the subject of women's writing. Her contribution, 'The Intellectual Status of Women', appears on pp. 30 ff.

MR BENNETT AND MRS BROWN

1. This essay should not be confused with the essay of the same title printed in the 'Literary Review' of the *New York Evening Post* on 17 November 1923 (*Essays*, III, pp. 384–88). Making up a story about a stranger in a train was a favourite amusement for Woolf. It

provides the basis for 'An Unwritten Novel' (*The Complete Shorter Fiction*, 2nd edn, ed. Susan Dick, Hogarth Press, 1989), and also occurs in the sketch 'Byron and Mr Briggs', where she refers to it as 'this familiar game' (*Essays* III, appendix II, pp. 482–3). In a talk on Woolf given on the fiftieth anniversary of her death, Nigel Nicolson recalled her playing this game with him on a train from Sissinghurst to London in the 1920s: 'Woolf assured him, in Sherlock Holmes fashion, that the man opposite puffing a cigar was a bus conductor from Leeds. "How do you know?" asked the young Nicolson. For the rest of the journey, Woolf whispered into his ear, weaving an imaginary tale around the alleged bus conductor' (*The Times*, 23 May 1991).

2. *The foundation of good fiction ... will be its portion*: the quotation is from Arnold Bennett's article 'Is the Novel Decaying?' in *Cassell's Weekly* (28 March 1923), which prompted the first version of this piece by Woolf. Arnold Bennett (1867–1931) was a very popular Edwardian novelist, well-established by this time.

3. *Edwardians and Georgians*: Edward VII reigned from 1901 to 1910; George V from 1910 until 1936.

4. *in or about December 1910*: this date can be linked with the end of the Edwardian era (the King died in May) and with the Post-Impressionist exhibition that took place in London during the last two months of the year.

5. *The Way of All Flesh*: was published by Grant Richards in 1903.

6. *Daily Herald*: founded in 1912, this progressive paper was floundering in the early 1920s, but was to be relaunched with success in 1930, when it attained the highest ever daily circulation, more than two million.

7. *Agamemnon*: Aeschylus' play was first performed in 458 BC. Woolf takes it as one of her texts in 'On Not Knowing Greek', see pp. 93ff.

8. *the Carlyles*: on their domestic arrangements see also 'Great Men's Houses', reprinted in *The Crowded Dance of Modern Life* (Penguin Books, 1993).

9. *from Richmond to Waterloo*: Leonard and Virginia Woolf lived in Richmond, just outside London, until March 1924.

10. *corn-chandler*: a corn merchant.

11. *Dr Watson in Sherlock Holmes*: Conan Doyle's stories about the detective Sherlock Holmes and his assistant, Dr Watson, appeared from 1891.

12. *War and Peace ... Villette*: *War and Peace* (1864–9) by Tolstoy;

Vanity Fair (1848) by Thackeray; *Tristram Shandy* (1767) by Sterne; *Madame Bovary* (1856) by Flaubert; *Pride and Prejudice* (1813) by Jane Austen; *The Mayor of Casterbridge* (1886) by Hardy; and *Villette* (1853), by Charlotte Brontë.

13. *when October comes round*: autumn was the main period for the publication of new novels.

14. *Mr Wells ... Mr Galsworthy*: H. G. Wells (1866–1946), the highly popular science-fiction writer and chronicler of lower-middle-class life; John Galsworthy (1867–1933), the Edwardian novelist famous for *The Forsyte Saga* (1922).

15. *Mile End Road*: a poor area in the East End of London.

16. *Surrey*: this county is Woolf's standard example for the new, affluent commuter-belt outside London.

17. *the pictures of Swanage and Portsmouth*: railway compartments had framed advertisements, often promoting the coastal towns reachable by rail.

18. *copyhold, not freehold*: the right to occupy rather than the full possession of a property.

19. *Hilda Lessways*: was published by Methuen in 1911; Woolf's quotations are all taken from the opening chapter.

20. *Maud*: Tennyson's poem was published by Edward Moxon in 1855.

21. *manufacture a three-volume novel*: the standard format for Victorian novels.

22. *humbugging*: cheap trickery, artistically false.

23. *called Albert or Balmoral*: after the Prince Regent or after Queen Victoria's private castle in Scotland.

24. *consumption*: tuberculosis.

25. *asseverating*: solemnly asserting.

26. *Factory Acts*: Acts of Parliament intended to limit the hours worked by children and women.

27. *Five Towns*: Tunstall, Burslem, Hanley, Stoke and Longton – the region known as 'The Potteries' and the setting for many of Bennett's novels.

28. *Ulysses*: publication of James Joyce's novel was completed in 1922. The Hogarth Press considered publishing it but didn't, partly due to Woolf's critical unease about it – 'It was a work which Virginia could neither dismiss nor accept' (Quentin Bell, *Virginia Woolf*, II, Hogarth Press 1972, p. 54) – but it was also due to the Hogarth Press's lack of resources for such a task.

29. *Mr Strachey's books*: *Eminent Victorians* was published in 1918 and *Queen Victoria* in 1921, both by Chatto & Windus.

30. *Lord Macaulay's essays*: his collected essays were published in 1843.
31. *Mr Prufrock*: Eliot's 'The Love Song of J. Alfred Prufrock' appeared in *Prufrock and Other Observations* (The Egoist Ltd, 1917). His *Poems* (1919) and *The Waste Land* (1922) were published by the Hogarth Press.
32. *infinite variety*: cf. Shakespeare, *Antony and Cleopatra*, II. ii. 235.

INDISCRETIONS

1. The quotation is from the first poem in William Blake's 'Rossetti Manuscript':

> Never seek to tell thy Love,
> Love that never told can be;
> For the gentle wind does move
> Silently, invisibly.

  (*The Poetical Works of William Blake*, ed. John Sampson, Clarendon, 1905).

2. *barber's block*: a rounded block on which wigs were made and displayed.
3. *Fanny Brawne*: Keats' lover.
4. *he had been put on . . . royally*: Shakespeare, *Hamlet*, V. ii. 397–8.
5. *sisterly to Wordsworth*: Wordsworth lived with his sister, Dorothy, before and after his marriage to Mary Hutchinson.
6. *her Mr Nicholls*: Charlotte Brontë married her Mr Nicholls in 1854.
7. *Mrs Thrale*: friend of Dr Johnson, and his hostess at her home in Streatham.
8. *any such contamination*: it was a favourite theme of Woolf's (in *A Room of One's Own*, for example) that writers should be free of (here, 'aloof from') their particular sex: to be one or the other, rather than both or neither, would interfere with the process of artistic creation.
9. *Landor . . . Marvell*: Walter Savage Landor (1775–1864), the classical poet and critic; Sir Thomas Browne (1605–82), writer and physician; and Andrew Marvell (1621–78), the poet, satirist and Cromwellian.
10. *Emerson . . . Ruskin*: Ralph Waldo Emerson (1803–82), the American essayist; Matthew Arnold (1822–88), poet, essayist and campaigner for improved education; and John Ruskin (1819–1900), art critic and Slade Professor of Fine Art at Oxford. For Harriet Martineau and Maria Edgeworth, see 'An Imperfect Lady', Note 1.

11. *Mrs Gaskell*: Elizabeth Gaskell (1810–65) the popular novelist and biographer of Charlotte Brontë.

12. *Herbert Spencer*: (1810–1903), inventor of evolutionary philosophy and social theorist.

13. *Madame de Sévigné*: (1629–96), French aristocrat and letter-writer.

ON NOT KNOWING GREEK

1. *John Paston*: the Paston family, whose fifteenth-century letters survive, included several 'John's. They lived about twenty miles from Norwich, on the coast.

2. *nimbus*: a surrounding cloud or halo.

3. *Euripides*: the Greek dramatist (485?–406? BC).

4. *Aeschylus killed by a stone*: according to legend, Aeschylus was killed by a tortoise dropped by an eagle mistaking his bald head for a rock.

5. *Son of him . . . Agamemnon*: the opening lines of Sophocles' *Electra*, as translated by R. C. Jebb (CUP, 1904). The play's date is uncertain; it was probably performed between 410 and 418 BC. It is not clear whether or not it preceded Euripides' *Electra*.

6. *Pentheus*: in Euripides' play, Pentheus, King of Thebes, is persuaded to dress as a woman so that he may witness the rites of Bacchus.

7. *an enormous audience*: Greek dramas were performed outside before the whole population of Athens, though the competition for the tragedy prize, the Dionysia, was celebrated in March.

8. *Tristram and Iseult*: the tragic story of Tristram's love for Iseult, the wife of his uncle, King Mark of Cornwall.

9. *the old story of Electra*: the outline of this, partly supplied in the next paragraph, is that Electra joined her brother Orestes in murdering Clytemnestra and her lover Aegisthus. They acted to avenge her murder of their father Agamemnon and his lover Cassandra when he returned from the Trojan War.

10. *οἴ 'γὼ τάλαιν . . . διπλῆν*: the first line (674) is spoken by Electra when she has been (wrongly) told that her brother Orestes is dead: 'Oh miserable that I am! I am lost this day' (in Jebb's translation). The second line (1415, translated as 'Strike again' on the next page of this essay) is Electra calling to Orestes within the house while he is murdering Clytemnestra: Jebb translates, 'Smite, if thou canst, once more!'

11. *I will dance with you*: in Jane Austen's, *Emma* (1816, ch. xxxviii). Emma's reply to Mr Knightley's question ' "Whom are you going

to dance with?"' is, in fact, '"With you, if you will ask me" ... "Indeed I will."'

12. *my behaviour is unseemly ... motherhood*: two quotations from *Electra* (617–18, 770). The second (for which Woolf gives both Greek and translation) is expanded in the words that follow as, 'A mother may be wronged, but she never comes to hate her child'. Jebb's Greek edition glosses δεινὸν as implying 'a mysterious power, a strangely potent tie' and he cites Isa., 49:15 – 'Can a woman forget her sucking child, that she should not have compassion on the son of her womb?'

13. *six pages of Proust*: the volumes that make up *A la Recherche du Temps Perdu* appeared from 1913 until 1927.

14. *Antigone*: by Sophocles, who also wrote an *Ajax*.

15. *Canterbury Tales*: written by Chaucer in the late fourteenth century.

16. *from habit and not from impulse*: this distinction, which Woolf is taking up as a useful one, was standard in the psychology of the period.

17. *Addison, Voltaire*: authors of neo-classical drama in England and France in the eighteenth century.

18. *British Museum*: this contains much sculpture taken from sites in Greece.

19. *that bird distraught ... rocky tomb*: from Sophocles' *Electra* (149–51). Electra gives two examples of perpetual mourning, Procne the nightingale and Niobe. The 'rocky tomb' is the stone on Mount Sipylus into which Niobe was transformed after the murder of her children by Hera in revenge for Niobe's boasting about their number. In this version of the myth, Procne has been transformed into the nightingale who mourns her son Itys, whom she had killed and served up to her husband in revenge for his rape of her sister Philomela. She is thus a murdering mother, as Sophocles makes explicit some lines earlier, when Electra identifies herself with this bird: 'like the nightingale, slayer of her offspring, I will wail without ceasing' (107ff.).

20. *the choruses*: all Greek dramas include such a group of choric speakers.

21. *white Colonus and its nightingale*: Sophocles' sequel to *Oedipus Tyrannus* was the play *Oedipus at Colonus*. The nightingale occurs at line 668ff., while 'love unconquered in fight' is from Sophocles' *Antigone*, line 781.

22. *1663 lines*: modern editions are set out as 1673 lines, but this is a recent convention.

23. *ὀμμάτων δ' ... Ἀθροδίτα*: the quotation (in fact two lines, 418–19) refers to Menelaus being deprived of the presence of Helen, taken away by Paris, but thinking he sees the ghost of her: 'in the

emptiness of the eyes, all Aphrodite [love] is gone'. Scholars are divided as to whether they think the eyes are the hungering eyes of Menelaus or the blank gaze of Helen's phantom; the ambiguity need not be resolved, since it only enhances the pathos which makes the lines so striking. The 'eyes' further recall Woolf's own dramatic use of the word 'eyeless' in the foregoing paragraph.

24. *Dostoevsky*: Woolf knew something of the problems of translating Dostoevksy at first hand since she had taken lessons in Russian and subsequently worked with S. S. Koteliansky on *Stavrogin's Confession* (Hogarth Press, 1922), the suppressed chapters of *The Possessed*.

25. *mirrors in odd corners*: Woolf uses this image differently in 'The Art of Biography' (CE, IV, p. 226), where she suggests that the modern biographer works against the presentation of a single fixed subject by 'hanging up looking-glasses at odd corners'.

26. ὀτοτοτοῖ ... πολλον: the quotation from *Agamemnon* (1072–3) is a series of cries of sorrow, uttered by Cassandra who foresees her own death, 'O woe, woe, woe! Alas! Apollo, Apollo!'

27. *For as the argument mounts from step to step*: Woolf's description of the discussion in the *Symposium* also recalls her memoir of the first meetings of the Bloomsbury set:

> The argument, whether it was about atmosphere or the nature of truth, was always tossed into the middle of the party. Now Hawtrey would say something; now Vanessa; now Saxon; now Clive; now Thoby. It filled me with wonder to watch those who were finally left in the argument piling stone upon stone, cautiously, accurately, long after it had completely soared above my sight. (*Moments of Being*, pp. 206–7)

28. *Protagoras*: in the Platonic dialogue of his name. He was a Sophis.

29. *Agathon's house*: this paragraph summarizes the setting of Plato's *Symposium*, though the time of the year is March. The quotation is taken from towards the end, at line 213. E. Alcibiades' praise of Socrates occurs at line 216. E, 217. Woolf is using Percy Bysshe Shelley's translation *The Banquet of Plato* (1840). Agathon was an Athenian dramatist.

30. *Alcibiades*: (450?–404 BC) Athenian statesman and pupil of Socrates whose ambition provoked the distrust of the Athenians.

31. *the European war*: the First World War, 1914–18.

32. *Wilfred Owen and Siegfried Sassoon*: the two most famous poets of the First World War were friends; Owen (1893–1918) died a week

before the armistice, but Sassoon (1866–1967) survived the war and became a noted autobiographical novelist.

33. *Yet being dead . . . grows not old*: the first quotation is half of the third line of Simonides' epitaph on the Lacedaemonian dead at Plataea, the second is the whole of his epigram on the Athenean dead at Plataea. Woolf has changed 'Hellas' to 'Greece'. (See *Select Epigrams from the Greek Authority*, ed. J. W. Mackail (Longmans, 1911), sections 3, II, I).

34. *Shelley takes twenty-one words*: the quotation occurs at I, line 196. E, and includes within itself a further quotation from Euripides (from *Stheneboea*, F. 663).

35. *θάλασσα . . . σελήνη*: the five single Greek words mean: sea, death, flower, star and moon.

36. *Professor Mackail says 'wan'*: Mackail entitles an epigram of Asclepiades (in his *Select Epigrams* at §10. XIV) 'Why so pale and wan, fond lover', although the line is in fact from the song in John Suckling's *Aglaura*, IV, i (1637).

37. *the age of Burne-Jones and Morris*: the late nineteenth century of the Pre-Raphaelites.

38. *ἅ̓τ ἐν . . . δακρύεις:* from *Electra*, lines 149–51, 'Who evermore weepest in thy rocky tomb', see Note 19.

39. *Homer*: (lived in the seventh century BC) the supposed author of the *Iliad* and the *Odyssey*.

40. *Wycherley*: William Wycherley (1640–1716), the Restoration dramatist of social mores, author of *The Country Wife* (1675).

41. *Racine*: Jean Racine (1639–99), the French neo-classical tragic dramatist.

42. *Penelope . . . Nausicaa*: Penelope is Odysseus' wife; Telemachus is their son; and Nausicaa is a princess who desires and helps Odysseus on his way home.

THE DUCHESS OF NEWCASTLE

1. *All I desire is fame*: from the preface to her *Poems and Fancies* (1653), sig. A3r.

2. *Garish in her dress*: in her review of Thomas Longueville's *The First Duke and Duchess of Newcastle* (1910) (*Times Literary Supplement*, 2 Feb. 1911, reprinted in *Essays*, I, p. 349) Woolf quotes the memoir of Count Grammont: 'It was worth while to see her dress; for she must have had at least sixty ells of gauze and silver tissue about her, not to mention a sort of pyramid upon her head, adorned with a

hundred thousand baubles. "I bet," said the King, "that it is the Duchess of Newcastle."'

3. *the few splendid phrases that Lamb scattered upon her tomb*: for example, 'the thrice noble, chaste, and virtuous, – but again somewhat fantastical, and original-brain'd, generous Margaret Newcastle', in Charles Lamb's essay 'Mackery End, in Hertfordshire' (*The Works of Charles and Mary Lamb*, ed. E. V. Lucas, Methuen & Co., 1903–5, vol. II). Lamb also praises her in 'The Two Races of Men', 'A Complaint of the Decay of Beggars in the Metropolis' and 'Detached Thoughts on Books and Reading' in the same volume. The Duke and Duchess's tomb is in Westminster Abbey.

4. *beyond the ruin of time*: this and the following biographical comments come from 'A True Relation of my Birth, Breeding, and Life', in *Natures Pictures drawn by Fancies Pencil to the Life* (1656), edited by C. H. Firth in *Memoirs of William Cavendish Duke of Newcastle and Margaret his wife* (1906).

5. *the impetuosity of her thought always outdid the pace of her fingers*: Woolf also comments on the Duchess's irrepressible prolific writing in *A Room of One's Own* (1929), situating it historically: 'Margaret too might have been a poet; in our day all that activity would have turned a wheel of some sort. As it was, what could bind, tame or civilize for human use that wild, generous, untutored intelligence? It poured itself out, higgledy-piggledy, in torrents of rhyme and prose, poetry and philosophy.'

6. *the Civil War*: from 1642–46.

7. *I fear ... I have enemies*: sentiments expressed in *Letters written by Margaret Newcastle, to her husband* (ed. R. W. Golding, Roxburghe Club, 1909).

8. *that nobody knew or could know the cause of anything*: in William Cavendish's *Philosophical and Physical Opinions* (2nd edn, 1663).

9. *He did approve . . .*: see 'A True Relation', ed. C. H. Firth, p. 162.

10. *corvets, voltoes*: leaps and vaults; William Cavendish ran a riding school and published *A New Method and Extraordinary Invention to Dress Horses, and Work Them, According to Nature by the Subtlety of Art* (1667).

11. *the Protectorate*: from 1653, within the period of Parliamentary rule (1649–60), a more centralized form of government placed Oliver Cromwell and then his son Richard as Lord Protectors.

12. *the Restoration*: in 1660, when Charles II became King.

13. *Horace Walpole sneered at them*: 'What a picture of foolish nobility was this stately poetic couple, retired to their little domain, and

intoxicating one another with circumstantial flattery on what was of consequence to no mortal but themselves' (*A Catalogue of the Royal and Noble Authors of England*, II, 1758, p. 9).

14. *Women live like Bats . . . and die like Worms*: quote from her 'Female Orations', in *Orations of Diverse Sorts* (1662), p. 226.

15. *the best bred women are those whose minds are civilest*: from CCXI *Sociable Letters* (1664), p. 51.

16. *why 'hogs have the measles' . . .*: questions like this, and the earlier one as to whether 'snails have teeth?', made up the sort of sub-heading found in *The World's Olio* (1655) and her works on natural philosophy.

17. *for there is more pleasure in making than in mending*: from *The World's Olio*, sig. A3v.

18. *our heads are full of fairies, 'dear to God as we are'*: from *Poems and Fancies*, sig. Aa2r.

19. *we are in utter darkness*: Margaret Cavendish discusses the limitations of our knowledge and the possibility of other, better worlds in *Poems and Fancies* (pp. 43ff.), and in the preface to *Blazing World*, first published at the end of *Observations Upon Experimental Philosophy* (1666).

20. *wrote of many matters . . . ipse dixit will not serve my turn*: her autodidacticism is recorded in William Cavendish's *Philosophical and Physical Opinions*, sig. A1v; *ipse dixit* means 'he himself said it'.

21. *Mr Stanley's account*: in Thomas Stanley, *The History of Philosophy* (1655–62).

22. *but half of his work on Passion*: Descartes' *The Passions of the Soul* (1649; trans., 1650).

23. *the little book called De Cive*: Cavendish could not read Latin, so she would have had to read Hobbes' text in its English translation, published as *Philosophical Rudiments Concerning Government and Society* in 1657. The Duke of Newcastle was a patron of Descartes and Hobbes.

24. *The palace of the Queen wherein she dwells . . . her pillow's laid*: this and the following extracts are from the poems 'Descending Down', 'The Claspe', and 'The City of the Fairies' in Margaret Cavendish's *Poems and Fancies* (1653).

25. *my Lady Sanspareille hath a strange spreading wit*: a character from *Youths Glory, and Deaths Banquet*, in *Playes* (1662).

26. *Sir Golden Riches, Moll Meanbred . . . and the rest*: characters from *The Lady Contemplation* in *Playes*.

27. *did beat her husband . . . bragging of myself*: remarks she made in CCXI *Sociable Letters* (1664), pp. 48–9, 87, 103, 207ff, 243.

28. *Sir Egerton Brydges . . . complained*: in *The Select Poems of Margaret Cavendish*, ed. Sir Egerton Brydges (Johnson and Warwick, 1813).

29. *of Shakespeare's fools*: from CCXI *Sociable Letters*, p. 244.

30. *a very comely woman*: Pepys in his diary for 26 April 1687 (*Samuel Pepys, Diaries and Correspondence*, ed. Richard Lord Braybrooke, H. Colburn, 1825).

TWO WOMEN

1. *I have no hesitation . . . herself*: from Charlotte Yonge's *Womankind* (1876).

2. *Queen Victoria so furious*: in Sir Theodore Martin's *Queen Victoria as I Knew Her* (1908).

3. *the essentials of . . . men*: the quotation is from Greg's 'Why are Women Redundant?', reprinted in *Literary and Social Judgements* (1868).

4. *Trollope's picture of four girls*: from *Miss Mackenzie* (1865).

5. *as Miss Nightingale said . . . dangerous*: Florence Nightingale as 'Cassandra' in her *Suggestions for Thought to the Searchers After Truth* (1860).

6. *Miss Martineau frankly hailed*: in her *Autobiography* (1877).

7. *Miss Garrett said*: in a letter to Emily Davies, 12 April 1862.

8. *Mrs Gurney*: supporter of the Girls' Public Day School Company, a scheme for the setting up of secondary schools for girls.

9. *navvies*: Catherine Marsh did some work with railway navvies, but came into her own distributing religious literature and lessons among the navvies constructing the Crystal Palace for the Great Exhibition of 1851. Her book *English Hearts and English Hands* (1858) was very popular.

10. *Saturday Review*: the article, entitled 'Feminine Wranglers', appeared on 23 July 1864.

11. *Lamartine . . . Turgenev*: Alphonse de Lamartine (1790–1869), the French poet, writer and politician; Prosper Mérimée (1803–70), French novelist and short-story writer, the author of *Carmen* (1845); Victor Hugo (1802–85), the leading French romantic poet, novelist and dramatist; Duc de Broglie (1821–1901), the French statesman and man of letters; Charles Sainte-Beuve (1804–69), the French literary critic, admired by Matthew Arnold and others as the founder of modern criticism; Ernest Renan (1823–92), the writer, philosopher and Professor of Hebrew who applied scientific historical investigation to Christianity in his *Vie de Jésus* (1863); Jenny Lind (1820–87), the Swedish-born soprano, nicknamed the 'Swedish Nightingale'; and Ivan Turgenev (1818–83), the Russian novelist and playwright much admired by Woolf.

THE ART OF FICTION

1. *Sir Walter Raleigh and Mr Percy Lubbock*: the two recent works of criticism alluded to are Sir Walter Raleigh's, *Some Authors* (posthumously published in 1923) and Percy Lubbock's, *The Craft of Fiction* (1922).

2. *Meredith*: George Meredith (1828–1909), was a friend of Woolf's parents and the author of *The Egoist* (1879). Meredith was much admired by Woolf, see 'On Re-reading Meredith' (*Essays*, II, p. 272), 'Small Talk about Meredith' and 'On Re-reading Novels' (*Essays*, III, pp. 5, 336).

3. *The Golden Bowl*: by Henry James (1905).

4. *Tristram Shandy*: by Laurence Sterne (1767).

5. *Pattern . . . features*: while the feminization of 'beauty' is conventional, that of 'pattern' is not. It is interesting that Woolf regenders beauty in the face of the quotation from Forster, where beauty is neutral, and that she attributes femininity to 'pattern', identified as anti-human.

6. *the teapot and the pug dog*: the pug dog is not a typical metonymy in Woolf for the domesticity she is always spurning as a subject for fiction or as a sphere for women's lives; the teapot, on the other hand, recalls numerous occasions in Woolf's novels when the afternoon tea-drinking ritual functions as a satire against Victorian constraints.

7. *Mr Roger Fry*: the influential art critic (1866–1934) and a close friend of Woolf; she published his biography in 1940.

8. *War and Peace . . . A la Recherche du Temps Perdu*: *War and Peace* (1864–9) by Leo Tolstoy; *The Brothers Karamazov* (1880) by Fyodor Dostoevsky; *A la Recherche du Temps Perdu* (1913–27) by Marcel Proust.

9. *Flaubert*: Gustave Flaubert (1821–80), the French realist novelist, author of *Madame Bovary* (1857).

10. *The novel, in short, might become a work of art*: the acerbic irony is typical of Woolf's anti-tea-table mode.

DOROTHY OSBORNE'S LETTERS

1. *Donne, says Sir Edmund Gosse*: in Gosse's *The Life and Letters of John Donne* (2 vols., 1899); Lady Bedford was Donne's patron.

2. *Horace Walpole*: (1717–97) wit, letter-writer, and author of *The Castle of Otranto* (1764).

3. *Duchess of Newcastle*: see 'The Duchess of Newcastle', pp. 107 ff.

4. *without unsexing herself*: the allusion to Lady Macbeth's 'Unsex me here' (*Macbeth*, I. v. 41) opens many questions about 'sexing' for a

writer, and specifically for a woman writer; *A Room of One's Own* (1929), the first version of which was written in the same autumn as this review essay, explores their possibilities in greater detail. In it Woolf discusses Dorothy Osborne – 'what a gift that untaught and solitary girl had for the framing of a sentence' – and compares her to the Duchess of Newcastle, as here.

5. *Evelina*: Fanny Burney's novel was published in 1778.

6. *Pride and Prejudice*: Jane Austen's novel was published in 1813.

7. *standish*: a stand for pen, ink and other writing implements.

8. *Temple*: Dorothy Osborne's letters were written to Sir William Temple (1628–99), the leading statesman of his day, who brought about the marriage between William of Orange and Mary. He also wrote a treatise on the nature of government and was a patron of Jonathan Swift.

9. *visit the wells at Epsom*: the district of Surrey famous for the mineral springs discovered there in 1618.

10. *The Hague*: the seat of the Dutch government and the centre of diplomatic activity in the seventeenth century when the Dutch Republic played a leading role in Europe.

11. *Mild Dorothea ... Swift called her*: in his ode 'Occasioned by Sir William Temple's Late Illness and Recovery' (1693), which Woolf probably read in T. P. Courtenay's two-volume *Memoirs of the Life, Works and Correspondence of Temple* (1836).

12. *Triple Alliance*: in 1668, between England, Holland and Sweden, negotiated by Temple and John de Witt to act as a check on Louis XIV of France.

13. *Treaty of Nimuegen*: between France and the Dutch allied to the English, in 1678–9.

MEMORIES OF A WORKING WOMEN'S GUILD

1. *a hot June morning in Newcastle*: changed in the other versions to Manchester, as though to fictionalize the proceedings (and Devonshire becomes Cornwall throughout). In a letter to Violet Dickinson sent from Sussex before the conference, Woolf had written: 'We're down here, but come up [to London] for a few days, and then retire to New Castle on Tyne to join the Cooperative Women' (*Letters*, II, late May 1913, p. 28).

2. *beating the bush*: in other editions, the more common phrase 'beating *about* the bush' was substituted. However, the original more clearly continues the shooting metaphor: 'beaters' were employed to scare birds into flight; here it is the women that are doing the shooting.

3. *my comfortable capitalistic head*: this strong phrase was subsequently diluted to become, 'it would not matter to me a single jot'.

4. *babies*: more specifically described as 'hot' babies in later versions of the text.

5. *Miss Kidd . . . Miss Lilian Harris*: these actual names were later changed to Miss Wick and Miss Janet Erskine.

6. *the ash-tray in which many cigarettes had come amiably to an end*: elsewhere, 'Miss Erskine may have been smoking a pipe – there was one on the table.' And further, 'She may have been reading a detective story – there was a book of that kind on the table.'

7. *They want baths and money*: the other versions included the following sentence: 'When people get together communally they always talk about baths and money: they always show the least desirable of their characteristics – their lust for conquest and their desire for possessions.'

8. *Einstein*: the scientist is elsewhere replaced by 'Cézanne and Shakespeare'.

9. *no working man or woman . . . or a writer with his pen*: Woolf is crossing a line, or not thinking twice, in making her habitual analogy of writing and painting to crafts into a direct comparison with paid labour, skilled and unskilled.

10. *lights*: the lungs of beasts sold cheaply by butchers, often as pet food.

11. *crudity*: in the other versions, 'illiteracy'.

12. *the ganger*: a work overseer.

13. *They read Dickens and Scott . . . Alice Meynell*: the absence of first names marks the first two out as classics in comparison with the other names on the list; but they, like Henry George and the rest, were in every sense popular writers in the nineteenth century.

14. *not Carlyle's please*: Carlyle's *The French Revolution: A History* was published in three volumes in 1837.

15. *B. Russell on China*: Bertrand Russell's *The Problem of China* was published in 1922.

WHY?

1. *Somerville*: the Oxford women's college, founded in 1879 and admitted to the University as a full college in 1957.

ROYALTY

1. *the Duke of Kent's wedding-day*: on 29 November, London had celebrated the wedding of the Duke of Kent and Princess Marina of Greece.

2. *Irving and Ellen Terry*: famous actors of the period; Henry Irving is also mentioned in the piece on 'Ellen Terry' herself (reprinted in *The Crowded Dance of Modern Life*, Penguin Books, 1992).

3. *Maeterlinck*: Maurice Maeterlinck (1862–1949), Belgian poet, essayist and dramatist, the author of *Pelléas and Mélisande* (1892).

4. *Whipsnade*: a zoo in Bedfordshire.

5. *Prometheus Unbound ... Wuthering Heights*: the original *Prometheus Unbound* (1820) is by Shelley, and *Wuthering Heights* (1847) by Emily Brontë.

THE LEANING TOWER

1. *trash*: a favourite word of Woolf's to refer (not necessarily negatively) to ephemeral literature.

2. *It is less than two hundred years since people took an interest in themselves*: a view regularly proposed in Woolf's several versions of the history of biography and autobiography.

3. *the Napoleonic war*: culminating in Napoleon's defeat in 1815 at Waterloo.

4. *villages like Brighton*: Brighton was by now a large town; this reminder of its rapid growth in the first half of the nineteenth century reinforces both the sense of distance from the pre-news era and the speed of contemporary change. But there was also a more local reason for choosing this example, as this paper was initially presented to a meeting in May of the Workers' Educational Association in Brighton, not far from the Woolfs' home at Rodmell, still a small village.

5. *today*: the piece was written during the air raids of 1940.

6. *We turn on the wireless*: Woolf's references to broadcasting (the 'wireless' or the 'loudspeaker') usually occur in the context of a wartime potential for propaganda. See also 'Thoughts on Peace in an Air Raid' and the notes to 'Thunder at Wembley' (reprinted in *The Crowded Dance of Modern Life*, Penguin Books, 1993).

7. *Trafalgar ... Waterloo*: the battle of Trafalgar (1805); the battle of Waterloo (1815).

8. *the Crimean War ... the Boer War*: the Crimean War (1854–6); the Indian Mutiny (1857–8); and the Boer War (1899–1902).

9. *Pecksniff, Becky Sharp, Mr Woodhouse*: characters in Dickens' *Martin Chuzzlewit* (1844), Thackeray's *Vanity Fair* (1848) and Jane Austen's *Emma* (1816).

10. *innumerable notes ... unconscious*: a particularly graphic example of Woolf's two-stage sequence from the multiplicity and heterogeneity

of external impressions and their subsequent 'unconscious' unification. She uses a similar metaphor in her essay 'Modern Novels':

> The mind, exposed to the ordinary course of life, receives upon its surface a myriad impressions – trivial, fantastic, evanescent or engraved with the sharpness of steel. From all sides they come, an incessant shower of innumerable atoms, composing in their sum what we might venture to call life itself . . .
> (*Essays*, III, p. 33)

11. *emotion recollected in tranquillity*: Wordsworth uses the phrase in his 'Preface' to the *Lyrical Ballads* (1800).

12. *Mr Desmond MacCarthy's answer*: in 'Lytton Strachey and the Art of Biography', *Sunday Times*, 5 Nov. 1933.

13. *Rupert Brooke's poems*: his *Poems* were published by Sidgwick and Jackson in 1911.

14. *A Room with a View*: was published by Edward Arnold in 1908.

15. *G. K. Chesterton's essays*: collections of Chesterton's *belles-lettres* were published between 1901 and 1934, the year of his death.

16. *Belloc . . . Middleton Murry*: Hilaire Belloc (1870–1953), poet, novelist, essayist and staunch Catholic; Lytton Strachey (1880–1932), biographer, essayist and close friend of Woolf; James Flecker (1884–1915), Edwardian lyric poet and playwright; Osbert (1892–1969) and Sacheverell Sitwell (1897–1988), aristocratic poets and brothers of the eccentric poet Edith Sitwell; John Middleton Murry (1889–1957), critic and editor, the husband of Katherine Mansfield.

17. *Nobody thinks it strange*: this defence of the difficulty of learning the craft of writing is a frequent refrain (cf. 'The Patron and the Crocus', pp. 65ff).

18. *Mr Auden . . . says*:

> Half-boys, we spoke of books and praised
> The acid and austere, behind us only
> The stuccoed suburb and expensive school.
>
> (Poem XXIV (To Christopher Isherwood),
> *Look, Stranger!*, Faber and Faber, 1936)

19. *In Germany, in Russia, in Italy, in Spain*: the 1930s saw the rise of the Nazi Party in Germany, Stalin's purges of the Communist Party, Mussolini's Abyssinian War (1935) and the Spanish Civil War (1936–9).

20. *Autumn Journal*: published by Faber and Faber in 1939.

21. *Marlborough*: an English public school in Wiltshire.

22. *humane letters: literae humaniores*, the Oxford degree in classical literature, ancient history and philosophy.

23. *the pedagogic, the didactic, the loud speaker strain*: the repetitions and assimilations here are typical of Woolf's mistrust of literature that parades its politics, and of her association of this with the new forms of mass communication, regarded as crudely propagandist.

24. *Mr Day Lewis ingeminating love . . .*: i.e., reiterating; the quotation is from C. Day Lewis's *A Hope for Poetry* (Basil Blackwell, 1934), and the poem (mis)quoted is Stephen Spender's 'After they have tired' from his *Poems* (Faber and Faber, 1933):

> We have at last come to a country
> Where light equal like the shine from snow strikes all faces,
> Here you may wonder
> How it was that works, money, interest, building, could
>   ever hide
> The palpable and obvious love of man for man.

25. *We are in a group, in a class-room*: whereas her general history of reading does not especially see the movement from public to private contexts as an advance, this return to the 'group' situation is unequivocally regarded as negative here, inseparable from the didacticism Woolf deplores in literature.

26. *Lover . . . lonely hills*: the extract is from Wordsworth's 'Song at the Feast of Brougham Castle' (1807).

27. *one dying, the other struggling to be born*: an allusion to Matthew Arnold's 'Stanzas from The Grand Chartreuse' (1855): 'wandering between two worlds, one dead/The other powerless to be born' (lines 85–6).

28. *to write about dolls and puppets*: an allusion to the opening and closing metaphor of Thackeray's *Vanity Fair* (1848):

> Ah! *Vanitas Vanitatum!* Which of us is happy in this world?
> Which of us has his desire? or, having it, is satisfied? – Come,
> children, let us shut up the box and the puppets, for our play
> is played out.

29. *Stevenson wrote*: spoken, rather than written, by Stevenson, according to his stepson Lloyd Osbourne in *An Intimate Portrait of Robert Louis Stevenson* (1924).

30. *with help from Dr Freud*: this passage is a fascinating transposition of Freud into Woolf's own terms. She sees psychoanalysis as capable of abolishing a contingently divided state of mind attributable to the effects (always bad, in her view) of the nineteenth century; whereas Freud sees the mind as irreducibly divided. Freud's unconscious as the source of the division becomes Woolf's

unconsciousness as a source of artistic inspiration derived – and this is the most striking alteration – from 'a mind no longer crippled'. In other words, for Woolf unconsciousness goes with the absence of division; for Freud it is the reverse.

31. *One of these parents wrote to the New Statesman*: Molly Fordham, on 13 April 1940.

32. *Winchester*: another famous English public school.

33. *twopence half-penny ... 35 guineas*: there were twelve pence in a shilling and twenty shillings to a pound. A guinea was one pound one shilling; professional payments were often made in guineas.

34. *real people, not ... featureless masses*: compare the reversal of this point about the possible characters of democratic fiction in 'This is the House of Commons' (reprinted in *The Crowded Dance of Modern Life*, Penguin Books, 1993).

35. *the different dialects, the clipped and cabined vocabulary*: for another more ambiguous suggestion concerning this contrast, see 'Memories of a Working Women's Guild', pp. 140.

36. *a common reader*: Johnson's phrase, adopted by Woolf for her two anthologies of her own essays:

> I rejoice to concur with the common reader; for by the common sense of readers uncorrupted with literary prejudices, after all the refinements of subtlety and the dogmatism of learning, must be finally decided all claim to poetical honours. (Samuel Johnson, 'Life of Gray' in *Lives of the Most Eminent English Poets* (1779–81).)

37. *Readers are requested to point out any defects ...*: Woolf is humorously turning the library's directive to report any damage to books into an invitation to criticism.

38. *pay dividends of pleasure*: a strikingly literal assimilation of texts to companies, and readers to shareholders.

39. *We must sample before we can select*: this extended version of Woolf's regular analogy between reading and eating makes tasting the necessary preliminary to taste (i.e., discrimination).

40. *the wigged and gowned*: judges and academics. Comparable contempt for institutional scholarship is expressed in 'How Should One Read a Book?' (reprinted in *The Crowded Dance of Modern Life*, Penguin Books, 1993; and *Three Guineas* (1938), where the point is illustrated by a photograph).

41. *an eminent Victorian who was also an eminent pedestrian*: Woolf is referring to her father, Leslie Stephen, the respected man of letters and mountaineer.